SOPHIE KINSELLA

SHOPAHOLIC

ties

THE KNOT

DELTA TRADE PAPERBACKS

SHOPAHOLIC TIES THE KNOT
A Delta Book/March 2003

Published by
Bantam Dell
A division of Random House, Inc.
New York, New York

Book design by Karin Batten

Library of Congress Cataloging-in-Publication Data

Kinsella, Sophie.
Shopaholic ties the knot / Sophie Kinsella.
p. cm.
ISBN 0-385-33617-9
1. Bloomwood, Becky (Fictitious character)—Fiction.
2. British—New York (State)—Fiction. 3. Manhattan (New York, N.Y.)—
Fiction. 4. Young women—Fiction. 5. Shopping—Fiction.
6. Weddings—Fiction. I. Title.

PR6061.I54 S57 2003
823'.92—dc21   2002073789

Manufactured in the United States of America
Published simultaneously in Canada
First published in 2002 by Transworld, United Kingdom

BVG   10 9 8 7 6

The Dress . . .

I stare at my reflection and feel a little glow of pleasure. It's a simple dress—but I look fantastic in it. It makes me look really thin! It makes my skin look radiant and . . . God, maybe this is the one!

There's silence in the shop.

"Do you feel it here?" says Cynthia, the owner of the boutique, clutching her stomach.

"I . . . don't know! I think so!" I give an excited little laugh. "I think I might!"

"I knew it. You see? When you find the right dress, it hits you. You can't plan for it. You just know when it's right."

"I've found my wedding dress!" I beam at Suze. "I've found it!"

"At last!" There's a ring of relief to Cynthia's voice. "Let's all have a glass of champagne to celebrate!"

An assistant is carrying past another dress, and I catch sight of an embroidered silk corset bodice, tied up with ribbons.

"Hey, that looks nice," I say. "What's that?"

"Never mind what it is!" says Cynthia, handing me a glass of champagne. "You've found your dress!" She lifts her glass, but I'm still looking at the ribboned bodice.

"Maybe I should just try that one on. Just quickly."

"You don't need to look any further." Cynthia's voice is slightly shrill. "This is the one!"

"Mmm . . ." I pull a tiny face. "You know, I'm not so sure it is."

For an awful moment I think Cynthia's going to throw the champagne at me.

"I thought this was the dress of your dreams!"

"It's the dress of *some* of my dreams," I explain. "I have a lot of dreams. Could we put it down as another possible?"

For Abigail,
who would have found
the brilliant solution in a flash

SHOPAHOLIC

ties

THE KNOT

SECOND UNION BANK
53 WALL STREET
NEW YORK, NY 10005

November 7, 2001

Miss Rebecca Bloomwood
Apt. B
251 W. 11th Street
New York, NY 10014

Dear Miss Bloomwood:

New Joint Account No.: 5039 2566 2319

We are pleased to confirm your new joint bank account with
Mr. Luke J. Brandon, and enclose explanatory documentation.
A debit card will be sent to you under separate cover.

We at Second Union Bank continually pride ourselves on
our highly individual approach to clients. Please contact me
personally at any time if you have a query, and I will help in any
way I can. No matter is too small for my attention.

With kind regards.

Yours sincerely,

Walt Pitman
Director of Customer Relations

December 12, 2001

Miss Rebecca Bloomwood
Apt. B
251 W. 11th Street
New York, NY 10014

Dear Miss Bloomwood:

Thank you for your letter of December 9 regarding your joint
account with Mr. Luke J. Brandon. I agree the relationship
between bank and client should be one of friendship and
cooperation, and in answer to your question, my favorite
color is red.

I regret, however, I am unable to reword entries on your
forthcoming statement as you request. The particular debit
item you refer to will appear on your next statement as "Prada,
New York." It cannot be changed to "Gas bill."

Yours sincerely,

Walt Pitman
Director of Customer Relations

January 7, 2002

Miss Rebecca Bloomwood
Apt. B
251 W. 11th Street
New York, NY 10014

Dear Miss Bloomwood:

Thank you for your letter of January 4 regarding your joint account with Mr. Luke J. Brandon, and for the chocolates, which I must return. I agree it is difficult to keep tabs on every tiny purchase, and was sorry to hear that "the odd little misunderstanding" had arisen between you.

Unfortunately, it is impossible to split the statement into half as you suggest, sending half to yourself and half to Mr. Brandon and "keeping it our little secret." All income and outgoings are itemized jointly.

That is why it is called a joint account.

Yours sincerely,

Walt Pitman
Director of Customer Relations

One

OK. DON'T PANIC. The answer will come to me any minute. I just have to think hard about what marriage is all about. It's about love, obviously. And companionship, and mutual support. And . . . soup?

My eye rests on a huge antique silver tureen, complete with ladle. Now, that would make a perfect wedding gift. I can just see it: Suze and Tarquin sitting by the fire, ladling soup into each other's bowls. It'll be all lovely and domestic and heartwarming, and every time they drink soup they'll think of me.

Perhaps I could even have it engraved. "To my best friends Suze and Tarquin on their wedding day with love and affection from Becky." And a little poem, maybe.

Mind you, engraving is quite expensive. I'd better check how much it would all come to.

"Excuse me, how much is this soup tureen?" I say, turning to Arthur Graham, who is the owner of Graham's Antiques. This shop has to be one of my favorites in the West Village. It's small and intimate like someone's home, and everywhere you turn, there's something you might want. Like that fantastic carved chair, and a hand-painted velvet throw, and that amazing grandfather clock over in the corner . . .

"The tureen?" Arthur comes over, dapper in his jacket and tie.

"This is very special. Eighteenth-century silver. Exquisite crafts-manship. You see this detail on the rim?"

"Beautiful!" I look obediently.

"And it's priced at . . ." He consults a little book. "Four thou-sand dollars."

"Oh, right." My smile falters, and I carefully put the ladle back. "Thanks. I'll . . . keep looking."

So maybe marriage isn't about soup. Maybe it's about . . . chess? I run my hand over a beautiful old chess set, all set up as though a game's in progress. But I'm not sure Suze knows how to play chess.

A clock? No.

A . . . an antique barometer?

Oh God, I'm really clutching at straws here. I can't believe it's Suze's wedding in two days and I still haven't got her and Tarquin a present. Or at least, not one I can actually give them. Months ago I bought them this gorgeous picnic hamper, filled with picnicware, a champagne cooler, really cool knives and forks, and even a rug. It took me ages to choose all the stuff, and I was so pleased with it. But Suze phoned last night to check what time we'd be arriving, and told me her aunt had just given her a fantastic present—a picnic hamper filled with Conran tableware!

Well, no way am I giving Suze the same present as someone else. So here I am in the only place I can think of where I'll find something unique. Except . . . what? She hasn't registered for gifts, because she says she hates the idea of asking people for things. And anyway, I'd never just get her some boring set of plates off a list. Suze is my best friend, and I'm going to be her bridesmaid, and my present has to be something really special.

I can feel myself starting to get anxious. OK, just think laterally. What do Suze and Tarquin enjoy doing?

"Do you have any horse saddles?" I ask in sudden inspiration. "Or . . . bridles?"

"Not at the moment."

Oh well. Anyway, I'd have to get two, wouldn't I? And they probably wouldn't even fit the horses properly . . .

A carved music stand? Except how would I get it home on the plane? And anyway, neither of them plays an instrument. A marble bust of Abraham Lincoln? A picture of . . .

Hang on a minute. I push the bust of Lincoln aside and look

carefully at the old trunk he's been resting on. Now that's rather nice. In fact it's very nice. I undo the straps and gently lift the lid, inhaling the smell of old leather.

Wow. This is stunning. All pale silk and leather straps, and a mirror, and little compartments to put your cuff links in. Suze will adore this, I know she will. She can use it to keep jumpers in and when she and Tarquin go on a cruise a porter can wheel it up the ramp for her and she'll look all glamorous and film-star-like.

And the point is, even if someone else gives them a suitcase or something, one of my great maxims of life is: you can never have too much luggage.

"How much is this trunk?" I ask Arthur Graham a little nervously. Please don't let it be $10,000—

"We've had that awhile." He frowns at it. "I could let you have it for . . . three hundred."

"Perfect." I breathe a sigh of relief. "I'll take it."

Mission accomplished! I've got Suze's wedding present! Thank goodness for that. Now all I need is my bridesmaid's dress, and I'm there.

"It's Miss Bloomwood, isn't it?" says Arthur, opening a large leather-bound notebook. "I'm sure we have your address . . . And yes. Here it is." He smiles at me. "Is that all for today?"

I don't need anything else. I don't even need to look around the rest of the shop.

"Um . . . Well." Idly I glance around again. It's always a good idea to have your eyes open when you're in antique shops, because there are some really good bargains out there. And it's all a good investment. I mean, this is how some people make their money.

Through the door to the back room I see the corner of a lace shawl, and feel a tug of desire. Antique shawls are *so* in at the moment. And since I'm buying the trunk, it occurs to me, Arthur might give it to me for half price. Or maybe even for free!

Oh, come on. I'll just have a quick look. But only at very small things, because I've promised Luke no more furniture.

"I'll have a bit of a browse." I smile back at Arthur. "Thanks."

I head happily into the back room and reach for the lace shawl, but close up it looks a bit ragged. I put it down again and pick up a cocktail shaker. This is nice. Maybe I should get it for Suze as well.

"This is cool!" I beam at Arthur, who has followed me in.

"It's fun, isn't it?" he agrees. "It goes with the 1930s cocktail cabinet."

"Cocktail cabinet?" I echo, feeling prickles of interest. "I didn't see a—"

"Here." He walks over to what I thought was a cupboard, unhooks the front flap, and displays the mirrored Art Deco fittings inside. "You see, here's where your bottles go . . . here are your highballs . . ."

I gaze at it, completely smitten. A real, genuine, 1930s cocktail cabinet. I've *always* wanted a cocktail cabinet.

Just think, if we had one of these in the apartment it would change our lives. Every night Luke and I would mix martinis, and dance to old-fashioned songs, and watch the sun go down. It'd be so atmospheric! We'd have to buy one of those old-fashioned record players with the big horns, and start collecting 78s, and I'd start wearing gorgeous vintage tea dresses.

We have to have this. We *have* to. This isn't some boring chair, or set of shelves. This is different. Luke will understand.

"How much is that?" I say, trying to sound nonchalant. I'm rather good at getting good prices in this shop. The trick is to sound as though you don't care whether you buy it or not.

"This?" Arthur looks at it thoughtfully, and I hold my breath. "This really should be seven hundred dollars. But since you're taking the trunk as well . . . I could let you have the pair for . . . eight hundred?"

Eight hundred dollars. For a wedding present *and* a unique cocktail cabinet that we'll treasure all our lives. I mean, this isn't like buying some pair of shoes that you'll forget about. This is a genuine investment for the future.

"I'll take them!" I beam at Arthur Graham.

"Excellent!" He smiles back. "You have a very good eye."

Luke and I've been living together in New York now for a year, and our apartment is on West 11th Street, in the really nice leafy, atmospheric bit. There are ornate little balconies on all the houses, and stone steps up to all the front doors, and trees all along the pavement. Right opposite us lives someone who plays jazz piano, and on summer evenings we stroll up to the roof terrace that we share with our neighbors, and sit on cushions and drink wine and listen. (At least, we did that one time and I'm sure we will again.)

As I let myself into the house, there's a pile of post for us in the hall, and I quickly flick through it.

Boring . . .

Boring . . .

British *Vogue*!

Boring . . .

Oh. My Saks Fifth Avenue store card bill.

I look at the envelope for moment, then remove it and put it in my bag. Not because I'm hiding it. Simply because there's no particular point in Luke seeing it. I read this really good magazine article recently, entitled "Too Much Information?" in which it said you should filter out the day's events rather than tell your partner every single tiny thing and overload his or her weary mind. It said your home should be a sanctuary, and that no one needs to know *everything*. Which, when you think about it, makes a lot of sense.

I put the rest of the post under my arm and start to walk up the stairs. There aren't any letters from England, but then, I wouldn't expect there to be today, because tonight we're flying home for the wedding! I just can't wait.

Suze is my first friend to take the plunge and get married. She's marrying Tarquin, who's a really sweet guy she's known all her life. (In fact, he's her cousin. But it's legal. They checked.) The wedding's going to be at her parents' house in Hampshire, and there's going to be loads of champagne, and a horse and carriage . . . and best of all, I'm going to be her bridesmaid!

At the thought, I feel a pang of yearning. I'm *so* looking forward to it. Not just being bridesmaid—but seeing Suze, my parents, and my home. It occurred to me yesterday I haven't been back to Britain for over six months, which suddenly seems like a really long time. I completely missed Dad getting elected captain of the golf club, which was his life ambition. And I missed the scandal when Siobhan at the church stole the roof money and used it to go to Cyprus. And worst of all, I missed Suze getting engaged—although she came out to New York two weeks later to show me her ring.

It's not that I mind exactly, because I'm having such a great time out here. My job at Barneys is perfect, and living in the West Village is even more perfect. I love walking through the tiny tucked-away streets, and buying cupcakes at the Magnolia Bakery on Saturday mornings and walking back through the market. Basically, I love everything I have here in New York. Except possibly Luke's mother.

But still. Your home's your home.

As I reach the second floor, I hear music coming from our apartment, and I feel a little fizz of anticipation inside. That'll be Danny, working away. He'll probably have finished by now! My dress will be ready!

Danny Kovitz lives upstairs from us, in his brother's apartment, and he's become one of my best friends since I've been in New York. He's a fabulous designer, really talented—but he's not that successful yet. Five years after leaving fashion school, he's still waiting for his big break to come along. But like he always says, making it as a designer is even harder than making it as an actor. If you don't know the right people or have an ex-Beatle as a father, you might as well forget it. I feel so sorry for him, because he does deserve to succeed. So as soon as Suze asked me to be her bridesmaid, I asked him to make my dress. The great thing is, Suze's wedding is going to be stuffed full of rich, important guests. So hopefully loads of people will ask me who designed my dress, and then a whole word-of-mouth buzz will start, and Danny will be made!

I just can't wait to see what he's done. All the sketches he's shown me have been amazing—and of course, a handmade dress will have far more workmanship and detail than you'd get off the peg. Like, the bodice is going to be a boned, hand-embroidered corset—and Danny suggested putting in a tiny beaded love-knot using the birthstones of all the bridal party, which is just so original.

My only slight worry—tiny niggle—is that the wedding's in two days' time, and I haven't actually tried the dress on yet. Or even seen it. This morning I rang Danny's doorbell to remind him I was leaving for England today, and after he'd eventually staggered to the door, he promised me he'd have it by lunchtime. He told me he always lets his ideas ferment until the very last minute—then he gets a surge of adrenaline and inspiration. It's just the way he works, he assured me, and he's never missed a deadline yet.

I open the door and call "Hello!" cheerfully. There's no response, so I push open the door to our all-purpose living room. The radio is blaring Madonna, the television is playing MTV, and Danny's novelty robot dog is trying to walk up the side of the sofa.

And Danny is slumped over his sewing machine in a cloud of gold silk, fast asleep.

"Danny?" I say in dismay. "Hey, wake up!"

With a start, Danny sits up and rubs his thin face. His curly hair is rumpled, and his pale blue eyes are even more bloodshot than they were when he answered the door this morning. His skinny frame is clad in an old gray T-shirt and a bony knee is poking out of his ripped jeans, complete with a scab that he got Rollerblading this past weekend. He looks like a ten-year-old with stubble.

"Becky!" he says blearily. "Hi! What are you doing here?"

"This is my apartment. Remember? You were working down here because your electricity fused."

"Oh. Yeah." He looks around dazedly. "Right."

"Are you OK?" I peer at him anxiously. "I got some coffee."

I hand him a cup and he takes a couple of deep gulps. Then his eyes land on the pile of mail in my hand and for the first time, he seems to wake up.

"Hey, is that British *Vogue*?"

"Er . . . yes," I say, putting it down where he can't reach it. "So—how's the dress doing?"

"It's going great! Totally under control."

"Can I try it on yet?"

There's a pause. Danny looks at the mound of gold silk in front of him as though he's never seen it before in his life.

"Not yet, no," he says at last.

"But it will be ready in time?"

"Of course! Absolutely." He puts his foot down and the sewing machine starts whirring busily. "You know what?" he says over the noise. "I could really do with a glass of water."

"Coming up!"

I hurry into the kitchen, turn on the tap, and wait for the cold to come through. The plumbing in this building is a little bit eccentric, and we're always on at Mrs. Watts, the owner, to fix it. But she lives miles away in Florida, and doesn't really seem interested. And other than that, the place is completely wonderful. Our apartment is huge by New York standards, with wooden floors and a fireplace, and enormous floor-to-ceiling windows.

(Of course, Mum and Dad weren't at all impressed when they came over. First they couldn't understand why we didn't live in a house. Then they couldn't understand why the kitchen was so small. Then they started saying wasn't it a shame we didn't have a garden, and did I know that Tom next door had moved into a house with a quarter of an acre? Honestly. If you had a quarter of an acre in New York, someone would just build ten office buildings on it.)

"OK! So how's it—" I walk back into the living room and break off. The sewing machine has stopped, and Danny's reading my copy of *Vogue*.

"Danny!" I wail. "What about my dress!"

"Did you see this?" says Danny, jabbing at the page. "'Hamish Fargle's collection demonstrated his customary flair and wit,'" he reads aloud. "Give me a break! He has zero talent. Zero. You know, he was at school with me. Totally ripped off one of my ideas—" He looks up at me, eyes narrowed. "Is he stocked at Barneys?"

"Erm . . . I don't know," I lie.

Danny is completely obsessed with being stocked at Barneys. It's the only thing he wants in the world. And just because I work there as a personal shopper, he seems to think I should be able to arrange meetings with the head buyer.

In fact, I have arranged meetings with the head buyer for him. The first time, he arrived a week late for the appointment and she'd gone to Milan. The second time, he was showing her a jacket and as she tried it on, all the buttons fell off.

Oh God. What was I thinking, asking him to make my dress?

"Danny, just tell me. Is my dress going to be ready?"

There's a long pause.

"Does it actually have to be ready for today?" says Danny at last. "Like literally *today*?"

"I'm catching a plane in six hours!" My voice rises to a squeak. "I've got to walk down the aisle in less than . . ." I break off and shake my head. "Look, don't worry. I'll wear something else."

"Something else?" Danny puts down *Vogue* and stares at me blankly. "What do you mean, something else?"

"Well . . ."

"Are you *firing* me?" He looks as though I've told him our ten-year marriage is over. "Just because I've run a tad over schedule?"

"I'm not firing you! But I mean, I can't be a bridesmaid without a dress, can I?"

"But what else would you wear?"

"Well . . ." I twist my fingers awkwardly. "I do have this one little reserve dress in my wardrobe . . ."

I can't tell him I've actually got three. And two on hold at Barneys.

"By whom?"

"Er . . . Donna Karan," I say guiltily.

"Donna Karan?" His voice cracks with betrayal. "You prefer Donna Karan to me?"

"Of course not! But I mean, the seams are actually sewn . . ."

"Wear my dress."

"Danny—"

"Wear my dress! Please!" He throws himself down on the floor and walks toward me on his knees. "It'll be ready. I'll work all day and all night."

"We haven't *got* all day and all night! We've got about . . . three hours!"

"Then I'll work all three hours. I'll do it!"

"You can really make a boned embroidered corset from scratch in three hours?" I say incredulously.

Danny looks abashed. "So . . . um . . . we may have to rethink the design very slightly . . ."

"In what way?"

He drums his fingers for a few moments, then looks up. "Do you have a plain white T-shirt?"

"A *T-shirt*?" I can't hide my dismay.

"It'll be great. I promise!" From outside comes the chugging sound of a van pulling up and Danny glances out of the window. "Hey, did you buy another antique?"

An hour later I stare at myself in the mirror. I'm wearing a full sweeping skirt made of gold silk—topped by my white T-shirt, which is now completely unrecognizable. Danny's ripped off the sleeves, sewn on sequins, gathered hems, created lines where there were none—and basically turned it into the most fantastic top I've ever seen.

"I love it." I beam at Danny. "I love it! I'll be the coolest brides-maid in the world!"

"It's pretty good, isn't it?" Danny gives a casual shrug, but I can see he's pleased with himself.

I take another gulp of my cocktail, draining the glass. "Delicious. Shall we have another one?"

"What was in that?"

"Erm . . ." I squint vaguely at the bottles lined up in the cocktail cabinet. "I'm not sure."

It took a while to get the cocktail cabinet up the stairs and into our apartment. To be honest, it's a bit bigger than I remembered, and I'm not sure it'll fit into that little alcove behind the sofa where I'd planned to put it. But still, it looks fantastic! It's standing proudly in the middle of the room, and we've already put it to good use. As soon as it arrived, Danny went upstairs and raided his brother Randall's drinks cupboard, and I got all the booze I could find in the kitchen. We've had a margarita each and a gimlet, and my invention called the Bloomwood, which consists of vodka, orange, and M&M's, which you scoop out with a spoon.

"Give me the top again. I want to pull in that shoulder tighter."

I peel off the top, hand it to him, and reach for my jumper, not bothering to be modest. I mean, this is Danny. He threads a needle and starts expertly gathering along the hem of the T-shirt. "So, these weird cousin-marrying friends of yours," he says. "What's that about?"

"They're not weird!" I hesitate for a moment. "Well, OK, Tarquin is a tiny bit weird. But Suze isn't weird at all. She's my best friend! You've met her!"

Danny raises an eyebrow. "So—couldn't they find anyone else to marry except their own family? Was it like, 'OK, Mom's taken . . . my sister, too fat . . . the dog . . . mmm, don't like the hair.' "

"Stop it!" I can't help giggling. "They just suddenly realized they were meant for each other."

"Like *Harry Met Sally*." He puts on a film-trailer voice. "They were friends. They came from the same gene pool."

"Danny . . ."

"OK." He relents, and snips off the thread. "So, what about you and Luke?"

"What about us?"

"D'you think you'll get married?"

"I . . . I have no idea!" I say, feeling a slight color coming to my cheeks. "I can't say it's ever crossed my mind."

Which is completely true.

Well, OK. It's not *completely* true. Maybe it has crossed my mind on the very odd occasion. Maybe just occasionally I've doodled "Becky Brandon" on my notepad to see what it looked like. And I might possibly have flicked through *Martha Stewart Weddings* once or twice. Just out of idle curiosity.

Perhaps, also, it's occurred to me that Suze is getting married and she's been going out with Tarquin for less time than me and Luke.

But you know. It's not a big deal. I'm really not into weddings. In fact, if Luke asked me, I'd probably say no.

Well . . . OK. I'd probably say yes.

But the point is, it's not going to happen. Luke doesn't want to get married "for a very long time, if at all." He said that in an interview in the *Telegraph* three years ago, which I found in his file of clippings. (I wasn't poking about. I was looking for an elastic band.) The piece was mainly about his business, but they asked him about personal stuff too—and then they captioned his picture *Brandon: marriage at the bottom of agenda.*

Which is absolutely fine by me. It's at the bottom of my agenda, too.

While Danny's finishing off the dress, I do a little housework. Which is to say I tip the dirty breakfast dishes into the sink where they can soak, dab at a spot on the counter—and then spend some time rearranging the spice jars in the spice rack, according to color. That's such a satisfying job. Almost as good as organizing my felt-tip pens used to be.

"So do you guys find it hard living together?" says Danny, coming to the door and watching me.

"No." I look at him in surprise. "Why?"

"My friend Kirsty just tried living with her boyfriend. Disaster.

All they did was fight. She said she doesn't know how anyone does it."

I slot the cumin jar next to fenugreek (what *is* fenugreek?), feeling rather smug. The truth is, Luke and I have had hardly any problems since living together. Except maybe the incident when I repainted the bathroom and got gold glitter paint on his new suit. But that doesn't count, because, as Luke admitted afterward, he completely overreacted, and anybody with sense would have seen that the paint was wet.

Now that I think about it, perhaps we've had the odd teeny little dispute about how many clothes I buy. Perhaps Luke has on occasion opened the wardrobe door and said in exasperation, "Are you *ever* going to wear any of these?"

Perhaps we've also had the odd argu-frank discussion about how many hours Luke works. He runs his own very successful financial PR company, Brandon Communications, which has branches in London and New York and is expanding all the time. He loves his work, and maybe once or twice I've accused him of loving work more than me.

But the point is, we're a mature, flexible couple who are able to talk things through. We went out to lunch not long ago and had a long talk, during which I sincerely promised I would try to shop a bit less and Luke sincerely promised he would try to work a bit less. And I reckon we're both making a pretty good effort.

"Living together has to be worked at," I say wisely. "You have to be flexible. You have to give as well as take."

"Really?"

"Oh yes. Luke and I share our finances, we share the chores . . . it's all a matter of teamwork. The point is, you can't expect everything to stay as it was before. You have to *accommodate*."

"Really?" Danny looks interested. "So who do you think accommodates more? You or Luke?"

I'm thoughtful for a moment.

"It's difficult to say, really," I say at last. "I expect it's about equal on both sides."

"So, like . . . all this stuff." Danny gestures around the cluttered apartment. "Is it mostly yours or mostly his?"

"Erm . . ." I look around, taking in all my aromatherapy candles, vintage lace cushions, and stacks of magazines. For an instant, my mind flicks back to the immaculate, minimalist apartment Luke had in London.

"You know . . ." I say at last. "A bit of both . . ."

Which is kind of true. I mean, Luke's got his laptop in the bedroom.

"The point is, there's no friction between us," I continue. "We think as one. We're like one unit."

"That's great," says Danny, reaching for an apple from the fruit bowl. "You're lucky."

"I know we are." I look at him confidingly. "You know, Luke and I are so in tune, sometimes there's almost a . . . sixth sense between us."

"Really?" Danny stares at me. "Are you serious?"

"Oh yes. I'll know what he's about to say, or I'll kind of *feel* when he's around . . ."

"Like The Force?"

"I suppose." I give a nonchalant shrug. "It's like a gift. I don't question it too closely—"

"Greetings, Obi-Wan Kenobi," says a deep voice behind us, and Danny and I both jump out of our skins. I swivel round—and there's Luke, standing at the door with an amused grin. His face is flushed from the cold and there are snowflakes in his dark hair, and he's so tall, the room suddenly seems a little smaller.

"Luke!" I exclaim. "You scared us!"

"Sorry," he says. "I assumed you would feel my presence."

"Yes. Well, I did kind of feel something . . ." I say, a little defiantly.

"Of course you did." He gives me a kiss. "Hi, Danny."

"Hi," says Danny, watching as Luke takes off his navy cashmere coat, then loosens his cuffs while simultaneously unknotting his tie, with the same assured, deft movements he always makes.

Once, after a few too many cocktails, Danny asked me, "Does Luke make love the same way he opens a champagne bottle?" And although I shrieked and hit him, and said it was none of his business, I could kind of see what he meant. Luke never fumbles or hesitates or looks confused. He always seems to know exactly what he wants, and he pretty much gets it, whether it's a champagne bottle opening smoothly or a new client for his company, or, in bed, for us to . . .

Well. Anyway. Let's just say, since we've been living together, my horizons have been broadened.

Now he picks up the post and starts to leaf briskly through it. "So how are you, Danny?"

"Good, thanks," says Danny, taking a bite of apple. "How's the world of high finance? Did you see my brother today?" Danny's brother Randall works in a financing company, and Luke's had lunch with him a couple of times.

"Not today, no," says Luke.

"OK, well, when you do," says Danny, "ask him if he's put on weight. Really casually. Just say, 'Why, Randall, you're looking well-covered.' And then maybe comment on his choice of entree. He is so paranoid that he's getting fat. It's hilarious."

"Brotherly love," says Luke. "Beautiful, isn't it?" He comes to the end of the post and looks at me with a slight frown.

"Becky, has our joint account statement come yet?"

"Er . . . no. Not yet." I give him a reassuring smile. "I expect it'll come tomorrow!"

Our bank statement actually came yesterday, but I put it straight in my underwear drawer. I'm slightly concerned about some of the entries, so I'm just going to see if there's anything I can do to rectify the situation. The truth is, despite what I said to Danny, I've been finding this whole joint account thing a bit tricky.

Don't get me wrong, I'm all for sharing money. In fact, hand on heart, I *love* sharing Luke's money. It gives me a real buzz! I just don't love it when he suddenly asks, "What was this seventy dollars in Bloomingdale's for?" and I can't remember. So I've worked out a whole new tactical response—which is so simple, it's brilliant.

It's to spill something on the statement, so he can't read it.

"I'm going to take a shower," says Luke, gathering up the post. And he's almost out of the room—when he stops. Very slowly he turns back and looks at the cocktail cabinet as though seeing it for the first time.

"What is that?" he says slowly.

"It's a cocktail cabinet!" I say brightly.

"Where has it come from?"

"It . . . umm . . . actually, I bought it today."

"Becky . . ." Luke closes his eyes. "I thought we said no more crap."

"It's not crap! It's genuine 1930s! We can make amazing cocktails every night!" I'm feeling a bit nervous at his expression, so I start to gabble. "Look, I know we said no more furniture. But this is different. I mean, when you see a one-off like this, you have to grab it!"

I trail away and bite my lip. Luke silently walks toward the cabinet. He runs a hand along the top, then picks up a cocktail shaker, his mouth tight.

"Luke, I just thought it would be fun! I thought you'd like it. The guy in the shop said I've got a really good eye . . ."

"A really good eye," echoes Luke as though in disbelief.

I gasp and scream as he throws the cocktail shaker in the air, and I'm wincing, waiting for it to land with a crash on the wooden floor—when Luke neatly catches it. Danny and I gape as he throws it again, twirls round, and rolls it down his arm.

I don't believe it. I'm living with Tom Cruise.

"I worked as a barman for a summer," says Luke, his face breaking into a smile.

I never knew that! Luke is so driven and businesslike and you think he doesn't care about anything except work . . . and then all of a sudden, he surprises you.

"Teach me how to do it!" I cry excitedly. "I want to be able to do that!"

"And me!" says Danny. He picks up the other cocktail shaker, gives it an inexpert twirl, then tosses it at me. I make a grab, but it lands on the sofa.

"Butterfingers!" mocks Danny. "Come on, Becky. You need to get in practice for catching the bouquet at this wedding."

"No, I don't!"

"Sure you do. You wanna be next, don't you?"

"Danny . . ." I try to give a lighthearted laugh.

"You two should definitely get married," Danny continues, ignoring me. He picks up the cocktail shaker and begins tossing it from hand to hand. "It's perfect. Look at you. You live together, you don't want to kill each other, you're not already related . . . I could make you a *fabulous* dress . . ." He puts down the shaker with a suddenly intent expression. "Hey, listen, Becky. Promise me, if you get married, I can make your dress."

This is appalling. If he carries on like this, Luke will think I'm trying to pressure him. He might even think I told Danny to bring up the subject deliberately.

I've got to redress the balance somehow. Quickly.

"Actually, I don't want to get married," I hear myself saying. "Not for at least ten years."

"Really?" Danny looks taken aback. "You don't?"

"Is that so?" Luke looks up with an unreadable expression. "I wasn't aware of that."

"Weren't you?" I reply, trying to sound nonchalant. "Well . . . now you know!"

"Why don't you want to get married for ten years?" says Danny.

"I . . . erm . . ." I clear my throat. "As it happens, I have a lot of things I want to do first. I want to concentrate on my career, and I want to . . . explore my full potential . . . and . . . get to know the real me first . . . and . . . be a whole . . . umm . . . rounded person."

I tail off and meet Luke's quizzical gaze slightly defiantly.

"I see," he says, nodding. "Well, that sounds very sensible." He looks at the cocktail shaker in his hand, then puts it down. "I'd better go and pack."

He wasn't supposed to *agree* with me.

Two

WE ARRIVE AT Heathrow at seven the next morning and pick up our rental car. As we drive along to Suze's parents' house in Hampshire, I peer blearily out of the window at the snowy country-side, the hedgerows and fields and little villages, as though I've never seen them before. After Manhattan, everything looks so tiny and pretty. For the first time I realize why Americans go around call-ing everything in England "quaint."

"Which way now?" says Luke, as we arrive at yet another little crossroads.

"Erm, you definitely turn left here. I mean . . . right. No, I mean left."

As the car swings round, I fish in my bag for the invitation, just to check the exact address.

Sir Gilbert and Lady Cleath-Stuart
request the pleasure of your company . . .

I stare, slightly mesmerized, at the grand swirly writing. God, I still can't quite believe Suze and Tarquin are getting married.

I mean, of course I *believe* it. After all, they've been going out for well over a year now, and Tarquin's basically moved into the flat I used to share with Suze—although they seem to be spending more and more time in Scotland. They're both really sweet and laid back, and everyone's agreed that they make a brilliant couple.

But just occasionally, when I'm not concentrating, my mind will suddenly yell, "Whaat? Suze and Tarquin?"

I mean, Tarquin used to be Suze's weird geeky cousin. For years he was just that awkward guy in the corner with the ancient jacket and a tendency to hum Wagner in public places. He was the guy who rarely ventured beyond the safe haven of his Scottish castle—and when he did, it was to take me on the worst date of my life (although we don't talk about that anymore).

But now he's . . . well, he's Suze's boyfriend. Still slightly awkward, and still prone to wearing woolly jumpers knitted by his old nanny. Still a bit tatty round the edges. But Suze loves him, and that's what counts.

Oh God, I can't start crying yet. I have to pace myself.

"Harborough Hall," reads Luke, pausing at a pair of crumbling stone pillars. "Is this it?"

"Erm . . ." I sniff, and try to look businesslike. "Yes, this is it. Just drive in."

I've been to Suze's house plenty of times before, but I always forget quite how impressive it is. We sweep down a great big long avenue lined with trees and into a circular gravel drive. The house is large and gray and ancient-looking, with pillars at the front and ivy growing over it.

"Nice house," says Luke as we head toward the huge front door. "How old is it?"

"Dunno," I say vaguely. "It's been in their family for years." I tug at the bell pull to see if by any remote chance it's been mended—but it obviously hadn't. I knock a couple of times with the heavy door knocker—and when there's no answer to that either, I push my way into the huge flagstoned hall, where an old Labrador is asleep by a crackling fire.

"Hello?" I call. "Suze?"

Suddenly I notice that Suze's father is also asleep by the fireplace, in a large winged armchair. I'm a bit scared of Suze's father, actually. I certainly don't want to wake him up.

"Suze?" I say, more quietly.

"Bex! I thought I heard something!"

I look up—and there's Suze standing on the staircase, in a tartan dressing gown with her blond hair streaming down her back and a huge excited smile.

"Suze!"

I bound up the stairs and give her a huge hug. As I pull away we're both a bit pink about the eyes, and I give a shaky laugh. God, I've missed Suze, even more than I'd realized.

"Come up to my room!" says Suze, tugging my hand. "Come and see my dress!"

"Is it really lovely?" I say excitedly. "In the picture it looked amazing."

"It's just perfect! Plus you *have* to see, I've got the coolest corsety thing from Rigby and Peller . . . and these really gorgeous knickers . . ."

Luke clears his throat and we both look round.

"Oh!" says Suze. "Sorry, Luke. There's coffee and newspapers and stuff in the kitchen, through there." She points down a corridor. "You can have bacon and eggs if you like! Mrs. Gearing will make them for you."

"Mrs. Gearing sounds like my kind of woman," says Luke with a smile. "I'll see you later."

Suze's room is light and airy and overlooks the garden. I say *garden*. It's about twelve thousand acres, with lawns running down from the back of the house to a clump of cedar trees and a lake, which Suze nearly drowned in once when she was three. There's also a walled rose garden to the left, all flower beds and gravel paths and hedges, which is where Tarquin proposed to Suze. (Apparently he got down on one knee and when he stood up, gravel was clinging to his trousers. That is so Tarquin.) On the right there's an old tennis court and then rough grass, extending all the way to a hedge, beyond which is the village church graveyard. As I look out of the window now, I can see a huge marquee billowing to the rear of the house, and a tented walkway being put up, which will snake past the tennis court and over the grass, all the way to the churchyard gate.

"You're not going to walk to the church?" I say, suddenly fearful for Suze's Emma Hope shoes.

"No, silly! I'm going in the carriage. But all the guests can walk back to the house, and there'll be people handing out hot whiskeys as they go."

"God, it's going to be spectacular!" I say, watching as a man in jeans begins to hammer a stake into the ground. And in spite of myself, I can't help feeling a twinge of envy. I've always dreamed of having some huge, amazing wedding, with horses and carriages and lots of hoopla, ever since . . .

Well, since . . .

To be completely, perfectly honest, ever since Princess Diana's wedding. I was six years old when we all watched it round at our neighbor Janice's house, and I can still remember goggling at her as she got out of the carriage in that dress. It was like Cinderella come to life. It was *better* than Cinderella. I wanted to be her so much, it hurt. Mum had bought me a commemorative book of photographs called *Diana's Big Day*—and the next day I spent ages making my own version called *Becky's Big Day*, with lots of drawings of me in a big frilly dress, wearing a crown. (And, in some versions, carrying a magic wand.)

Maybe I've moved on a little since then. I don't dream about wearing a crumpled cream-colored lampshade for a wedding dress. I've even given up on marrying a member of the royal family. But still, whenever I see a wedding, part of me turns back into that starry-eyed six-year-old.

"I know! Isn't it going to be great?" Suze beams happily. "Now, I must just brush my teeth . . ."

She disappears into the bathroom and I wander over to her dressing table, where the announcement of the engagement is stuck in the mirror. The Hon. Susan Cleath-Stuart and The Hon. Tarquin Cleath-Stuart. Blimey. I always forget Suze is so grand.

"I want a title," I say, as Suze comes back into the room with a hairbrush in her hair. "I feel all left out. How do I get one?"

"Ooh, no you don't," says Suze, wrinkling her nose. "They're crap. People send you letters saying Dear Ms. Hon."

"Still. It'd be so cool. What could I be?"

"Erm . . ." Suze tugs at a tangle in her hair. "Dame Becky Bloomwood?"

"That makes me sound about ninety-three," I say doubtfully.

"What about . . . Becky Bloomwood MBE. Those MBE things are quite easy to get, aren't they?"

"Easy-peasy," says Suze confidently. "You could get one for services to industry or something. I'll nominate you, if you like. Now come on, I want to see your dress!"

"OK!" I heave my case onto the bed, click it open, and carefully draw out Danny's creation. "What do you think?" I proudly hold it up against myself and swoosh the gold silk around. "It's pretty cool, isn't it?"

"It's fantastic!" says Suze, staring at it with wide eyes. "I've never seen anything like it!" She fingers the sequins on the shoulder. "Where did you get it? Is this the one from Barneys?"

"No, this is the one from Danny. Remember, I told you he was making me a dress?"

"That's right." She screws up her face. "Which one's Danny, again?"

"My upstairs neighbor," I remind her. "The designer. The one we bumped into on the stairs that time?"

"Oh yes," says Suze, nodding. "I remember."

But the way she says it, I can tell she doesn't really.

I can't blame her—she only met Danny for about two minutes. He was on his way to visit his parents in Connecticut and she was pretty jet-lagged at the time and they barely spoke. Still. It's weird to think that Suze doesn't really know Danny, and he doesn't know her, when they're both so important to me. It's like I've got two completely separate lives, and the longer I'm in New York, the farther they split apart.

"OK, here's mine," says Suze excitedly.

She opens a wardrobe door and unzips a calico cover—and there's a simply stunning dress, all drifting white silk and velvet with long sleeves and a traditional long train.

"Oh God, Suze," I breathe, my throat tight. "You're going to be so completely beautiful. I still can't believe you're getting married! 'Mrs. Cleath-Stuart.' "

"Ooh, don't call me that!" says Suze, wrinkling her nose. "It sounds like my mother. But actually it *is* quite handy marrying someone in the family," she adds, closing the wardrobe, "because I can keep my name and take his, all at the same time. So I can keep being S C-S for my frames." She reaches into a cardboard box and pulls out a beautiful glass frame, all spirals and whorls. "Look, this is the new range—"

Suze's career is designing photograph frames, which sell all over the country, and last year she diversified into photograph albums, wrapping paper, and gift boxes too.

"The whole theme is shell shapes," she says proudly. "D'you like it?"

"It's beautiful!" I say, running my finger round the spirals. "How did you come up with it?"

"I got the idea from Tarkie, actually! We were out walking one day and he was saying how he used to collect shells when he was a child and about all the different amazing shapes in nature . . . and then it hit me!"

I look at her face, all lit up, and have a sudden image of her and Tarquin walking hand in hand on the blustery moors, in Aran sweaters by The Scotch House.

"Suze, you're going to be so happy with Tarquin," I say heart-feltly.

"D'you think?" She flushes with pleasure. "Really?"

"Definitely. I mean, look at you! You're simply glowing!"

Which is true. I hadn't really noticed it before, but she looks completely different from the old Suze. She's still got the same delicate nose and high cheekbones, but her face is rounder, and kind of softer. And she's still slim, but there's a kind of a fullness . . . almost a . . .

My gaze runs down her body and stops.

Hang on a minute.

No. Surely . . .

No.

"Suze?"

"Yes?"

"Suze, are you . . ." I swallow. "You're not . . . pregnant?"

"No!" she replies indignantly. "Of course not! Honestly, what-ever can have given you—" She meets my eye, breaks off, and shrugs. "Oh, all right then, yes I am. How did you guess?"

"How did I guess? From you . . . I mean, you *look* pregnant."

"No, I don't! No one else has guessed!"

"They must have. It's completely obvious!"

"No, it isn't!" She sucks in her stomach and looks at herself in the mirror. "You see? And once I've got my Rigby and Peller on . . ."

I can't get my head round this. Suze is pregnant!

"So—is it a secret? Don't your parents know?"

"Oh no! Nobody knows. Not even Tarkie." She pulls a face. "It's a bit tacksville, being pregnant on your wedding day, don't you think? I thought I'd pretend it's a honeymoon baby."

"But you must be at least three months gone."

"Four months. It's due at the beginning of June."

I stare at her. "So how on earth are you going to pretend it's a honeymoon baby?"

"Um . . ." She thinks for a moment. "It could be a bit premature."

"Four whole *months*?"

"Well, OK then. I'll think of something else," says Suze airily. "It's ages away. Anyway, the important thing is, don't tell anyone."

"OK. I won't." Gingerly I reach out and touch her stomach. Suze is having a baby. She's going to be a mother. And Tarquin's going to be a father. God, it's like we're all suddenly growing up or something.

Suze is right on one point at least. Once she's squeezed into her corset, you can't see the bulge at all. In fact, as we both sit in front of her dressing table on the morning of the wedding, grinning excitedly at each other, she actually looks *thinner* than me, which is a tad unfair.

We've had such a great couple of days, chilling out, watching old videos and eating endless KitKats. (Suze is eating for two, and I need energy after my transatlantic flight.) Luke brought some paperwork with him and has spent most of the time in the library— but for once I don't mind. It's just been so nice to be able to spend some time with Suze. I've heard all about the flat she and Tarquin are buying in London and I've seen pictures of the gorgeous hotel on Antigua where she and Tarquin are going for their honeymoon, and I've tried on most of the new clothes in her wardrobe.

There's been loads going on all over the house, with florists and caterers and relations arriving every minute. What's a bit weird is, none of the family seems particularly bothered by it. Suze's mother has been out hunting both the days that I've been here, and her father has been in his study. Mrs. Gearing, their housekeeper, is the one who's been organizing the marquee and flowers and everything—and even she seems pretty relaxed. When I asked Suze about it she just shrugged and said, "I suppose we're used to throwing big parties."

Last night there was a grand drinks party for Suze and Tarquin's relations who have all come down from Scotland, and I was expecting everyone to be talking about the wedding then, at least. But every time I tried to get anyone excited about the flowers, or how romantic it all was, I got blank looks. It was only when Suze mentioned that Tarquin was going to buy her a horse as a wedding present that they all suddenly got animated, and started talking about breeders they knew, and horses they'd bought, and how their great chum had a very nice young chestnut mare Suze might be interested in.

I mean, honestly. No one even *asked* me what my dress was like.

Anyway. I don't care, because it looks wonderful. We both look wonderful. We've both been made up by a fantastic makeup artist, and our hair is up in sleek chignons. The photographer has taken so-called "candid" pictures of me buttoning Suze into her dress (he made us do it three times, in fact my arms were aching by the end). Now Suze is umming and aahing over about six family tiaras while I take sips of champagne. Just to keep me from getting nervous.

"What about your mother?" says the hairdresser to Suze, as she pulls wispy blond tendrils round her face. "Does she want a blow-dry?"

"I doubt it," says Suze, pulling a face. "She's not really into that kind of stuff."

"What's she wearing?" I ask.

"God knows," says Suze. "The first thing that comes to hand, probably." She meets my eye, and I pull a tiny sympathetic face. Last night Suze's mother came downstairs for drinks in a dirndl skirt and patterned woolly jumper, with a large diamond brooch on the front. Mind you, Tarquin's mother looked even worse. I really don't know where Suze has managed to get her sense of style.

"Bex, could you just go and make sure she doesn't put on some hideous old gardening dress?" says Suze. "She'll listen to you, I know she will."

"Well . . . OK," I say doubtfully. "I'll try."

As I let myself out of the room, I see Luke coming along the corridor in his morning dress.

"You look very beautiful," he says with a smile.

"Do I?" I do a little twirl. "It's a lovely dress, isn't it? And it fits so well—"

"I wasn't looking at the dress," says Luke. His eyes meet mine with a wicked glint and I feel a flicker of pleasure. "Is Suze decent?" he adds. "I just wanted to wish her well."

"Oh yes," I say. "Go on in. Hey, Luke, you'll never guess!"

I've been absolutely dying to tell Luke about Suze's baby for the last two days, and now the words slip out before I can stop them.

"What?"

"She's . . ." I can't tell him, I just can't. Suze would kill me. "She's . . . got a really nice wedding dress," I finish lamely.

"Good!" says Luke, giving me a curious look. "There's a surprise. Well, I'll just pop in and have a quick word. See you later."

I cautiously make my way to Suze's mother's bedroom and give a gentle knock.

"Hellooo?" thunders a voice in return, and the door is flung open by Suze's mother, Caroline. She's about six feet tall with long rangy legs, gray hair in a knot, and a weatherbeaten face that creases into a smile when she sees me.

"Rebecca!" she booms, and looks at her watch. "Not time yet, is it?"

"Not quite!" I smile gingerly and run my eyes over her outfit of ancient navy blue sweatshirt, jodhpurs, and riding boots. She's got an amazing figure for a woman her age. No wonder Suze is so skinny. I glance around the room, but I can't see any telltale suit-carriers or hatboxes.

"So, um, Caroline . . . I was just wondering what you were planning to wear today. As mother of the bride!"

"Mother of the bride?" She stares at me. "Good God, I suppose I am. Hadn't thought of it like that."

"Right! So, you . . . haven't got a special outfit ready?"

"Bit early to be dressing up, isn't it?" says Caroline. "I'll just fling something on before we go."

"Well, why don't I help you choose?" I say firmly, and head toward the wardrobe. I throw open the doors, preparing myself for a shock—and gape in astonishment.

This has got to be the most extraordinary collection of clothes I've ever seen. Riding habits, ball dresses, and thirties suits are jostling for space with Indian saris, Mexican ponchos . . . and an extraordinary array of tribal jewelry.

"These clothes!" I breathe.

"I know." Caroline looks at them dismissively. "A load of old rubbish, really."

"Old *rubbish*? My God, if you found any of these in a vintage shop in New York . . ." I pull out a pale blue satin coat edged with ribbon. "This is fantastic."

"D'you like it?" says Caroline in surprise. "Have it."

"I couldn't!"

"Dear girl, I don't want it."

"But surely the sentimental value . . . I mean, your memories—"

"My memories are in here." She taps her head. "Not in there." She surveys the melee of clothes, then picks up a small piece of bone on a leather cord. "Now, *this* I'm rather fond of."

"That?" I say, trying to summon some enthusiasm. "Well, it's—"

"It was given to me by a Masai chief, many years ago now. We were driving at dawn to find a pride of elephants, when a chieftain flagged us down. A tribeswoman was in a fever after giving birth. We helped bring down her temperature and the tribe honored us with gifts. Have you been to the Masai Mara, Rebecca?"

"Er . . . no. I've never actually been to—"

"And this little lovely." She picks up an embroidered purse. "I bought this at a street market in Konya. Bartered for it with my last packet of cigarettes before we trekked up the Nemrut Dagi. Have you been to Turkey?"

"No, not there, either," I say, feeling rather inadequate. God, I feel undertraveled. I scrabble around in my mind, trying to think of somewhere I've been that will impress her—but it's a pretty paltry lineup, now that I think about it. France a few times, Spain, Crete . . . and that's about it. Why haven't I been anywhere exciting? Why haven't I been trekking round Mongolia?

I was going to go to Thailand once, come to think of it. But then I decided to go to France instead and spend the money I saved on a Lulu Guinness handbag.

"I haven't really traveled much at all," I admit reluctantly.

"Well, you must, dear girl!" booms Caroline. "You must broaden your horizons. Learn about life from real people. One of the dearest friends I have in the world is a Bolivian peasant woman. We ground maize together on the plains of the Llanos."

"Wow."

A little clock on the mantelpiece chimes the half hour, and I suddenly realize we're not getting anywhere.

"So anyway . . . did you have any ideas for a wedding outfit?"

"Something warm and colorful," says Caroline, reaching for a thick red and yellow poncho.

"Erm . . . I'm not so sure that would be entirely appropriate . . ." I push between the jackets and dresses, and suddenly see a flash of apricot silk. "Ooh! This is nice." I haul it out—and I don't believe it. It's Balenciaga.

"My going-away outfit," says Caroline reminiscently. "We traveled on the Orient Express to Venice, then explored the caves of Postojna. Do you know that region?"

"You have to wear this!" I say, my voice rising to a squeak of excitement. "You'll look spectacular. And it's so romantic, wearing your own going-away outfit!"

"I suppose it might be rather fun." She holds it up against herself with red, weatherbeaten hands that make me wince every time I look at them. "That should still fit, shouldn't it? Now, there must be a hat around here somewhere . . ." She puts down the suit and starts rooting around on a shelf.

"So—you must be really happy for Suze," I say, picking up an enameled hand mirror and examining it.

"Tarquin's a dear boy." She turns round and taps her beaky nose confidentially. "Very well endowed."

This is true. Tarquin is the fifteenth richest person in the country, or something. But I'm a bit surprised at Suze's mother bringing it up.

"Well, yes . . ." I say. "Although I don't suppose Suze really needs the money . . ."

"I'm not talking about money!" She gives me a knowing smile and suddenly I realize what she means.

"Oh!" I feel myself blushing furiously. "Right! I see!"

"All the Cleath-Stuart men are the same. They're famous for it. Never a divorce in the family," she adds, plonking a green felt hat on top of her head.

Gosh. I'm going to look at Tarquin a bit differently now.

It takes me a while to persuade Caroline out of the green felt hat and into a chic black cloche. As I'm walking back along the corridor toward Suze's room, I hear some familiar voices in the hall downstairs.

"It's common knowledge. Foot-and-mouth was caused by carrier pigeons."

"Pigeons? You're telling me that this huge epidemic, which has wiped out stocks of cattle across Europe, was caused by a few harmless pigeons?"

"Harmless? Graham, they're vermin!"

Mum and Dad! I hurry to the banisters—and there they are, standing by the fireplace. Dad's in morning dress with a top hat under his arm, and Mum's dressed in a navy jacket, floral skirt, and bright red shoes, which don't quite match her red hat.

"Mum?"

"Becky!"

"Mum! Dad!" I hurry down the stairs and envelop them both in a hug, breathing in the familiar scent of Yardley's talc and Tweed.

This trip is getting more emotional by the minute. I haven't seen my parents since they came out to visit me in New York four months ago. And even then, they only stayed for three days before going off to Florida to see the Everglades.

"Mum, you look amazing! Have you done something to your hair?"

"Maureen put some highlights in," she says, looking pleased. "And I popped next door to Janice this morning, so she could do my face. You know, she's taken a course in professional makeup. She's a real expert!"

"I can . . . see!" I say feebly, looking at the lurid stripes of blusher and highlighter painted on Mum's cheeks. Maybe I can manage to wipe them off accidentally on purpose.

"So, is Luke here?" says Mum, looking around with bright eyes, like a squirrel searching for a nut.

"Somewhere around," I say—and Mum and Dad exchange glances.

"He is here, though?" Mum gives a tense little laugh. "You did fly on the same plane, didn't you?"

"Mum, don't worry. He's here. Really."

Mum still doesn't look convinced—and I can't honestly blame her. The truth is, there was this tiny incident at the last wedding we all attended. Luke didn't turn up, and I was completely desperate, and I resorted to . . . um . . .

Well. It was only a tiny white lie. I mean, he *could* have been there, mingling somewhere. If they hadn't had that stupid group photograph, no one would ever have known.

"Jane! Graham! Hello!"

There's Luke, striding through the front door. Thank God for that.

"Luke!" Mum gives a relieved trill of laughter. "You're here! Graham, he's here!"

"Of course he's here!" says my father, rolling his eyes. "Where did you think he was? On the moon?"

"How are you, Jane?" says Luke with a smile, and kisses her on the cheek.

Mum's face is pink with happiness, and she's clutching onto Luke's arm as though he might vanish in a puff of smoke. He gives me a little smile, and I beam happily back. I've been looking forward to this day for so long, and now it's actually here. It's like Christmas. In fact, it's better than Christmas. Through the open front door I can see wedding guests walking past on the snowy gravel in morning dress and smart hats. In the distance, the church bells are pealing, and there's a kind of excited, expectant atmosphere.

"And where's the blushing bride?" says Dad.

"I'm here," comes Suze's voice. We all look up—and there she is, floating down the stairs, clutching a stunning bouquet of roses and ivy.

"Oh, Suzie," says Mum, and claps a hand to her mouth. "Oh, that dress! Oh . . . Becky! You're going to look—" She turns to me with softened eyes and for the first time seems to take in my dress. "Becky . . . is that what you're wearing? You'll freeze!"

"No, I won't. The church is going to be heated."

"It's lovely, isn't it?" says Suze. "So unusual."

"But it's only a T-shirt!" She gives a dissatisfied tug at the sleeve. "And what's this frayed bit? It isn't even finished properly!"

"It's customized," I explain. "It's completely unique."

"Unique? Don't you have to match the others?"

"There aren't any others," explains Suze. "The only other person I would have asked is Tarquin's sister, Fenny. But she said if she was a bridesmaid again she'd jinx her chances of marriage. You know what they say, 'Three times a bridesmaid.' Well, she's been one about ninety-three times! And she's got her eye on this chap who works in the City, so she doesn't want to take any chances."

There's a short silence. I can see Mum's brain working hard. Oh God, *please* don't—

"Becky love, how many times have you been a bridesmaid?" she says, a little too casually. "There was Uncle Malcolm and Aunt Sylvia's wedding . . . but I think that's it, isn't it?"

"And Ruthie and Paul's," I remind her.

"You weren't a bridesmaid at that," says Mum at once. "You were a . . . flower girl. So it's twice, including today. Yes, twice."

"Did you get that, Luke?" says Dad with a grin. "Twice."

Honestly, what are my parents *like*?

"Well, anyway!" I say, trying quickly to think of another subject. "So . . . er . . ."

"Of course, Becky has a good ten years before she needs to worry about anything like that . . ." says Luke conversationally.

"What?" Mum stiffens, and her eyes dart from Luke to me and back again. "What did you say?"

"Becky wants to wait at least ten years before she gets married," says Luke. "Isn't that right, Becky?"

There's a stunned silence. I can feel my face growing hot.

"Um . . ." I clear my throat and try to give a nonchalant smile. "That's . . . that's right."

"Really?" says Suze, staring at me, wide-eyed. "I never knew that! Why?"

"So I can . . . um . . . explore my full potential," I mumble, not daring to look at Mum. "And . . . get to know the real me."

"Get to know the real you?" Mum's voice is slightly shrill. "Why

do you need ten years to do that? I could show it to you in ten minutes!"

"But Bex, how old will you be in ten years' time?" says Suze,
wrinkling her brow.

"I won't necessarily need ten whole years exactly," I say, feeling
a little rattled. "You know, maybe . . . eight will be long enough."

"Eight?" Mum looks as though she wants to burst into tears.

"Luke," says Suze, looking perturbed. "Did you know about
this?"

"We discussed it the other day," says Luke with an easy smile.

"But I don't understand," she persists. "What about the—"

"The time?" Luke cuts her off neatly. "You're right. I think we
should all get going. You know, it's five to two."

"Five minutes?" Suze suddenly looks petrified. "Really? But I'm
not ready! Bex, where are your flowers?"

"Er . . . in your room, I think. I put them down somewhere . . ."

"Well, get them! And where's Daddy got to? Oh shit, I want a
cigarette—"

"Suze, you can't *smoke*!" I say in horror. "It's bad for the—" I
stop myself just in time.

"For the dress?" suggests Luke helpfully.

"Yes. She might . . . drop ash on it."

By the time I've found my flowers in Suze's bathroom, redone my
lipstick, and come downstairs again, only Luke is left in the hall.

"Your parents have gone over," he says. "Suze says we should go
over too, and she'll come with her father in the carriage. And I've
found a coat for you," he adds, proffering a sheepskin jacket. "Your
mother's right, you can't walk over like that."

"OK," I agree reluctantly. "But I'm taking it off in the church."

"Did you know your dress is unraveling at the back, by the
way?" he says as he puts it on.

"Really?" I look at him in dismay. "Does it look awful?"

"It looks very nice." His mouth twitches into a smile. "But you
might want to find a safety pin after the service."

"Bloody Danny!" I shake my head. "I knew I should have gone for Donna Karan."

As Luke and I make our way over the gravel to the tented walkway, the air is still and silent and a watery sun is coming out. The pealing bells have diminished to a single chiming, and there's no one about except a sole scurrying waiter. Everyone else must already be inside.

"Sorry if I brought up a sensitive subject just then," says Luke as we begin to walk toward the church.

"Sensitive?" I raised my eyebrows. "Oh, what, *that*. That's not a sensitive subject at all!"

"Your mother seemed a bit upset . . ."

"Mum? Honestly, she's not bothered either way. In fact . . . she was joking!"

"Joking?"

"Yes!" I say, a little defiantly. "Joking."

"I see." Luke takes my arm as I stumble slightly on the matting. "So you're still determined to wait eight years before you get married."

"Absolutely." I nod. "At least eight years."

In the distance I can hear hooves on gravel, which must be Suze's carriage setting off.

"Or you know, maybe six," I add casually. "Or . . . five, possibly. It all depends."

There's a long silence, broken only by the soft, rhythmic sound of our footsteps on the walkway. The atmosphere is growing very strange between us, and I don't quite dare look at Luke. I clear my throat and rub my nose, and try to think of a comment about the weather.

We reach the church gate, and Luke turns to look at me—and suddenly his face is stripped of its usual quizzical expression.

"Seriously, Becky," he says. "Do you really want to wait five years?"

"I . . . I don't know," I say, confused. "Do you?"

There's a moment of stillness between us, and my heart starts to thump.

Oh my God. Oh my God. Maybe he's going to . . . Maybe he's about to—

"Ah! The bridesmaid!" The vicar bustles out of the porch and Luke and I both jump. "All set to walk up the aisle?"

"I, er . . . think so," I say, aware of Luke's gaze. "Yes."

"Good! You'd better get inside!" adds the vicar to Luke. "You don't want to miss the moment!"

"No," he says, after a pause. "No, I don't."

He drops a kiss on my shoulder and walks inside without saying anything else, and I stare after him, still completely confused.

Did we just talk about . . . Was Luke really saying . . .

Then there's the sound of hooves, and I'm jolted out of my reverie. I turn to see Suze's carriage coming down the road like something out of a fairy tale. Her veil is blowing in the wind and she's smiling radiantly at some people who have stopped to watch, and I've never seen her look more beautiful.

I honestly wasn't planning to cry. In fact, I'd already planned a way to stop myself doing so, which is to recite the alphabet backward in a French accent. But even as I'm helping Suze straighten her train I'm feeling damp around the eyes. And as the organ music swells and we start to process slowly forward into the packed church, I'm having to sniff hard every two beats, along with the organ. Suze is holding tightly to her father's arm and her train is gliding along the old stone floor. I'm walking behind, trying not to tap my heels on the floor, and hoping no one will notice my dress unraveling.

We reach the front—and there's Tarquin waiting, with his best man. He's as tall and bony as ever, and his face still reminds me of a stoat, but I have to admit he's looking pretty striking in his sporran and kilt. He's gazing at Suze with such transparent love and admiration that I can feel my nose starting to prickle again. He turns briefly, meets my eye, and grins nervously—and I give an embarrassed little smile back. To be honest, I'll never be able to look at him again without thinking about what Caroline said.

The vicar begins his "Dearly beloved" speech, and I feel myself relax with pleasure. I'm going to relish every single, familiar word. This is like watching the start of a favorite movie, with my two best friends playing the main parts.

"Susan, wilt thou take this man to be thy wedded husband?" The vicar's got huge bushy eyebrows, which he raises at every question, as though he's afraid the answer might be no. "Wilt thou love him, comfort him, honor, and keep him in sickness and in health; and, forsaking all others, keep thee only unto him, so long as ye both shall live?"

There's a pause—then Suze says, "I will," in a voice as clear as a bell.

I wish bridesmaids got to say something. It wouldn't have to be anything very much, just a quick "Yes" or "I do."

When we come to the bit where Suze and Tarquin have to hold hands, Suze gives me her bouquet, and I take the opportunity to turn round and have a quick peek at the congregation. The place is crammed to the gills, in fact there isn't even room for everyone to sit down. There are lots of strapping men in kilts and women in velvet suits, and there's Fenny and a whole crowd of her London friends, all wearing Philip Treacy hats, it looks like. And there's Mum, squashed right up against Dad, with a tissue pressed to her eyes. She looks up and sees me and I give a little smile—but all she does is sob again.

I turn back and Suze and Tarquin are kneeling down, and the vicar is intoning severely, "Those whom God has joined together, let no man put asunder."

I look at Suze as she beams radiantly at Tarquin. She's completely lost in him. She belongs to him now. And to my surprise, I suddenly feel slightly hollow inside. Suze is married. It's all changed.

It's a year since I went off to live in New York, and I've loved every minute of it. Of course I have. But subconsciously, I realize, I've always had it in the back of my mind that if everything went wrong, I could come back to Fulham and have my old life with Suze.

Suze doesn't need me anymore. She's got someone else, who will always come first in her life. I watch as the vicar places his hands on Suze's and Tarquin's heads to bless them—and my throat feels a little tight as I remember all the times we've had together. The time I cooked a horrible curry to save money and she kept saying how delicious it was even while her mouth was burning. The time she tried to seduce my bank manager so he would extend my overdraft. Every time I've got myself into trouble, she's been there for me.

And now it's all over.

Suddenly I feel in need of a little reassurance. I turn round and quickly scan the rows of guests, looking for Luke's face. For a few moments I can't spot him, and although I keep wearing my confident smile, I feel a ridiculous panic rising inside me, like a child realizing she's been left behind at school; that everyone else has been collected but her.

Until suddenly I see him. Standing behind a pillar toward the back, tall and dark and solid, his eyes fixed on mine. Looking at me and no one else. And as I gaze back at him, I feel restored. I've been collected too; it's OK.

We emerge into the churchyard, the sound of bells behind us, and a crowd of people who have gathered outside on the road start to cheer.

"Congratulations!" I cry, giving Suze a huge hug. "And to you, Tarquin!"

I've always been a teeny bit awkward around Tarquin. But now I see him with Suze—married to Suze—the awkwardness seems to melt away.

"I know you'll be really happy," I say warmly, and give him a kiss on the cheek, and we both laugh as someone throws confetti at us. Guests are already piling out of the church like sweets out of a jar, talking and laughing and calling to each other in loud confident voices. They swarm around Suze and Tarquin, kissing and hugging and shaking hands, and I move away a little, wondering where Luke is.

The whole churchyard is filling up with people, and I can't help staring at some of Suze's relations. Her granny is coming out of the church very slowly and regally, holding a stick, and is being followed by a dutiful-looking young man in morning dress. A thin, pale girl with huge eyes is wearing an enormous black hat, holding a pug and chain-smoking. There's a whole army of almost identical brothers in kilts standing by the church gate, and I remember Suze telling me about her aunt who had six boys before finally getting twin girls.

"Here. Put this on." Luke's voice is suddenly in my ear, and I turn round, to see him holding out the sheepskin jacket. "You must be freezing."

"Don't worry. I'm fine!"

"Becky, there's snow on the ground," says Luke firmly, and drapes the coat round my shoulders. "Very good wedding," he adds.

"Yes." I look up at him carefully, wondering if by any chance we can work the conversation back to what we were talking about before the service. But now Luke's looking at Suze and Tarquin, who are being photographed under the oak tree. Suze looks absolutely radiant, but Tarquin looks as though he's facing gunfire.

"He's a very nice chap," he says, nodding toward Tarquin. "Bit odd, but nice."

"Yes. He is. Luke—"

"Would you like a glass of hot whiskey?" interrupts a waiter, coming up with a tray. "Or champagne?"

"Hot whiskey," I say gratefully. "Thanks." I take a few sips and close my eyes as the warmth spreads through my body. If only it could get down to my feet, which, to be honest, are completely freezing.

"Bridesmaid!" cries Suze suddenly. "Where's Bex? We need you for a photograph!"

My eyes open.

"Here," I shout, slipping the sheepskin coat off my shoulders. "Luke, hold my drink—"

I hurry through the melee and join Suze and Tarquin. And it's funny, but now that all these people are looking at me, I don't feel cold anymore. I smile my most radiant smile, and hold my flowers nicely, and link arms with Suze when the photographer tells me to, and, in between shots, wave at Mum and Dad, who have pushed their way to the front of the crowd.

"We'll head back to the house soon," says Mrs. Gearing, coming up to kiss Suze. "People are getting chilly. You can finish the pictures there."

"OK," says Suze. "But let's just take some of me and Bex together."

"Good idea!" says Tarquin at once, and heads off in obvious relief to talk to his father, who looks exactly like Tarquin but forty years older. The photographer takes a few shots of me and Suze beaming at each other, then pauses to reload his camera. Suze accepts a glass of whiskey from a waiter and I reach surreptitiously behind me to see how much of my dress has unraveled.

"Bex, listen," comes a voice in my ear. I look round, and Suze is gazing at me earnestly. She's so close I can see each individual speck of glitter in her eyeshadow. "I need to ask you something. You don't really want to wait ten years before you get married, do you?"

"Well . . . no," I admit. "Not really."

"And you do think Luke's the one? Just . . . honestly. Between ourselves."

There's a long pause. Behind me I can hear someone saying, "Of course, our house is fairly modern. I think it was built in 1853—"

"Yes," I say eventually, feeling a deep pink rising through my cheeks. "Yes. I think he is."

Suze looks at me searchingly for a few moments longer—then abruptly seems to come to a decision. "Right!" she says, putting down her whiskey. "I'm going to throw my bouquet."

"What?" I stare at her in bewilderment. "Suze, don't be stupid. You can't throw your bouquet yet!"

"Yes I can! I can throw it when I like."

"You ought to throw it when you leave for your honeymoon!"

"I don't care," says Suze obstinately. "I can't wait any longer. I'm going to throw it now."

"But you're supposed to do it at the *end*!"

"Who's the bride? You or me? If I wait till the end it won't be any fun! Now, stand over there." She points with an imperious hand to a small mound of snowy grass. "And put your flowers down. You'll never catch it if you're holding things! Tarkie?" She raises her voice. "I'm going to throw my bouquet now, OK?"

"OK!" Tarquin calls back cheerfully. "Good idea."

"Go on, Bex!"

"Honestly! I don't even want to catch it!" I say, slightly grumpily. But I suppose I am the only bridesmaid—so I put my flowers down on the grass, and go and stand on the mound as instructed.

"I want a picture of this," Suze is saying to the photographer. "And where's Luke?"

The slightly weird thing is, no one else is coming with me. Everyone else has melted away. Suddenly I notice that Tarquin and his best man are going around murmuring in people's ears, and gradually all the guests are turning to me with bright, expectant faces.

"Ready, Bex?" calls Suze.

"Wait!" I cry. "You haven't got enough people! There should be lots of us, all standing together . . ."

I feel so stupid, up here on my own. Honestly, Suze is doing this all wrong. Hasn't she *been* to any weddings?

"Wait, Suze!" I cry again, but it's too late.

"Catch, Bex!" she yells. "Caaatch!"

The bouquet comes looping high through the air, and I have to jump slightly to catch it. It's bigger and heavier than I expected, and for a moment I just stare dazedly at it, half secretly delighted and half completely furious with Suze.

And then my eyes focus. And I see the little envelope. *To Becky.*

An envelope addressed to me in Suze's bouquet?

I look up bewilderedly at Suze, and with a shining face she nods toward the envelope.

With trembling fingers, I open the card. There's something lumpy inside. It's . . .

It's a ring, all wrapped up in cotton wool. I take it out, feeling dizzy. There's a message in the card, written in Luke's handwriting. And it says . . .

It says *Will You* . . .

I stare at it in disbelief, trying to keep control of myself, but the world is shimmering, and blood is pounding through my head.

I look up dazedly, and there's Luke, coming forward through the people, his face serious but his eyes warm.

"Becky—" he begins, and there's a tiny intake of breath around the churchyard. "Will you—"

"Yes! Yeee-esssss!" I hear the joyful sound ripping through the churchyard before I even realize I've opened my mouth. I'm so charged up with emotion, my voice doesn't even *sound* like mine. In fact, it sounds more like . . .

Mum.

I don't believe it.

As I whip round, she claps a hand over her mouth in horror. "Sorry!" she whispers, and a ripple of laughter runs round the crowd.

"Mrs. Bloomwood, I'd be honored," says Luke, his eyes crinkling into a smile. "But I believe you're already taken."

Then he looks at me again.

"Becky, if I had to wait five years, then I would. Or eight—or even ten." He pauses, and there's complete silence except for a tiny gust of wind, blowing confetti about the churchyard. "But I hope that one day—preferably rather sooner than that—you'll do me the honor of marrying me?"

My throat's so tight, I can't speak. I give a tiny nod, and Luke takes my hand. He unfolds my fingers and takes out the ring. My heart is hammering. Luke wants to marry me. He must have been planning this all along. Without saying a thing.

I look at the ring, and feel my eyes start to blur. It's an antique diamond ring, set in gold, with tiny curved claws. I've never seen another quite like it. It's perfect.

"May I?"

"Yes," I whisper, and watch as he slides it onto my finger. He looks at me again, his eyes more tender than I've ever seen them, and kisses me, and the cheering starts.

I don't believe it. I'm engaged.

Three

OK. Now, I may be engaged, but I'm not going to get carried away.

No way.

I know some girls go mad, planning the biggest wedding in the universe and thinking about nothing else . . . but that's not going to be me. I'm not going to let this take over my life. I mean, let's get our priorities right here. The most important thing is not the dress, or the shoes, or what kind of flowers we have, is it? It's making the promise of lifelong commitment. It's pledging our troth to one another.

I pause, halfway through putting on my moisturizer, and gaze at the reflection in my old bedroom mirror. "I, Becky," I murmur solemnly. "I, Rebecca. Take thee, Luke."

Those ancient words just send a shiver up your spine, don't they?

"To be thine . . . mine . . . husband. For better, for richer . . ."

I break off with a puzzled frown. That doesn't sound quite right. Still, I can learn it properly nearer the time. The point is, the vows are what matters, nothing else. We don't have to go over the top. Just a simple, elegant ceremony. No fuss, no hoopla. I mean, Romeo and Juliet didn't need a big wedding with sugared almonds and vol-au-vents, did they?

In fact, maybe we should even get married in secret, like they did! Suddenly I'm gripped by a vision of Luke and me kneeling before an Italian priest in the dead of night, in some tiny stone chapel. God, that would be romantic. And then somehow Luke would think I was dead, and he'd commit suicide, and so would I, and it would be incredibly tragic, and everyone would say we did it for love and the whole world should learn from our example . . .

"Karaoke?" Luke's voice outside the bedroom door brings me back to reality. "Well, it's certainly a possibility . . ."

The door opens and he holds out a cup of coffee to me. He and I have been staying here at my parents' house since Suze's wedding, and when I left the breakfast table, he was refereeing my parents as they argued over whether or not the moon landings actually happened.

"Your mother's already found a possible date for the wedding," he says. "What do you think about the—"

"Luke!" I put up a hand to stop him. "Luke. Let's just take this one step at a time, shall we?" I give him a kind smile. "I mean, we've only just got engaged. Let's just get our heads round that first. There's no need to dash into setting dates."

I glance at myself in the mirror, feeling quite grown-up and proud of myself. For once in my life I'm not getting overexcited.

"You're right," says Luke after a pause. "No, you are right. And the date your mother suggested would be a terrible hurry."

"Really?" I take a thoughtful sip of coffee. "So . . . just out of interest . . . when was it?"

"June 22nd. This year." He shakes his head. "Crazy, really. It's only a few months away."

"Madness!" I say, rolling my eyes. "I mean, there's no hurry, is there?"

June 22nd. Honestly! What is Mum thinking?

Although . . . I suppose a summer wedding would be nice in theory.

There's nothing actually *stopping* us getting married this year.

And if we did make it June, I could start looking at wedding dresses straight away. I could start trying on tiaras. I could start reading *Brides*! Yes!

"On the other hand," I add casually, "there's no *real* reason to delay, is there? I mean, now we've decided, in one sense, we might as well just . . . do it. Why hang around?"

"Are you sure? Becky, I don't want you to feel pressured—"

"It's OK. I'm quite sure. Let's get married in June!" I give him an exhilarated beam. "Shall we go and register today?"

Oops. That just kind of slipped out.

"Today?" says Luke, looking taken aback. "You're not serious."

"Of course not!" I give a lighthearted laugh. "I'm joking! Although, you know, we *could* go and start looking at a few things, purely for information . . ."

"Becky, I'm busy today, remember?" He glances at his watch. "In fact, I must get going."

"Oh yes," I say, trying to muster some enthusiasm. "Yes, you don't want to be late, do you?"

Luke's spending the day with his mother, Elinor, who is over in London on her way to Switzerland. The official version is that she's going there to stay with some old friends and "enjoy the mountain air." Of course everyone knows she's really going to have her face lifted for the zillionth time.

Then this afternoon, Mum, Dad, and I are going up to meet them for tea at Claridges. Everyone has been exclaiming about what a lucky coincidence it is that Elinor's over here, so the two families will be able to meet. But every time I think about it, my stomach turns over. I wouldn't mind if it was Luke's real parents—his dad and stepmum, who are really lovely and live in Devon. But they've just gone out to Australia, where Luke's sister has moved, and they probably won't be back until just before the wedding. So all we're left with to represent Luke is Elinor.

Elinor Sherman. My future mother-in-law.

OK . . . let's not think about that.

"Luke . . ." I pause, trying to find the right words. "How do you think it'll be? Our parents meeting for the first time? You know— your mother . . . and my mother . . . I mean, they're not exactly similar, are they?"

"It'll be fine! They'll get on wonderfully, I'm sure."

He honestly hasn't a clue what I'm talking about.

I know it's a good thing that Luke adores his mother. I know sons should love their mothers. And I know he hardly ever saw her when he was tiny, and he's trying to make up for lost time . . . but still. *How* can he be so devoted to Elinor?

As I arrive downstairs in the kitchen, Mum's tidying up the break-fast things with one hand and holding the portable phone in the other.

"Yes," she's saying. "That's right. Bloomwood, B-l-o-o-m-w-o-o-d. Of Oxshott, Surrey. And you'll fax that over? Thank you.

"Good." She puts away the phone and beams at me. "That's the announcement gone in the Surrey *Post*."

"*Another* announcement? Mum, how many have you done?"

"Just the standard number!" she says defensively. "The *Times,* the *Telegraph,* the Oxshott *Herald,* and the Esher *Gazette*."

"And the Surrey *Post*."

"Yes. So only . . . five."

"Five!"

"Becky, you only get married once!" says Mum.

"I know. But honestly . . ."

"Now, listen." Mum is rather pink in the face. "You're our only daughter, Becky, and we're not going to spare any expense. We want you to have the wedding of your dreams. Whether it's the an-nouncements, or the flowers, or a horse and carriage like Suzie had . . . we want you to have it."

"Mum, I wanted to talk to you about that," I say awkwardly. "Luke and I will contribute to the cost—"

"Nonsense!" says Mum briskly. "We wouldn't hear of it."

"But—"

"We've always hoped we'd be paying for a wedding one day. We've been putting money aside especially, for a few years now."

"Really?" I stare at her, feeling a sudden swell of emotion. Mum and Dad have been saving all this time, and they never said a word. "I . . . I had no idea."

"Yes, well. We weren't going to tell you, were we? Now!" Mum snaps back into businesslike mode. "Did Luke tell you we've found a date? You know, it wasn't easy! Everywhere's booked up. But I've spoken to Peter at the church, he's had a cancellation, and he can fit us in at three on that Saturday. Otherwise it would be a question of waiting until November."

"November?" I pull a face. "That's not very weddingy."

"Exactly. So I told him to pencil it in. I've put it on the calendar, look."

I glance over at the fridge calendar, which has a different recipe using Nescafé for each month. And sure enough, there in June is a big felt-tipped "BECKY'S WEDDING."

I stare at it, feeling slightly weird. I am going to get married. It's something I've secretly thought about for so long—and now it really is happening.

"I've been having a few ideas about the marquee," adds Mum. "I saw a beautiful striped one in a magazine somewhere, and I thought, 'I must show that to Becky . . .' "

She reaches behind her and hauls out a stack of glossy magazines. *Brides. Modern Bride. Wedding and Home.* All shiny and succulent and inviting, like a plate of sticky doughnuts.

"Gosh!" I say, forcing myself not to reach greedily for one. "I haven't read any of those bridal things yet. I don't even know what they're like!"

"Neither have I," says Mum at once, as she flicks expertly through an issue of *Wedding and Home.* "Not properly. I've just glanced through for the odd idea. I mean, they're really just adverts mainly . . ."

I hesitate, my fingers running over the cover of *You and Your Wedding.* I can hardly believe I'm actually allowed to read these now. Openly! I don't have to sidle up to the rack and take tiny, guilty peeks, like stuffing a biscuit into my mouth and all the time wondering if someone will see me.

The habit's so ingrained I almost can't break it, even though I've got an engagement ring on my finger now.

"I suppose it makes sense to have a very brief look," I say casually. "You know, just for basic information . . . just to be aware what's available . . ."

Oh, sod it. Mum's not even listening, anyway, so I might as well give up pretending I'm not going to read every single one of these magazines avidly from cover to cover. Happily I sink into a chair and reach for *Brides,* and for the next ten minutes we're both completely silent, gorging on pictures.

"There!" says Mum suddenly. She turns her magazine round so I can see a picture of a billowing white and silver striped marquee. "Isn't that nice?"

"Very pretty." I run my gaze down interestedly to the picture of the bridesmaids' dresses, and the bride's bouquet . . . and then my eye comes to rest on the dateline.

"Mum!" I exclaim. "This is from last year! How come you were looking at wedding magazines last year!"

"I've no idea!" says Mum shiftly. "I must have . . . picked it up in a doctor's waiting room or something. Anyway. Are you getting any ideas?"

"Well . . . I don't know," I say vaguely. "I suppose I just want something simple."

A vision of myself in a big white dress and sparkly tiara suddenly pops into my head. Getting out of a carriage at St. Paul's Cathedral . . . my handsome prince waiting for me . . . cheering crowds . . .

OK, stop. I'm *not* going to go over the top. I've already decided that.

"I agree," Mum is saying. "You want something elegant and tasteful. Oh, look, grapes covered with gold leaf. We could do that!" She turns a page. "Look, identical twin bridesmaids! Don't they look pretty? Do you know anyone with twins, love?"

"No," I say regretfully. "I don't think so. Ooh, you can buy a special wedding countdown alarm clock! And a wedding organizer with matching bridal diary for those special memories. Do you think I should get one of those?"

"Definitely," says Mum. "If you don't, you'll only wish you had." She puts down her magazine. "You know, Becky, one thing I will say to you is, don't do this by half-measures. Remember, you only do it once—"

"Hellooo?" We both look up as there's a tap on the back door. "It's only me!" Janice's bright eyes look through the glass, and she gives a little wave. Janice is our next-door neighbor and I've known her forever. She's wearing a floral shirtwaister in a virulent shade of turquoise, and eye shadow to match, and there's a folder under her arm.

"Janice!" cries Mum. "Come on in and have a coffee."

"I'd love one," says Janice. "I've brought my Canderel." She comes in and gives me a hug. "And here's the special girl! Becky love, congratulations!"

"Thanks," I say, with a bashful grin.

"Just look at that ring!"

"Two carats," says Mum at once. "Antique. It's a family heir-loom."

"A family heirloom!" echoes Janice breathlessly. "Oh, Becky!" She picks up a copy of *Modern Bride* and gives a wistful little sigh. "But how are you going to organize the wedding, living in New York?"

"Becky doesn't have to worry about a thing," says Mum firmly. "I can do it all. It's traditional, anyway."

"Well, you know where I am if you want any help," says Janice. "Have you set a date yet?"

"June 22nd," says Mum over the shriek of the coffee grinder. "Three o'clock at St. Mary's."

"Three o'clock!" says Janice. "Lovely." She puts down the magazine and gives me a suddenly earnest look. "Now, Becky, there's something I want to say. To both of you."

"Oh yes?" I say, slightly apprehensively, and Mum puts down the coffeepot.

Janice takes a deep breath. "It would give me great pleasure to do your wedding makeup. You and the whole bridal party."

"Janice!" exclaims my mother in delight. "What a kind thought! Think of that, Becky. Professional makeup!"

"Er . . . fantastic!"

"I've learned such a lot on my course, all the tricks of the trade. I've got a whole book full of photographs you can browse through, to choose your style. In fact I've brought it with me, look!" Janice opens the folder and begins to flip over laminated cards of women who look as though they had their makeup applied during the seventies. "This look is called Prom Princess, for the younger face," she says breathlessly. "Now, here we have Radiant Spring Bride, with extra-waterproof mascara . . . Or Cleopatra, if you wanted something more dramatic?"

"Great!" I say feebly. "Perhaps I'll have a look nearer the time."

There is no way in a million years I'm letting Janice near my face.

"And you'll be getting Wendy to do the cake, will you?" asks Janice as Mum puts a cup of coffee in front of her.

"Oh, no question," says Mum. "Wendy Prince, who lives on Maybury Avenue," she adds to me. "You remember, she did Dad's

retirement cake with the lawnmower on it? The things that woman
can do with a nozzle!"

I remember that cake. The icing was virulent green and the
lawnmower was made out of a painted matchbox. You could still
see "Swan" through the green.

"You know, there are some really amazing wedding cakes in
here," I say, tentatively holding out an issue of *Brides*. "From this
special place in London. Maybe we could go and have a look."

"Oh, but love, we have to ask Wendy!" says Mum in surprise.
"She'd be devastated if we didn't. You know her husband's just had
a stroke? Those sugar roses are what's keeping her going."

"Oh, right," I say, putting down the magazine guiltily. "I didn't
know. Well . . . OK then. I'm sure it'll be lovely."

"We were very pleased with Tom and Lucy's wedding cake."
Janice sighs. "We've saved the top tier for the first christening. You
know, they're with us at the moment. They'll be round to offer their
congratulations, I'm sure. Can you believe they've been married a
year and a half already!"

"Have they?" Mum takes a sip of coffee and gives a brief smile.

Tom and Lucy's wedding is still a very slightly sore point in our
family. I mean, we love Janice and Martin to bits so we never say
anything, but to be honest, we're none of us very keen on Lucy.

"Are there any signs of them . . ." Mum makes a vague, euphemistic gesture. "Starting a family," she adds in a whisper.

"Not yet." Janice's smile flickers briefly. "Martin and I think they
probably want to *enjoy* each other first. They're such a happy young
couple. They just dote on each other! And of course, Lucy's got her
career—"

"I suppose so," says Mum consideringly. "Although it doesn't do
to wait *too* long . . ."

"Well, I know," agrees Janice. They both turn to look at me—
and suddenly I realize what they're driving at.

For God's sake, I've only been engaged a day! Give me a chance!

I escape to the garden and wander round for a bit, sipping my coffee. The snow is starting to melt outside, and you can just see
patches of green lawn and bits of rosebush. As I pick my way down
the gravel path, I find myself thinking how nice it is to be in an

English garden again, even if it is a bit cold. Manhattan doesn't have any gardens like this. There's Central Park, and there's the odd little flowery square. But it doesn't have any proper English gardens, with lawns and trees and flower beds.

I've reached the rose arbor and am looking back at the house, imagining what a marquee will look like on the lawn, when suddenly there's a rumble of conversation from the garden next door. I wonder if it's Martin, and I'm about to pop my head over the fence and say "Hello!" when a girl's voice comes clearly over the snow, saying: "Define *frigid*! Because if you ask me—"

It's Lucy. And she sounds furious! There's a mumbled reply, which can only be Tom.

"And you're such a bloody expert, are you?"

Mumble mumble.

"Oh, give me a break."

I edge surreptitiously toward the fence, wishing desperately I could hear both sides.

"Yeah, well, maybe if we had more of a life, maybe if you actually organized something once in a blue moon, maybe if we weren't stuck in such a bloody rut . . ."

Lucy's voice is so hectoring. And now Tom's voice is raised defensively in return.

"We went out to . . . all you could do was complain . . . made a real bloody effort . . ."

Crack!

Shit. *Shit.* I've stepped on a twig.

For an instant I consider running. But it's too late, their heads have already appeared over the garden fence, Tom's all pink and distressed, and Lucy's tight with anger.

"Oh, hi!" I say, trying to look relaxed. "How are *you*? I'm just . . . um . . . having a little stroll . . . and I dropped my . . . hanky."

"Your hanky?" Lucy looks suspiciously at the ground. "I can't see any hanky."

"Well . . . erm . . . So . . . how's married life?"

"Fine," says Lucy shortly. "Congratulations, by the way."

"Thanks."

There's an awkward pause, and I find myself running my eyes over Lucy's outfit, taking in her top (black polo-neck, probably

M&S), trousers (Earl Jeans, quite cool, actually), and boots (high-heeled with laces, Russell & Bromley).

This is something I've always done, checking out people's clothes and listing them in my mind like on a fashion page. I thought I was the only one who did it. But then I moved to New York—and there, everyone does it. Seriously, everybody. The first time you meet anyone, whether it's a rich society lady or a doorman, they give you a swift, three-second top-to-toe sweep. You can see them costing your entire outfit to the nearest dollar before they even say hello. I call it the Manhattan Onceover.

"So how's New York?"

"It's great! Really exciting . . . I love my job . . . it's such a great place to live!"

"I've never been," says Tom wistfully. "I wanted to go there for our honeymoon."

"Tom, don't start that again," says Lucy sharply. "OK?"

"Maybe I could come and visit," says Tom. "I could come for the weekend."

"Er . . . yes! Maybe! You could both come . . ." I tail off lamely as Lucy rolls her eyes and stomps toward the house. "Anyway, lovely to see you and I'm glad married life is treating you . . . er . . . treating you, anyway."

I hurry back into the kitchen, dying to tell Mum what I just heard, but it's empty.

"Hey, Mum!" I call. "I just saw Tom and Lucy!"

I hurry up the stairs, and Mum is halfway down the loft ladder, pulling down a big white squashy bundle all wrapped up in plastic.

"What's that?" I ask, helping her to get it down.

"Don't say anything," she says, with suppressed excitement. "Just . . ." Her hands are trembling as she unzips the plastic cover. "Just . . . look!"

"It's your wedding dress!" I say in astonishment as she pulls out the white frothy lace. "I didn't know you still had that!"

"Of course I've still got it!" She brushes away some sheets of tissue paper. "Thirty years old, but still as good as new. Now, Becky, it's only a thought . . ."

"What's a thought?" I say, helping her to shake out the train.

"It might not even fit you . . ."

Slowly I look up at her. She's serious.

"Actually, I don't think it will," I say, trying to sound casual. "I'm sure you were much thinner than me! And . . . shorter."

"But we're the same height!" says Mum in puzzlement. "Oh, go on, try it, Becky!"

Five minutes later I stare at myself in the mirror in Mum's bedroom. I look like a sausage roll in layered frills. The bodice is tight and lacy, with ruffled sleeves and a ruffled neckline. It's tight down to my hips where there are more ruffles, and then it fans out into a tiered train.

I have never worn anything less flattering in my life.

"Oh, Becky!" I look up—and to my horror, Mum's in tears. "I'm so silly!" she says, laughing and brushing at her eyes. "It's just . . . my little girl, in the dress I wore . . ."

"Oh, Mum . . ." Impulsively I give her a hug. "It's a . . . a really lovely dress . . ."

How exactly do I add, But I'm not wearing it?

"And it fits you perfectly," gulps Mum, and rummages for a tissue. "But it's your decision." She blows her nose. "If you don't think it suits you . . . just say so. I won't mind."

"I . . . well . . ."

Oh God.

"I'll . . . think about it," I manage at last, and give Mum a lame smile.

We put the wedding dress back in its bag, and have some sandwiches for lunch, and watch an old episode of *Changing Rooms* on the new cable telly Mum and Dad have had installed. And then, although it's a bit early, I go upstairs and start getting ready to see Elinor. Luke's mother is one of those Manhattan women who always look completely and utterly immaculate, and today of all days I want to match her in the smartness stakes.

I put on the DKNY suit I bought myself for Christmas, brand-new tights, and my new Prada sample sale shoes. Then I survey my appearance carefully, looking all over for specks or creases. I'm not going to be caught out this time. I'm not going to have a single stray thread or crumpled bit which her beady X-ray eyes can zoom in on.

I've just about decided that I look OK, when Mum comes busting into my bedroom. She's dressed smartly in a purple Windsmoor suit and her face is glowing with anticipation.

"How do I look?" she says with a little laugh. "Smart enough for Claridges?"

"You look lovely, Mum! That color really suits you. Let me just . . ."

I reach for a tissue, dampen it under the tap, and wipe at her cheeks where she's copied Janice's badger-look approach to blusher.

"There. Perfect."

"Thank you, darling!" Mum peers at herself in the wardrobe mirror. "Well, this will be nice. Meeting Luke's mother at last."

"Mmm," I say noncommittally.

"I expect we'll get to be quite good friends! What with getting together over the wedding preparations . . . You know, Margot across the road is such good friends with her son-in-law's mother, they take holidays together. She says she hasn't lost a daughter, she's gained a friend!"

Mum sounds really excited. How can I prepare her for the truth?

"And Elinor certainly sounds lovely! The way Luke describes her. He seems so fond of her!"

"Yes, he is," I admit grudgingly. "Incredibly fond."

"He was telling us this morning about all the wonderful charity work she does. She must have a heart of gold!"

As Mum prattles on, I tune out and remember a conversation I had with Luke's stepmum, Annabel, when she and his dad came out to visit us.

I completely adore Annabel. She's very different from Elinor, much softer and quieter, but with a lovely smile that lights up her whole face. She and Luke's father live in a sleepy area of Devon near the beach, and I really wish we could spend more time with them. But Luke left home at eighteen, and he hardly ever goes back. In fact, I get the feeling he thinks his father slightly wasted his life by settling down as a provincial lawyer, instead of conquering the world.

When they came to New York, Annabel and I ended up having an afternoon alone together. We walked around Central Park talking about loads of different things, and it seemed as though no subject was off-limits. So at last I took a deep breath and asked her what I've always wanted to know—which is how she can stand Luke being so dazzled by Elinor. I mean, Elinor may be his biological mother, but Annabel has been there for him all his life. She was the one who looked after him when he was ill and helped him with his homework and cooked his supper every night. And now she's been pushed aside.

For an instant I could see the pain in Annabel's face. But then she kind of smiled and said she completely understood it. That Luke had been desperate to know his real mother since he was a tiny child, and now that he was getting the chance to spend time with her, he should be allowed to enjoy it.

"Imagine your fairy godmother came along," she said. "Wouldn't you be dazzled? Wouldn't you forget about everyone else for a while? He needs this time with her."

"She's not his fairy godmother!" I retorted. "She's the wicked old witch!"

"Becky, she's his natural mother," Annabel said, with a gentle reproof. Then she changed the subject. She wouldn't bitch about Elinor, or anything.

Annabel is a saint.

"It's such a shame they didn't get to see each other while Luke was growing up!" Mum is saying. "What a tragic story." She lowers her voice, even though Luke's left the house. "Luke was telling me only this morning how his mother was desperate to take him with her to America. But her new American husband wouldn't allow it! Poor woman. She must have been in misery. Leaving her child behind!"

"Well, yes, maybe," I say, feeling a slight rebellion. "Except . . . she didn't *have* to leave, did she? If she was in so much misery, why didn't she tell the new husband where to go?"

Mum looks at me in surprise. "That's very harsh, Becky."

"Oh . . . I suppose so." I give a little shrug and reach for my lip liner.

I don't want to stir things up before we even begin. So I won't say what I really think, which is that Elinor never showed any interest in Luke until his PR company started doing so well in New York. Luke has always been desperate to impress her—in fact, that's the real reason he expanded to New York in the first place, though he won't admit it. But she completely ignored him, like the cow she is, until he started winning a few really big contracts and being mentioned in the papers and she suddenly realized he could be useful to her. Just before Christmas, she started her own charity—the Elinor Sherman Foundation—and made Luke a director. Then she had a great big gala concert to launch it—and guess who spent about twenty-five hours a day helping her out with it until he was so exhausted, Christmas was a complete washout?

But I can't say anything to him about it. When I once brought up the subject, Luke got all defensive and said I'd always had a problem with his mother (which is kind of true) and she was sacrificing loads of her time to help the needy and what more did I want, blood?

To which I couldn't really find a reply.

"She's probably a very lonely woman," Mum is musing. "Poor thing, all on her own. Living in her little flat. Does she have a cat to keep her company?"

"Mum . . ." I put a hand to my head. "Elinor doesn't live in a 'little flat.' It's a duplex on Park Avenue."

"A duplex? What—like a maisonette?" Mum pulls a sympathetic little face. "Oh, but it's not the same as a nice house, is it?"

Oh, I give up. There's no point.

As we walk into the foyer at Claridges, it's full of smart people having tea. Waiters in gray jackets are striding around with green and white striped teapots, and everyone's chattering brightly and I can't see Luke or Elinor anywhere. As I peer around, I'm seized by sudden hope. Maybe they're not here. Maybe Elinor couldn't make it! We can just go and have a nice cup of tea on our own! Thank God for—

"Becky?"

I swivel round—and my heart sinks. There they are, on a sofa in the corner. Luke's wearing that radiant expression he gets whenever he sees his mother, and Elinor's sitting on the edge of her seat in a houndstooth suit trimmed with fur. Her hair is a stiff lacquered helmet and her legs, encased in pale stockings, seem to have got even thinner. She looks up, apparently expressionless—but I can see from the flicker of her eyelids that she's giving both Mum and Dad the Manhattan Onceover.

"Is that her?" whispers Mum in astonishment, as we give our coats in. "Goodness! She's very . . . young!"

"No, she's not," I mutter. "She's had a lot of help."

Mum gazes at me incomprehendingly for a moment before the penny drops. "You mean . . . she's had a *face-lift*?"

"Not just one. So keep off the subject, OK?"

We both stand waiting as Dad hands in his coat, and I can see Mum's mind working, digesting this new piece of information, trying to fit it in somewhere.

"Poor woman," she says suddenly. "It must be terrible, to feel so insecure. That's living in America for you, I'm sure."

As we approach the sofa, Elinor looks up and her mouth extends by three millimeters, which is her equivalent to a smile.

"Good afternoon, Rebecca. And felicitations on your engagement. Most unexpected."

What's that supposed to mean?

"Thanks very much!" I say, forcing a smile. "Elinor, I'd like to introduce my parents, Jane and Graham Bloomwood."

"How do you do?" says Dad with a friendly smile, and holds out his hand. He looks so distinguished in his dark gray suit, I feel a twinge of pride. He's actually very handsome, my dad, even though his hair is going a bit gray.

"Graham, don't stand on ceremony!" exclaims Mum. "We're going to be family now!" Before I can stop her she's enveloping a startled Elinor in a hug. "We're so pleased to meet you, Elinor! Luke's told us all about you!" As she stands up again I see she's rumpled Elinor's collar, and can't help giving a tiny giggle.

"Isn't this nice?" Mum continues as she sits down. "Very grand!" She looks around, her eyes bright. "Now, what are we going to have? A nice cup of tea, or something stronger to celebrate?"

"Tea, I think," says Elinor. "Luke . . ."

"I'll go and sort it out," says Luke, leaping to his feet.

I hate the way he behaves around his mother. Normally he's so strong and assured. But with Elinor it's as though she's the president of some huge multinational and he's some junior minion. He hasn't even said hello to me yet.

"Now, Elinor," says Mum. "I've brought you a little something. I saw them yesterday and I couldn't resist!"

She pulls out a package wrapped in gold paper and hands it to Elinor. A little stiffly, Elinor takes off the paper—and pulls out a blue padded notebook, with the words "His Mum" emblazoned on the front in swirly silver writing. She stares at it as though Mum's presented her with a dead rat.

"I've got a matching one!" says Mum triumphantly. She reaches in her bag and brings out an equivalent "Her Mum" notebook, in pink. "They're called the Mums' Planning Kit! There's a space for us to write in our menus, guest lists . . . color schemes . . . and here's a plastic pocket for swatches, look . . . This way we can keep coordinated! And this is the ideas page . . . I've already jotted down a few thoughts, so if you want to contribute anything . . . or if there's any particular food you like . . . The point is, we want you to be involved as much as possible." She pats Elinor's hand. "In fact, if you'd like to come and stay for a while, so we could really get to know each other . . ."

"My schedule is rather full, I'm afraid," says Elinor with a wintry smile as Luke reappears, holding his mobile.

"The tea's on its way. And . . . I've just had rather a nice phone call." He looks around with a suppressed smile. "We've just landed NorthWest Bank as a client. We're going to manage the launch of an entire new retail division. It's going to be huge."

"Luke!" I exclaim. "That's wonderful!"

Luke's been wooing NorthWest for absolutely ages, and last week he admitted he'd thought he'd lost them to another agency. So this is really fantastic.

"Well done, Luke," says Dad.

"That's brilliant, love!" chimes in Mum.

The only one who hasn't said anything is Elinor. She's not even paying attention, but looking in her Hermès bag.

"What do you think, Elinor?" I say deliberately. "It's good news, isn't it?"

"I hope this won't interfere with your work for the foundation," she says, and snaps her bag shut.

"It shouldn't," says Luke easily.

"Of course, Luke's work for your foundation is voluntary," I point out sweetly. "Whereas this is his business."

"Indeed." Elinor gives me a stony look. "Well, Luke, if you don't have time—"

"Of course I've got time," says Luke, shooting me a glance of annoyance. "It won't be a problem."

Great. Now they're both pissed off with me.

Mum has been watching this exchange in slight bewilderment, and as the tea arrives her face clears in relief.

"Just what the doctor ordered!" she exclaims as a waiter places a teapot and silver cake stand on our table. "Elinor, shall I pour for you?"

"Have a scone," says Dad heartily to Elinor. "And some clotted cream?"

"I don't think so." Elinor shrinks slightly as though cream particles might be floating through the air and invading her body. She takes a sip of tea, then looks at her watch. "I must go, I'm afraid."

"What?" Mum looks up in surprise. "Already?"

"Luke, could you fetch the car?"

"Absolutely," says Luke, draining his cup.

"What?" Now it's my turn to stare. "Luke, what's going on?"

"I'm going to drive my mother to the airport," says Luke.

"Why? Why can't she take a taxi?"

As the words come out of my mouth I realize I sound a bit rude—but honestly. This was supposed to be a nice family meeting. We've only been here about three seconds.

"There are some things I need to discuss with Luke," says Elinor, picking up her handbag. "We can do so in the car." She stands up and brushes an imaginary crumb off her lap. "So nice to meet you," she says to Mum.

"You too!" exclaims Mum, leaping up in a last-ditch attempt at friendliness. "Lovely to meet you, Elinor! I'll get your number from Becky and we can have some nice chats about what we're going to wear! We don't want to clash with each other, do we?"

"Indeed," says Elinor, glancing at Mum's shoes. "Good-bye, Rebecca." Elinor nods at Dad. "Graham."

"Good-bye, Elinor," says Dad in an outwardly polite voice—but as I glance at him I can tell he's not at all impressed. "See you later,

Luke." As they disappear through the doors, he looks at his watch. "Twelve minutes."

"What do you mean?" says Mum.

"That's how long she gave us."

"Graham! I'm sure she didn't mean . . ." Mum breaks off as she notices the blue "His Mum" book, still lying on the table amid the wrapping paper. "Elinor's left her wedding planner behind!" she cries, grabbing it. "Becky, run after her."

"Mum . . ." I take a deep breath. "I wouldn't bother. I'm not sure she's that interested."

"I wouldn't count on her for any help," says Dad. He reaches for the clotted cream and piles a huge amount onto his scone.

"Oh." Mum looks from my face to Dad's—then slowly subsides into her seat, clutching the book. "Oh, I see."

She takes a sip of tea, and I can see her struggling hard to think of something nice to say.

"Well . . . she probably just doesn't want to interfere!" she says at last. "It's completely understandable."

But even she doesn't look that convinced. God, I hate Elinor.

"Mum, let's finish our tea," I say. "And then why don't we go to the sales?"

"Yes," says Mum after a pause. "Yes, let's do that! Now you mention it, I could do with some new gloves." She takes a sip of tea and looks more cheerful. "And perhaps a nice bag."

"We'll have a lovely time," I say, and squeeze her arm. "Just us."

FRANTON, BINTON AND OGLEBY

ATTORNEYS AT LAW

739 THIRD AVENUE

SUITE 503

NEW YORK, NY 10017

Miss Rebecca Bloomwood
251 W. 11th Street, Apt. B
New York, NY 10014

February 11, 2002

Dear Miss Bloomwood:

May we be the very first to congratulate you on your engagement to Mr. Luke Brandon, the report of which we saw in *The
New York Observer*. This must be a very happy time for you, and we
send you our wholehearted good wishes.

We are sure that at this time, you will be inundated with many
unwanted, even tasteless offers. However, we offer a unique and
personal service to which we would like to draw your attention.

As divorce lawyers with over 30 years' experience between us,
we know the difference a good attorney can make. Let us all
hope and pray that you and Mr. Brandon never reach that
painful moment. But if you do, we are specialists in the following areas:

• **Contesting** prenuptial agreements
• **Negotiating** alimony
• **Obtaining** court injunctions
• **Uncovering** information (with the help of our in-house pri-
  vate detective)

We do not ask that you contact us now. Simply place this letter
with your other wedding memorabilia—and should the need
arise you will know where we are.

Many congratulations again!

Ernest P. Franton
Associate Partner

ANGELS OF ETERNAL PEACE CEMETERY
WESTCHESTER HILLS, WESTCHESTER COUNTY, NEW YORK

Miss Rebecca Bloomwood
251 W. 11th Street, Apt. B
New York, NY 10014

February 13, 2002

Dear Miss Bloomwood:

May we be the very first to congratulate you on your engagement to Mr. Luke Brandon, the report of which we saw in *The New York Observer*. This must be a very happy time for you, and we send you our wholehearted good wishes.

We are sure that at this time, you will be inundated with many unwanted, even tasteless offers. However, we offer a unique and personal service to which we would like to draw your attention.

A wedding gift with a difference.

What better way for your guests to show their appreciation of the love you have for each other, than by giving you adjoining cemetery plots? In the peace and tranquility of our meticulously tended gardens, you and your husband will rest together as you have lived together, for all eternity.*

A pair of plots in the prestigious Garden of Redemption is currently available at the special offer price of $6,500. Why not add it to your wedding list—and let your loved ones give you the gift that will truly last forever?**

Again, many congratulations, and may you have a long and blissful married life together.

Hank Hamburg
Director of Sales

---

* In case of divorce, plots can be moved to opposite sides of cemetery.
** Hamburg Family Mortuaries, Inc., reserves the right to reallocate grave space, giving 30 days' notice in the event of redevelopment of the land (see attached terms and conditions).

Four

Who cares about bloody Elinor, anyway?

We'll have a lovely wedding, with or without her help. As Mum said, it's her loss, and she'll regret it on the day, when she doesn't feel part of the celebrations. We cheered up quite a lot after we left Claridges, actually. We went to the Selfridges sale and Mum found a nice new bag and I got some volumizing mascara, while Dad went and had a pint of beer, like he always does. Then we all went out for supper, and by the time we got home we were all a lot more cheerful and finding the whole situation quite funny.

The next day, when Janice came round for coffee, we told her all about tea with Elinor and she was really indignant on our behalf, and said if Elinor thought she was getting her makeup done for free, she had another think coming! Then Dad joined in and did a good imitation of Elinor looking at the clotted cream as if it was about to mug her and we all started giggling hysterically—until Luke came downstairs and asked what was funny, and we had to pretend we were laughing at a joke on the radio.

I really don't know what to do about Luke and his mother. Part of me thinks I should be honest. I should tell him how upset she made us all, and how Mum was really hurt. But the trouble is, I've tried to be honest with him in the past about Elinor and it's always led to a huge row. And I *really* don't want to have any rows now, while we're just engaged, and all blissful and happy. So I didn't say anything.

The following day we left to come back to New York, and when we said good-bye, Mum gave Luke a huge affectionate hug, as though to make up for the way she feels about Elinor. After all, he can't help his mother, can he? Then she hugged me, and wrote down my fax number for the zillionth time and promised she'd be in touch as soon as she'd talked to some caterers.

Apart from the small issue of Elinor, everything is going perfectly. Just to prove it, on the plane back to New York, I did this quiz in *Wedding and Home* on "Are You Ready for Marriage?" And we got the top marks! It said, "Congratulations! You are a committed and loving couple, able to work through your problems. The lines of communication are open between you and you see eye to eye on most issues."

OK, maybe I did cheat a tiny bit. Like for the question "Which part of your wedding are you most looking forward to?" I was going to put (a) "Choosing my shoes" until I saw that (c) "Making a life-long commitment" got ten points whereas (a) only got two.

But then, I'm sure everyone else has a little peek at the answers too. They probably factor it in somehow.

At least I didn't put (d) "Dessert" (no points).

"Becky?"

"Yes?"

We arrived back at the apartment an hour ago and Luke is going through the post. "You haven't seen that joint account statement, have you? I'll have to give them a ring."

"Oh, it came. Sorry, I forgot to tell you."

I hurry into the bedroom and take the statement from its hiding place, feeling a slight beat of apprehension.

Come to think of it, there was a question about financial matters in that quiz. I think I ticked (b) "We have similar patterns of expenditure and money is never an issue between us."

"Here you are," I say lightly, handing him the sheet of paper.

"I just don't see why we keep going overdrawn on this account," Luke's saying. "Our household expenses can't increase every month . . ." He peers at the page, which is covered in thick white blobs. "Becky . . . why has this statement got Wite-Out all over it?"

"I know!" I say apologetically. "I'm sorry about that. The bottle was there, and I was moving some books, and it just . . . tipped over."

"But it's almost impossible to read!"

"Is it?" I say innocently. "That's a shame. Still, never mind. These things happen . . ." And I'm about to pluck it from his fingers when suddenly his eyes narrow.

"Does that say . . ." He starts scraping at the statement with his fingernail, and suddenly a big blob of Wite-Out falls off.

Damn. I should have used tomato ketchup, like last month.

"Miù Miù. I *thought* so. Becky, what's Miù Miù doing in here?" He scrapes again, and Wite-Out starts to shower off the page like snow.

Oh God. Please don't see—

"Sephora . . . and Joseph . . . No wonder we're overdrawn!" He gives me an exasperated look. "Becky, this account is supposed to be for household expenses. Not skirts from Miù Miù!"

OK. Fight or flight.

I cross my arms defiantly and lift my chin. "So . . . a skirt isn't a household expense. Is that what you're saying?"

Luke stares at me. "Of course that's what I'm saying!"

"Well, you know, maybe that's the problem. Maybe the two of us just need to clarify our definitions a little."

"I see," says Luke after a pause, and I can see his mouth twitching slightly. "So you're telling me that you would classify a Miù Miù skirt as a household expense."

"I . . . might! It's 'in the household,' isn't it? And anyway," I continue quickly. "Anyway. At the end of the day, what does it matter? What does *any* of it matter? We have our health, we have each other, we have the . . . the beauty of life. Those are the things that matter. Not money. Not bank accounts. Not the mundane, soul-destroying details." I make a sweeping gesture with my hand, feeling as though I'm making an Oscar-winning speech. "We're on this planet for all too short a time, Luke. All too short a time. And when we come to the end, which will count for more? A number on a piece of paper—or the love between two people? Knowing that a few meaningless figures balanced—or knowing that you were the person you wanted to be?"

As I reach the end, I'm choked by my own brilliance. I look up in a daze, half expecting Luke to be near tears and whispering, "You had me at 'And.' "

"Very stirring," says Luke crisply. "Just for the record, in my book 'household expenses' means joint expenses pertaining to the running of this apartment and our lives. Food, fuel, cleaning products, and so on."

"Fine!" I shrug. "If that's the narrow . . . frankly *limited* definition you want to use—then fine."

The doorbell rings and I open it to see Danny standing in the hallway.

"Danny, is a Miù Miù skirt a household expense?" I say.

"Absolutely," says Danny, coming into the living area.

"You see?" I raise my eyebrows at Luke. "But fine, we'll go with your definition . . ."

"So did you hear?" says Danny morosely.

"Hear what?"

"Mrs. Watts is selling."

"What?" I stare at him. "Are you serious?"

"As soon as the lease is up, we're out."

"She can't do that!"

"She's the owner. She can do what she likes."

"But . . ." I stare at Danny in dismay, then turn to Luke, who is putting some papers into his briefcase. "Luke, did you hear that? Mrs. Watts is selling!"

"I know."

"You *knew*? Why didn't you tell me?"

"Sorry. I meant to." Luke looks unconcerned.

"What will we do?"

"Move."

"But I don't want to move. I like it here!"

I look around the room with a pang. This is the place where Luke and I have been happy for the last year. I don't want to be uprooted from it.

"So you want to hear where this leaves me?" says Danny. "Randall's getting an apartment with his girlfriend."

I look at him in alarm. "He's throwing you out?"

"Practically. He says I have to start contributing, otherwise I can start looking for a new place. Like, how am I supposed to do that?" Danny raises his hands. "Until I have my new collection ready, it just won't be possible. He might as well just . . . order me a cardboard box."

"So, er . . . how is the new collection coming on?" I ask cautiously.

"You know, being a designer isn't as easy as it looks," says Danny defensively. "You can't just be creative to order. It's all a matter of inspiration."

"Maybe you could get a job," says Luke, reaching for his coat.

"A job?"

"They must need designers at, I don't know, Gap?"

"Gap?" Danny stares at him. "You think I should spend my life designing *polo shirts*? So how about, ooh, two sleeves right here, three buttons on the placket, some ribbing . . . How can I contain my excitement?"

"What will we do?" I say plaintively to Luke.

"About Danny?"

"About our apartment!"

"We'll find somewhere," says Luke reassuringly. "Which reminds me. My mother wants to have lunch with you today."

"She's back?" I say in dismay. "I mean . . . she's back!"

"They had to postpone her surgery." Luke pulls a little face. "The clinic was placed under investigation by the Swiss medical authorities while she was there and all the procedures were put on hold. So . . . one o'clock, La Goulue?"

"Fine." I shrug unenthusiastically.

Then, as the door closes behind Luke, I feel a bit bad. Maybe Elinor's had a change of heart. Maybe she wants to bury the hatchet and get involved with the wedding. You never know.

I'd planned to be really cool and only tell people I was engaged if they asked me "How was your trip?"

But when the time comes I find myself running into the personal shopping department at Barneys where I work, thrusting out my hand, and yelling "Look!"

Erin, who works there with me, looks up startled, peers at my hand, then claps her hands over her mouth. "Oh my God! Oh my God!"

"I know!"

"You're engaged? To Luke?"

"Yes, of course to Luke! We're getting married in June!"

"What are you going to wear?" she gabbles. "I'm so jealous! Let me see the ring! Where did you get it? When I get engaged I'm going straight to Harry Winstons. And forget a month's salary, we're talking at least three years' . . ." She tails off as she examines my ring. "Wow."

"It's Luke's family's," I say. "His grandmother's."

"Oh right. So . . . it isn't new?" Her face falls slightly. "Oh well . . ."

"It's . . . vintage," I say carefully—and her entire expression lifts again.

"Vintage! A vintage ring! That's such a cool idea!"

"Congratulations, Becky," says Christina, my boss, and gives me a warm smile. "I know you and Luke will be very happy together."

"Can I try it on?" says Erin. "No! I'm sorry. Forget I mentioned it. I just . . . A vintage ring!"

She's still gazing at it as my first client, Laurel Johnson, comes into the department. Laurel is president of a company that leases private jets and is one of my favorite clients, even though she tells me all the time how she thinks everything in the store is overpriced and she'd buy all her clothes from Kmart if it weren't for her job.

"What's this I see?" she says, taking off her coat and shaking out her dark curly hair.

"I'm engaged!" I say, beaming.

"Engaged!" She comes over and scrutinizes the ring with dark, intelligent eyes. "Well, I hope you'll be very happy. I'm sure you will be. I'm sure your husband will have sense enough to keep his dick out of the little blonde who came to work as his intern and told him she'd never met a man who filled her with awe before. *Awe.* I ask you. Did you ever hear such a—" She stops mid-track, claps her hand to her mouth, and gives me a rueful look. "Damn."

"Never mind," I say comfortingly. "You were provoked."

Laurel has made a New Year's resolution not to talk about her ex-husband or his mistress anymore, because her therapist, Hans, has told her it isn't healthy for her. Unfortunately she's finding this resolution quite hard to keep. Not that I blame her. He sounds like a complete pig.

"You know what Hans told me last week?" she says as I open the door of my fitting room. "He told me to write down a list of everything I wanted to say about that woman—and then tear it up. He said I'd feel a sense of freedom."

"Oh right," I say interestedly. "So what happened?"

"I wrote it all down," says Laurel. "And then I mailed it to her."

"Laurel!"

"I know. I know. Not helpful."

"Well, come on in," I say, trying not to laugh, "and tell me what you've been up to. I'm a little behind this morning . . ."

One of the best things about working as a personal shopper is you get really close to your clients. In fact, some of them feel like friends. When I first met Laurel, she'd just split up with her husband. She was really low, and had zero self-confidence. Now, I'm not trying to boast, but when I found her the perfect Armani dress to wear to this huge ballet gala that he was going to be at—when I watched her staring at herself in the mirror, raising her chin and smiling and feeling like an attractive woman again—I honestly felt I'd made a difference to her life.

This morning Laurel is looking for a couple of suits for work. I know her so well now it's easy to pick out what will sit well on her tall frame. We have a nice easy chat, and talk about the new Brad Pitt movie, and Laurel tells me all about her new, very sexy golf coach.

"My entire game has fallen to pieces," she says, pulling a face. "I'm no longer aiming to hit the ball in the hole. I'm just aiming to look thin and attractive and the ball can go where the hell it likes."

As she gets changed back into her own daywear I come out of the fitting room, holding a pile of clothes.

"I can't possibly wear that," comes a muffled voice from Erin's room.

"If you just try it—" I can hear Erin saying.

"You know I never wear that color!" The voice rises, and I freeze.

That's a British accent.

"I'm not wasting my time anymore! If you bring me things I can't wear—"

Tiny spiders are crawling up and down my back. I don't believe it. It can't be—

"But you asked for a new look!" says Erin helplessly.

"Call me when you've got what I asked for."

And before I can move, here she is, walking out of Erin's fitting room, as tall and blonde and immaculate as ever, her lips already curving into a supercilious smile. Her hair is sleek and her blue eyes are sparkling and she looks on top of the world.

Alicia Billington.

Alicia Bitch Longlegs.

I meet her eyes—and it's like an electric shock all over my body. Inside my tailored gray trousers, I can feel my legs starting to tremble. I haven't laid eyes on Alicia Billington for well over a year. I should be able to deal with this. But it's as though that time has concertinaed into nothing. The memories of all our encounters are as strong and sore as ever. What she did to me. What she tried to do to Luke.

She's looking at me with the same patronizing air she used to use when she was a PR girl and I was a brand-new financial reporter. And although I tell myself firmly that I've grown up a lot since then, that I'm a strong woman with a successful career and nothing to prove . . . I can still feel myself shrinking inside. Turning back into the girl who always felt a bit of a flake, who never knew quite what to say.

"Rebecca!" she says, looking a me as though highly amused. "Well, I never!"

"Hi, Alicia," I say, and somehow force myself to smile courteously. "How are you?"

"I had heard you were working in a shop, but I thought that must be a joke." She gives a little laugh. "Yet . . . here you are. Makes sense, really."

I don't just "work in a shop"! I want to yell furiously. I'm a personal shopper! It's a skilled profession! I help people!

"And you're still with Luke, are you?" She gives me mock concerned look. "Is his company finally back on track? I know he went through a rough time."

I cannot believe this girl. It was she who tried to sabotage Luke's company. It was she who set up a rival PR company that went bust. It was she who lost all her boyfriend's money—and apparently had to be bailed out by her dad.

And now she's behaving as though she won.

I swallow several times, trying to find the right response. I know I'm worth more than Alicia. I should be able to come up with the perfect, polite, yet witty retort. But somehow it doesn't come.

"I'm living in New York myself," she says airily. "So I expect we'll see each other again. Maybe you'll sell me a pair of shoes." She gives me a final patronizing smile, hoists her Chanel bag on her shoulder, and walks out of the department.

When she's left, there's silence all around.

"Who was *that*?" says Laurel at last, who has come out of the fitting room only half dressed, without me noticing.

"That was . . . Alicia Bitch Longlegs," I say, half dazed.

"Alicia Bitch Fatass more like," says Laurel. "I always say, there's no bitch like an English bitch." She gives me a hug. "Don't worry about it. Whoever she is, she's just jealous."

"Thanks," I say, and rub my head, trying to clear my thoughts. But I'm still a bit shell-shocked, to be honest. I never thought I'd have to set eyes on Alicia again.

"Becky, I'm so sorry!" says Erin, as Laurel goes back into the fitting room. "I had no idea you and Alicia knew each other!"

"I had no idea she was a client of yours!"

"She doesn't show up very often." Erin pulls a face. "I never met anyone so fussy. So what's the story between you two?"

Oh, nothing! I want to say. She just trashed me to the tabloids and nearly ruined Luke's career, and has been a complete bitch to me from the very first moment I met her. Nothing to speak of.

"We just have a bit of a history," I say at last.

"You know she's engaged too? To Peter Blake. Very old money."

"I don't understand." My brow wrinkles. "I thought she got married last year. To a British guy. Ed . . . somebody?"

"She did! Except she didn't. Oh my God, didn't you hear the story?" A pair of customers are wandering past the personal shopping area, and Erin lowers her voice. "They had the wedding and they were at the reception—when in walks Peter Blake as someone's date. Alicia hadn't known he was coming, but apparently the minute she found out who he was, she totally zeroed in on him. So they started chatting and were really getting on—like, *really* getting on . . . but what can Alicia do, she's married!" Erin's face is shiny with glee. "So she went up to the priest and said she wanted an annulment."

"She did *what*?"

"She asked for an annulment! At her own wedding reception! She said they hadn't consummated it so it didn't count." Erin gives a little gurgle of laughter. "Can you believe it?"

I can't help giving a halfhearted laugh in response. "I can believe anything of Alicia."

"She said she always gets what she wants. Apparently the wedding is going to be to *die* for. But she's a complete bridezilla. Like, she's practically forced one of the ushers to have a nose job, and she's sacked every florist in New York . . . the wedding planner's going nuts! Who's your wedding planner?"

"My mum," I reply, and Erin's eyes widen.

"Your mom's a wedding planner? I never knew that!"

"No, you moron!" I giggle, starting to cheer up. "My mum's organizing the wedding. She's got it all under control already."

"Oh right." Erin nods. "Well—that probably makes things easier. So you can keep your distance."

"Yes. It should be really simple. Cross fingers!" I add, and we both laugh.

Five

I ARRIVE AT LA Goulue at one o'clock on the dot, but Elinor isn't there yet. I'm shown to a table and sip my mineral water while I wait for her. The place is busy, as it always is at this time, mostly with smartly dressed women. All around me is chatter and the gleam of expensive teeth and jewels, and I take the opportunity to eavesdrop shamelessly. At the table next to mine, a woman wearing heavy eyeliner and an enormous brooch is saying emphatically, "You simply cannot furnish an apartment these days under one hundred thousand dollars."

"So I said to Edgar, 'I am a human being,' " says a red-haired girl on my other side.

Her friend chews on a celery stick and looks at her with bright, avid eyes. "So what did he say?"

"One room, you're talking thirty thousand."

"He said, 'Hilary—' "

"Rebecca?"

I look up, a bit annoyed to miss what Edgar said, to see Elinor approaching the table, wearing a cream jacket with large black buttons and carrying a matching clutch bag. To my surprise she's not alone. A woman with a shiny chestnut bob, wearing a navy blue suit and holding a large Coach bag, is with her.

"Rebecca, may I present Robyn de Bendern," says Elinor. "One of New York's finest wedding planners."

"Oh," I say, taken aback. "Well . . . Hello!"

"Rebecca," says Robyn, taking both my hands and gazing intently into my eyes. "We meet at last. I'm so delighted to meet you. *So* delighted!"

"Me too!" I say, trying to match her vivacity while simultaneously racking my brain. Did Elinor mention meeting a wedding planner? Am I supposed to know about this?

"Such a pretty face!" says Robyn, without letting go of my hands. She's taking in every inch of me, and I find myself reciprocating. She looks in her forties, immaculately made up with bright hazel eyes, sharp cheekbones, and a wide smile exposing a row of immaculate teeth. Her air of enthusiasm is infectious, but her eyes are appraising as she takes a step back and sweeps over the rest of me.

"Such a young, fresh look. My dear, you'll make a stunning bride. Do you know yet what you'll be wearing on the day?"

"Er . . . a wedding dress?" I say stupidly, and Robyn bursts into peals of laughter.

"That humor!" she cries. "You British girls! You were quite right," she adds to Elinor, who gives a gracious nod.

Elinor was right? What about?

Have they been talking about me?

"Thanks!" I say, trying to take an unobtrusive step backward. "Shall we . . ." I nod toward the table.

"Let's," says Robyn, as though I've made the most genius suggestion she's ever heard. "Let's do that." As she sits down I notice she's wearing a brooch of two intertwined wedding rings, encrusted with diamonds.

"You like this?" says Robyn. "The Gilbrooks gave it to me after I planned their daughter's wedding. Now *that* was a drama! Poor Bitty Gilbrook's nail broke at the last minute and we had to fly her manicurist in by helicopter . . ." She pauses as though lost in memories, then snaps to. "So, Rebecca." She beams at me and I can't help beaming back. "Lucky, lucky girl. Tell me, are you enjoying every moment?"

"Well—"

"What I always say is, the first week after you're engaged is the most precious time of all. You have to *savor* it."

"Actually, it's been a couple of weeks now—"

"Savor it," says Robyn, lifting a finger. "Wallow in it. What I always say is, no one else can have those memories for you."

"Well, OK!" I say with a grin. "I'll . . . wallow in it!"

"Before we start," says Elinor, "I must give you one of these." She reaches into her bag and puts an invitation down on the table. What's this?

Mrs. Elinor Sherman requests the pleasure of your company . . .

Wow. Elinor's holding an engagement party! For us!

"Gosh!" I look up. "Well . . . thanks. I didn't know we were having an engagement party!"

"I discussed the matter with Luke."

"Really? He never mentioned it to me."

"It must have slipped his mind." Elinor gives me a cold, gracious smile. "I will have a stack of these delivered to your apartment and you can invite some friends of your own. Say . . . ten."

"Well . . . er . . . thanks."

"Now, shall we have some champagne, to celebrate?"

"What a lovely idea!" says Robyn. "What I always say is, if you can't celebrate a wedding, what can you celebrate?" She gives me a twinkling smile and I smile back. I'm warming to this woman. But I still don't know what she's doing here.

"Erm . . . I was just wondering, Robyn," I say hesitantly. "Are you here in a . . . professional capacity?"

"Oh no. No, no, nooooo." Robyn shakes her head. "It's not a profession. It's a *calling.* The hours I put in . . . the sheer love I put into my job . . ."

"Right." I glance uncertainly at Elinor. "Well, the thing is—I'm not sure I'm going to need any help. Although it's very kind of you—"

"No help?" Robyn throws back her head and peals with laughter. "You're not going to need any help? Please! Do you know how much organization a wedding takes?"

"Well—"

"Have you ever done it before?"

"No, but—"

"A lot of girls think your way," says Robyn, nodding. "Do you know who those girls are?"

"Um—"

"They're the girls who end up *weeping* into their wedding cake, because they're too stressed out to enjoy the fun! Do you want to be those girls?"

"No!" I say in alarm.

"Right! Of course you don't!" She sits back, looking like a teacher whose class has finally cracked two plus two. "Rebecca, I will take that strain off you. I will take on the headaches, the hard work, the sheer *stress* of the situation . . . Ah, here's the champagne!"

Maybe she has got a point, I think as a waiter pours champagne into three flutes. Maybe it would be a good idea to get a little extra help. Although how exactly she'll coordinate with Mum . . .

"I will become your best friend, Becky," Robyn's saying, beaming at me. "By the time of your wedding, I'll know you *better* than your best friend does. People call my methods unorthodox; they say I get too close. But when they see the results . . ."

"Robyn is unparalleled in this city," says Elinor, taking a sip of champagne, and Robyn gives a modest smile.

"So let's start with the basics," she says, and takes out a large, leather-bound notebook. "The wedding's on June 22nd . . ."

"Yes."

"Rebecca and Luke . . ."

"Yes."

"At the Plaza Hotel . . ."

"What?" I stare at her. "No, that's not—"

"I'm taking it that both the ceremony and reception will take place there?" She looks up at Elinor.

"I think so," says Elinor, nodding. "Much easier that way."

"Excuse me—"

"So—the ceremony in the Terrace Room?" She scribbles for a moment. "And then the reception in the Ballroom. Lovely. And how many?"

"Wait a minute!" I say, planting a hand on her notebook. "What are you talking about?"

"Your wedding," says Elinor. "To my son."

"At the Plaza Hotel," says Robyn with a beam. "I don't need to tell you how lucky you are, getting the date you wanted! Luckily it was a client of mine who made the cancellation, so I was able to snap it right up for you then and there . . ."

"I'm not getting married at the Plaza Hotel!"

Robyn looks sharply at Elinor, concern creasing her brow. "I thought you'd spoken to John Ferguson?"

"I have," replies Elinor crisply. "I spoke with him yesterday."

"Good! Because as you know, we're on a very tight schedule. A Plaza wedding in less than five months? There are some wedding planners who would simply say, impossible! I am not that wedding planner. I did a wedding once in three days. Three days! Of course, that was on a beach, so it was a little different—"

"What do you mean, the Plaza's booked?" I turn in my chair. "Elinor, we're getting married in Oxshott. You know we are."

"Oxshott?" Robyn wrinkles her brow. "I don't know it. Is it up-state?"

"Some provisional arrangements have been made," says Elinor dismissively. "They can easily be cancelled."

"They're not provisional!" I stare at Elinor in fury. "And they can't be cancelled!"

"You know, I sense some tension here," says Robyn brightly. "So I'll just go make a few calls . . ." She picks up her mobile and moves off to the side of the restaurant, and Elinor and I are left glaring at each other.

I take a deep breath, trying to stay calm. "Elinor, I'm not getting married in New York. I'm getting married at home. Mum's already started organizing it. You know she has!"

"You are not getting married in some unknown backyard in England," says Elinor crisply. "Do you know who Luke is? Do you know who *I* am?"

"What's that got to do with anything?"

"For someone with a modicum of intelligence, you're very naive." Elinor takes a sip of champagne. "This is the most important social event in all our lives. It must be done properly. Lavishly. The Plaza is unsurpassed for weddings. You must be aware of that."

"But Mum's already started planning!"

"Then she can stop planning. Rebecca, your mother will be grateful to have the wedding taken off her hands. It goes without saying, I will fund the entire event. She can attend as a guest."

"She won't want to attend as some guest! It's her daughter's wedding! She wants to be the hostess! She wants to organize it!"

"So!" A cheerful voice interrupts us. "Are we resolved?" Robyn appears back at the table, putting her mobile away.

"I've booked an appointment for us to see the Terrace Room after lunch," says Elinor frostily. "I would be glad if you would at least be courteous enough to come and view it with us."

I stare at her mutinously, tempted to throw down my napkin and say no way. I can't believe Luke knows anything about this. In fact, I feel like ringing him up right now and telling him exactly what I think.

But then I remember he's at a board lunch . . . and I also remember him asking me to give his mother a chance. Well, fine. I'll give her a chance. I'll go along and see the room, and walk around and nod politely and say nothing. And then tonight I'll tell her equally politely that I'm still getting married in Oxshott.

"All right," I say at last.

"Good." Elinor's mouth moves a few millimeters. "Shall we order?"

Throughout lunch, Elinor and Robyn talk about all the New York weddings they've ever been to, and I eat my food silently, resisting their attempts to draw me into the conversation. Outwardly I'm calm, but inside I can't stop seething. How dare Elinor try and take over? How dare she just hire a wedding planner without even consulting me? How dare she call Mum's garden an "unknown backyard"?

She's just an interfering cow, and if she thinks I'm going to get married in some huge anonymous New York hotel instead of at home with all my friends and family, she can just think again.

We finish lunch and decline coffee, and head outside. It's a brisk, breezy day with clouds scudding along the blue sky.

As we walk toward the Plaza, Robyn smiles at me. "I can understand if you're a little tense. It can be very stressful, planning a New York wedding. Some of my clients get very . . . wound up, shall we say."

I'm not planning a New York wedding! I want to yell. I'm planning an Oxshott wedding! But instead I just smile and say, "I suppose."

"I have one client in particular who's really quite demanding . . ." Robyn exhales sharply. "But as I say, it is a stressful business . . . Ah. Here we are! Isn't it an impressive sight?"

As I look up at the opulent facade of the Plaza I grudgingly have to admit it looks pretty good. It stretches up above Plaza Square like a wedding cake, with flags flying above a grand porticoed entrance.

"Have you been to a wedding here before?" asks Robyn.

"No. I've never been inside at all."

"Ah! Well . . . In we go . . ." says Robyn, ushering Elinor and me up the steps, past uniformed porters, through a revolving door, and into an enormous reception hall with a high, ornate ceiling, a marble floor, and huge gilded pillars. Directly in front of us is a light, bright area filled with palms and trellises where people are drinking coffee and a harp is playing and waiters in gray uniforms are hurrying around with silver coffeepots.

I suppose, if I'm honest, this is quite impressive too.

"Along here," says Robyn, taking my arm and leading us to a cordoned-off staircase. She unclasps a heavy rope cordon and we head up a grand staircase, and through another vast marble hall. Everywhere I look are ornate carvings, antiques, wall hangings, the hugest chandeliers I've ever seen . . .

"This is Mr. Ferguson, the executive director of catering."

Out of nowhere, a dapper man in a jacket has appeared. He shakes my hand and beams at me.

"Welcome to the Plaza, Rebecca! And may I say, you've made a very wise choice. There's nothing in the world like a Plaza wedding."

"Right!" I say politely. "Well, it seems a very nice hotel . . ."

"Whatever your fantasy, whatever your cherished dream, we'll do everything we can to create it for you. Isn't that right, Robyn?"

"That's right!" says Robyn fondly. "You simply couldn't be in better hands."

"Shall we go and look at the Terrace Room first?" Mr. Ferguson's eyes twinkle. "This is the room where the ceremony will take place. I think you'll like it."

We sweep back through the vast marble hall and he opens a pair of double doors, and we walk into an enormous room, surrounded by a white balustraded terrace. At one end is a marble fountain, at the other steps up to a raised area. Everywhere I look, people are scurrying around, arranging flowers and draping chiffon and placing gilt chairs in angled rows on the richly patterned carpet.

Wow.

This is actually . . . quite nice.

Oh, sod it. It's amazing.

"You're in luck!" says Mr. Ferguson with a beam. "We have a wedding on Saturday, so you can see the room 'in action,' as it were."

"Nice flowers," says Robyn politely, then leans toward me and whispers, "We'll have something far more special than these."

More special than these? They're the hugest, most spectacular flower arrangements I've ever seen in my life! Cascading roses, and tulips, and lilies . . . and are those orchids?

"So, you'll come in through these double doors," says Robyn, leading me along the terrace, "and then the bugles will play . . . or trumpets . . . whatever you wish . . . You'll pause in front of the grotto, arrange your train, have some photographs. And then the string orchestra will begin . . ."

"String orchestra?" I echo dazedly.

"I've spoken to the New York Phil," she adds to Elinor. "They're checking their tour schedule, so, fingers crossed . . ."

The *New York Phil*?

"The bride on Saturday is having seven harpists," says Mr. Ferguson. "And a soprano soloist from the Met."

Robyn and Elinor look at each other.

"Now *that's* an idea," says Robyn, and reaches for her notebook. "I'll get onto it."

"Shall we go and look at the Baroque Room now?" suggests Mr. Ferguson, and leads us to a large, old-fashioned elevator.

"The night before the wedding, you'll probably want to take a suite upstairs and enjoy the spa facilities," he says pleasantly as we travel upward. "Then on the day, you can bring in your own professional hair and makeup people." He smiles. "But I expect you've already thought of that."

"I . . . er . . ." My mind flicks madly back to Janice and Radiant Spring Bride. "Kind of . . ."

"The guests will be served cocktails as they pass along the corridor," explains Robyn as we leave the elevator. "Then this is the Baroque Room, where hors d'oeuvres will be served before we go into the Grand Ballroom. I expect you haven't even given hors d'oeuvres a thought yet!"

"Well . . . um . . . you know . . ." I'm about to say that everyone likes minisausages.

"But for example," she continues, "you could consider a caviar bar, an oyster bar, a Mediterranean meze table, sushi, perhaps . . ."

"Right," I gulp. "That . . . sounds good."

"And of course, the space itself can be themed however you like." She gestures around the room. "We can transform it into a Venetian carnival, a Japanese garden, a medieval banqueting hall . . . wherever your imagination takes you!"

"And then into the Grand Ballroom for the main reception!" says Mr. Ferguson cheerfully. He throws open a pair of double doors and . . . oh my God. This room is the most spectacular of all. It's all white and gold, with a high ceiling and theatrical boxes, and tables set around the vast, polished dance floor.

"That's where you and Luke will lead the dancing," says Robyn with a happy sigh. "I always say, that's the moment of a wedding I love the most. The first dance."

I gaze at the shining floor, and have a sudden vision of Luke and me whirling round among the candlelight and everyone looking on.

And seven harps.

And the New York Phil.

And caviar . . . and oysters . . . and cocktails . . .

"Rebecca, are you all right?" says Mr. Ferguson, suddenly seeing my expression.

"I think she's a little overwhelmed," says Robyn with a little laugh. "It's a lot to take in, isn't it?"

"Well . . . yes. I suppose so."

I take a deep breath and turn away for a moment. OK, let's not get carried away. This may all be very glitzy, but I am *not* going to be swayed by any of it. I've decided I'm going to get married in England—and that's what I'm going to do. End of story.

Except . . . just look at it all.

"Come and sit down," says Robyn, patting a gilt chair beside her. "Now, I know from your point of view it still seems far off. But we're on a pretty tight schedule . . . so I just wanted to talk to you about your overall view of the wedding. What's your fantasy? What, for you, is the image of pure romance? A lot of my clients say Scarlett and Rhett, or Fred and Ginger . . ." She looks at me with sparkling eyes, her pen poised expectantly over the page.

This has gone far enough. I have to tell this woman that none of this is actually going to happen. Come on, Becky. Get back to reality.

"I . . ."

"Yes?"

"I've always loved the end of *Sleeping Beauty,* when they dance together," I hear myself saying.

"The ballet," says Elinor approvingly.

"No, actually, I meant . . . the Disney film."

"Oh!" Robyn looks momentarily puzzled. "I'll have to catch that again! Well . . . I'm sure that will be inspirational too . . ."

She starts writing in her book and I bite my inner lip.

I have to call a halt to all this. Come on. Say something!

For some reason my mouth stays closed. I look around, taking in the molded ceiling; the gilding; the twinkling chandeliers.

Robyn follows my gaze and smiles at me. "Becky, you know, you're a very lucky girl." She squeezes my arm affectionately. "We're going to have so much fun!"

HOUSE OF LORDS
APPPOINTMENTS COMMISSION

NOMINATION FORM

Please summarize here why you are suitable for recommendation as a nonparty political peer and how you, personally, would make an effective contribution to the work of the House of Lords. Please support this with a CV clearly showing your major achievements and highlighting relevant skills and experience.

APPLICATION TO BE A LIFE PEER

Name: Rebecca Bloomwood

Address: Apt. B
251 W. 11th Street
New York, NY 10014

Preferred title: Baroness Rebecca Bloomwood of Harvey Nichols

Major achievements:

Patriotism
I have served Great Britain for many years, bolstering the economy through the medium of retail.

Trade Relations
Since living in New York I have promoted international trade between Britain and America, e.g., I always buy imported Twinings tea and Marmite.

Public Speaking
I have appeared on television chairing debates on current affairs (in the world of fashion).

Cultural Expertise
I am a collector of antiques and fine art, most notably 1930s cocktail cabinets and barware.

Personal contribution if appointed:
As a new member of the House of Lords, I would personally be very willing to take on the role of fashion consultant, an area hitherto neglected—yet vital to the very lifeblood of democracy.

February 21, 2002

Miss Rebecca Bloomwood
Apt. B
251 W. 11th Street
New York, NY 10014

Dear Miss Bloomwood:

Thank you for your letter of February 20.

I am afraid I could not comment on whether or not a Miù Miù
skirt is a household expense.

Yours sincerely,

Walt Pitman
Director of Customer Relations

Six

I'M NOT GOING to get married in New York. Of course I'm
not. It's unthinkable. I'm going to get married at home, just like I
planned, with a nice marquee in the garden. There's absolutely no
reason to change my plans. None at all.

Except . . . it would be amazing. Walking down that aisle in
front of four hundred people, to the sound of a string orchestra,
with amazing flower arrangements everywhere. Having the huge,
dreamy, Lady Di wedding I always fantasized about but thought was
beyond my grasp. I mean, it'd be *Becky's Big Day* come to life.

Then we'd all sit down to some incredible dinner . . . Robyn
gave me some sample dinner menus, and the food! Rosace of Maine
Lobster . . . Fowl Consommé with Quenelles of Pheasant . . . Wild
Rice with Pignoli Nuts . . .

I know Oxshott and Ashtead Quality Caterers are good—but
I'm not sure they even know what a pignoli nut is. (To be honest, I
don't either. But that's not the point.)

And maybe Elinor's right, Mum would be *grateful* if we took the
whole thing off her hands. Yes. Maybe she's finding the organization
more of a strain than she's letting on. Maybe she's already wishing
she hadn't volunteered to do the whole thing. Whereas if we get
married at the Plaza, she won't have to do anything, just turn up.
Plus Mum and Dad wouldn't have to pay for a thing . . . I mean, it
would be doing them a favor!

So as I'm walking back to Barneys, I take out my mobile and dial the number for home. As Mum answers I can hear the closing music of *Crimewatch* in the background, and I suddenly feel a wave of nostalgia for home. I can just imagine Mum and Dad sitting there, with the curtains drawn and the gas-effect fire flickering cozily.

"Hi, Mum?"

"Becky!" exclaims Mum. "I'm so glad you've phoned! I've been trying to fax you through some menus from the catering company, but your machine won't work. Dad says, have you checked your paper recently?"

"Um . . . I don't know. Listen, Mum—"

"And listen to this! Janice's sister-in-law knows someone who works at a balloon printing company! She says if we order two hundred or more balloons we can have the helium for free!"

"Great! Look, I was just thinking about the wedding, actually . . ."

Why do I suddenly feel nervous?

"Oh yes? Graham, turn the television down."

"It was just occurring to me . . . just as a possibility"—I give a shrill laugh—"that Luke and I could get married in America!"

"America?" There's a long pause. "What do you mean, America?"

"It was just a thought! You know, since Luke and I live here already . . ."

"You've lived there for one year, Becky!" Mum sounds quite shocked. "This is your home!"

"Well, yes . . . but I was just thinking . . ." I say feebly.

Somehow I was hoping that Mum would say "What a fantastic idea!" and make it really easy.

"How would we organize a wedding in America?"

"I don't know!" I swallow. "Maybe we could have it at a . . . a big hotel."

"A *hotel*?" Mum sounds as though I've gone mad.

"And maybe Elinor would help . . ." I plow on. "I'm sure she'd contribute . . . you know, if it was more expensive . . ."

There's a sharp intake of breath at the other end of the phone and I wince. Damn. I should never have mentioned Elinor.

"Yes, well. We don't want her contributions, thank you. We can manage very well by ourselves. Is this Elinor's idea, then, a hotel? Does she think we can't put on a nice wedding?"

"No!" I say hastily. "It's just . . . it's nothing! I was just . . ."

"Dad says, if she's so keen on hotels, she can stay at one instead of with us."

Oh God. I'm just making everything worse.

"Look . . . forget it. It was a silly idea." I rub my face. "So—how are the plans going?"

We chat for a few more minutes, and I hear all about the nice man from the marquee company and how his quote was very reasonable, and how his son was at school with cousin Alex, isn't it a small world? By the end of our conversation Mum sounds completely mollified and all talk of American hotels has been forgotten.

I say good-bye, turn off the phone, and exhale sharply. Right. Well, that's decided. I might as well call Elinor and tell her. No point in hanging around.

I turn on my mobile again, dial two digits, and then stop.

On the other hand—is there any point in rushing straight into a decision?

I mean, you never know. Maybe Mum and Dad will talk it over this evening and change their minds. Maybe they'll come out to have a look. Maybe if they actually *saw* the Plaza . . . if they saw how magical it was all going to be . . . how luxurious . . . how glamorous . . . I can't quite bear to give it up. Not quite yet.

When I get home, Luke is sitting at the table, frowning over some papers.

"You came home early!" I say, pleased.

"I had some papers to go over," says Luke. "Thought I'd get some peace and quiet here."

"Oh, right."

As I get near I see that they're all headed "The Elinor Sherman Foundation." I open my mouth to say something—then close it again.

"So," he says, looking up with a little smile, "what did you think of the Plaza?"

"You *knew* about it?" I stare at him.

"Yes. Of course I did. I would have come along too if I hadn't had a lunch appointment."

"But, Luke . . ." I take a deep breath, trying not to overreact. "You know my mother's planning a wedding in England."

"It's early days, surely?"

"You shouldn't have just fixed up a meeting like that!"

"My mother thought it would be a good way to surprise you. So did I."

"Spring it on me, you mean!" I retort crossly, and Luke looks at me, puzzled.

"Didn't you like the Plaza? I thought you'd be overwhelmed!"

"Of course I *liked* it. That's not the point."

"I know how much you've always wanted a big, magnificent wedding. When my mother offered to host a wedding at the Plaza, it seemed like a gift. In fact, it was my idea to surprise you. I thought you'd be thrilled."

He looks a bit deflated and immediately guilt pours over me. It hadn't occurred to me that Luke might have been in on the whole thing.

"Luke, I am thrilled! It's just . . . I don't think Mum would be very happy, us getting married in America."

"Can't you talk her round?"

"It's not that easy. Your mother's been pretty high-handed, you know—"

"High-handed? She's only trying to give us a wonderful wedding."

"If she really wanted to, she could give us a wonderful wedding in England," I point out. "Or she could help Mum and Dad—and they could *all* give us a wonderful wedding! But instead, she talks about their garden as an 'unknown backyard'!" Resentment flares up inside me again as I remember Elinor's dismissive voice.

"I'm sure she didn't mean—"

"Just because it isn't in the middle of New York! I mean, she doesn't know anything about it!"

"OK, fine," says Luke shortly. "You've made your point. You don't want the wedding. But if you ask me, my mother's being incredibly generous. Offering to pay for a wedding at the Plaza, plus she's arranged us a pretty lavish engagement party . . ."

"Who said I want a lavish engagement party?" I retort before I can stop myself.

"That's a bit churlish, isn't it?"

"Maybe I don't care about all the glitz and the glamour and the . . . the material things! Maybe my family is more important to me! And tradition . . . and . . . and honor. You know, Luke, we're only on this planet for a short time . . ."

"Enough!" says Luke in exasperation. "You win! If it's really going to be a problem, forget it! You don't have to come to the engagement party if you don't want to—and we'll get married in Oxshott. Happy now?"

"I . . ." I break off, and rub my nose. Of course, it is a fairly amazing offer. And if I *could* somehow persuade Mum and Dad, maybe we'd all have the most fantastic time of our lives.

"It's not necessarily a question of getting married in Oxshott," I say at last. "It's a question of . . . of . . . coming to the right decision. Look, you were the one saying we didn't have to rush into anything . . ."

Luke's expression softens, and he gets up.

"I know." He sighs. "Look, Becky, I'm sorry."

"I'm sorry too," I mumble.

"Oh, this is ridiculous." He puts his arms around me and kisses my forehead. "All I wanted to do was give you the wedding you've always dreamed of. If you really don't want to get married at the Plaza, then of course we won't."

"What about your mother?"

"We'll just explain to her how you feel." Luke gazes at me for a few moments. "Becky, it doesn't matter to me where we get married. It doesn't matter to me whether we have pink flowers or blue flowers. What matters to me is we're going to become a couple—and the whole world is going to know it."

He sounds so sure and steady, I feel a sudden lump in my throat.

"That's what matters to me too," I say, and swallow hard. "That's the most important thing."

"OK. So let's agree. You can make the decision. Just tell me where to turn up—and I'll turn up."

"OK." I smile back at him. "I promise to give you at least forty-eight hours' notice."

"Twenty-four will do." He kisses me again, then points to the sideboard. "That arrived, by the way. An engagement present."

I look over and gape. It's a robin's-egg-blue box, tied up with white ribbon. A present from Tiffany!

"Shall I open it?"

"Go ahead."

Excitedly I untie the ribbon and open the box to find a blue glass bowl nestling in tissue paper, and a card reading "With best wishes from Marty and Alison Gerber."

"Wow! This is nice! Who are the Gerbers?"

"I don't know. Friends of my mother's."

"So . . . will everyone who comes to the party bring us a present?"

"I expect so."

"Oh . . . right."

Gosh. When Tom and Lucy had their engagement party, only about three people brought presents. And they certainly weren't from Tiffany. I stare at the bowl thoughtfully, running my finger over its gleaming surface.

You know, maybe Luke does have a point. Maybe it would be churlish to throw Elinor's generosity back in her face.

OK, what I'll do is, I'll wait until the engagement party's over. And *then* I'll decide.

The engagement party is at six o'clock the following Friday. I mean to get there early, but we have a frantic day at work, with three big emergencies—one of which involves our most demanding celebrity client, who clearly has *not* got over her recent breakup, whatever she may say in *People* magazine. Anyway, so I don't arrive until ten past six, feeling a little flustered. On the plus side, I'm wearing a completely fabulous black strapless dress, which fits me perfectly. (Actually, it was earmarked for Regan Hartman, one of my clients. But I'll just tell her I don't think it would suit her after all.)

Elinor's duplex is in a grand building on Park Avenue, with the most enormous marble-floored foyer and walnut-lined elevators that always smell of expensive scent. As I step out at the sixth floor I can hear the hubbub and tinkle of piano music. There's a queue of people waiting at the door, and I wait politely behind an elderly

couple in matching fur coats. I can just see through to the apartment, which is dimly lit and already seems to be full of people.

To be honest, I've never really liked Elinor's apartment. It's all
done in pale blue, with silk sofas and heavy curtains and the dullest
pictures in the world hanging on the walls. I can't believe she really
likes any of them. In fact, I can't believe she ever *looks* at any of
them.

"Good evening." A voice interrupts my thoughts and I realize
I've reached the head of the queue. A woman in a black trouser suit,
holding a clipboard, is giving me a professional smile.

"May I have your name?"

"Rebecca Bloomwood," I say modestly, expecting her to gasp, or
at least light up with recognition.

"Bloomwood . . . Bloomwood . . ." The woman looks down the
list, turns a page, and runs her finger to the bottom before looking
up. "I don't see it."

"Really?" I stare at her. "It must be there somewhere!"

"I'll look again . . ." The woman goes up to the top and runs her
eyes down more slowly. "No," she says at last. "I'm afraid not.
Sorry." She turns to a blond woman who has just arrived. "Good
evening! May I take your name?"

"But . . . but . . . the party's for me!"

"Vanessa Dillon."

"Ah yes," says the door woman, and crosses off her name with a
smile. "Please go in. Serge will take your coat. Could you please step
aside, miss?" she adds coldly to me. "You're blocking the doorway."

"You have to let me in! I must be on the list!" I peer inside the
door, hoping to see Luke, or even Elinor—but it's just a load of people I don't recognize. "Please! Honestly, I'm supposed to be here!"

The woman in black sighs. "Do you have your invitation with
you?"

"No! I don't have one. I'm the . . . the engagee!"

"The what?" She stares at me blankly.

"The party's for *me*! And Luke . . . oh God . . ." I peer again into
the party and suddenly spot Robyn, dressed in a silver beaded top
and floaty skirt.

"Robyn!" I call, as discreetly as I can. "Robyn! They won't let
me in!"

"Becky!" Robyn's face lights up. "At last!" She beckons gaily with her champagne glass with one hand, while with the other she moves a pair of men in dinner jackets out of my path. "Come on, belle of the ball!"

"You see?" I say desperately. "I'm not gate-crashing! The party's being given *for me!*"

The blond woman stares at me for a long time—then shrugs. "OK. You can go in. Serge will take your coat. Do you have a gift?"

A gift? Has she listened to anything I've been saying?

"No, I don't."

The woman rolls her eyes as though to say, "That figures"—then turns to the next person in the queue, and I hurry in before she changes her mind.

"I can't stay long," says Robyn as I join her. "I have three re-hearsal dinners to go to. But I particularly wanted to see you tonight, because I have exciting news. A *very* talented event de-signer is going to be working on your wedding! Sheldon Lloyd, no less!"

"Wow!" I say, trying to match her tone even though I have no idea who Sheldon Lloyd is. "Gosh."

"You're bowled over, aren't you? What I always say is, if you want to make things happen, make them happen now! So I've been speaking with Sheldon and we've been tossing around some ideas. He thought your Sleeping Beauty concept was *fabulous,* by the way. Really original." She looks around and lowers her voice. "His idea is . . . we turn the Terrace Room into an enchanted forest."

"Really?"

"Yes! I'm so thrilled, I just have to show you!"

She opens her bag and pulls out a sketch, and I stare at it in disbelief.

"We'll have birch trees imported from Switzerland, and gar-lands of fairy lights. You'll walk down an avenue of trees, with their branches hanging over you. Pine needles will give off a wonderful scent as you walk, flowers will magically blossom as you pass, and trained songbirds will sing overhead. . . . What do you think about an animatronic squirrel?"

"Erm . . ." I pull a little face.

"No, I wasn't sure about that, either. OK . . . we'll forget the woodland creatures." She takes out a pen and scores out an entry. "But otherwise . . . it's going to be fabulous. Don't you think?"

"I . . . Well . . ."

Should I tell her I'm still not quite decided about whether to get married in New York?

Oh, but I can't. She'll stop all the preparations on the spot. She'll go and tell Elinor, and there'll be a terrible fuss.

And the thing is, I'm sure we will end up going for the Plaza in the end. Once I've worked out exactly how to win Mum round. I mean, we'd be mad not to.

"You know, Sheldon has worked for many Hollywood stars," says Robyn, lowering her voice still further. "When we meet him you can look at his portfolio. I'm telling you, it's quite something."

"Really?" I feel a sparkle of excitement. "It all sounds . . . fantastic!"

"Good!" She looks at her watch. "Now, I have to run. But I'll be in touch." She squeezes my hand, downs her champagne, and hurries toward the door—and I stare after her, still a little dazzled.

Hollywood stars! I mean, if Mum knew about that, wouldn't she see the whole thing differently? Wouldn't she realize what an amazing opportunity this is?

The trouble is, I can't quite pluck up courage to bring up the subject again. I didn't even dare tell her about this party. She'd only get all upset and say, "Doesn't Elinor think we can throw a nice engagement party?" or something. And then I'd feel even more guilty than I already do. Oh God. I just need a way to introduce the idea into her head once more, without her immediately getting upset. Maybe if I spoke to Janice . . . if I told her about the Hollywood stars . . .

A burst of laughter nearby brings me out of my thoughts, and I realize I'm standing all alone. I take a sip of champagne and look for someone to join. The slightly weird thing is, this is supposed to be an engagement party for me and Luke. But there must be at least a hundred people here, and I don't know any of them. At least, I dimly recognize the odd face here and there—but not really well enough to bound up and say hello. I try smiling at a woman coming in, but she eyes me suspiciously and pushes her way toward a group standing by the window. You know, whoever said Americans were friendlier than the British can't ever have been to New York.

Danny should be here somewhere, I think, peering through the throng. I invited Erin and Christina too—but they were both still hard at it when I left Barneys. I expect they'll be along later.

Oh come on, I've got to talk to someone. I should at least let Elinor know I'm here. I'm just elbowing my way past a group of women in matching black Armani when I hear someone saying "Do you know the bride?"

I freeze behind a pillar, trying to pretend I'm not eavesdropping.

"No. Does anybody?"

"Where do they live?"

"The West Village somewhere. But apparently they're moving to this building."

I stare at the pillar in bemusement. What's that?

"Oh really? I thought it was impossible to get in here."

"Not if you're related to Elinor Sherman!" The women laugh gaily and move off into the melee, and I stare blankly at a molded curlicue.

They must have got that wrong. There's no way we're moving here. No way.

I wander aimlessly around for another few minutes, find myself a glass of champagne, and try to keep a cheerful smile on my face. But try as I might, it keeps slipping. This isn't exactly how I pictured my engagement party would be. First of all the door-people try to stop me going in. Then I don't know anybody. Then the only things to eat are low-fat, high-protein cubes of fish—and even then, the wait staff look taken aback when you actually eat them.

I can't help thinking back slightly wistfully to Tom and Lucy's engagement party. It wasn't nearly as grand as this, of course. Janice made a big bowl of punch and there was a barbecue, and Martin sang "Are You Lonesome Tonight?" on the karaoke machine. But still. At least it was fun. At last I knew people. I knew more people at that party than I do at this one—

"Becky! Why are you hiding?" I look up and feel a swoosh of relief. There's Luke.

"Luke! At last!" I say, moving forward—then gasp in joy as I see a familiar, balding, middle-aged man standing beside him, grinning cheerfully at me. "Michael!" I throw my arms around him and give him a big hug.

Michael Ellis has to be one of my favorite people in the world. He's based in Washington, where he heads up an incredibly successful advertising agency. He's also Luke's partner in the American arm of Brandon Communications, and has been like a mentor figure to him. And to me, for that matter. If it weren't for some advice Michael gave me a while ago, I'd never have moved to New York in the first place.

"Luke said you might be coming!" I say, beaming at him.

"You think I'd miss this?" Michael twinkles at me. "Congratulations!" He raises his glass toward me. "You know, Becky, I'll bet you're regretting not taking up my offer of a job now. You could have had real prospects in Washington. Whereas instead . . ." He shakes his head. "Look at the way things have turned out for you. Great job, got your man, a wedding at the Plaza . . ."

"Who told you about the Plaza?" I say in surprise.

"Oh, just about everybody I've spoken to. Sounds like it's going to be some event."

"Well . . ." I give a bashful shrug.

"Is your mom excited about it?"

"I . . . er . . . well . . ." I take a sip of champagne to avoid having to answer.

"She's not here tonight, I take it?"

"No. Well, it is quite a long way!" My laugh is a little shrill, and I take another sip, draining my glass.

"Let me get you another," says Luke, taking my glass. "And I'll find my mother. She was asking where you were . . . I've just asked Michael to be best man," he adds as he walks off. "Luckily he said yes."

"Really?" I say, and beam at Michael in delight. "Fantastic! I can't think of a better choice."

"I'm very honored to be asked," says Michael. "Unless you want me to marry you, of course. I'm a bit rusty, but I could probably remember the words . . ."

"Really?" I say in surprise. "Are you secretly a minister, as well as everything else?"

"No." He throws back his head and laughs. "But a few years back, some friends wanted me to marry them. I pulled some strings and got registered as an officiant."

"Well, I think you'd make a great minister! Father Michael. People would flock to your church."

"An atheist minister." Michael raises his eyebrows. "I guess I wouldn't be the first." He takes a sip of champagne. "So how's the shopping business?"

"It's great, thanks." I beam at him.

"You know, I recommend you to everyone I meet. 'You need clothes, go to Becky Bloomwood at Barneys.' I tell busboys, businessmen, random people I meet on the street . . ."

"I wondered why I kept getting all these strange people through." I smile at him.

"Seriously, I wanted to ask a small favor." Michael lowers his voice slightly. "I'd be grateful if you could help out my daughter, Lucy. She just broke up with a guy and I think she's going through a patch of lacking self-confidence. I told her I knew who could fix her up."

"Absolutely," I say, feeling touched. "I'd be glad to help."

"You won't bankrupt her, though. Because she's only on a lawyer's salary."

"I'll try not to," I say, laughing. "How about you?"

"You think I need help?"

"To be honest, you look pretty good already." I gesture to his immaculate dark gray suit, which I'm certain didn't give him much change out of $3,000.

"I always dress up when I know I'm going to be seeing the beautiful people," says Michael. He looks around the party with an amused expression, and I follow his gaze. A nearby group of six middle-aged women are talking at each other animatedly, seemingly without taking breath. "Are these your friends?"

"Not really," I admit. "I don't know many people here."

"I guessed as much." He gives me a quizzical smile and takes a sip of champagne. "So . . . how are you getting along with your future mother-in-law?" His expression is so innocent, I want to laugh.

"Oh, like a house on fire," I say, grinning. "Can't you tell?"

"What are you talking about?" says Luke, suddenly appearing at my shoulder. He hands me a full glass of champagne and I shoot a glance at Michael.

"We were just talking about wedding plans," says Michael easily. "Have you decided on a honeymoon location yet?"

"We haven't really talked about it." I look at Luke. "But I've had some ideas. We need to go somewhere really nice and hot. And glamorous. And somewhere I've never been before."

"You know, I'm not sure I'll be able to fit in much of a honeymoon," says Luke with a small frown. "We've just taken on North-West and that means we may be looking at expanding again. So we might have to make do with a long weekend."

"A long weekend?" I stare at him in dismay. "That's not a honeymoon!"

"Luke," says Michael reprovingly. "That won't do. You have to take your wife on a nice honeymoon. As best man, I insist. Where have you never been, Becky? Venice? Rome? India? Africa?"

"I haven't been to any of them!"

"I see." Michael raises his eyebrows. "This could turn out to be some honeymoon."

"Everyone has seen the world except me. I never even had a gap year. I never did Australia, or Thailand . . ."

"Neither did I," says Luke, shrugging.

"I haven't *done* anything! You know, Suze's mother's best friend in the whole world is a Bolivian peasant." I look at Luke impressively. "They ground maize together on the plains of the Llanos!"

"Looks like it's Bolivia," says Michael to Luke.

"You want to grind maize on our honeymoon?"

"I just think maybe we should broaden our horizons a bit. Like . . . go backpacking, maybe."

"Becky, are you aware of the concept of backpacking?" says Luke mildly. "All your possessions in one rucksack. Which you have to *carry*. Not FedEx."

"I could do that!" I say indignantly. "Easily! And we'd meet loads of really interesting people—"

"I know interesting people already."

"You know bankers and PR people! Do you know any Bolivian peasants? Do you know any homeless people?"

"I can't say I do," says Luke. "Do you?"

"Well . . . no," I admit after a pause. "But that's not the point. We should!"

"OK, Becky," says Luke lifting a hand. "I have a solution. You organize the honeymoon. Anywhere you want, as long as it doesn't take more than two weeks."

"Really?" I gape at him. "Are you serious?"

"I'm serious. You're right, we can't get married and not have a proper honeymoon." He smiles at me. "Surprise me."

"Well, OK. I will!"

I take a sip of champagne, feeling all bubbly with excitement. How cool is this? I get to choose the honeymoon! Maybe we should go to an amazing spa in Thailand, or something. Or some spectacular safari . . .

"Speaking of homeless," says Luke to Michael, "we'll be out on the streets in September."

"Really?" says Michael. "What happened?"

"The lease on our apartment is up—and the owner's selling. Everyone out."

"Oh!" I say, suddenly diverted from pleasant visions of me and Luke standing on top of one of the pyramids. "That reminds me. Luke, I heard this really odd conversation just now. Some people were saying that we were going to move to this building. Where did they get that from?"

"It's a possibility," says Luke.

"What?" I stare at him blankly. "What do you mean, it's a possibility? Have you gone mad?"

"Why not?"

I lower my voice a little. "Do you really think I want to live in this stuffy building full of horrible old women who look at you as though you smell?"

"Becky—" interrupts Michael, jerking his head meaningfully.

"It's true!" I turn to him. "Not one of the people who lives in this building is nice! I've met them, and they're all absolutely—"

Abruptly I halt, as I realize what Michael's trying to tell me.

"Except . . . for . . . Luke's mother," I add, trying to sound as natural as possible. "Of course."

"Good evening, Rebecca," comes a chilly voice behind me, and I stand up, cheeks flaming.

There she is, standing behind me, wearing a long white Grecian-style dress that falls in pleats to the ground. She's so thin and pale, she looks just like one of her own pillars.

"Hello, Elinor," I say politely. "You look lovely. I'm sorry I was a little late."

"Rebecca," she replies, and offers me a cheek. "I hope you've been circulating? Not just sitting here with Luke?"

"Er . . . kind of . . ."

"This is a good opportunity for you to meet some important people," she says. "The president of this building, for example."

"Right." I nod. "Well, er . . . maybe."

This is probably not the moment to tell her that there's no way in a million years I'm moving to this building.

"I'll introduce you to her later. But now I'm about to make the toast," she says. "If you would both come over to the podium."

"Excellent!" I say, trying to sound enthusiastic, and take a gulp of champagne.

"Mother, you've met Michael," says Luke.

"Indeed," says Elinor with a gracious smile. "How do you do?"

"Very well, thank you," says Michael pleasantly. "I intended to come to the launch of your foundation but unfortunately couldn't make it up from Washington. I hear it went very well, though?"

"It did. Thank you."

"And now another happy occasion." He gestures around the room. "I was just saying to Luke, how lucky he was to have landed such a beautiful, talented, accomplished girl as Becky."

"Indeed." Elinor's smile freezes slightly.

"But you must feel the same way."

There's silence.

"Of course," says Elinor at last. She extends her hand and, after a tiny hesitation, places it on my shoulder.

Oh God. Her fingers are all cold. It's like being touched by the ice queen. I glance at Luke, and he's glowing with pleasure.

"So! The toast!" I say brightly. "Lead the way!"

"See you later, Michael," says Luke.

"Have a good one," replies Michael, and gives me the tiniest of winks. "Luke," he adds more quietly as she moves away, "on the subject of your mother's charity, I'd like to have a word later."

"Right," says Luke after a pause. "Fine."

Is it my imagination or does he look slightly defensive?

"But do the toast first," says Michael pleasantly. "We're not here to talk business."

As I walk through the room with Luke and Elinor, I can see people starting to turn and murmur. A little podium has been set up at one end of the room, and as we step up onto it I start to feel a little nervous for the first time. Silence has fallen around the room and the entire assembled gathering is looking at us.

Two hundred eyes, all giving me the Manhattan Onceover.

Trying to stay unself-conscious, I search among the crowd for faces I recognize. But apart from Michael at the back, there isn't a single one.

I keep smiling, but inside I feel a bit low. Where are my friends? I know Christina and Erin are on their way—but where's Danny? He promised he was going to come.

"Ladies and gentlemen," says Elinor graciously, "welcome. It gives me enormous pleasure to welcome you here tonight on this happy occasion. Particularly Marcia Fox, president of this building, and Guinevere von . . ."

"I don't care about your stupid list!" comes a high-pitched voice from the door, and a couple of heads at the back turn to look.

". . . von Landlenburg, associate of the Elinor Sherman Foundation . . ." says Elinor, her jaw growing more rigid.

"Let me in, you stupid cow!"

There's a scuffling sound and a small scream, and the whole room turns to see what's going on.

"Get your hands off me. I'm pregnant, OK? If anything happens I'll sue!"

"I don't believe it!" I shriek in delight, and jump down off the podium. "Suze!"

"Bex!" Suze appears through the door, looking tanned and healthy, with beads in her hair and a sizable bump showing through her dress. "Surprise!"

Seven

"We thought we'd surprise you!" says Suze after the fuss has died down and Elinor has made her toast—in which she mentions me and Luke once, and the Elinor Sherman Foundation six times. "Like a last bit of our honeymoon! So we turned up at your flat . . ."

"And I was, as ever, running perfectly on time . . ." puts in Danny, giving me an apologetic grin.

"So Danny said why didn't we come along to the party and give you a bit of a shock?"

"It's so great to see you." I give her an affectionate hug. "And Tarquin." We all glance toward Tarquin, who has been surrounded by a group of avidly interested New York ladies.

"Do you live in a castle?" I can hear one of them saying.

"Well . . . um, yes. Actually, I do."

"Do you know Prince Charles?" says another, goggling.

"We've played polo once or twice . . ." Tarquin looks around, desperate to escape.

"You *have* to meet my daughter," says one of the ladies, putting a clamplike arm round his shoulders. "She loves England. She visited Hampton Court *six times*."

"He is spectacular," says a low voice in my ear, and I look round to see Danny gazing over my shoulder at Tarquin. "Utterly spectacular. Is he a model?"

"Is he a *what*?"

"I mean, this story about him being a farmer." Danny drags on his cigarette. "It's bullshit, right?"

"You think Tarquin should be a *model*?" I can't help a snort of laughter erupting through me.

"What?" says Danny defensively. "He has a fantastic look. I could design a whole collection around him. Prince Charles meets . . . Rupert Everett . . . meets—"

"Danny, you do know he's straight?"

"Of course I know he's straight! What do you take me for?" Danny gives a thoughtful pause. "But he went to English boarding school, right?"

"Danny!" I give him a shove and look up. "Hi, Tarquin! You managed to get away!"

"Hello!" says Tarquin, looking a bit harassed. "Suze, darling, have you given Becky the stuff from her mother?"

"Oh, it's back at the hotel," says Suze, and turns to me. "Bex, we dropped in on your mum and dad on the way to the airport. They are so obsessed!" She giggles. "They can't talk about anything but the wedding."

"I'm not surprised," says Danny. "It sounds like it's going to be fairly amazing. Catherine Zeta-Jones, eat your heart out."

"Catherine Zeta-Jones?" says Suze interestedly. "What do you mean?"

I feel my body stiffen all over. Shit. Think.

"Danny," I say casually. "I think the editor of *Women's Wear Daily* is over there."

"Really? Where?" Danny's head swivels round. "I'll be back in a second." He disappears off into the party and I subside in relief.

"When we were there, they were having this huge argument about how big the marquee should be," says Suze with another giggle. "They made us sit on the lawn, pretending to be guests."

I don't want to hear about this. I take a gulp of champagne and try to think of another topic.

"Have you told Becky the other thing that happened?" says Tarquin, looking suddenly grave.

"Er . . . no, not yet," says Suze guiltily, and Tarquin gives a deep, solemn sigh.

"Becky, Suze has something she needs to confess."

"That's right." Suze bites her lip and looks abashed. "We were at your parents' house, and I asked to look at your mum's wedding dress. So we were all admiring it, and I was holding a cup of coffee . . ." She hangs her head. "And then—I don't know how it happened, but . . . I spilled my coffee on the dress."

I stare at her incredulously. "On the dress? Are you serious?"

"We offered to clean it, of course," says Tarquin. "But I'm not sure it will be wearable. We're so incredibly sorry, Becky. And we'll pay for another dress, of course." He looks at his empty glass. "Can I get anyone another drink?"

"So the dress is . . . ruined?" I say, just to be sure.

"Yes, and it wasn't easy, I can tell you!" says Suze as soon as Tarquin is out of earshot. "The first time I tried, your mum whisked it away just in time. Then she started getting all worried and saying she'd better put it away. I had to practically *throw* my coffee cup at it, just as she was packing it up—and even then it only just caught the train. Of course, your mum hates me now," she adds gloomily. "I shouldn't think I'll get invited to the wedding."

"Oh, Suze. She doesn't really. And thank you *so* much. You're a complete star. I honestly didn't think you'd manage it."

"Well, I couldn't let you look like a lamb cutlet, could I?" Suze grins. "The weird thing is, in her wedding pictures, your mum looks really lovely in it. But in real life . . ." She pulls a little face.

"Exactly. Oh, Suze, I'm so glad you're here." Impulsively I give her a hug. "I thought you'd be all . . . married. What's being married like, anyway?"

"Kind of the same," says Suze after a pause. "Except we have more plates—"

I feel a tapping on my shoulder and look up to see a red-haired woman wearing a pale silk trouser suit.

"Laura Redburn Seymour," she says, extending her hand. "My husband and I have to go, but I just wanted to say I just heard about your wedding plans. I got married in exactly the same place, fifteen years ago. And let me tell you, when you walk down that aisle, there's no feeling like it." She clasps her hands and smiles at her husband, who looks exactly like Clark Kent.

"Gosh," I say. "Well . . . thank you!"

"Were you brought up in Oxshott, then?" asks Suze cheerfully. "That's a coincidence!"

Oh, fuck.

"I'm sorry?" says Laura Redburn Seymour.

"Oxshott!" says Suze. "You know!"

"Ox? What ox?" Laura Redburn Seymour looks confusedly at her husband.

"We don't believe in hunting," says Clark Kent a little coldly. "Good evening. And congratulations again," he adds to me.

As the two walk off, Suze stares at me in puzzlement. "Bex. Did that make any sense?"

"I . . . erm . . ." I rub my nose, playing for time.

I really don't know why, but I have a strong feeling that I don't want to tell Suze about the Plaza.

OK. I do know why. It's because I know exactly what she'll say.

"Yes!" I say at last. "I think it did, kind of."

"No, it didn't! She didn't get married in Oxshott. Why did she think you would be walking up the same aisle as her?"

"Well . . . you know . . . they're American. Nothing they say makes sense . . . So, er . . . wedding dress shopping! Shall we go tomorrow?"

"Ooh, definitely!" says Suze, her brow immediately unfurling. "Where shall we go? Does Barneys have a bridal department?"

Thank God Suze is so sweet and unsuspicious.

"Yes, it does," I say. "I've had a quick look, but I haven't tried anything on yet. The only thing is, I haven't got an appointment, and it's a Saturday tomorrow." I wrinkle my brow. "We could try Vera Wang but that'll probably be all booked up . . ."

"I want to go baby shopping as well. I've got a list."

"I've bought a couple of things," I say, looking fondly at her bump. "You know. Just little presents."

"I want a really nice mobile . . ."

"Don't worry, I've got you one of those. And some really cute little outfits!"

"Bex! You shouldn't have!"

"There was a sale on at Baby Gap!" I say defensively.

"Excuse me?" interrupts a voice, and we both look up to see a lady in black and pearls approaching. "I couldn't help overhearing your conversation just now. My name is Cynthia Harrison. I'm a great friend of Elinor's and also of Robyn, your wedding planner. You're in very good hands there!"

"Oh, right!" I say politely. "That's nice to hear!"

"If you're looking for a wedding dress, may I invite you both along to my new bridal boutique, Dream Dress?" Cynthia Harrison beams at me. "I've been selling wedding dresses for twenty years, and this very week I've opened a store on Madison Avenue. We have a huge selection of designer gowns, shoes, and accessories. Personal service in a luxurious environment. All your bridal needs catered to, however great or small."

She stops rather abruptly, as though she's been reading off a card.

"Well . . . OK! We'll come tomorrow!"

"Shall we say eleven o'clock?" suggests Cynthia, and I glance at Suze, who nods.

"Eleven it is. Thank you very much!"

As Cynthia Harrison departs, I grin at Suze excitedly. But she's peering over at the other side of the room.

"What's up with Luke?" she says.

"What do you mean?" I turn round and stare. Luke and Michael are in the corner of the room, away from everyone else, and it looks as though they're arguing.

As I watch, Luke raises his voice defensively, and I catch the words "the bigger picture, for God's sake!"

"What are they talking about?" says Suze.

"I've got no idea!"

I strain as hard as I can, but I can only hear the odd phrase.

". . . simply don't feel . . . appropriate . . ." Michael is saying.

". . . short term . . . feel it's entirely appropriate . . ."

Luke looks really rattled.

". . . wrong impression . . . abusing your position . . ."

". . . had enough of this!"

I watch in dismay as Luke stalks off, out of the room. Michael looks completely taken aback by his reaction. For a moment he's stock still—then he reaches for his glass and takes a slug of whiskey.

I can't believe it. I've never known Luke and Michael to have a cross word before. I mean, Luke adores Michael. He practically sees him as a father figure. What on earth can be going on?

"I'll be back in a minute," I murmur to Suze, and hurry, as discreetly as possible, over to where Michael is still standing, staring into space.

"What was all that about?" I demand as soon as I reach him. "Why were you and Luke fighting?"

Michael looks up, startled—then quickly composes his features into a smile.

"Just a little business disagreement," he says. "Nothing to worry about. So, have you decided on a honeymoon location yet?"

"Michael, come on. It's me! Tell me what's going on." I lower my voice. "What did you mean, Luke's abusing his position? What's happened?"

There's a long pause and I can see Michael weighing up whether or not to tell me.

"Did you know," he says at last, "that at least one member of staff from Brandon Communications has been redeployed to work for the Elinor Sherman Foundation?"

"What?" I stare at him in shock. "Are you serious?"

"I've recently discovered that a new assistant at the company has been assigned to work for Luke's mother. Brandon Communications is still paying her salary—but essentially she's Elinor's full-time lackey. Naturally she's unhappy about the situation." Michael sighs. "All I wanted to do was raise the point, but Luke's very defensive."

"He hasn't said anything about this to me!" I say incredulously.

"He hasn't said anything about it to anybody. I only found out because it so happens that this assistant knows my daughter, and felt she could call me up." Michael lowers his voice. "The real danger is that she might complain to the investors. Then Luke would be in trouble."

"It's his mother," I say at last. "You know what a hold she's got over him. He'll do anything to impress her."

"I know," says Michael. "And I can understand that. Everyone has their own hang-ups." He looks at his watch. "I have to go, I'm afraid."

"You can't leave! Not without talking to him again!"

"I'm not sure that would do any good right now." Michael looks at me kindly. "Becky, don't let this spoil your evening. And don't go and give Luke a hard time. It's obviously a very sensitive topic." He squeezes my arm. "I'm sure it'll all work out."

"I won't. I promise!" I force myself to smile brightly. "And thanks for coming, Michael. It meant a lot to us. Both of us."

I give him a warm hug and watch as he walks away. Then, when he's gone, I head out of the room. I have to talk to Luke, as quickly as possible.

Obviously, Michael's right. It's a very sensitive subject, so I won't go charging in. I'll just ask a few probing, tactful questions, and gently steer him in the right direction. Just like a future wife should.

Eventually I find him upstairs, sitting in a chair in his mother's bedroom, staring into space.

"Luke, I just spoke to Michael!" I exclaim. "He told me you were sending the Brandon Communications staff over to work for your mother's charity!"

Oops. That didn't quite come out right.

"One assistant," says Luke without turning his head. "OK?"

"Can't she hire her own assistant? Luke, what if your investors find out?"

"Becky, I'm not completely stupid. This whole charity thing will be good for the company too." At last he turns his head to look at me. "This business is all about image. When I'm photographed handing over some enormous check to a deserving charity, the positive effect will be enormous. These days, people want to be associated with companies that give something back. I've already planned a photo opportunity in the *New York Post* in a couple of weeks' time, plus a couple of carefully placed features. The effect on our profile will be huge!"

"So why didn't Michael see it like that?"

"He wasn't listening. All he could talk about was how I was 'setting the wrong precedent.' "

"Well, maybe he has a point! I mean, surely you hire staff in order to work for you, not to send off to other companies—"

"This is a one-off example," says Luke impatiently. "And in my opinion, the benefits to the company will far outweigh any costs."

"Michael's your partner! You should listen to him. You should trust him."

"And he should trust me!" retorts Luke angrily. "There won't be a problem with the investors. Believe me, when they see the publicity we're going to generate, they'll be more than happy. If Michael could just *understand* that, instead of quibbling over stupid details . . . Where is he, anyway?"

"Michael had to go," I say—and see Luke's face tighten in shock.

"He left? Oh, well. Great."

"It wasn't like that. He had to." I sit down on the bed and take hold of Luke's hand. "Luke, don't fight with Michael. He's been such a good friend. Come on, remember everything he's done for you? Remember the speech he made on your birthday?"

I'm trying to lighten the atmosphere, but Luke doesn't seem to notice. His face is taut and defensive and his shoulders are hunched up. He's not going to listen to a word I say. I give an inward sigh and take a sip of champagne. I'll just have to wait until a better time.

There's silence for a few minutes—and after a while we both relax. It's as though we've called a truce.

"I'd better go," I say at last. "Suze doesn't know anybody down there."

"How long is she in New York for?" asks Luke, looking up.

"Just a few days."

I look idly around the room. I've never been in Elinor's bedroom before. It's immaculate, like the rest of the place, with pale walls and lots of expensive-looking custom-made furniture.

"Hey, guess what," I say, suddenly remembering. "Suze and I are going to choose a wedding dress tomorrow!"

Luke looks at me in surprise. "I thought you were going to wear your mother's wedding dress."

"Yes. Well." I frown. "The thing is, there was this awful accident . . ."

And all I can say is thank God. Thank God for Suze and her well-aimed cup of coffee.

As we approach the window of Dream Dress on Madison Avenue the next morning, I suddenly realize what Mum was asking me to do. *How* could she want me to dress up in white frills, instead of one of these gorgeous, amazing, Oscar-winner creations? We open the door and silently look around the hushed showroom, with its champagne-colored carpet and painted trompe l'oeil clouds on the ceiling—and, hanging in gleaming, glittery, sheeny rows on two sides of the room, wedding dresses.

I can feel overexcitement rising through me like a fountain. Any minute I might giggle out loud.

"Rebecca!" Cynthia has spotted us and is coming forward with a beam. "I'm so glad you came. Welcome to Dream Dress, where our motto is—"

"Ooh, I bet I know!" interrupts Suze. "Is it 'Live out your dream at Dream Dress'?"

"No. It's not." Cynthia smiles.

"Is it 'Dreams come true at Dream Dress'?"

"No." Cynthia's smile tightens slightly. "It's 'We'll find your Dream Dress.'"

"Oh, lovely!" Suze nods politely.

Cynthia ushers us into the hushed room and seats us on a cream sofa. "I'll be with you in a moment," she says pleasantly. "Have a browse through some magazines meanwhile." Suze and I grin excitedly at each other—then she reaches for *Contemporary Bride,* and I pick up *Martha Stewart Weddings.*

I adore *Martha Stewart Weddings.*

Secretly, I want to *be Martha Stewart Weddings.* I just want to crawl inside the pages with all those beautiful people getting married in Nantucket and South Carolina and riding to the chapel on horses and making their own place-card holders out of frosted russet apples.

I stare at a picture of a wholesome-looking couple standing in a poppy field against a staggeringly beautiful backdrop of mountains. You know, maybe we should get married in a poppy field too, and I could have barley twined round my hair and Luke could make us a loving seat with his own bare hands because his family has worked in wood crafting for six generations. Then we'd ride back to the house in an old country wagon—

"What's 'French white-glove service'?" says Suze, peering puzzledly at an ad.

"I dunno." I look up dazedly. "Hey, Suze, look at this. Shall I make my own bouquet?"

"Do what?"

"Look!" I point to the page. "You can make your own flowers out of crepe paper for an imaginative and individual bouquet."

"You? Make paper flowers?"

"I could!" I say, slightly nettled by her tone. "I'm a very creative person, you know."

"And what if it rains?"

"It won't rain—" I stop myself abruptly.

I was about to say, "It won't rain in the Plaza."

"I just . . . know it won't rain," I say instead, and quickly turn a page. "Ooh, look at those shoes!"

"Ladies! Let's begin." We both look up to see Cynthia coming back, a clipboard in her hand. She sits down on a small gilt chair and we both look at her attentively.

"Nothing in your life," she says, "can prepare you for the experience of buying your wedding dress. You may think you know about buying clothes." Cynthia gives a little smile and shakes her head. "Buying a wedding dress is different. We at Dream Dresses like to say, you don't choose your dress . . ."

"Your dress chooses you?" suggests Suze.

"No," says Cynthia with a flash of annoyance. "You don't *choose* your dress," she repeats, turning to me, "you *meet* your dress. You've met your man . . . now it's time to meet your dress. And let me assure you, there is a dress waiting for you. It might be the first dress you try on." Cynthia gestures to a halter-top sheath hanging up nearby. "It might be the twentieth. But when you put on the right dress . . . it'll hit you here." She clasps her solar plexus. "It's like falling in love. You'll know."

"Really?" I look around, feeling tentacles of excitement. "How will I know?"

"Let's just say . . . you'll know." She gives me a wise smile. "Have you had any ideas at all yet?"

"Well, obviously I've had a few thoughts . . ."

"Good! It's always helpful if we can narrow the search down a little. So before we start, let me ask you a few basic questions." She unscrews her pen. "Were you after something simple?"

"Absolutely," I say, nodding my head. "Really simple and elegant. Or else quite elaborate," I add, my eye catching sight of an amazing dress with roses cascading down the back.

"Right. So . . . simple or elaborate . . ." She scribbles on her notebook. "Did you want beading or embroidery?"

"Maybe."

"OK . . . now. Sleeves or strapless?"

"Possibly strapless," I say thoughtfully. "Or else sleeves."

"Did you want a train?"

"Ooh, yes!"

"But you wouldn't mind if you didn't have a train, would you?" puts in Suze, who is leafing through *Wedding Hair.* "I mean, you could always have one of those really long veils for the procession."

"That's true. But I do like the idea of a train . . ." I stare at her, gripped by a sudden thought. "Hey, Suze, if I waited a couple of years to get married, your baby would be two—and it could hold my train up!"

"Oh!" Suze claps her hand over her mouth. "That would be so sweet! Except, what if it fell over? Or screamed?"

"I wouldn't mind! And we could get it a really gorgeous little outfit . . ."

"If we could just get back to the subject . . ." Cynthia smiles at us and surveys her clipboard. "So we're after something either simple or elaborate, with sleeves or strapless, possibly with beading and/or embroidery and either with a train or without."

"Exactly!" My eye follows hers around the shop. "But you know, I'm quite flexible."

"Right." Cynthia stares at her notes silently for a few moments. "Right," she says again. "Well, the only way you can know is by trying a few dresses on . . . so let's get started!"

Why have I never done this before? Trying on wedding dresses is simply the most fun I've had ever, in my whole life. Cynthia shows me into a large fitting room with gold and white cherub wallpaper and a big mirror and gives me a lacy basque and high satin shoes to put on—and then her assistant brings in dresses in lots of five. I try on silk chiffon sheaths with low backs, ballerina dresses with tight bodices and layers of tulle, dresses made from duchesse satin and lace, starkly plain dresses with dramatic trains, simple dresses, glittery dresses . . .

"When you see the right one, you'll know," Cynthia keeps saying as the assistant heaves the hangers up onto the hooks. "Just . . . keep trying."

"I will!" I say happily, as I step into a strapless dress with beaded lace and a swooshy skirt. I come outside and parade around in front of Suze.

"That's fantastic!" she says. "Even better than the one with the little straps."

"I know! But I still quite like that one with the lace sleeves off the shoulder . . ." I stare critically at myself. "How many have I tried on now?"

"That takes us up to . . . thirty-five," says Cynthia, looking at her list.

"And how many have I marked so far as possibles?"

"Thirty-two."

"Really?" I look up in surprise. "Which ones didn't I like?"

"The two pink dresses and the coatdress."

"Oh no, I still quite like the coatdress. Put it down as a possible." I parade a bit more, then look around the shop, trying to see if there's anything I haven't looked at yet. I stop in front of a rail of baby flower-girls' dresses and sigh, slightly more heavily than I meant to. "God, it's tricky, isn't it? I mean . . . one dress. *One.*"

"I don't think Becky's ever bought one thing before," says Suze to Cynthia. "It's a bit of a culture shock."

"I don't see why you can't wear more than one. I mean, it's supposed to be the happiest day of your life, isn't it? You should be allowed *five* dresses."

"That would be cool!" says Suze. "You could have a really sweet romantic one for walking in, then a more elegant one to walk out . . . then one for cocktails . . ."

"And a really sexy one for dancing . . . and another one for . . ."

"For Luke to rip off you," says Suze, her eyes gleaming.

"Ladies," says Cynthia, giving a little laugh. "Rebecca. I know it's hard . . . but you are going to have to choose sometime! For a June wedding, you're already leaving it very late."

"How can I be leaving it late?" I say in astonishment. "I've only just got engaged!"

Cynthia shakes her head. "In wedding dress terms, that's late.

What we recommend is that if brides think they may have a short engagement, they begin to look for a dress *before* they get engaged."

"Oh God." I give a gusty sigh. "I had no idea it was all going to be so difficult."

"Try on that one at the end," suggests Suze. "The one with the chiffon trumpet sleeves. You haven't tried that, have you?"

"Oh," I say, looking at it in surprise. "No, I haven't."

I carry the dress back to the fitting room, clamber out of the swooshy skirt, and step into it.

It skims sleekly over my hips, hugs my waist, and falls to the floor in a tiny, rippling train. The neckline flatters my face, and the color is just right against my skin. It feels good. It looks good.

"Hey," says Suze, sitting up as I come out. "Now, that's nice."

"It's nice, isn't it?" I say, stepping up onto the podium.

I stare at my reflection and a feel a little glow of pleasure. It's a simple dress—but I look fantastic in it. It makes me look really thin! It makes my skin look radiant and . . . God, maybe this is the one!

There's silence in the shop.

"Do you feel it here?" says Cynthia, clutching her stomach.

"I . . . don't know! I think so!" I give an excited little laugh. "I think I might!"

"I knew it. You see? When you find the right dress, it just hits you. You can't plan for it, you can't work it out on paper. You just know when it's right."

"I've found my wedding dress!" I beam at Suze. "I've found it!"

"At last!" There's a ring of relief to Cynthia's voice. "Let's all have a glass of champagne to celebrate!"

As she disappears I admire myself again. It just shows, you can't tell. Who would have thought I'd go for trumpet sleeves?

An assistant is carrying past another dress and I catch sight of an embroidered silk corset bodice, tied up with ribbons.

"Hey, that looks nice," I say. "What's that?"

"Never mind what that is!" says Cynthia, handing me a glass of champagne. "You've found your dress!" She lifts her glass, but I'm still looking at the ribboned bodice.

"Maybe I should just try that one on. Just quickly."

"You know what I was thinking?" says Suze, looking up from *Brides*. "Maybe you should have a dress that *isn't* a wedding dress. Like a color!"

"Wow!" I stare at Suze, my imagination gripped. "Like red or something."

"Or a trouser suit!" suggests Suze, showing me a magazine picture. "Don't those look cool?"

"But you've found your dress!" chips in Cynthia, her voice slightly shrill. "You don't need to look any further! This is The One!"

"Mmm . . ." I pull a tiny face. "You know . . . I'm not so sure it is."

For an awful moment I think Cynthia's going to throw the champagne at me.

"I thought this was the dress of your dreams!"

"It's the dress of *some* of my dreams," I explain. "I have a lot of dreams. Could we put it down as another possible?"

"Right," she says at last. "Another possible. I'll just write that down."

As she walks off, Suze leans back on the sofa and beams at me. "Oh, Bex, it's going to be so romantic! Tarkie and I went to look at the church you're getting married in. It's beautiful!"

"It is nice," I agree, quelling an automatic wave of guilt.

Although nothing's been decided yet. I haven't definitely chosen the Plaza. We still might get married in Oxshott.

Maybe.

"Your mum's planning to put this gorgeous arch of roses over the gate, and bunches of roses on all the pews . . . and then everyone will get a rose buttonhole. She thought maybe yellow, but it depends on the other colors . . ."

"Oh, right. Well, I'm not really sure yet . . ." I tail off as I see the shop door opening behind me.

Robyn is coming into the shop, dressed in a mauve suit and clutching her Mulberry bag. She catches my eye in the mirror and gives a little wave.

What's Robyn doing here?

"And then on the tables, maybe some sweet little posies . . ."

Robyn's heading toward us. I'm not sure I like this.

"Hey, Suze!" I turn with what I hope is a natural smile. "Why don't you go and look at those . . . um . . . ring cushions over there?"

"What?" Suze stares at me as though I've gone mad. "You're not having a ring cushion, are you? *Please* don't tell me you've turned into an American."

"Well, then . . . the tiaras. I might have one of those!"

"Bex, what's wrong?"

"Nothing!" I say brightly. "I just thought you might want to . . . oh, hi, Robyn!" As she approaches, I force myself to give her a friendly smile.

"Becky!" says Robyn, clasping her hands. "Isn't that gown beautiful? Don't you look adorable? Is that the one, do you think?"

"I'm not sure yet." My smile is so fixed, it's hurting. "So, Robyn, how on earth did you know I'd be here? You must be telepathic!"

"Cynthia told me you'd be coming in. She's an old friend." Robyn turns to Suze. "And is this your chum from England?"

"Oh . . . yes. Suze, Robyn, Robyn, Suze."

"Suze? The maid of honor herself? Oh, it's a pleasure to meet you, Suze! You'll look simply wonderful in—" She stops abruptly as her gaze takes in Suze's stomach. "Dear, are you *expecting*?"

"I'll have had the baby by then," Suze assures her.

"Good!" Robyn's face relaxes. "As I say, you'll look wonderful in violet!"

"Violet?" Suze looks puzzled. "I thought I was wearing blue."

"No, definitely violet!"

"Bex, I'm sure your mum said—"

"Well, anyway!" I interrupt hurriedly. "Robyn, I'm a bit tied up here—"

"I know, and I don't want to get in your way. But since I'm here, there's just a couple of things . . . Two seconds, I promise!" She reaches into her bag and pulls out her notebook. "First of all, the New York Philharmonic will unfortunately be on tour at the time of the wedding, but I'm working on an alternative. Now, what else . . ." She consults her notebook.

"Great!" I dart a quick glance at Suze, who's staring at Robyn with a puzzled frown on her face. "You know, maybe you should just give me a call sometime, and we can talk about all this . . ."

"It won't take long! So the other thing was . . . we've scheduled in a tasting at the Plaza on the 23rd in the chef's dining room. I passed on your views on monkfish, so they're having a rethink on that . . ." Robyn flips a page. "Oh, and I still really need that guest list from you!" She looks up and wags her finger in mock reproof. "We'll be needing to think about invitations before we know it! Especially for the overseas guests!"

"OK. I'll . . . I'll get into it," I mumble.

I don't dare look at Suze.

"Great! And I'm meeting you at Antoine's on Monday, ten o'clock. Those cakes . . . you are going to swoon. Now I have to run." She closes her notebook and smiles at Suze. "Nice to meet you, Suze. See you at the wedding!"

"See you there!" says Suze in a too-cheerful voice. "Absolutely."

The door closes behind Robyn and I swallow hard, my face tingling.

"So, ahm . . . I might as well get changed."

I head to the fitting room without meeting Suze's eye. A moment later, she's in there with me.

"Who was that?" she says lightly as I unzip the dress.

"That was . . . Robyn! She's nice, isn't she?"

"And what was she talking about?"

"Just . . . wedding chitchat . . . you know . . . Can you help me out of this corset?"

"Why does she think you're getting married at the Plaza?"

"I . . . um . . . I don't know!"

"Yes you do! And that woman at the party!" Suddenly Suze's voice is as severe as she can manage. "Bex, what's going on?"

"Nothing!"

Suze grabs my shoulder. "Bex, stop it! You're not getting married at the Plaza. Are you?"

I stare at her, feeling my face grow hotter and hotter.

"It's . . . an option," I say at last.

"What do you mean, it's an option?" Suze stares at me, her grip on me loosening. "How can it be an option?"

I adjust the dress on the hanger, playing for time, trying to stifle the guilt rising inside me. If I behave as though this is a completely normal situation, then maybe it will be.

"It's just that . . . well, Elinor's offered to throw this really spectacular wedding for me and Luke. And I haven't quite decided whether or not to take her up." I see Suze's expression. "What?"

"What do you mean 'what?' " expostulates Suze. "What about

(a) your mum's already *organizing* your wedding? What about (b) Elinor is a complete cow? What about (c) you've gone off your head? Why on *earth* would you want to get married at the Plaza?"

"Because . . . because . . ." I close my eyes briefly. "Suze, you have to see it. We're going to have a great big string orchestra, and caviar, and an oyster bar . . . and Tiffany frames for everyone on the tables . . . and Cristal champagne . . . and the whole place will be this magical enchanted forest, and we're going to have real birch trees and songbirds . . ."

"Real birch trees?" Suze pulls a face. "What do you want those for?"

"It's going to be like *Sleeping Beauty*! And I'm going to be the princess, and Luke's going to be the . . ." I tail off feebly to see Suze staring at me reproachfully.

"What about your mum?"

There's silence, and I pretend to be preoccupied unhooking my basque. I don't want to have to think about Mum right at the moment.

"Bex! What about your mum?"

"I'll just have to . . . talk her round," I say at last.

"Talk her *round*?"

"She said herself I shouldn't do the wedding by halves!" I say defensively. "If she came and saw the Plaza, and saw all the plans—"

"But she's done such a lot of preparation already! When we were there she could talk about nothing else. Her and—what's your neighbor called?"

"Janice."

"That's right. They're calling your kitchen the control center. There's about six pin boards up, and lists, and bits of material everywhere . . . And they're so happy doing it." Suze stares at me earnestly. "Becky, you can't just tell them it's all off. You can't."

"Elinor would fly them over!" There's a guilty edge to my voice, which I pretend I can't hear. "I mean, they'd have a fantastic time! It would be a once-in-a-lifetime experience for them too! They could stay in the Plaza, and dance all night, and see New York . . . They'd have the most fabulous holiday ever!"

I'm trying desperately to paint a picture that, deep down, I know isn't true. As I meet Suze's eyes I can feel shame pouring over me, and I quickly look away.

"Have you said this to your mum?"

"No. I . . . I haven't told her anything about it. Not yet. Not until I'm 100 percent sure." There's a pause while Suze's eyes narrow.

"Bex, you are going to do something about this, aren't you?" she says suddenly. "Promise me you're not just going to bury your head in the sand and pretend it isn't happening."

"Honestly! I wouldn't do that!" I say indignantly.

"This is me, remember!" retorts Suze. "I know what you're like! You used to throw all your bank statements into the trash and hope a complete stranger would pay off your bills!"

This is what happens. You tell your friends your most personal secrets, and they use them against you.

"I've grown up a lot since then," I say, trying to sound dignified. "And I will sort it out. I just need to . . . to think it through."

There's a long silence. Outside, I can hear Cynthia saying "Here at Dream Dress, our motto is, you don't *choose* your dress . . ."

"Look, Bex," says Suze at last. "I can't make this decision for you. No one can. All I can say is, if you're going to pull out of your mum's wedding, you're going to have to do it quickly."

THE PINES
43 Elton Road
Oxshott
Surrey

FAX MESSAGE

TO BECKY BLOOMWOOD

FROM MUM

20 March 2002

Becky, darling! Wonderful news!

You might have heard that Suzie spilt her coffee all over the wedding dress. She was devastated, poor thing.

But I took the dress to the cleaners . . . and they worked miracles! It's as white as snow again and you'll be able to wear it after all!

Much love and talk soon,

Mum xxxxxxxxx

Eight

OK. SUZE IS right. I can't dither anymore. I have to decide.
The day after she's left to go home I sit down in my fitting room
at lunchtime with a piece of paper and a pen. I'm just going to have
to do this logically. Work out the pros and cons, weigh them all
up—and make a rational decision. Right. Let's go.

For Oxshott

1. Mum will be happy
2. Dad will be happy
3. It'll be a lovely wedding

I stare at the list for a few seconds—then make a new heading.

For New York

1. I get to have the most amazing wedding in the world

I bury my head in my hands. It isn't any easier on paper.
In fact it's harder, because it's thrusting the dilemma right in my
face, instead of where I want it—which is in a little box at the back
of my mind where I don't have to look at it.

"Becky?"

"Yes?" I look up, automatically covering up the sheet of paper
with my hand. Standing at the door of my fitting room is Elise, one

of my clients. She's a thirty-five-year-old corporate lawyer who's just been assigned to Hong Kong for a year. I'll quite miss her actually. She's always nice to chat to, even though she doesn't really have a sense of humor. I think she'd *like* to have one—it's just that she doesn't quite understand what jokes are for.

"Hi, Elise!" I say in surprise. "Do we have an appointment? I thought you were leaving today."

"Tomorrow. But I wanted to buy you a wedding gift before I go."

"Oh! You don't have to do that!" I exclaim, secretly pleased.

"I just need to find out where you're registered."

"Well, actually, we haven't registered yet," I say, feeling a flicker of frustration. It's not *my* fault we haven't registered yet. It's Luke's! He keeps saying he's too busy to spend a day in the shops, which frankly just doesn't make sense.

"You haven't?" Elise frowns. "So how can I buy you a gift?"

"Well . . . um . . . you could just . . . buy something. Maybe."

"Without a list?" Elise stares at me blankly. "But what would I get?"

"I don't know! Anything you felt like!" I give a little laugh. "Maybe a . . . toaster?"

"A toaster. OK." Elise roots around in her bag for a piece of paper. "What model?"

"I've no idea! It was just off the top of my head! Look, Elise, just . . . I don't know, get me something in Hong Kong."

"Are you registering there too?" Elise looks alert. "Which store?"

"No! I just meant . . ." I sigh. "OK, look. When we register, I'll let you know the details. You can probably do it online."

"Well. OK." Elise puts her piece of paper away, giving me a re-proving look. "But you really should register. People will be wanting to buy you gifts."

"Sorry," I say. "But anyway, have a fabulous time in Hong Kong."

"Thanks." Elise hesitates, then awkwardly comes forward and pecks me on the cheek. "Bye, Becky. Thanks for all your help."

When she's gone, I sit down again and look at my piece of paper, trying to concentrate.

But I can't stop thinking about what Elise said.

What if she's right? What if there are loads of people out there, all trying to get us presents and unable to?

Suddenly I feel a fresh stab of fear. What if they abandon the attempt in frustration? Or what if they all buy us nasty green glass decanters, like the one Auntie Jean bought for Mum and Dad that *still* gets brought out every Christmas?

This is serious. I pick up my phone and speed-dial Luke's number.

As it rings, I suddenly remember promising the other day to stop phoning him at work with what he called "wedding trivia." I'd made him stay on the line for half an hour while I described three different table settings, and apparently he missed a really important call from Japan.

But surely this is an exception?

"Listen!" I say urgently as he picks up. "We need to register! We can't put it off any longer!"

"Becky, I'm in a meeting. Can this wait?"

"No! It's important!"

There's silence—then I hear Luke saying, "If you could excuse me for a moment—"

"OK," he says, returning to the phone. "Start again. What's the problem?"

"The problem is, people are trying to buy us presents! We need a list! If there's nothing for them to buy, who knows what they might get us!"

"Well, let's register, then."

"I've been wanting to!" I squeak in frustration. "You know I have! I've been waiting and *waiting* for you to have a spare day, or even an evening—"

"I've been tied up with things," he says, a defensive edge to his voice. "That's just the way it is."

I know why he's so defensive. It's because he's been working every night on some stupid promotion for Elinor's charity. And he knows what I think about that.

"Well, we need to get started," I say. "We need to decide what we want."

"Look, Becky. Do I really need to be there?"

"Of course you need to be there! Don't you care what plates we have?"

"Frankly, no."

"*No?*" I take a deep breath, about to launch into a tirade along the lines of, "If you don't care about our plates, then maybe you don't care about our relationship!"

Then, just in time I realize, this way I get to choose everything exactly as I want it.

"Well, OK," I say. "I'll do it."

"Great. And I agreed we'd have a drink with my mother tonight, at her apartment. Six thirty."

"Oh," I say, pulling a face. "All right. See you then. Shall I call you after I've been to Tiffany to let you know what I registered?"

"Becky," says Luke, deadpan. "If you call me again with any more wedding talk during office hours, it's entirely possible we may not be *having* a wedding."

"Fine!" I say. "Fine! If you're not interested, I'll just organize it all and see you at the altar, shall I? Would that suit you?"

There's a pause, and I can tell Luke's laughing.

"Do you want an honest answer or the *Cosmo* 'Does Your Man Really Love You?' full marks answer?"

"Give me the full marks answer," I say after a moment's thought.

"I want to be involved in every tiny detail of our wedding," says Luke earnestly. "I understand that if I show any lack of interest at any stage it is a sign that I am not committed to you as a woman and beautiful, caring, all-round special person, and, frankly, don't deserve you."

"That was pretty good, I suppose," I say, a little grudgingly. "Now give me the honest answer."

"See you at the altar."

"Ha-di-ha. Well, all I can say is, you'll be sorry when I put you in a pink tuxedo."

"You're right," says Luke. "I will. Now I have to go. Really. I'll see you later."

"Bye."

I put down the phone, reach for my coat, and pick up my bag. As I'm zipping it up, I glance at my piece of paper again and bite my lip. Maybe I should stay here and think a bit more, and try to come to a decision.

But then . . . whether we get married in England or America, we'll need a wedding present list, won't we? So in a way it's *more* sensible to go and register first—and decide about which country to get married in later.

Exactly.

OK, so perhaps I should have realized that lots of brides might want to register at Tiffany. And this is a very busy time of day, and they only have so many members of staff available at one time. I told them it was an emergency, and I have to say, they were very sympathetic, but even so, they couldn't fit me in right at that moment. They asked if I could possibly come back at two o'clock, or tomorrow.

But I'm *working* at two o'clock. And tomorrow I'll be so busy, I already know I won't get a proper lunch hour. God, how are you supposed to plan a wedding and have a job at the same time? As I walk back to Barneys, I'm fizzing with frustration. Now that I've decided to register, I can't wait a minute longer. I want to do it *now*, while I'm all excited, and before anyone goes and buys us a green decanter. I'm just wondering whether I should quickly call all our relations to let them know there *will* be a list . . . when my eye is caught by an ad for Crate and Barrel. "Walk right in and register," it says, above a picture of a big shiny tea kettle.

I stop still in the middle of the street. There's a huge Crate and Barrel about two minutes away. I mean, it's not Tiffany—but it's presents, isn't it? It's all cool pans and stuff . . . Oh, I'm going. I start to walk again, quicker and quicker, until I'm almost running down the sidewalk.

It's only as I'm pushing my way into the store, out of breath, that I realize I don't know anything about registering. In fact, I don't know much about wedding lists at all. For Tom and Lucy's wedding I chipped in with Mum and Dad, and Mum organized it all—and the only other person I know who's got married is Suze, and she and Tarquin didn't have a list.

I look randomly around the shop, wondering where to start. It's bright and light, with colorful tables here and there laid out as though for dinner, and lots of displays full of gleaming glasses, racks of knives, and stainless-steel cookware.

As I wander toward a pyramid of shiny saucepans, I notice a girl in a high swingy ponytail who is going around marking things on a form. I edge nearer, trying to see what she's doing, and spot the

words "Crate and Barrel Registry" on the paper. She's registering!
OK, I can watch what she does.

"Hey," she says, looking up. "You know anything about cookware? You know what this thing is?"

She holds up a pan, and I can't help hiding a smile. Honestly.
These Manhattanites don't know anything. She's probably never
cooked a meal in her life!

"It's a frying pan," I say kindly. "You use it to fry things with."

"OK. What about this?"

She holds up another pan with a ridged surface and two looped
handles. Blimey. What on earth's that for?

"I . . . um . . . I think it's an . . . omelette . . . griddle . . .
skillet . . . pan."

"Oh, right." She looks at it puzzledly and I back quickly away. I
pass a display of pottery cereal bowls and find myself at a computer
terminal marked "Registry." Maybe this is where you get the forms.

"Welcome to Crate and Barrel," says a cheerful message on the
screen. "Please enter the choice you require."

Distractedly I punch a few times at the screen. I'm half listening
to a couple behind me arguing about plates.

"I just don't want to *be* taupe stoneware," the girl is saying almost tearfully.

"Well, what do you want to be?" retorts the man.

"I don't know!"

"Are you saying *I'm* taupe stoneware, Marie?"

Oh God, I must stop eavesdropping. I look down at the screen
again, and stop in surprise. I've arrived at the place where you look
up people's lists so you can buy them a gift. I'm about to press
"Clear" and walk away, when I pause.

It would be quite cool to see what other people put down,
wouldn't it?

Cautiously I enter the name "R. Smith" and press "Enter."

To my astonishment the screen starts filling up with a whole se-
ries of couples' names.

Rachel Smith and David Forsyth, Oak Springs, Miss.
Annie M. Winters and Rod Smith, Raleigh, N.C.
Richard Smith and Fay Bullock, Wheaton, Ill.
Leroy Elms and Rachelle F. Smith . . .

This is so cool! OK, let's see what Rachel and David chose. I

press "Enter" and a moment later the machine starts spewing out
pieces of paper.

Glass Caviar/Shrimp Server	4
Footed Cake Platter with Dome	1
Water Lily Bowl	2
Classic Decanter 28 oz.	

Wow, that all sounds really nice. I definitely want a water lily
bowl. And a shrimp server.

OK, now let's see what Annie and Rod chose. I press "Enter"
again, and another list starts appearing in front of me.

Gosh, Annie and Rod are keen on barware! I wonder why they
want three ice buckets.

This is completely addictive! Let's see what Richard and Fay are
getting. And then Leroy and Rachelle . . . I print them both out, and
am just wondering whether to try another name, like Brown, when a
voice says, "Can I help you, miss?" My head jerks up and I see a sales-
man wearing a name badge reading "Bud" smiling at me. "Are you
having some trouble locating the list you want?"

I feel myself prickle with embarrassment.

I *can't* admit I'm just snooping.

"I . . . actually . . . I've just found it." I grab randomly for
Richard and Fay's list. "They're friends of mine. Richard and Fay." I
clear my throat. "I want to buy them a wedding present. That's why
I'm here. Also, I want to register myself."

"Well, let's deal with the purchase first. What would you like to
buy?"

"Umm . . . well . . ." I look down at the list. "Um . . ."

Come on. I'm not really going to buy a present for a pair of
complete strangers. Just admit the truth. I was nosy.

"Actually . . . I think I'll leave it for another day," I say. "But I
would like to register a list myself."

"No problem!" says Bud cheerily. "Here's the form for you to fill
in as you go around . . . you'll see that most of our merchandise
breaks down into sections . . ."

"Oh, right. What sort of—"

"Kitchenware, flatware, hollowware, barware, stemware, glassware . . ." He pauses for breath. "And miscellaneous."

"Right . . ."

"It can be a little overwhelming, deciding what you're going to want in your new home." He smiles at me. "So what I suggest is, you start with the basics. Think about your everyday needs—and work up from there. If you need me, just give me a shout!"

"Great! Thanks very much!"

Bud moves away and I look around the store with a fizz of anticipation. I haven't been so excited since I used to write out lists for Father Christmas. And even then, Mum would stand over my shoulder, saying things like "I'm not sure Father Christmas can give you the *real* ruby slippers, darling. Why not ask for a nice coloring book instead?"

Now, no one's telling me what I can or can't have. I can write down anything I like! I can ask for those plates over there . . . and that jug . . . and that chair . . . I mean, if I wanted to, I could ask for everything! The whole shop!

You know. In theory.

But I'm not going to get carried away. I'll start with everyday needs, just as Bud suggested. Feeling pleasantly grown-up, I wander toward a display of kitchen equipment and start perusing the shelves.

Ooh. Lobster crackers! Let's get some of those. And those cute little corn holders. And those sweet little plastic daisies. I don't know what they're for, but they look so gorgeous!

I note the numbers carefully down on my list. OK. What else? As I look around again, my attention is caught by a gleaming array of chrome.

Wow. We just have to have a frozen yogurt maker. And a waffle maker. And a bread cooker, and a juicer, and a Pro Chef Premium Toaster Oven. I write down all the numbers and look around with a sigh of satisfaction. Why on earth have I never registered before? Shopping without spending any money!

You know, I should have got married a long time ago.

"Excuse me?" The girl with the ponytail is over in the knife section. "Do you know what poultry shears are?" She holds up a piece of equipment I've never seen before in my life.

"They're . . . shears for poultry . . . I guess . . ."

For a moment we stare at each other blankly, then the girl shrugs, says "OK," and writes it down on her list.

Maybe I'll get some poultry shears too. And one of those cool herb-chopper things. And a professional blowtorch for making crème brûlée.

Not that I've ever made crème brûlée—but you know. When I'm married, I'm bound to. I have a sudden vision of myself in an apron, nonchalantly brûléeing with one hand and drizzling a home-made fruit coulis with the other, while Luke and an assortment of witty guests look on admiringly.

"So where else are you registering?" says the girl, picking up an egg whisk and peering at it.

I look at her in surprise. "What do you mean? Are you allowed more than one list?"

"Of course! I'm having three. Here, Williams-Sonoma, and Bloomies. It's really cool there, you scan everything on this gun—"

"Three lists!" I can't keep the elation out of my voice.

And actually, when you think about it, why stop at three?

So by the time I arrive at Elinor's apartment that evening I've made appointments to register at Tiffany, Bergdorf, Bloomingdale's, and Barneys, ordered the Williams-Sonoma catalogue, and started an online wedding list.

I haven't managed to think any more about where we're going to get married—but then, first things first.

As Elinor opens the door, music is playing and the apartment smells pleasantly of flowers. Elinor's wearing a wrap dress and her hair looks slightly softer than usual—and as she kisses me she gives my hand a little squeeze.

"Luke's already here," she says as we walk along the corridor. "That's a pretty pair of shoes. Are they new?"

"Er, actually, they are. They're Dolce and Gabbana! Thanks!" I can't help gaping at her in astonishment. I've never known Elinor to compliment me before. Not once.

"You look like you've lost a little weight," she adds. "It suits you."

I'm so gobsmacked I stop, right in the middle of the doorway— then have to hurry to catch up. Is Elinor Sherman finally, after all this time, going to start making an effort to be nice to me? I can't quite believe it.

But then . . . come to think of it, she was quite nice at the end of the engagement party too. She said it had been a mistake about me not being on the door list and that she was really sorry.

Actually no, she didn't exactly say she was sorry—she said she would sue the party planners. But still. That shows concern, doesn't it?

God, maybe Elinor has a hidden nice side, I find myself thinking. Maybe there's a whole different persona under that icy exterior. Yes! She's all vulnerable and insecure but she's put up a protective shell around herself. And I'm the only one who can see beneath it, and when I coax the true Elinor into the world, all New York society will marvel, and Luke will love me even more, and people will call me The Girl Who Changed Elinor Sherman, and—

"Becky?" Luke's voice penetrates my thoughts. "Are you all right?"

"Yes," I say, realizing with a start that I'm blundering into the coffee table. "Yes, I'm fine!"

I sit down next to him on the sofa, Elinor hands me a glass of icy-cold wine, and I sip it, gazing out the window over the glittering Manhattan lights stretching into the distance. Elinor and Luke are in the middle of some discussion about the foundation, and I nibble a salted almond and tune out. Somehow I've arrived in the middle of a dreamlike picture in which Elinor is saying to a crowded room, "Becky Bloomwood is not only a model daughter-in-law, but a valued friend," and I'm smiling modestly as people start applauding, when there's a snapping sound, and I come to, slightly spilling my drink.

Elinor has closed the crocodile notebook she's been writing in. She puts it away, turns down the music slightly, and looks directly at me.

"Rebecca," she says.

"Yes?"

"I asked you here tonight because there's something I'd like to discuss with you." She refreshes my drink and I smile at her.

"Oh yes?"

"As you know, Luke is a very wealthy young man."

"Oh. Right," I say, a little embarrassed. "Well . . . yes, I suppose so."

"I've been speaking with my lawyers . . . and with Luke's lawyers . . . and we are all agreed. So if I could just give you this . . ." She gives me a glittering smile and hands over a thick white envelope—then hands another to Luke.

As I take it I feel a tingle of anticipation. You see? Elinor's already becoming friendlier. This is just like *Dallas*. She's probably making me an associate of some family company or something, to welcome me into the dynasty. God, yes! And I'll get to go to board meetings and everything and we'll mount some amazing takeover together and I'll wear big earrings . . .

Excitedly, I open the envelope and pull out a thick, typed document. But as I read the words I can feel my excitement ebb away.

> *Memorandum of Agreement*
> *Between Luke James Brandon (hereinafter called "The Groom")*
> *and Rebecca Jane Bloomwood (hereinafter called "The Bride") of—*

I don't get it. Memorandum of what agreement? Is this—

Surely this isn't a—

I look bewilderedly at Luke, but he's flipping over the pages, looking as taken aback as me.

"Mother, what's this?" he says.

"It's simply a precaution," says Elinor with a distant smile. "A form of insurance."

Oh my God. It is. It's a prenuptial contract.

Feeling slightly sick, I flip through the contract. It's about ten pages long, with headings like "Property Settlement in the Case of Divorce."

"Insurance against what, exactly?" Luke's voice is unreadable.

"Let's not pretend we're living in a fairy-tale world," says Elinor crisply. "We all know what might happen."

"What's that, exactly?"

"Don't be obstructive, Luke. You know perfectly well what I mean. And bearing in mind Rebecca's . . . shall we say, history of spending?" She glances meaningfully at my shoes—and with a start of humiliation I realize why she asked me about them.

She wasn't trying to be nice. She was gathering ammunition to attack me.

Oh, how could I be so *stupid*? There is no soft center to Elinor. It just doesn't exist.

"Let me get this straight," I say, breathing hard. "You think I'm just after Luke for his money."

"Becky, of course she doesn't," exclaims Luke.

"Yes, she does!"

"A prenuptial contract is simply a sensible premarital step."

"Well, it's a step I really don't think we need to take," says Luke with a little laugh.

"I would beg to differ," says Elinor. "I'm only trying to protect you. Both of you," she adds unconvincingly.

"What do you think, I'm going to . . . divorce Luke and get all his money?"

Just like you did with your husbands, I'm about to add, but stop myself just in time. "You think that's why I want to marry him?"

"Becky—"

"You may, of course, look the contract over in your own time—"

"I don't need to look it over."

"Do I take it you're refusing to sign?" Elinor gives me a triumphant look as though I've confirmed every suspicion she had.

"No!" I say in a trembling voice. "I'm not refusing to sign! I'll sign whatever you like! I'm not going to have you think I want Luke's money!" I grab the pen off the table and furiously start scrawling my signature on the first page, so hard I rip the paper.

"Becky, don't be stupid!" exclaims Luke. "Mother—"

"It's fine! I'll sign every single . . . bloody . . ."

My face is hot and my eyes a little blurry as I turn the pages, signing again and again without even looking at the text above. *Rebecca Bloomwood. Rebecca Bloomwood.*

"Well, I'm not signing it," says Luke. "I never wanted a prenup! And I'm certainly not going to sign something I've never seen before in my life."

"There. Done." I put down my pen and pick up my bag. "I think I'll go now. Bye, Elinor."

"Becky—" says Luke. "Mother, what on *earth* possessed you to do this?"

As I head out of Elinor's apartment my head is still pounding. I wait for the lift for a few seconds—but when it doesn't come, head for the stairs instead. I feel shaky with fury, with mortification. She thinks I'm a gold digger.

Is that what everyone thinks?

"Becky!" Luke is coming down the stairs after me, three at a time. "Becky, wait. I'm so sorry. I had no idea . . ." As we reach the ground floor he envelops me in his arms and I stand there rigidly.

"Believe me. That was as much of a shock for me as it was for you."

"Well . . . you know . . . I think you should sign it," I say, staring at the floor. "You should protect yourself. It's only sensible."

"Becky. This is me. This is *us*." Gently he lifts my chin until I haven't got anywhere to look except into his dark eyes. "I know you're angry. Of course you are. But you have to excuse my mother. She's lived in America a long time. Prenups are standard issue here. She didn't mean—"

"She did," I say, feeling a fresh surge of humiliation. "That's exactly what she meant. She thinks I've got some plan to . . . to take all your money and spend the whole lot on shoes!"

"That's not your plan?" Luke feigns shock. "You're telling me this now? Well, if you're going to change the ground rules, perhaps we *should* have a prenup—"

I give a half-smile—but I'm still raw inside.

"I know loads of people have prenups here," I say. "I know that. But she shouldn't just . . . draw one up without consulting either of us! Do you know how she made me feel?"

"I know." Luke strokes my back soothingly. "I'm furious with her."

"You're not."

"Of course I am."

"No, you're not! You're never furious with her! That's the trouble." I break away from his arms, trying to keep calm.

"Becky?" Luke stares at me. "Is something else wrong?"

"It's not just this. It's . . . everything! The way she's taken over the wedding. The way she was so supercilious and horrible with my parents . . ."

"She's naturally a very formal person," says Luke defensively. "It doesn't mean she's trying to be supercilious. If your parents really got to know her—"

"And the way she uses you!" I know I'm on dangerous ground—but now I've started, I can't stop everything pouring out. "You've given her hours and hours of your time. You've provided staff for her charity. You've even fallen out with Michael because of her. I just don't understand it! You *know* Michael cares about you. You *know* he's only got your best interests at heart. But because of your mother, you're not even talking to him."

Luke's face flinches, and I can see I've touched a nerve.

"And now she wants us to move to this building. Don't you see? She just wants to get her claws into you! She'll have you running errands for her all day long, and she'll never leave us alone . . . Luke, you're already giving her so much!"

"What's wrong with that?" Luke's expression is gradually becoming tighter. "She's my mother."

"I know she is! But come on. She was never even interested in you before you became a success over here. Remember our first trip to New York? You were so desperate to impress her—and she didn't even make the effort to see you! But now that you've made it here, you've got a name, you've got contacts in the media, you've got resources—and all of a sudden she wants to get all the credit and just *use* you . . ."

"That's not true."

"It is true! You just can't see it! You're too dazzled by her!"

"Look, Becky, it's easy for you to criticize," says Luke hotly. "You have a fantastic relationship with your mother. I barely saw mine when I was growing up—"

"Exactly!" I cry, before I can stop myself. "That proves my point! She didn't give a shit about you then either!"

Oh, bugger. I shouldn't have said that. A flash of pain passes through Luke's eyes and suddenly he looks about ten years old.

"You know that's not true," he says. "My mother wanted me. It wasn't her fault."

"I know. I'm sorry—" I move toward him, but he jerks away.

"Put yourself in her shoes for a change, Becky. Think about what she's gone through. Having to leave behind her child; having to put on a brave face. She's been used to hiding her feelings for so long, no wonder her manner can be a little awkward."

Listening to him, I almost want to cry. He's got it all worked out. He's still like the boy who made every excuse in the world for why his mother never came to see him.

"But now we're having a chance to forge our relationship once again," Luke is saying. "Maybe she is a bit tactless now and then. But she's doing her best."

Yeah, right, I want to say. She's really trying hard with me.

Instead I give a tiny shrug and mumble, "I suppose so."

Luke walks over and takes hold of my hand. "Come back upstairs. We'll have another drink. Forget this ever happened."

"No." I exhale sharply. "I think I'll . . . go home. You go. I'll see you later."

As I make my way home it starts to rain, big splashy drops that puddle in the gutters and drip off canopies. They spatter on my hot cheeks and wet my hair and make marks on my new suede-trimmed shoes. But I barely notice them. I'm still too wound up by the evening; by Elinor's gimlet gaze; by my own humiliation; by my frustration with Luke.

The moment I get inside the apartment there's a crack of thunder outside. I switch all the lights on and the television, and pick up the post. There's an envelope from Mum and I open it first. A swatch of fabric falls out and a long letter smelling faintly of her perfume.

Darling Becky,

Hope all's well in the Big Apple!

Here's the color we were thinking of for the table napkins. Janice says we should have pink but I think this pale plum is very pretty, especially with the colors we were thinking of for the flowers. But let me know what you think, you're the bride, darling!

The photographer that Dennis recommended came round yesterday and we were all very impressed. Dad has heard good things about him at the golf club, which is always a good sign. He can do color and black-and-white, and includes a photograph album in the price, which seems a very good deal. Also, he can turn the picture you like best into one hundred mini jigsaw puzzles to send to all the guests as a little thank-you!

The most important thing of all, I told him, is that we have lots of pictures of you by the flowering cherry tree. We planted that when you were born, and it's always been my secret dream that our little baby Rebecca would grow up and one day stand beside it on her wedding day. You are our only child and this day is so important to us.

Yours with lots of love,
Mum

By the end, I'm crying. I don't know why I ever thought I wanted to get married in New York. I don't know why I let Elinor even show me the stupid Plaza. Home is where I want to get married. With Mum and Dad, and the cherry tree, and my friends, and everything that really matters to me.

That's it, I've made my choice.

"Becky?"

I give a startled jump and turn round. There's Luke, standing at the door, out of breath and drenched from head to foot. His hair is plastered to his head and raindrops are still running down his face. "Becky . . ." he says urgently. "I'm sorry. I'm so sorry. I shouldn't have let you go like that. I saw the rain . . . I don't know what I was thinking—" He breaks off as he sees my tear-stained face. "Are you all right?"

"I'm fine." I wipe my eyes. "And Luke . . . I'm sorry too."

Luke gazes at me for a long time, his face trembling, his eyes burning.

"Becky Bloomwood," he says at last. "You're the most generous-spirited . . . giving . . . loving . . . I don't deserve . . ."

He breaks off and comes toward me, his face almost fierce with intent. As he kisses me, raindrops spatter from his hair onto my mouth and mingle with the warm salty taste of him. I close my eyes and let my body gradually unwind, the pleasure gradually begin. I can already feel him hard and determined, gripping my hips and wanting me right now, right this minute, to say sorry, to say he loves me, to say he'll do anything for me . . .

God, I love make-up sex.

Nine

I WAKE UP THE next morning all snug and contented and happy with myself. As I lie in bed, curled up against Luke, I'm full of a strong inner resolve. I've sorted out my priorities. Nothing will change my mind now.

"Luke?" I say, as he makes a move to get out of bed.

"Mmm?" He turns and kisses me, and he's all warm and delicious and lovely.

"Don't go. Stay here. All day."

"All day?"

"We could pretend we were ill." I stretch luxuriously out on the pillows. "Actually, I do feel rather ill."

"Oh, really? Which bit?"

"My . . . tummy."

"Looks fine to me," says Luke, peeking under the duvet. "Feels fine . . . Sorry. You don't get a note."

"Spoilsport."

I watch as he gets out of bed, puts on a robe, and heads for the bathroom.

"Luke?" I say again as he reaches the door.

"What?"

I open my mouth to tell him I made a big decision last night. That I want to get married in Oxshott, just like we originally planned. That I'm going to cancel the Plaza. That if Elinor is furious, then so be it.

Then I close it again.

"What is it?" says Luke.

"Just . . . don't use up all my shampoo," I say at last.

I can't face bringing up the subject of the wedding. Not now, when everything's so lovely and happy between us. And anyway, Luke doesn't care where we get married. He said so himself.

I've taken the morning off work for the cake-tasting meeting with Robyn, but our appointment's not until ten. So after Luke's gone I slowly pad around the apartment, making myself some breakfast and thinking about what I'm going to say to Elinor.

The thing is to be direct. Firm and direct but pleasant. Grown-up and professional, like businesspeople who have to fire other businesspeople. Stay calm and use phrases like "We chose to go another way."

"Hello, Elinor," I say to my reflection. "I have something I need to say to you. I have chosen to go another way."

No. She'll think I'm becoming a lesbian.

"Hello, Elinor," I try again. "I've been bouncing around your wedding-scenario proposal. And while it has many merits . . ."

OK, come on. Just do it.

Ignoring my butterflies, I pick up the phone and dial Elinor's number.

"Elinor Sherman is unable to take your call . . ."

She's out.

I can't just leave her a message saying the wedding's off. Can I? Could I?

No.

I put the phone down hurriedly, before the bleep sounds. OK. What shall I do now?

Well, it's obvious. I'll call Robyn. The important thing is that I tell *someone,* before anything else gets done.

I gather my thoughts for a moment, then dial Robyn's number.

"Hello! Do I hear wedding bells? I hope so, because this is Robyn de Bendern, the answer to your wedding planning prayers. I'm afraid I'm unavailable at present, but your call is so important to me . . ."

Robyn's probably already on her way to meet me at the cake-maker's studio, it occurs to me. I could call her there. Or I could leave a message.

But as I hear her bright, chirruping voice, I feel a pang of guilt.

Robyn's already put so much into this. In fact, I've already become quite fond of her. I just can't tell her it's all off over the phone. Feeling suddenly firm, I put down the phone and reach for my bag.

I'll be a grown-up, go along to the cake studio, and break the news to her face-to-face.

And I'll deal with Elinor later.

To be honest, I don't really like wedding cake. I always take a piece because it's bad luck or something if you don't, but actually all that fruitcake and marzipan and icing like blocks of chalk makes me feel a bit sick. And I'm so nervous at the thought of telling Robyn it's all off that I can't imagine eating anything.

Even so, my mouth can't help watering as I arrive at the cake studio. It's big and light, with huge windows and the sweetest, most delicious sugary-buttery smell wafting through the air. There are huge mounted cakes on display, and rows of flower decorations in transparent boxes, and people at marble tables, carefully making roses out of icing and painting strands of sugar ivy.

As I hover at the entrance, a skinny girl in jeans and strappy high heels is being led out by her mother, and they're in the middle of a row.

"You only had to taste it," the mother is saying furiously. "How many calories could that be?"

"I don't care," retorts the girl tearfully. "I'm going to be a size two on my wedding day if it kills me."

Size two!

Anxiously I glance at my thighs. Should I be aiming for size two as well? Is that the size brides are supposed to be?

"Becky!" I look up to see Robyn, who seems a little flustered. "Hello! You made it."

"Robyn." As I see her, I feel my stomach clench with apprehension. "Listen. I need to talk to you. I tried calling Elinor, but she was . . . Anyway. There's something I need to . . . tell you."

"Absolutely," says Robyn distractedly. "Antoine and I will be with you in a moment, but we have a slight crisis on our hands." She lowers her voice. "There was an accident with one of the cakes. Very unfortunate."

"Miss Bloomwood?" I look up to see a man with gray hair and

twinkling eyes in a white chef's outfit. "I am Antoine Montignac. The cake maker of cake makers. Perhaps you have seen me in my television show?"

"Antoine, I don't think we've quite resolved the problem with the . . . other client . . ." says Robyn anxiously.

"I come in a moment." He dismisses her with his hand. "Miss Bloomwood. Sit down."

"Actually, I'm not sure I really want to . . ." I begin. But before I know what I'm doing, I've been seated on a plushy chair at a polished table, and Antoine is spreading glossy portfolios in front of me.

"I can create for you the cake that will surpass all your dreams," he announces modestly. "No image is beyond my powers of creativity."

"Really?" I look at a photograph of a spectacular six-tier cake decorated with sugar tulips, then turn the page to see one in the shape of five different butterflies. These are the hugest cakes I've ever seen in my life. And the decorations!

"So, are these all fruitcakes inside?"

"Fruitcake? *Non, non, non!*" Antoine laughs. "This is very English notion, the fruitcake at the wedding. This particular cake . . ." He points to the butterfly cake. "It was a light angel sponge, each tier layered with three different fillings: burnt orange caramel, passion-fruit-mango, and hazelnut soufflé."

Gosh.

"If you like chocolate, we can construct a cake purely from different varieties of chocolate." He turns to another page. "This was a dark chocolate sponge layered with chocolate fondant, white chocolate cream, and a Grand Marnier truffle filling."

I had no idea wedding cakes could be anything like this. I flip through dazedly, looking at cake after spectacular cake.

"If you do not want the traditional tiers, I can make for you a cake to represent something you love. A favorite painting . . . or a sculpture . . ." He looks at me again. "A Louis Vuitton trunk, perhaps . . ."

A Louis Vuitton trunk wedding cake! How cool would that be?

"Antoine? If you could just come here a moment?" Robyn pokes her head out of a small meeting room to the right—and although she's smiling, she sounds pretty harassed.

"Excuse me, Miss Bloomwood," says Antoine apologetically. "Davina. Some cake for Miss Bloomwood to taste."

A smiling assistant disappears through a pair of double doors—

then returns with a glass of champagne and a china plate holding two slices of cake and a sugar lily. She hands me a fork and says, "This one is passion-fruit-mango, strawberry, and tangerine mousseline, and this is caramel creme with pistachio and mocha truffle. Enjoy!"

Wow. Each slice is a light sponge, with three different pastel-colored fillings. I don't know where to start!

OK . . . let's go for mocha truffle.

I put a piece in my mouth and nearly swoon. Now *this* is what wedding cakes should all be like. Why don't we have these in England?

I take a few sips of champagne and nibble the sugar lily, which is all yummy and lemony—then take a second piece and munch blissfully, watching a girl nearby as she painstakingly makes a spray of lilies of the valley.

You know, maybe I should get Suze a nice cake for her baby's christening. I mean, I'll get a present as well—but I could always buy a cake as a little extra.

"Do you know how much these cakes are?" I ask the girl as I polish off the second slice.

"Well . . . it really varies," she says, looking up. "But I guess they start at about a thousand dollars."

I nearly choke on my champagne. A thousand dollars? They *start* at $1,000?

For a *cake*?

I mean, how much have I eaten, just now? That must have been at least $50 worth of cake on my plate!

"Would you like another slice?" says the girl, and glances at the meeting room. "It looks like Antoine is still held up."

"Ooh, well . . . Why not! And could I try one of those sugar tulips? You know. Just for research purposes."

"Sure," says the girl pleasantly. "Whatever you like."

She gives me a tulip and a spray of tiny white flowers, and I crunch through them happily, washing them down with champagne.

Then I look idly around and spy a huge, elaborate flower, yellow and white with tiny drops of dew. Wow. That looks yummy. I reach over a display of sugar hearts, pick it up, and it's almost in my mouth when I hear a yell.

"Stooooop!" A guy in whites is pounding across the studio toward me. "Don't eat the jonquil!"

"Oops!" I say, stopping just in time. "Sorry. I didn't realize. Is it very special?"

"It took me three hours to make," he says, taking it gently from my hand. "No harm done, though." He smiles at me, but I notice there's sweat on his forehead.

Hmm. Maybe I should just stick to the champagne from now on. I take another sip, and am looking around for the bottle, when raised voices start coming from the side room where Robyn and Antoine are closeted.

"I deed not do this deliberately! Mademoiselle, I do not have a vendetta."

"You do! You bloody hate me, don't you?" comes a muffled voice.

I can hear Robyn's voice, saying something soothing, which I can't make out.

"It's just one thing after another!" The girl's voice is raised now—and as I hear it clearly, I freeze, glass halfway to my mouth.

I don't believe it.

It can't be.

"This bloody wedding is jinxed!" she's exclaiming. "Right from the word *go,* everything's gone wrong."

The door swings open and now I can hear her properly.

It is. It's Alicia.

I feel my whole body stiffen.

"First the Plaza couldn't fit us in! Now this fiasco with the cake! And do you know what I just heard?"

"What?" says Robyn fearfully.

"My maid of honor dyed her hair red! She won't match the others! Of all the bloody inconsiderate, selfish . . ."

The door is flung open and out stalks Alicia, her stilettos echoing like gunfire on the wooden floor. When she sees me, she stops dead and I look at her, my heart thumping hard.

"Hi, Alicia," I say, forcing myself to sound relaxed. "Sorry to hear about your cake. That was delicious, by the way, Antoine."

"What?" says Alicia blankly. Her eyes flash to my engagement ring, to my face, back to my ring, to my shoes, to my bag—taking in my skirt on the way—and finally back to my ring. It's like the Manhattan Onceover in a hall of mirrors.

"You're getting married?" she says at last. "To Luke?"

"Yes." I glance nonchalantly at the diamond on my left hand, then smile innocently up at her.

I'm starting to relax now. I'm starting to enjoy this.

(Also, I just gave Alicia the Manhattan Onceover myself. And my ring is a teeny bit bigger than hers. Not that I'm comparing or anything.)

"How come you didn't say?"

You didn't ask, I want to reply, but instead I just give a little shrug.

"So where are you getting married?" Alicia's old supercilious expression is returning and I can see her getting ready to pounce.

"Well . . . as it happens . . ." I clear my throat.

OK, this is the moment. This is the time to make the big announcement. To tell Robyn I've changed my mind. I'm going to get married in Oxshott.

"Actually . . ."

I take a deep breath. Come on. It's like a Band-Aid. The quicker I do it, the quicker it'll be over. Just say it.

And I really am on the brink of it—when I make the fatal mistake of looking up. Alicia's looking as patronizing and smug as she ever did. I feel years of feeling stupid and small welling up in me like a volcano—and I just can't help it, I hear my voice saying, "Actually, we're getting married at the Plaza."

Alicia's face snaps in shock, like an elastic band. "The Plaza? Really?"

"It should be rather lovely," I add casually. "Such a beautiful venue, the Plaza. Is that where you're getting married?"

"No," says Alicia, her chin rather tight. "They couldn't fit us in at such short notice. When did you book?"

"Oh . . . a week or two ago," I say, and give a vague shrug.

Yes! Yes! Her expression!

"It's going to be wonderful," puts in Robyn enthusiastically. "I spoke to the designer this morning, by the way. He's ordered two hundred birch trees, and they're going to send over some samples of pine needles . . ."

I can see Alicia's brain working hard.

"*You're* the one having the enchanted forest in the Plaza," she says at last. "I've heard about that. Sheldon Lloyd's designing it. Is that true?"

"That's the one," I say, and smile at Robyn, who beams back as though I'm an old ally.

"Mees Bloomwood." Antoine appears from nowhere and presses my hand to his lips. "I am now completely at your service. I apologize for the delay. One of these irritating little matters . . ."

Alicia's face goes rigid.

"Well," she says. "I'll be off then."

"Au revoir," says Antoine, without even looking up.

"Bye, Alicia," I say innocently. "Have a lovely wedding."

As she stalks out, I subside back in my seat, heart still pumping wth exhilaration. That was one of the best moments of my life. Finally getting the better of Alicia Bitch Longlegs. Finally! I mean, how often has she been horrible to me? Answer: approximately one thousand times. And how often have I had the perfect put-down at my lips? Answer: never.

Until today!

I can see Robyn and Antoine exchanging looks, and I'm dying to ask them what they think of Alicia. But . . . it wouldn't be becoming in a bride-to-be.

Plus if they bitch about her, they might bitch about me too.

"Now!" says Robyn. "On to something more pleasant. You've seen the details of Becky's wedding, Antoine."

"Indeed," says Antoine, beaming at me. "Eet will be a most beautiful event."

"I know," I hear myself saying happily. "I'm so looking forward to it!"

"So . . . we discuss the cake . . . I must fetch some pictures for you . . . meanwhile, can I offer you some more champagne, perhaps?"

"Yes, please," I say, and hold out my glass. "That would be lovely!"

The champagne fizzes, pale and delicious, into my glass. Then Antoine disappears off again and I take a sip, smiling to hide the fact that inside, I'm feeling a slight unease.

Now that Alicia's gone, there's no need to pretend anymore. What I should do is put my glass down, take Robyn aside, apologize for having wasted her time—and inform her that the wedding is off and I'm getting married in Oxshott. Quite simple and straightforward.

That's what I should do.

But . . . something very strange has happened since this morning. I can't quite explain it—but somehow, sitting here, drinking champagne and eating thousand-dollar cake, I just don't *feel* like someone who's going to get married in a garden in Oxshott.

If I'm really honest, hand on heart—I feel exactly like someone who's going to have a huge, luxurious wedding at the Plaza.

More than that, I *want* to be someone who's going to have a huge, luxurious wedding at the Plaza. I *want* to be that girl who swans around expensive cake shops and has people running after her and gets treated like a princess. If I call off the wedding, then it'll all stop. Everyone will stop making a fuss. I'll stop being that special, glossy person.

Oh God, what's happened to me? I was so resolved this morning.

Determinedly I close my eyes and force myself to think back to Mum and her flowering cherry tree. But even that doesn't work. Perhaps it's the champagne—but instead of being overcome with emotion, and thinking: I *must* get married at home, I find myself thinking: Maybe we can incorporate the cherry tree into the enchanted forest.

"All right, Becky?" says Robyn, beaming at me. "Penny for them!"

"Oh!" I say, my head jerking up guiltily. "I was just thinking that . . . the um . . . wedding will be fantastic."

What am I going to do? Am I going to say something?

Am I *not* going to say anything?

Come *on,* Becky. Decide.

"So—you want to see what I have in my bag?" says Robyn brightly.

"Er . . . yes, please."

"Ta-daah!" She pulls out a thick, embossed card, covered in swirly writing, and hands it to me.

> *Mrs. Elinor Sherman*
> *requests the honour of your presence*
> *at the marriage of*
> *Rebecca Bloomwood*
> *to her son*
> *Luke Brandon*

I stare at it, my heart thumping hard.

This is real. This is really real. Here it is, in black and white.

Or at least, bronze and taupe.

I take the stiff card from her and turn it over and over in my fingers.

"What do you think?" Robyn beams. "It's exquisite, isn't it? The card is 80 percent linen."

"It's . . . lovely." I swallow. "It seems very soon to be sending out invitations, though."

"We aren't sending them out yet! But I always like to get the invitations done early. What I always say is, you can't proofread too many times. We don't want to be asking our guests to wear 'evening press,' like one bride I could mention . . ." She trills with laughter.

"Right." I stare down at the words again.

Saturday June 21st at seven o'clock
at the Plaza Hotel
New York City

This is serious. If I'm going to say anything, I have to say it now. If I'm going to call this wedding off, I have to do it now. Right this minute.

My mouth remains closed.

Does this really mean I'm choosing the Plaza after all? That I'm selling out? That I'm choosing the gloss and glitter? That I'm going with Elinor instead of Mum and Dad?

"I thought you'd like to send one to your mother!" says Robyn.

My head jerks up sharply—but Robyn's face is blithely innocent. "Such a shame she isn't here to get involved with the preparations. But she'll love to see this, won't she?"

"Yes," I say after a long pause. "Yes, she'll . . . love it."

I put the invitation into my bag and snap the clasp shut, feeling slightly sick.

So this is it. New York it is.

Mum will understand. When I tell her all about it properly, she'll come round. She has to.

Antoine's new mandarin and lychee cake is fabulous. But somehow as I nibble at it, my appetite's gone.

After I've tried several more flavors and am no nearer a decision, Antoine and Robyn exchange looks and suggest I probably need time to think. So with one last sugar rose for my purse, I say good-bye and head to Barneys, where I deal with all my clients perfectly pleasantly, as though nothing's on my mind.

But all the time I'm thinking about the call I've got to make. About how I'm going to break the news to Mum. About how I'm going to *explain* to Mum.

I won't say anything as strong as I definitely want to get married in the Plaza. Not initially. I'll just tell her that it's there as a possibility, if we both want it. That's the key phrase. *If we both want it.*

The truth is, I didn't present it properly to her before. She'll probably leap at the chance once I explain it all to her fully. Once I tell her about the enchanted forest and the string orchestra, and the dance band and the thousand-dollar cake. A lovely luxury wedding, all expenses paid! I mean, who wouldn't leap at it?

But my heart's thumping as I climb the stairs to our apartment. I know I'm not being honest with myself. I know what Mum really wants.

I also know that if I make enough fuss, she'll do anything I ask her.

I close the door behind me and take a deep breath. Two seconds later, the doorbell rings behind me and I jump with fright. God, I'm on edge at the moment.

"Hi," I say, opening it. "Oh, Danny, it's you. Listen, I need to make quite an important phone call. So if you wouldn't mind—"

"OK, I have to ask you a favor," he says, coming into the apartment and completely ignoring me.

"What is it?"

"Randall's been pressuring me. He's like, where exactly do you sell your clothes? Who exactly are your customers? Do you have a business plan? So I'm like, of course I have a business plan, Randall. I'm planning to buy up Coca-Cola next year, what do you think?"

"Danny?"

"So then he starts saying if I don't have any genuine client base I should give up and he's not going to subsidize me anymore. He used the word *subsidize*! Can you believe it?"

"Well," I say distractedly. "He does pay your rent. And he bought you all those rolls of pink suede you wanted . . ."

"OK," says Danny after a pause. "OK. So the pink suede was a mistake. But Jesus! He just wouldn't leave it alone. I told him about your dress—but he was like, Daniel, you can't base a commercial enterprise on one customer who lives downstairs." Danny chews the skin on his thumb nervously. "So I told him I just had a big order from a department store."

"Really? Which one?"

"Barneys."

I look at him, my attention finally caught.

"*Barneys?* Danny, why did you say Barneys?"

"So you can back me up! If he asks you, you stock me, OK? And all your clients are falling over themselves to buy my stuff, you've never known anything like it in the history of the store."

"You're mad. He'll never fall for it. And what will you say when he wants some money?"

"I'll have money by then!"

"What if he checks up? What if he goes to Barneys to look?"

"He won't check up," says Danny scornfully. "He only has time to talk to me once a month, let alone make unscheduled visits to Barneys. But if he meets you on the stairs, go along with my story. That's all I'm asking."

"Well . . . all right," I say at last.

Honestly. As if I haven't got enough to worry about already.

"Danny, I really must make this call . . ." I say helplessly.

"So did you find somewhere else to live yet?" he says, flopping down into an armchair.

"We haven't had time."

"You haven't even thought about it?"

"Elinor wants us to move to her building and I've said no. That's as far as we've got."

"Really?" Danny stares at me. "But don't you want to stay in the Village?"

"Of course I do! There's no way I'm moving there."

"So what are you going to do?"

"I . . . don't know! I've just got too many other things to think about at the moment. Speaking of which—"

"Pre-wedding stress," says Danny knowingly. "The solution is a double martini." He opens up the cocktail cabinet and a sheaf of wedding list brochures falls out onto the floor.

"Hey!" he says reproachfully, picking them up. "Did you register without me? I cannot believe that! I have been dying to register my entire life! Did you ask for a cappuccino maker?"

"Er . . . yes. I think so—"

"Big mistake. You'll use it three times, then you'll be back at Starbucks. Listen, if you ever want me to take delivery of any presents, you know I'm right upstairs . . ."

"Yeah, right." I give him a look. "After Christmas."

Christmas is still a slightly sore point with me. I thought I'd be really clever and order a load of presents off the Internet. But they never arrived, so I spent Christmas Eve rushing round the shops buying replacements. Then on Christmas morning we went upstairs to have a drink with Danny and Randall—to find Danny sitting in the silk robe I'd bought for Elinor, eating the chocolates that were meant for Samantha at work.

"Hey, what was I supposed to think?" he says defensively. "It was Christmas, they were gift-wrapped . . . it was like, Yes, Daniel, there *is* a Santa Claus—" He reaches for the Martini bottle and sloshes it into the cocktail shaker. "Strong? Extra strong?"

"Danny, I *really* have to make this phone call. I'll be back in a minute."

I unplug the phone and take it into the bedroom, then close the door and try to focus my thoughts again.

Right. I can do this. Calm and collected. I dial our home number and wait with slight dread as the ringing tone sounds.

"Hello?" comes a tinny-sounding voice.

"Hello?" I reply puzzledly. Even allowing for long distance, that's not Mum's voice.

"Becky! It's Janice! How are you, love?"

This is bizarre. Did I dial next-door's number by mistake?

"I'm . . . fine."

"Oh, good! Now, while you're on the phone, which do you prefer, Evian or Vittel?"

"Vittel," I say automatically. "Janice—"

"Lovely. And for sparkling water? It's only that a lot of people drink water these days, you know, what with being healthy . . . What do you think of Perrier?"

"I . . . I don't know. Janice—" I take a deep breath. "Is Mum there?"

"Didn't you know, love? Your parents have gone away! To the Lake District."

I feel a plunge of frustration. How can I have forgotten about their trip to the Lake District?

"I've just popped in to see to the plants. If it's an emergency I can look up the number they left—"

"No, it's . . . it's OK."

My frustration has started to subside. Instead I'm feeing a tiny secret relief. This kind of lets me off the hook for the moment. I mean, it's not my fault if they're away, is it?

"Are you sure?" says Janice. "If it's important, I can easily get the number . . ."

"No, honestly, it's fine! Nothing important," I hear myself saying. "Well, lovely to speak to you . . . bye then!" I thrust down the receiver, trembling slightly.

It's only for a few more days. It won't make any difference either way.

I walk back into the living room to find Danny reclining on the sofa, flipping channels.

"All OK?" he says, lifting his head.

"Fine," I say. "Let's have that drink."

"In the shaker," he says, nodding his head toward the cabinet, just as the front door opens.

"Hi!" I call. "Luke, is that you? You're just in time for a—"

I stop abruptly as Luke enters the room and stare at him in dismay. His face is pale and hollow, his eyes even darker than usual. I've never seen him look like this before.

Danny and I glance at each other and I feel my heart plunge in dread.

"Luke!" I gulp. "Are you OK?"

"I've been trying to call for an hour," he says. "You weren't at work, the line here was busy . . ."

"I was probably on my way home. And then I had to make a call." Anxiously I take a step toward him. "What's happened, Luke? Is it work?"

"It's Michael," says Luke. "I've just heard. He's had a heart attack."

Ten

MICHAEL'S ROOM IS on the fourth floor of the George Washington University Hospital. We walk along the corridors in silence, both staring straight ahead. We arrived in Washington last night. Our hotel bed was very big and comfortable, but even so, neither of us slept very well. In fact, I'm not sure Luke slept at all. He hasn't said much, but I know he's feeling eaten up with guilt.

"He could have died," he said last night, as we were both lying awake in the darkness.

"But he didn't," I replied, and reached for his hand.

"But he could have."

And when you think about it, it's true. He could have. Every time I think about it I feel a horrible lurch in my tummy. I've never before known anyone close to me to be ill. I mean, there was my great-aunt Muriel, who had something wrong with her kidneys—but I only met her about twice. And all my grandparents are still alive except Grandpa Bloomwood, who died when I was two, so I never even knew him.

In fact, I've hardly ever been into a hospital before, unless you count *ER* and *Terms of Endearment*. As we walk along, past scary signs like "Oncology" and "Renal Unit," I realize yet again how sheltered my life has been.

We arrive at room 465 and Luke stops.

"This is it," he says. "Ready?" He knocks gently and, after a moment, pushes the door open.

Michael is lying asleep in a big clanky metal bed, with about six huge flower arrangements on the table next to him and more around the room. There's a drip attached to his hand and another tube going from his chest to some machine with little lights. His face is pale and drawn and he looks . . . vulnerable.

I don't like this. I've never seen Michael in anything other than an expensive suit, holding an expensive drink. Big and reassuring and indestructible. Not lying in a bed in a hospital gown.

I glance at Luke and he's staring at Michael, pale-faced. He looks like he wants to cry.

Oh God. Now *I* want to cry.

Then Michael opens his eyes, and I feel a swoosh of relief. His eyes, at least, are exactly the same. The same warmth. The same flash of humor.

"Now, you didn't have to come all this way," he says. His voice sounds dry and even more gravelly than usual.

"Michael," says Luke, taking an eager step forward. "How are you feeling?"

"Better. Better than I was feeling." Michael's eyes run quizzically over Luke. "How are *you* feeling? You look terrible."

"I feel terrible," says Luke. "I feel absolutely . . . ." He breaks off and swallows.

"Really?" says Michael. "Maybe you should have some tests run. It's a very reassuring process. I now know that I have angina. On the other hand, my lymph is fine and I'm not allergic to peanuts." His eyes rest on the fruit basket in Luke's hand. "Is that for me?"

"Yes!" says Luke, seeming to come to. "Just a little . . . Shall I put it here?"

He clears a space among the exotic flower arrangements, and as he does so I notice one of the attached cards has a White House heading. Gosh.

"Fruit," says Michael, nodding. "Very thoughtful. You've been talking to my doctor. They're extremely strict here. Visitors who bring candy are marched to a little room and forced to jog for ten minutes."

"Michael . . ." Luke takes a deep breath, and I can see his hands gripping the handle of the fruit basket. "Michael, I just wanted to say . . . I'm sorry. About our argument."

"It's forgotten. Really."

"It's not. Not by me."

"Luke." Michael gives Luke a kind look. "It's not a big deal."

"But I just feel—"

"We had a disagreement, that's all. Since then I've been thinking about what you said. You do have a point. If Brandon Communications is publicly associated with a worthy cause, it can only do the company profile good."

"I should never have acted without consulting you," mutters Luke.

"Well. As you said, it's your company. You have executive control. I respect that."

"And I respect your advice," says Luke at once. "I always will."

"So. Shall we agree to bury the hatchet?" Michael extends his hand, all bruised from where the drip needle goes into it—and after a moment, Luke gently takes it.

Now I'm completely choked.

"I'll just get some . . . water . . . ." I mumble, and back out of the room, breathing hard.

I *can't* burst into tears in front of Michael. He'll think I'm completely pathetic.

Or else he'll think I'm crying because I know something he doesn't. He'll think we've seen his medical charts and it wasn't angina at all. It was a brain clot that is inoperable except by a specialist from Chicago who's turned down Michael's case because of an old feud between the hospitals . . .

OK, look, I *must* stop confusing this with *ER*.

I walk to a nearby reception area, taking deep breaths to calm myself down, and sit down next to a middle-aged woman. There are people sitting on upholstered seats and a couple of patients in wheelchairs with drips, and I see a frail old woman greeting what must be her grandchildren. As she sees them, her whole face lights up and suddenly she looks ten years younger—and to my horror I find myself sniffing again.

"Are you all right?" I look up and see the middle-aged woman offering me a tissue. She smiles—but her eyes are red-rimmed. "It gets to you, doesn't it?" she says as I blow my nose. "Is a relation of yours in here?"

"Just a friend. How about you?"

"My husband, Ken," says the woman. "He's had bypass surgery. He's doing fine, though." She gives a half-smile. "He hates to see me upset."

"God. I'm . . . really sorry."

I feel a shiver go down my back as I try to imagine how I'd be feeling if it were Luke in that hospital bed.

"He should be be OK, if he starts looking after himself. These men. They take it all for granted." She shakes her head. "But coming in here . . . it teaches you what's important, doesn't it?"

"Absolutely," I say fervently.

We sit quietly for a while, and I think anxiously about Luke. Maybe I'll get him to start going to the gym a bit more. And eating that low-fat spread stuff that lowers your cholesterol. Just to be on the safe side.

"I should go back," says the woman, looking at her watch. She smiles at me. "Good to meet you."

"You too." I watch as she walks off down the corridor, then stand up and head back to Michael's room, shaking back my hair and putting on a cheerful expression. No more dissolving into tears.

"Hi!" says Luke as I enter. He's sitting on a chair by Michael's bed, and the atmosphere is a lot more relaxed, thank goodness.

"I was just telling Luke," says Michael as I sit down. "My daughter's on at me to retire. Or at least downscale. Move to New York."

"Really? Ooh, yes, do! We'd love that."

"It's a good idea," says Luke. "Bearing in mind you currently do about six full-time jobs."

"I really like your daughter," I say enthusiastically. "We had such fun when she came into Barneys. How's her new job going?"

Michael's daughter is an attorney who specializes in patent law, and just exudes extreme cleverness. On the other hand, she hadn't spotted that she was choosing colors that did nothing for her skin tone until I pointed it out to her.

"Very well indeed, thanks. She just moved to Finerman Wallstein," Michael adds to Luke. "Very swanky offices."

"I know them," says Luke. "I use them for personal matters. In fact, last time I went in there was a few weeks ago. Just about my will. Next time, I'll call in on her."

"Do that," says Michael. "She'd like it."

"Have you made a will, Luke?" I say with interest.

"Of course I've made a will." Luke stares at me. "Haven't you?"

"No," I say—then look from Luke to Michael. "What? What is it?"

"Everyone should make a will," says Michael gravely.

"It never even *occurred* to me you might not have made one," says Luke, shaking his head.

"It never even occurred to me to make one!" I say defensively. "I mean, I'm only twenty-seven."

"I'll make an appointment with my lawyer," says Luke. "We need to sort this out."

"Well. OK. But honestly . . ." I give a little shrug. Then a thought occurs to me. "So, who have you left everything to?"

"You," says Luke. "Minus the odd little bequest."

"Me?" I gape at him. "Really? Me?"

"It is customary for husbands to leave their property to their wives," he says with a small smile. "Or do you object?"

"No! Of course not! I just . . . kind of . . . didn't expect it."

I feel a strange glow of pleasure inside me. Luke's leaving everything to me!

I don't know why that should be a surprise. I mean, we live together. We're getting married. It's obvious. But still, I can't help feeling a bit proud.

"Do I take it you're not planning to leave anything to me?" inquires Luke mildly.

"Of course!" I exclaim. "I mean—of course I will!"

"No pressure," says Luke, grinning at Michael.

"I will!" I say, growing flustered. "I just hadn't really thought about it!"

To cover my confusion I reach for a pear and start munching it. Come to think of it, why *have* I never made a will?

I suppose because I've never really thought I'll die. But I could easily, couldn't I? I mean, our train could crash on the way back to New York. Or an ax murderer could break into our apartment . . .

And who would get all my stuff?

Luke's right. This is an emergency.

"Becky? Are you OK?" I look up to see Luke putting on his coat. "We must go."

"Thanks for coming," says Michael, and squeezes my hand as I bend to kiss him. "I really appreciate it."

"And I'll be in touch about the wedding," says Luke, and smiles at Michael. "No skiving your best-man duties."

"Absolutely not!" says Michael. "But that reminds me, I got a little confused at the engagement party, talking to different people. Are you two getting married in New York or England?"

"New York," says Luke, frowning in slight puzzlement. "That has been finally decided, hasn't it, Becky? I never even asked how your mother took the news."

"I . . . um . . ." I play for time, wrapping my scarf around my neck.

I can't admit the truth. I can't admit that Mum still doesn't know about the Plaza.

Not here. Not now.

"Yes!" I say, feeling my cheeks flame. "Yes, she was fine. New York it is!"

As we get onto the train, Luke looks pale and drained. I think it upset him more than he's letting on, seeing Michael looking so helpless. He sits staring out of the darkening window, and I try to think of something that will cheer him up.

"Look!" I say at last. I reach into my bag and take out a book I bought just the other day called *The Promise of Your Life*. "We need to talk about composing our wedding vows."

"Composing them?" Luke frowns. "Aren't they always the same?"

"No! That's old hat. Everyone writes their own these days. Listen to this. 'Your wedding vows are the chance for you to show the world what you mean to each other. Together with the proclamation by the officiant that you are now married, they are the linchpin of the entire ceremony. They should be the most beautiful and moving words spoken at your wedding.' "

I look up expectantly at Luke, but he's gazing out of the window again.

"It says in this book, we must think about what sort of couple we are," I press on. "Are we Young Lovers or Autumn Companions?"

Luke isn't even listening. Perhaps I should find a few specific examples. My eye falls on a page marked Summertime Wedding, which would be quite appropriate.

"'As the roses bloom in summertime, so did my love bloom for you. As the white clouds soar above, so does my love soar,'" I read aloud.

I pull a face. Maybe not. I flick through a few more pages, glancing down as I go.

> You helped me through the pain of rehab . . .
> Though you are incarcerated for murder, our love will
> shine like a beacon . . .

"Ooh, look," I say suddenly. "This is for high school sweethearts. 'Our eyes met in a math class. How were we to know that trigonometry would lead to matrimony?' "

"Our eyes met across a crowded press conference," says Luke. "How were we to know love would blossom as I announced an exciting new range of unit trusts investing in European growth companies with tracking facility, fixed-rate costs, and discounted premiums throughout the first accounting period?"

"Luke—"

Well, OK. Maybe this isn't the time for vows. I shut the book and look anxiously at Luke. "Are you all right?"

"I'm fine."

"Are you worried about Michael?" I reach for his hand. "Because honestly, I'm sure he's going to be fine. You heard what he said. It was just a wake-up call."

There's silence for a while—then Luke turns his head.

"While you were going to the rest room," he says slowly, "I met the parents of the guy in the room next to Michael's. He had a heart attack last week. Do you know how old he is?"

"How old?" I say apprehensively.

"Thirty-three."

"God, really? That's awful!"

Luke's only a year older than that.

"He's a bond trader, apparently. Very successful." He exhales slowly. "It makes you think, doesn't it? Think about what you're doing with your life. And wonder."

"Er . . . yes," I say, feeling as though I'm walking across eggshells. "Yes, it does."

Luke's never spoken like this before. Usually if I start conversations about life and what it all means—which, OK, I don't do very often—he either brushes me off or turns it into a joke. He certainly never confesses to doubting what he's doing with his life. I really want to encourage him—but I'm worried I might say the wrong thing and put him off.

Now he's staring silently out of the window again.

"What exactly were you thinking?" I prompt gently.

"I don't know," says Luke after a pause. "I suppose it just makes you see things differently for a moment."

He looks at me—and just for an instant I think I can see deep inside him, to a part of him I rarely have access to. Softer and quieter and full of doubts like everyone else.

Then he blinks—and it's as though he's closed the camera shutter. Back into normal mode. Businesslike. Sure of himself.

"Anyway. I'm glad Michael and I were able to make up," he says, taking a sip from the water bottle he's carrying.

"Me too."

"He saw my point of view in the end. The publicity that we'll get through the foundation will benefit the company enormously. The fact that it's my mother's charity is largely irrelevant."

"Yes," I say reluctantly. "I suppose so."

I really don't want to get into a conversation about Luke's mother right now, so I open the vows book again.

"Hey, here's one in rhyme . . ."

As we arrive back at Penn Station, it's crowded with people. Luke heads off to a rest room, and I head to a kiosk to buy a candy bar. I walk straight past a stand of newspapers—then stop. Hang on a minute. What was that?

I retrace my steps and stare at the *New York Post*. Right at the top, flagging an inside feature, is a little picture of Elinor.

I grab the paper and turn quickly to the inside page.

There's a headline, "How to Fight Charity Fatigue." Then there's a picture of Elinor with a frosty smile, standing on the steps of some big building and handing over a check to some man in a suit. My eyes run puzzledly over the caption. *Elinor Sherman has battled against apathy to raise money for a cause she believes in.*

Wasn't the photo opportunity supposed to be for Luke?

I scan the piece quickly, searching for any mention of Brandon Communications. For any mention of Luke. But I get to the end of the page—and his name hasn't appeared once. It's as though he doesn't figure at all.

I stare down at the page in disbelief.

After everything he's done for her. *How* can she treat him like this?

"What's that?"

I give a startled jump at Luke's voice. For an instant I consider hiding the paper under my coat. But then, there's no point, is there? He'll see it sooner or later.

"Luke . . ." I hesitate—then swivel the page so he can see it.

"Is that my mother?" Luke looks astounded. "She never told me anything was set up. Let me have a look."

"Luke . . ." I take a deep breath. "It doesn't mention you any-where. Or the company."

I wince as I see him scanning the page; as I watch the sheer disbelief growing on his face. It's been a hard enough day already, without discovering that his mother has completely screwed him.

"Didn't she even tell you she was doing the interview?"

Luke doesn't reply. He takes out his mobile, jabs in a number, and waits for a few moments. Then he makes a noise of frustration.

"I forgot. She's gone back to Switzerland."

I'd forgotten that too. She's gone to "visit her friends" again, in time for the wedding. This time she's staying for two whole months, which means she's having the full works. She must have done the interview just before she left.

I try to take Luke's hand, but he doesn't respond. God knows what he's thinking.

"Luke . . . maybe there's some explanation—"

"Let's forget it."

"But—"

"Just forget it." There's an edge to his voice that makes me flinch. "It's been a long, difficult day. Let's just get home."

THE LAST WILL AND TESTAMENT OF
Rebecca Bloomwood

I, REBECCA JANE BLOOMWOOD, do make, publish, and declare this to be my Last Will and Testament.

FIRST: I hereby revoke all former Wills and Codicils by me made.

SECOND: (a) I give and bequeath to SUSAN CLEATH-STUART my collection of shoes, all my jeans, my tan leather coat, all my makeup except the Chanel lipstick, my leather floor cube, my red Kate Spade handbag,[1] my silver ring with the moonstone, and my painting of two elephants.

(b) I give and bequeath to my mother JANE BLOOMWOOD all my remaining handbags, my Chanel lipstick, all my jewelry, my Barneys white cotton duvet set, my waffle-weave dressing gown, my suede cushions, my Venetian glass vase, my collection of jam spoons, and my Tiffany watch.[2]

(c) I give and bequeath to my father GRAHAM BLOOMWOOD my chess set, my CDs of classical music that he gave me for Christmas, my Bill Amberg weekend bag, my titanium desk lamp, and the incomplete manuscript of my self-help book *Manage Money the Bloomwood Way,* all rights of which are hereby passed to him.

(d) I give and bequeath to my friend DANNY KOVITZ all my old copies of *British Vogue,*[3] my lava lamp, my customized denim jacket, and my juicer.

(e) I give and bequeath to my friend ERIN GAYLER my Tse cashmere jumper, my Donna Karan evening dress, all my Betsey Johnson dresses, and my Louis Vuitton hair bobbles.

THIRD: I bequeath all the rest, residue, and remainder of my property of whatsoever kind or character and wheresoever situated, apart from any clothes found in carrier bags at the bottom of the wardrobe,[4] to LUKE JAMES BRANDON.

1. Unless she would prefer the new DKNY bag with the long straps.
2. Also my Tiffany keyring, which I have lost, but must be in the apartment somewhere.
3. Plus any other magazines I subsequently buy.
4. Which are to be disposed of discreetly, in secret.

Eleven

THIS IS NOT a good time.

In fact, it's horrendous. Ever since he saw that piece in the paper, Luke has been really withdrawn and silent. He won't talk about it, and the atmosphere in the apartment is getting really tense, and I just don't know how to make things better. A few days ago I tried buying some soothing scented candles, but they didn't really smell of anything except candle wax. So then yesterday I tried rearranging the furniture to make it more feng shui and harmonious. But Luke came into the living room just as I'd jammed a sofa leg into the DVD player, and I don't think he was very impressed.

I wish he'd open up to me, like they do on *Dawson's Creek*. But whenever I say, "Do you want to talk?" and pat the sofa invitingly, instead of saying, "Yes, Becky, I have some issues I'd like to share," he either ignores me or tells me we've run out of coffee.

I know he's tried calling his mother, but the patients at her stupid Swiss clinic aren't allowed mobile phones, so he hasn't been able to speak to her. I also know that he's been on the phone to Michael several times. And that the assistant who had been assigned to work for the Elinor Sherman Foundation is now back working for Brandon Communications. When I asked him about it, though, he just shut off and wouldn't say anything. It's as though he can't bring himself to admit any of it has happened.

The only thing that is going at all well at the moment is the wedding preparations. Robyn and I have had several meetings with the event designer, whose ideas for the room are absolutely spectacular. Then we had the dessert tasting at the Plaza the other day, and I nearly swooned at all the amazing, out-of-this-world sweets there were to choose from. It was champagne all the way through, and deferential waiters, and I was treated exactly like a princess . . .

But if I'm really honest, even that didn't feel quite as relaxed and wonderful as it should. Even while I was sitting there, being served poached white peaches with pistachio mousse and anise biscotti on a gilded plate, I couldn't help feeling little pricks of guilt through the pleasure, like tiny pinpoints of light through a blanket.

I think I'll feel a lot better when I've broken the news to Mum.

I mean, not that there's any reason to feel bad. Because I couldn't do anything about it while they were in the Lake District, could I? I wasn't exactly going to interrupt their nice relaxing holiday. But they get back tomorrow. So then what I'll do is very calmly phone up Mum, and tell her that I really appreciate everything she's done, and it doesn't mean I'm not grateful, but that I've decided . . .

No. That *Luke* and I have decided . . .

No. That Elinor has very kindly offered . . . That we have decided to accept . . .

Oh God. My insides are churning, just thinking about it.

OK, I won't think about it yet. Anyway, I don't want to come out with some stilted, awkward speech. Much better just to wait until the moment and be spontaneous.

As I arrive at Barneys, Christina is sorting through a rack of evening jackets.

"Hi!" she says as I walk in. "Did you sign those letters for me?"

"What?" I say distractedly. "Oh, sorry. I forgot. I'll do it today."

"Becky?" Christina looks at me more closely. "Are you all right?"

"I'm fine! I'm just . . . I don't know, the wedding . . ."

"I saw India from the bridal atelier last night. She said you'd reserved a Richard Tyler dress?"

"Oh yes, I have."

"But I could have sworn I heard you telling Erin the other day about a dress at Vera Wang."

I look away and fiddle with the zip of my bag. "Well. The thing is, I've kind of reserved more than one dress."

"How many?"

"Four," I say after a pause. I needn't tell her about the one at Kleinfeld.

Christina throws back her head in a laugh. "Becky, you can't wear more than one dress! You're going to have to fix on one in the end, you know."

"I know," I say weakly, and disappear into my fitting room before she can say anything else.

My first client is Laurel, who is here because she's been invited on a corporate weekend, dress "casual," and her idea of casual is a pair of track pants and a Hanes T-shirt.

"You look like shit," she says as soon as she walks in. "What's wrong?"

"Nothing!" I smile brightly. "I'm just a bit preoccupied at the moment."

"Are you fighting with your mother?"

My head jerks up.

"No," I say cautiously. "Why do you ask that?"

"It's par for the course," says Laurel, taking off her coat. "All brides fight with their mothers. If it's not over the ceremony, it's over the floral arrangements. I threw a tea strainer at mine because she cut three of my friends off the guest list without asking."

"Really? But then you made up."

"We didn't speak for five years afterward."

"Five years?" I stare at her, aghast. "Just over a wedding?"

"Becky, there's no such thing as *just* a wedding," says Laurel. She picks up a cashmere sweater. "This is nice."

"Mmm," I say distractedly. Oh God, now I'm really worried.

What if I fall out with Mum? What if she gets really offended and says she never wants to see me again? And then Luke and I have children and they never get to know their grandparents. And every Christmas they buy presents for Granny and Grandpa Bloomwood, just in case, but every year they sit under the tree unopened, and we quietly put them away, and one year our little girl says, "Mummy, why does Granny Bloomwood hate us?" and I have to choke back my tears and say, "Darling, she doesn't hate us. She just—"

"Becky? Are you all right?"

I snap into the present, to see Laurel peering at me concernedly. "You know, you really don't look yourself. Maybe you need a break."

"I'm fine! Honestly." I summon up a professional smile. "So . . . here are the skirts I was thinking of. If you try this beige one, with the off-white shirt . . ."

As Laurel tries on different pieces, I sit on a stool, nodding and making the odd absent comment, while my mind still frets on the subject of Mum. I feel like I've got so far into this mess, I've lost all sense of proportion. Will she flip out when I tell her about the Plaza? Won't she? I just can't tell.

I mean, take what happened at Christmas. I thought Mum was going to be devastated when I told her Luke and I weren't coming home, and it took me ages to pluck up the courage to tell her. But to my astonishment, she was really nice about it and told me that she and Dad would have a lovely day with Janice and Martin, and I mustn't worry. So maybe this will be the same. When I explain the whole story to her, she'll say, "Oh darling, don't be silly, of course you must get married wherever you want to."

Or else she'll burst into tears, say how could I deceive her like this, and she'll come to the Plaza over her dead body.

"So I was going into Central Park for my marathon training, and who should I see, standing right there like a Barbie doll?"

Laurel's voice filters into my mind and I look up.

"Not the blond intern?"

"Right! So my heart starts thumping, I'm walking toward her and I'm wondering what I'm going to say. Do I yell at her? Do I hit her? Do I completely ignore her? You know, which will give me most satisfaction? And of course half of me wants to run away and hide . . ."

"So what happened?" I say eagerly.

"When I got up close, it wasn't even her. It was some other girl!" Laurel puts a hand to her head. "It's like, now she's messing with my mind. Not content with taking my husband, wrecking my life, stealing my jewelry . . ."

"She's stolen your jewelry?" I say in surprise. "What do you mean?"

"I must have told you this. No? Things started going missing around the time Bill was taking her back to our apartment. An emerald pendant my grandmother gave me. A couple of bracelets. Of course, I had no idea what was going on, so I thought I was being careless. But then it all came out, and I realized. It had to be her."

"Couldn't you do anything?" I say, appalled.

"Oh, I did. I called the police." Laurel's chin tightens as she buttons up her dress. "They went and asked her some questions, but they didn't get anywhere. Of course they didn't." She gives me a strange little smile. "Then Bill found out. He went crazy. He went to the police and told them . . . well, I don't know exactly what he told them. But that same afternoon the police called me back and said they were dropping the case. It was obvious they thought I was just some vindictive, spurned wife. Which of course I was."

She stares at herself in the mirror and slowly the animation seeps out of her face. "You know, I always thought he would come to his senses," she says quietly. "I thought he'd last a month. Maybe two. Then he'd crawl back, I'd send him away, he'd crawl back again, we'd fight, but eventually . . ." She exhales slowly. "But he's not. He's not coming back."

She meets my eye in the mirror and I feel a sudden pang of outrage. Laurel's the nicest person in the world. Why would her stupid husband leave her?

"I like this dress," she adds, sounding more cheerful. "But maybe in the black."

"I'll go and get one for you," I say. "We have it on this floor."

I walk out of the personal shopping department and head toward the rack of Dries van Noten dresses. It's still early for regular shoppers and the floor is nearly empty. But as I'm searching for another dress in Laurel's size, I'm suddenly aware of a familiar figure in the corner of my vision. I turn, puzzled, but the figure has gone.

Weird. Eventually I find the dress, and pick out a matching fringed stole. I turn around—and there he is again. It's Danny. What on earth is he doing in Barneys? As I get nearer, I stare at him. His eyes are bloodshot, his hair is awry, and he's got a wild, fidgety look.

"Danny!" I say—and he visibly jumps. "What are you doing here?"

"Oh!" he says. "Nothing! Just . . . browsing."

"Are you OK?"

"I'm fine! Everything's fine." He glances at his watch. "So—I guess you're in the middle of something?"

"I am, actually," I say regretfully. "I have a client waiting. Otherwise we could go and have a coffee."

"No. That's fine," he says. "You go. I'll see you later."

"OK," I say, and walk back to my fitting room, rather puzzled.

Laurel decides to take three of the outfits I chose for her, and when she leaves she gives me a big hug. "Don't let the wedding get you down," she says. "You shouldn't listen to me. I have a somewhat jaded view. I know you and Luke will be happy."

"Laurel." I squeeze her tightly back. "You're the best."

God, if I ever meet that stupid husband of hers I'm going to let him have it.

When she's gone, I consult my schedule for the rest of the day. I've got an hour before my next client, so I decide to wander up to the bridal department and look at my dress again. It's definitely between this one and the Vera Wang. Or maybe the Tracy Connop.

Definitely one of those three, anyway.

As I walk out onto the sales floor again, I stop in surprise. There's Danny, standing by a rack of tops, fingering one casually. What on earth is he still doing here? I'm about to call out to him, and say does he want to come and see my dress and then go for a quick cappuccino? But then, to my astonishment, he glances around, surreptitiously bends down, and reaches for something in his canvas bag. It's a T-shirt with glittery sleeves, on a hanger. He shoves it onto the rack, looks around again, and reaches for another one.

I stare at him in utter stupefaction. What does he think he's doing?

He looks around again—then reaches into his bag and pulls out a small laminated sign, which he props up at the end of the display.

What the hell is he up to?

"Danny!" I say, heading toward him.

"What?" He gives a startled jump, then turns and sees me. "Sssh! Jesus, Becky!"

"What are you doing with those T-shirts?" I hiss.

"I'm stocking myself."

"What do you mean, stocking yourself?"

He jerks his head toward the laminated sign and I read it in disbelief.

THE DANNY KOVITZ COLLECTION
AN EXCITING NEW TALENT AT BARNEYS

"They're not all on Barneys hangers," says Danny, thrusting another two T-shirts on the rack. "But I figure that won't matter."

"Danny . . . you can't do this! You can't just . . . put your stuff on the racks!"

"I'm doing it."

"But—"

"I have no choice, OK?" says Danny, turning his head. "Randall's on his way here right now, expecting to see a Danny Kovitz line at Barneys."

I stare at him in horror.

"I thought you said he would never check!"

"He wouldn't have!" Danny shoves another hanger onto the rack. "But his stupid girlfriend has to poke her nose in. She never showed any interest in me before, but as soon as she hears the word Barneys, it's like Oh, Randall, you should support your brother! Go to Barneys tomorrow and buy one of his pieces! So I'm saying, you *really* don't have to do that—but now Randall's got the idea in his head, he's like, well, maybe I will pop in and take a look! So I'm up sewing all fucking night . . ."

"You made all of these last night?" I say incredulously, and reach for one of the T-shirts. A piece of leather braid falls off, onto the floor.

"So maybe the finish isn't quite up to my usual standards," says Danny defensively. "Just don't manhandle them, OK?" He starts to count the hangers. "Two . . . four . . . six . . . eight . . . ten. That should be enough."

"Danny . . ." I glance around the sales floor to see Carla, one of the assistants, giving us an odd look. "Hi!" I call brightly. "Just . . . helping one of my clients . . . for his girlfriend . . ." Carla gives us another suspicious look, then moves away. "This isn't going to work!" I mutter as soon as she's out of earshot. "You're going to have to take these down. You wouldn't even be stocked on this floor!"

"I need two minutes," he says. "That's all. Two minutes for him to come in, see the sign, then go. Come on, Becky. No one's even going to . . ." He freezes. "Here he is."

I follow his gaze and see Danny's brother Randall walking across the floor toward us.

For the millionth time I wonder how on earth Randall and Danny can have come from the same parents. While Danny is wiry and constantly on the move, Randall fills his double-breasted suit comfortably, and always wears the same disapproving frown.

"Hello, Daniel," he says, and nods to me. "Becky."

"Hi, Randall," I say, and give what I hope is a natural smile. "How are you?"

"So here they are!" says Danny triumphantly, moving away from the rack and gesturing to the T-shirts. "My collection. In Barneys. Just like I said."

"So I see," says Randall, and carefully scrutinizes the rack of clothes. I feel sure he's about to look up and say, "What on earth are you playing at?" But he says nothing—and with a slight dart of shock I realize that he's been completely taken in.

There again, why is that such a surprise? Danny's clothes don't look so out of place, up there on the rack.

"Well, congratulations," says Randall at last. "This is quite an achievement." He pats Danny awkwardly on the shoulder, then turns to me. "Are they selling well?"

"Er . . . yes!" I say. "Very popular, I believe."

"So, for how much do they retail?" He reaches for a T-shirt, and both Danny and I involuntarily draw breath. We watch, frozen, while he searches for the label, then looks up with a deep frown. "These have no price tags."

"That's because . . . they're only just out," I hear myself saying hurriedly. "But I think they're priced at . . . erm . . . eighty-nine dollars."

"I see." Randall shakes his head. "Well, I never was one for high fashion—"

"Telling me," Danny whispers in my ear.

"But if they're selling, they must have something. Daniel, I take my hat off to you." He reaches for another one, with rivets round the neck, and looks at it with a fastidious dismay. "Now, which one shall I buy?"

"Don't buy one!" says Danny at once. "I'll . . . make you one. As a gift."

"I insist," says Randall. "If I can't support my own brother—"

"Randall, please." Danny's voice crackles with sincerity. "Allow me to make a gift to you. It's the least I can do after all your kindness to me over the years. Really."

"Well, if you're sure," says Randall at last, with a shrug. He looks at his watch. "I must go. Good to see you, Becky."

"I'll walk to the elevator with you," says Danny, and darts me a jubilant look.

As they walk away, I feel a giggle of relief rising in me. I can't quite believe we got away with it so easily.

"Hey!" comes a voice behind me suddenly. "Look at these! They're new, aren't they?" A manicured hand appears over my shoulder and plucks one of Danny's T-shirts off the rail before I can stop it. My head whips round and I feel a plunge of dismay. It's Lisa Farley, a sweet but completely dippy client of Erin's. She's about twenty-two, doesn't seem to have a job, and always says whatever pops into her head, never mind whether someone might be offended. (She once asked Erin in all innocence, "Doesn't it bother you, having such a weird-shaped mouth?")

Now she's holding the T-shirt up against her, looking down at it appraisingly.

Damn it. I should have whipped them down off the rack straight away.

"Hi, Becky!" she says cheerily. "Hey, this is cute! I haven't seen these before."

"Actually," I say quickly, "these aren't for sale yet. In fact, I need to . . . um . . . take them back to the stock room." I try to grab for the T-shirt, but she moves away.

"I'll just take a look in the mirror. Hey, Tracy! What do you think?"

Another girl, wearing the new Dior print jacket, is coming toward us.

"Of what?"

"These new T-shirts. They're cool, aren't they?" She reaches for another one and hands it to Tracy.

"If you could just give them back to me—" I say helplessly.

"This one's nice!"

Now they're both searching through the hangers with brisk

fingers, and the poor T-shirts just can't take the strain. Hems are un-raveling, bits of glitter and strings of diamante are coming loose, and sequins are shedding all over the floor.

"Oops, this seam just came apart." Lisa looks up in dismay. "Becky, it just fell apart. I didn't pull it."

"That's OK," I say weakly.

"Is everything supposed to fall off like this? Hey, Christina!" Lisa suddenly calls out. "This new line is so fun!"

Christina?

I wheel round and feel a lurch of horror. Christina is standing at the entrance to the personal shopping department, in conversation with the head of personnel.

"What new line?" she says, looking up. "Oh, hi, Becky."

Shit. I have to stop this right now.

"Lisa—" I say desperately. "Come and see the new Marc Jacobs coats we've got in!"

Lisa ignores me.

"This new . . . what's it called . . ." She squints at the label. "Danny Kovitz! I can't believe Erin didn't tell me these were coming in! Naughty naughty!" She wags a finger in mock reproach.

I watch in dismay as Christina looks up, alert. There's nothing to galvanize her like someone suggesting her department is less than perfect.

"Excuse me a minute," she says to the head of personnel, and comes across the floor toward us, her dark hair gleaming under the lights.

"What didn't Erin tell you about?" she says pleasantly.

"This new designer!" says Lisa. "I never even heard of him be-fore."

"Ow!" says Tracy suddenly, and draws her hand away from the T-shirt. "That was a pin!"

"A pin?" echoes Christina. "Give me that!"

She takes the ragged T-shirt and stares at it bewilderedly. Then she catches sight of Danny's laminated sign.

Oh, I'm so *stupid*. Why didn't I take that down, at least?

As she reads it, her expression changes. She looks up and meets my eye, and I feel my whole body prickle with fear. I've never been in trouble with Christina before. But I've heard her telling people off over the phone, and I know she can be pretty fierce.

"Do you know anything about this, Becky?" she asks pleasantly.

"I . . ." I clear my throat. "The thing is . . ."

"I see. Lisa, I'm afraid there's been a little confusion." She gives Lisa a professional smile. "These items are not for sale. Becky—I think I'd better see you in my office."

"Christina, I'm . . . sorry," I say, feeling my face flush beetroot. "I really am . . ."

"What happened?" says Tracy. "Why aren't they for sale?"

"Is Becky in trouble?" says Lisa in dismay. "Will she get fired? Don't fire Becky! We like her better than Erin . . . Oh." She claps her hand over her mouth. "Sorry, Erin. I didn't see you there."

"That's all right," says Erin, giving a rather pinched smile.

"Christina, all I can do is apologize," I say humbly. "I never meant to cause any trouble. I never meant to mislead the customers . . ."

"In my office," says Christina, lifting a hand to stop me. "If you have anything to say, Becky, then you can say it—"

"Stop!" comes a melodramatic voice behind us, and we all whip round, to see Danny heading toward us, his eyes even wilder than usual. "Just stop right there! Don't blame Becky for this!" he says, placing himself in front of me. "She had nothing to do with it. If you're going to fire anyone—fire me!"

"Danny, she can't fire you," I mutter. "You're not employed by Barneys."

"And you would be?" inquires Christina.

"Danny Kovitz."

"Danny Kovitz. Ah." Light dawns on Christina's face. "So it was you who . . . assembled these garments. And planted them on our racks."

"What? He's not a real designer?" says Tracy in horror. "I knew it! *I* wasn't fooled." She thrusts the hanger she's holding back onto the rack as though she's been contaminated.

"Isn't that breaking the law?" says Lisa, wide-eyed.

"It may well be," says Danny defensively. "But shall I tell you why I'm reduced to criminal measures? Do you know the impossibility of getting a break in this so-called business of fashion?" He glances around to make sure his audience is listening. "I put every ounce of my life-force into my work. I weep, I cry out in pain, I squeeze myself dry of creative blood. But the fashion establishment isn't interested in new talent! They aren't interested in nurturing the newcomer who dares to be a little different!" His voice rises impassionedly. "If I have to take desperate measures, can you blame me? If you cut me, do I not bleed?"

"Wow," breathes Lisa. "I had no idea it was so tough out there."

"You did cut me," puts in Tracy, who looks far less impressed by Danny's speech. "With your stupid pin."

"Christina, you have to give him a chance!" exclaims Lisa. "Look! He's so dedicated!"

"I just want to bring my ideas to people who will love them," begins Danny again. "My only desire is that someone, someday, will wear one of my garments and feel themselves transformed. But as I crawl toward them on my hands and knees, the doors keep being slammed in my face—"

"Enough already!" says Christina, half exasperated, half amused. "You want your big break? Let me have a look at these clothes."

There's a sudden intrigued quiet. I glance quickly at Danny. Perhaps this is going to be it! Christina will spot his genius and Barneys will buy his entire collection and he'll be made! Then Gwyneth Paltrow will wear one of his T-shirts on Leno, and there'll be a rush for them, and suddenly he'll be famous and have his own boutique!

Christina reaches for a T-shirt with spattered dye and rhinestones on the front, and as she runs her eye up and down it, I hold my breath. Lisa and Tracy raise their eyebrows at each other, and although Danny is motionless, I can see his face tightening with hope. There's dead silence as she puts it down—and as she reaches for a second T-shirt we all give an intake of breath, as though the Russian judge's hand has hovered over the perfect six scorecard. With a critical frown, she stretches it out to look at it properly . . . and as she does so, one of the sleeves comes off in her hand, leaving a ragged seam behind.

Everyone stares at it speechlessly.

"That's the look," says Danny, a little too late. "It's a . . . a deconstructive approach to design . . ."

Christina is shaking her head and putting the T-shirt back. "Young man. You certainly have flair. You may even have talent. Unfortunately these are not enough. Until you can finish off your work properly, you're not going to get very far."

"My designs are usually immaculately finished!" says Danny at once. "Perhaps this particular collection was a little hurried . . ."

"I suggest you go back to the beginning, make a few pieces, very carefully . . ."

"Are you saying I'm careless?"

"I'm saying you need to learn how to follow a project through to the end." Christina smiles kindly at him. "Then we'll see."

"I can follow a project through!" says Danny indignantly. "It's one of my strengths! It's one of my— Would I be making Becky's wedding dress otherwise?" He grabs me, as though we're about to sing a duet. "The most important outfit of her whole life? She believes in me, even if nobody else does. When Becky Bloomwood walks down the aisle at the Plaza Hotel in a Danny Kovitz creation, you won't be calling me careless then. And when the phones start ringing off their hooks—"

"What?" I say stupidly. "Danny—"

"You're making Becky's wedding dress?" Christina turns to me. "I thought you were wearing Richard Tyler."

"Richard Tyler?" echoes Danny blankly.

"I thought you were wearing Vera Wang," says Erin, who wandered over to the little scene two minutes ago and has been staring agog ever since.

"I heard you were wearing your mother's dress," chips in Lisa.

"*I'm* making your dress!" says Danny, his eyes wide with shock. "Aren't I? You promised me, Becky! We had an agreement!"

"The Vera Wang sounds perfect," says Erin. "You have to have that."

"I'd go for Richard Tyler," says Tracy.

"What about the dress your mother was married in, though?" says Lisa. "Wouldn't that be so romantic?"

"The Vera Wang would be divine," says Erin determinedly.

"But how can you pass up your own mother's wedding dress?" demands Lisa. "How can you set aside a whole family tradition like that? Becky, don't you agree?"

"The point is to look good!" says Erin.

"The point is to be romantic!" retorts Lisa.

"But what about my dress?" comes Danny's plaintive voice. "What about loyalty to your best friend? What about that, Becky?"

Their voices seem to be drilling into my head, and they're all staring at me avidly, waiting for an answer . . . and with no warning I feel myself snap.

"I don't know, OK?" I cry desperately. "I just . . . don't know what I'm going to do!"

Suddenly I feel almost tearful—which is completely ridiculous. I mean, it's not like I won't *have* a dress.

"Becky, I think we need to have a little chat," says Christina, giving me a shrewd look. "Erin, clear all this up, please, and apologize to Carla, would you? Becky, come with me."

We go into Christina's smart beige suede office and she closes the door. She turns round—and for an awful moment I think she's going to yell at me. But instead she gestures for me to sit down and gives me a long, penetrating look through her tortoiseshell glasses.

"How are you, Becky?"

"I'm fine!"

"You're fine. I see." Christina gives a skeptical nod. "What's going on in your life at the moment?"

"Nothing much," I say brightly. "You know! Same old same old . . ."

"Wedding plans going all right?"

"Yes!" I say at once. "Yes! Absolutely no problems there."

"I see." Christina is silent for a moment, tapping her teeth with a pen. "You visited a friend in the hospital recently. Who was that?"

"Oh, yes. That was . . . a friend of Luke's, actually. Michael. He had a heart attack."

"That must have been a shock for you."

For a moment I'm silent.

"Well . . . yes, I suppose it was," I say at last, running a finger along the arm of my chair. "Especially for Luke. The two of them have always been really close, but they'd had a falling out, and Luke was already feeling really guilty. Then we got the call about Michael—I mean, if he'd died, Luke never would have been able to . . ." I break off and rub my face, feeling emotion rising. "And then of course, there's all this tension between Luke and his mother at the moment, which doesn't help. She completely used him. In fact, she more than used him, she abused him. He feels utterly betrayed by her. But he won't talk to me about it." My voice starts to tremble. "He won't talk to me about anything at the moment. Not the wedding, not the honeymoon . . . Not even where we're going to live! We're being chucked out of our apartment, and we haven't found anywhere else to go yet, and I don't know when we're even going to start looking . . ."

To my astonishment a tear starts trickling down the side of my nose. Where did that come from?

"But you're fine, apart from that," says Christina.

"Oh, yes!" I brush at my face. "Apart from that, everything's great!"

"Becky!" Christina shakes her head. "This is no good. I want you to take some vacation days. You're due some, anyway."

"I don't need a vacation!"

"I'd noticed you've been tense recently, but I had no idea it was this bad. It was only when Laurel talked to me this morning—"

"Laurel?" I say, taken aback.

"She's worried too. She told me she thought you'd lost your sparkle. Even Erin has noticed it. She says she told you about a Kate Spade sample sale yesterday, and you barely looked up. This is not the Becky I hired."

"Are you firing me?" I say dolefully.

"I'm not firing you! I'm *worried* about you. Becky, that's some combination of events you just told me about. Your friend . . . and Luke . . . and your apartment . . ."

She reaches for a bottle of mineral water, pours out two glasses, and hands one to me. "And that's not all. Is it, Becky?"

"What do you mean?" I say apprehensively.

"I think there's another complication you're not telling me about. To do with the wedding." She meets my eyes. "Am I right?"

Oh my God.

How did she find out? I've been so careful, I've been so—

"Am I right?" repeats Christina gently.

For a few more moments I'm completely motionless. Then, very slowly I nod.

It's almost a relief to think that the secret's out.

"How did you find out?" I say, sinking back into my chair.

"Laurel told me."

"*Laurel?*" A fresh shock runs through me. "But I never—"

"She said it was obvious. Plus you let a few little things slip out . . . You know, keeping a secret is never as easy as you might think."

"I just . . . can't believe you know. I haven't dared tell anybody!" I push my hair back off my hot face. "God knows what you think of me now."

"Nobody thinks any the worse of you," says Christina. "Really."

"I never meant things to get this far."

"Of course you didn't! Don't blame yourself."

"But it's all my fault!"

"No it's not. It's perfectly normal."

"*Normal?*"

"Yes! All brides argue with their mothers over the wedding. You're not the only one, Becky!"

I stare at her confusedly. What did she just say?

"I can understand the strain it's been putting you under." Christina looks at me sympathetically. "Especially if you and your mother have always been close in the past?"

Christina thinks . . .

Suddenly I realize she's waiting for an answer.

"Er . . . yes!" I gulp. "It has been . . . rather difficult."

Christina nods, as though I've confirmed every suspicion she had. "Becky, I don't often give you advice, do I?"

"Well . . . no."

"But I want you to listen to me on this. I want you to remember, this is your wedding. Not your mother's. It's yours and Luke's, and you only get one shot. So do it the way *you* want to. Believe me, if you don't, you'll regret it."

"Mmm. The thing is . . ." I swallow. "It's not *quite* that simple—"

"It is that simple. It's exactly that simple. Becky, it's your wedding. *It's your wedding.*"

Her voice is clear and emphatic and I stare at her, glass halfway to my lips, feeling as though a shaft of light is cutting through the cloud.

It's my wedding. I've never thought of it like that before.

It's not Mum's wedding. It's not Elinor's wedding. It's mine.

"It's easy to fall into the trap of wanting to please your mother too much," Christina is saying. "It's a natural, generous instinct. But sometimes you have to put yourself first. When I got married—"

"You were married?" I say in surprise. "I didn't know that."

"A long time ago. It didn't work out. Maybe it didn't work out because I hated every moment of the wedding. From the processional music to the vows that my mother insisted on writing." Her hand tenses around a plastic water stirrer. "From the lurid blue cocktails to that tacky, *tacky* dress . . ."

"Really? That's awful!"

"It's water under the bridge now." The water stirrer snaps and she gives me a slightly brittle smile. "But just bear my words in mind. It's your day. Yours and Luke's. Do it the way you want, and don't feel guilty about it. And Becky?"

"Yes?"

"Remember, you and your mother are both adults now. So have an adult conversation." She raises her eyebrows. "You might be surprised at how it turns out."

Christina is so right.

As I make my way home, I can suddenly see everything clearly. My whole approach to the wedding has changed. I feel full of a fresh, clean determination. This is *my* wedding. It's *my* day. And if I want to get married in New York, then that's where I'll get married. If I want to wear a Vera Wang dress, then that's what I'll wear. It's ridiculous to feel guilty about it.

I've been putting off talking to Mum for far too long. I mean, what am I expecting her to do, burst into tears? We're both adults. We'll have a sensible, mature conversation and I'll put forward my point of view calmly, and the whole thing will be sorted out, once and for all. God, I feel liberated. I'm going to call her straight away.

I march into the bedroom, dump my bag on the bed, and dial the number.

"Hi, Dad," I say as he answers. "Is Mum there? There's something I need to talk to her about. It's rather important."

As I glance at my face in the mirror, I feel like a newsreader on NBC, all crisp and cool and in charge.

"Becky?" says Dad puzzledly. "Are you all right?"

"I'm very well," I say. "I just have to discuss a . . . a couple of issues with Mum."

As Dad disappears off the line I take a deep breath and push my hair back, feeling suddenly very grown-up. Here I am, about to have an adult-to-adult, straight-down-the-line conversation with my mother, for probably the first time in my life.

You know, maybe this is the beginning of a whole new relationship with my parents. A new mutual respect. A shared understanding of life.

"Hello, darling?"

"Hi, Mum." I take a deep breath. Here goes. Calm and mature. "Mum—"

"Oh, Becky, I was going to give you a ring. You'll never guess who we saw up in the Lake District!"

"Who?"

"Auntie Zannie! You used to dress up in all her old necklaces, do you remember? And her shoes. We were laughing about it, the sight you made, tottering around . . ."

"Mum. There's something important I need to discuss with you."

"And they've still got the same grocer in the village. The one who used to sell you strawberry ice-cream cones. Do you remember the time you ate too many and weren't very well? We laughed about that too!"

"Mum—"

"And the Tivertons still live in the same house . . . but . . ."

"What?"

"I'm afraid, love . . . Carrot the donkey has . . ." Mum lowers her voice. "Gone to donkey heaven. But he was very old, darling, and he'll be very happy up there . . ."

This is impossible. I don't feel like a grown-up. I feel about six years old.

"They all send you their love," Mum says, eventually coming to the end of her reminiscences, "and of course they'll all be at the wedding! So, Dad said you wanted to talk about something?"

"I . . ." I clear my throat, suddenly aware of the echoey silence on the line; of the distance between us. "Well, I wanted to . . . um . . ."

Oh God. My mouth is trembling and my newsreader voice has turned into a nervous squeak.

"What is it, Becky?" Mum's voice rises in concern. "Is something wrong?"

"No! It's just that . . . that . . ."

It's no good.

I know what Christina said is right. I know there's no need to feel guilty. It's my wedding, and I'm a grown-up, and I should have it wherever I like. I'm not asking Mum and Dad to pay. I'm not asking them to make any effort.

But even so.

I can't tell Mum I want to get married in the Plaza over the phone. I just can't do it.

"I thought I'd come home and see you," I hear myself saying in a rush. "That's all I wanted to say. I'm coming home."

Finerman Wallstein

Attorneys at Law
Finerman House
1398 Avenue of the Americas
New York, NY 10105

Miss Rebecca Bloomwood
251 W. 11th Street, Apt. B
New York, NY 10014

April 18, 2002

Dear Miss Bloomwood:

Thank you for your letter of April 16 regarding your will. I
confirm that under the fourth clause, section (e) I have added the
line "And also my new denim high-heeled boots," as requested.

With kind regards,

Jane Cardozo

Twelve

As soon as I see Mum, I feel nervous. She's standing next to Dad at Terminal 4, scanning the arrivals gate, and as she sees me her whole face lights up with a mixture of delight and anxiety. She was quite taken aback when I told her I was coming home without Luke—in fact, I had to reassure her several times that everything was still OK between us.

Then I had to reassure her that I hadn't been sacked.

And then promise I wasn't being chased by international loan sharks.

You know, when I think back over the last few years, I sometimes feel a teeny bit bad about everything I've put my parents through.

"Becky! Graham, she's here!" She runs forward, elbowing a family in turbans out of the way. "Becky, love! How are you? How's Luke? Is everything all right?"

"Hi, Mum," I say, and give her a huge hug. "I'm well. Luke sends his love. Everything's fine."

Except one tiny matter—I've been planning a big wedding in New York behind your back.

Stop it, I instruct my brain firmly, as Dad gives me a kiss and takes my luggage. There's no point mentioning it yet. There's no point even thinking about it yet. I'll bring the subject up later, when we're all at home, when there's a natural opening in the conversation.

Which there's bound to be.

"So, Becky, did you think any more about getting married in America?"

"Well, Mum. It's funny you should ask that . . ."

Exactly. I'll wait for some opportunity like that.

But although I act as relaxed as I can, I can't think about anything else. All the while that Mum and Dad are finding the car, disagreeing on which way the exit is, and arguing over whether £3.60 for an hour's parking is a reasonable amount, I've got an anxious knot in my stomach that tightens every time the words *wedding, Luke, New York,* or *America* are mentioned, even in passing.

This is just like the time when I told my parents I was doing the Further Maths GCSE. Tom next door was doing Further Maths and Janice was really smug about it, so I told Mum and Dad I was too. then the exams came, and I had to pretend I was sitting an extra paper (I spent three hours in Top Shop instead). And then the results came out and they kept saying, "But what did you get in Further Maths?"

So then I made up this story that it took the examiners longer to mark Further Maths than the other subjects because it was harder. And I honestly think they would have believed me, except then Janice came running in, saying, "Tom got an A in Further Maths, what did Becky get?"

Bloody Tom.

"You haven't asked about the wedding yet," says Mum as we zoom along the A3 toward Oxshott.

"Oh! No, I haven't, have I?" I force a bright note into my voice. "So—er . . . how are preparations going?"

"To be honest, we haven't done very much," says Dad as we approach the turning for Oxshott.

"It's early days yet," says Mum easily.

"It's only a wedding," adds Dad. "People get far too het up about these things in my opinion. You can put it all together at the last minute."

"Absolutely!" I say in slight relief. "I couldn't agree more!"

Well, thank goodness for that. I sink back in my seat and feel the anxiety drain out of me. This is going to make everything a lot easier. If they haven't arranged very much yet, it'll take no time to call it all off. In fact, it sounds like they're really not bothered about it. This is going to be fine. I've been worrying about nothing!

"Suzie phoned, by the way," says Mum as we start to get near home. "She said, would you like to meet up later on today? I said I was sure you would . . . Oh, and I should warn you." Mum turns in her seat. "Tom and Lucy."

"Hmm?" I resign myself to hearing the details of the latest kitchen they've had put in, or which promotion Lucy has won at work.

"They've split up." Mum lowers her voice, even though it's just the three of us in the car.

"Split up?" I stare at her, taken aback. "Are you serious? But they've only been married for . . ."

"Not even two years. Janice is devastated, as you can imagine."

"What happened?" I say blankly, and Mum purses her lips.

"That Lucy ran off with a drummer."

"A drummer?"

"In a band. Apparently he's got a pierced . . ." She pauses disapprovingly, and my mind ranges wildly over all the possibilities, some of which I'm sure Mum's never heard of. (To be honest, I hadn't either, till I moved to the West Village.) "Nipple," she says at last, to my slight relief.

"Let me get this straight. Lucy's run off . . . with a drummer . . . with a pierced nipple."

"He lives in a trailer," puts in Dad, signaling left.

"After all the work Tom did on that lovely conservatory," says Mum, shaking her head. "Some girls have no gratitude."

I can't get my head round this. Lucy works for Wetherby's Investment Bank. She and Tom live in Reigate. Their curtains match their sofa. How on earth did she meet a drummer with a pierced nipple?

Suddenly I remember that conversation I overheard in the garden when I was here last. Lucy didn't exactly sound happy. But then she didn't exactly sound like she was about to run off, either.

"So how's Tom?"

"He's coping," says Dad. "He's at home with Janice and Martin at the moment, poor lad."

"If you ask me, he's well out of it," says Mum crisply. "It's Janice

I feel sorry for. After that lovely wedding she put on. They were all fooled by that girl."

We pull up outside the house, and to my surprise there are two white vans parked in the drive.

"What's going on?" I say.

"Nothing," says Mum.

"Plumbing," says Dad.

But they've both got slightly strange expressions. Mum's eyes are bright, and she glances at Dad a couple of times as we walk up to the front door.

"So, are you ready?" says Dad casually. He puts his key into the lock and swings open the door.

"Surprise!" cry Mum and Dad simultaneously, and my jaw drops to the ground.

The old hall wallpaper has gone. The old hall carpet has gone. The whole place has been done in light, fresh colors, with pale carpet and new lighting everywhere. As my eye runs disbelievingly upward I see an unobtrusive man in overalls repainting the banisters; on the landing are two more, standing on a stepladder and putting up a candelabra. Everywhere is the smell of paint and newness. And money being spent.

"You're having the house done up," I say feebly.

"For the wedding!" says Mum, beaming at me.

"You said—" I swallow. "You said you hadn't done much."

"We wanted to surprise you!"

"What do you think, Becky?" says Dad, gesturing around. "Do you like it? Does it meet with your approval?"

His voice is jokey. But I can tell it really matters to him whether I like it. To both of them. They're doing all this for me.

"It's . . . fantastic," I say huskily. "Really lovely."

"Now, come and look at the garden!" says Mum, and I follow her dumbly through to the French windows, where I see a team of uniformed gardeners working away in the flower beds.

"They're going to plant 'Luke and Becky' in pansies!" says Mum. "Just in time for June." And we're having a new water feature put in, right by where the entrance to the marquee will be. I saw it in *Modern Garden*."

"It sounds . . . great."

"And it lights up at night, so when we have the fireworks—"

"What fireworks?" I say, and Mum looks at me in surprise.

"I sent you a fax about the fireworks, Becky! Don't say you've forgotten."

"No! Of course not!"

My mind flicks back to the pile of faxes Mum's been sending me, and which I've been guiltily thrusting under the bed, some skimmed over, some completely unread.

What have I been doing? Why haven't I paid attention to what's been going on?

"Becky, love, you don't look at all well," says Mum. "You must be tired after the flight. Come and have a nice cup of coffee."

We walk into the kitchen, and I feel my insides gripped with new horror.

"Have you installed a new kitchen too?"

"Oh, no!" says Mum gaily. "We just had the units repainted. They look pretty, don't they? Now. Have a nice croissant. They come from the new bakery."

She hands me a basket—but I can't eat. I feel sick.

"Becky?" Mum peers at me. "Is something wrong?"

"No!" I say quickly. "Nothing's wrong. It's all . . . perfect."

What am I going to do?

"You know . . . I think I'll just go and unpack," I say, and manage a weak smile. "Sort myself out a bit."

As I close my bedroom door behind me, the weak smile is still pasted to my face, but inside my heart is thumping wildly.

This is not going as planned.

This is not going remotely as planned. New wallpaper? Water features? Fireworks displays? How come I didn't know about any of this? I should have been more attentive. This is all my own fault. Oh God, oh God . . .

How can I tell Mum and Dad this has all got to be called off? How can I do it?

I can't.

But I have to.

But I can't, I just can't.

It's *my* wedding, I remind myself firmly, trying to regain my New York kick-ass confidence. I can have it where I like.

But the words ring false in my brain, making me wince. Maybe that was true at the beginning. Before anything had been done, before any effort had been made. But now . . . this isn't just my wedding anymore. This is Mum's and Dad's gift to me. It's the biggest present they've ever given me in my life, and they've invested it with all the love and care they can muster.

And I'm proposing to reject it. To say thanks, but no thanks.

What have I been thinking?

Heart thumping, I reach into my pocket for the notes I scribbled on the plane, trying to remember all my justifications.

Reasons why our wedding should be at the Plaza:

1. Wouldn't you love a trip to New York, all expenses paid?
2. The Plaza is a fantastic hotel.
3. You won't have to make any effort.
4. A marquee would only mess up the garden.
5. You won't have to invite Auntie Sylvia.
6. You get free Tiffany frames.

They seemed so convincing when I was writing them. Now they seem like jokes. Mum and Dad don't know anything about the Plaza. Why would they want to fly off to some snooty hotel they've never clapped eyes on? Why would they want to give up hosting the wedding they've always dreamed of? I'm their only daughter. Their one and only child.

So . . . what am I going to do?

I sit staring at the page, breathing hard, letting my thoughts fight it out. I'm scrabbling desperately for a solution, a loophole to wriggle through, unwilling to give up until I've tried every last possibility. Round and round, over the same old ground.

"Becky?"

Mum comes in and I give a guilty start, crumpling the list in my hand.

"Hi!" I say brightly. "Ooh. Coffee. Lovely."

"It's decaffeinated," says Mum, handing me a mug reading *You Don't Have to Be Mad to Organize a Wedding But Your Mother Does*. "I thought maybe you were drinking decaffeinated these days."

"No," I say in surprise. "But it doesn't matter."

"And how are you feeling?" Mum sits down next to me and I

surreptitiously transfer my screwed-up piece of paper from one hand to the other. "A little bit tired? Sick, too, probably."

"Not too bad." I give a slightly heavier sigh than I meant to. "The airline food was pretty grim, though."

"You must keep your strength up!" Mum squeezes my arm. "Now, I've got something for you, darling!" She hands me a piece of paper. "What do you think?"

I unfold the paper and stare at it in bewilderment. It's house details. A four-bedroom house in Oxshott, to be precise.

"It's nice, isn't it?" Mum's face is glowing. "Look at all the features!"

"You're not going to move, are you?"

"Not for us, silly! You'd be just round the corner from us! Look, it's got a built-in barbecue, two en-suite bathrooms . . ."

"Mum, we live in New York."

"You do at the moment. But you won't want to stay in New York forever, will you? Not in the long term."

There's a sudden thread of concern in her voice; and although she's smiling, I can see the tension in her eyes. I open my mouth to answer—then realize, to my own surprise, that Luke and I haven't ever talked properly about the long term.

I suppose I've always assumed that we'll come back to Britain one day. But when?

"You're not planning to stay there for good, surely?" she adds, and gives a little laugh.

"I don't know," I say confusedly. "I don't know what we want to do."

"You couldn't bring up a family in that poky flat! You'll want to come home! You'll want a nice house with a garden! Especially now."

"Now what?"

"Now . . ." She makes a euphemistic circling gesture.

"What?"

"Oh, Becky." Mum sighs. "I can understand if you're a little . . . shy about telling people. But it's all right, darling! These days, it's perfectly acceptable. There's no stigma!"

"*Stigma?* What are you—"

"The only thing we'll need to know"—she pauses delicately—"is how much to let the dress out by? For the day?"

Let out the dress? What on . . .

Hang on.

"Mum! You haven't got the idea that I'm . . . I'm . . ." I make the same euphemistic gesture that she made.

"You're not?" Mum's face falls in disappointment.

"No! Of course I'm not! Why on earth would you think that?"

"You said you had something important to discuss with us!" says Mum, defensively taking a sip of coffee. "It wasn't Luke, it wasn't your job, and it wasn't your bank manager. And Suzie's having a baby, and you two girls always do things together, so we assumed . . ."

"Well, I'm not, OK? And I'm not on drugs either, before you ask."

"So, then, what *did* you want to tell us?" She puts her coffee down and looks at me anxiously. "What was so important that you had to come home?"

There's silence in the bedroom. My fingers tighten around my mug.

This is it. This is my lead-in moment. This is my opportunity to confess everything. If I'm going to do it, I have to do it right now. Before they go any further. Before they spend any more money.

"Well, it's . . ." I clear my throat. "It's just that . . ."

I stop, and take a sip of coffee. My throat is tight and I feel slightly sick. How can I possibly do this?

I close my eyes and allow the glitter of the Plaza to flash before my eyes, trying to summon up all the excitement and glamour again. The gilded rooms, the plushiness everywhere. Images of myself sweeping around that huge shiny dance floor before an admiring crowd.

But somehow . . . it doesn't seem quite as overpowering as it did before. Somehow it doesn't seem as convincing.

Oh God. What do I want? What do I really want?

"I knew it!"

I look up to see Mum gazing at me in dismay. "I knew it! You and Luke *have* fallen out, haven't you?"

"Mum—"

"I just knew it! I said to your father several times, 'I can feel it in my bones, Becky's coming home to call off the wedding.' He said nonsense, but I could just *feel* it, here." Mum clasps her chest. "A mother knows these things. And I was right, wasn't I? You do want to cancel the wedding, don't you?"

I stare at her dumbly. She knows I came home to cancel the wedding. How does she know that?

"Becky? Are you all right?" Mum puts an arm round my shoulders. "Darling, listen. We won't mind. All Dad and I want is the best for you. And if that means calling off the wedding, then that's what we'll do. Love, you mustn't go ahead with it unless you're 100 percent sure—110 percent!"

"But . . . but you've made so much effort . . ." I mumble. "You've spent all this money . . ."

"That doesn't matter! Money doesn't matter!" She squeezes me tight. "Becky, if you have any doubts at all, we'll cancel straight away. We just want you to be happy. That's all we want."

Mum sounds so sympathetic and understanding, for a few instants I can't speak. Here she is, offering me the very thing I came home to ask for. Without any questions, without any recriminations. Without anything but love and support.

As I look at her kind, cozy, familiar face, I know, beyond any doubt, that it's impossible.

"It's all right," I manage at last. "Mum, Luke and I haven't fallen out. The . . . the wedding's still on." I rub my face. "You know, I think I'll just go outside and . . . and get some air."

As I step out into the garden, a couple of of the hired gardeners look up and say hello, and I smile weakly back. I feel completely paranoid, as though my secret is so huge, I must somehow be giving it away. As though people must be able to see it, bulging out of me, or floating above my head in bubble captions.

I have another wedding planned.

For the same day as this one.

My parents have no idea.

Yes, I know I'm in trouble.

Yes, I know I've been stupid.

Oh, just piss off and leave me alone, can't you see how completely stressed out I am?

"Hello, Becky."

I give a start of surprise and turn round. Standing at the garden fence in the next-door garden, looking mournfully at me, is Tom.

"Tom! Hi!" I say, trying not to give away my shock at his appearance.

But . . . blimey. He looks awful, all pale and miserable and wearing absolutely terrible clothes. Not that Tom's ever been a style king—but while he was with Lucy, he did acquire a veneer of OKness. In fact, his hair went through quite a groovy stage. But now it's back to greasy hair and the maroon jumper Janice gave him five Christmases ago.

"Sorry to hear about . . ." I pause awkwardly.

"That's all right."

He hunches his shoulders miserably and looks around at all the gardeners digging and clipping away behind me. "So, how are the wedding preparations going?"

"Oh . . . fine," I say brightly. "You know, it's all lists at this stage. Things to do, things to check, little details to . . . to . . . finalize . . ."

Like which continent to get married in. Oh God. Oh God.

"So . . . er, how are your parents?"

"I remember the preparations for our wedding." Tom shakes his head. "Seems a million years ago now. Different people."

"Oh, Tom." I bite my lip. "I'm sorry. Let's change the—"

"You know the worst thing?" says Tom, ignoring me.

"Er . . ." Your hair, I nearly say.

"The worst thing is, I thought I understood Lucy. We understood each other. But all the time . . ." He breaks off, reaches in his pocket for a handkerchief, and blows his nose. "I mean, now I look back, of course I can see there were signs."

"Really?"

"Oh, yes," says Tom. "I just didn't pick up on them."

"Such as . . ." I prompt gently, trying not to give away how curious I am.

"Well." He thinks for a moment. "Like the way she kept saying if she had to live in Reigate for one more minute she'd shoot herself."

"Right," I say, slightly taken aback.

"Then there was the screaming fit she had in Furniture Village . . ."

"Screaming fit?"

"She began yelling, 'I'm twenty-seven! I'm twenty-seven! What am I doing here?' Security had to come in the end, and calm her down."

"But I don't understand. I thought she loved Reigate! You two seemed so . . ."

Smug is the word I'm searching for.

"So . . . happy!"

"She was happy until all the wedding presents were unwrapped," says Tom thoughtfully. "Then . . . it was like she suddenly looked around and realized . . . this was her life now. And she didn't like what she saw. Including me, I expect."

"Oh, Tom."

"She started saying she was sick of the suburbs, and she wanted to have a bit of life while she was young. But I thought, we've just repainted the house, we're halfway through the new conservatory, this isn't a good time to move—" He looks up, his eyes full of misery. "I should have listened, shouldn't I? Maybe I should even have got the tattoo."

"She wanted you to get a *tattoo*?"

"To match hers."

Lucy Webster with a tattoo! I almost want to laugh. But then, as I look at Tom's miserable face, I feel a surge of anger. OK, Tom and I haven't always seen eye to eye over the years. But he doesn't deserve this. He is what he is. And if Lucy wasn't happy with that, then why did she get married to him in the first place?

"Tom, you can't blame yourself," I say firmly. "It sounds like Lucy was having her own problems."

"Do you think?"

"Of course. She was very lucky to have you. More fool her, not appreciating it." Impulsively I lean across the fence and give him a hug. As I draw away again, he stares at me with huge eyes, like a dog.

"You've always understood me, Becky."

"Well, we've known each other a long time."

"No one else knows me like you do."

His hands are still round my shoulders, and he doesn't seem about to let go, so I step backward under the pretext of gesturing at the house, where a man in overalls is painting a window frame.

"Have you seen all the work Mum and Dad are having done? It's incredible."

"Oh, yes. They're really pushing the boat out. I heard about the fireworks display. You must be very excited."

"I'm really looking forward to it," I say automatically. It's what I've said at once, every time anyone's mentioned the wedding to me. But now, as I watch our old, familiar house being smartened up, like a lady putting on makeup, I start to feel a strange sensation. A strange tugging at my heart.

With a sudden pang, I realize I *am* looking forward to it.

I'm looking forward to seeing our garden all bedecked with balloons. To seeing Mum all dressed up and happy. Getting ready in my own bedroom, at my own dressing table. Saying good-bye to my old life properly. Not in some impersonal suite in a hotel . . . but here. At home, where I grew up.

While I was in New York, I couldn't begin to envisage this wedding. It seemed so tiny and humdrum in comparison to the glamour of the Plaza. But now that I'm here, it's the Plaza that's starting to seem unreal. It's the Plaza that's slipping away, like an exotic, far-off holiday, which I'm already starting to forget. It's been a lot of fun playing the part of a New York princess bride, tasting sumptuous dishes and discussing vintage champagne and million-dollar flower arrangements. But that's the point. I've been playing a part.

The truth is, this is where I belong. Right here in this English garden I've known all my life.

So what am I going to do?

Am I really going to . . .

I can barely even think it.

Am I really even contemplating canceling that whole, huge, expensive wedding?

Just the thought of it makes my insides shrivel up.

"Becky?" Mum's voice penetrates my thoughts and I look up dazedly, to see her standing at the patio doors, holding a tablecloth. "Becky! There's a phone call for you inside."

"Oh. OK. Who is it?"

"Someone called Robin," says Mum. "Hello, Tom, love!"

"Robin?" I frown puzzledly as I walk back toward the house. "Robin who?"

I'm not sure I know any Robins. Apart from Robin Anderson

who used to work for *Investment Monthly,* but I hardly knew him, really—

"I didn't catch the surname, I'm afraid," says Mum. "But she seems very nice. She said she was calling from New York . . ."

Robyn?

I can't move. I'm pinioned with horror to the patio steps.

Robyn is on the phone . . . here?

This is all wrong. Robyn doesn't belong in this world, she belongs in New York. This is like when people go back in time and mess up World War II.

"Is she a friend?" Mum's saying innocently. "We've just had a nice little chat about the wedding . . ."

The ground wobbles beneath me.

"What . . . what did she say?" I manage.

"Nothing in particular!" Mum stares at me in surprise. "She asked me what color I was going to wear . . . and she kept saying something odd about violinists. You don't want violinists at the wedding, do you, love?"

"Of course not!" My voice rises shrilly. "What would I want violinists for?"

"Becky, darling, are you all right?" Mum peers at me. "I'll tell her you'll call back, shall I?"

"No! Don't talk to her again! I mean . . . it's fine. I'll take it."

I hurry into the house, heart thumping. What am I going to say? Should I tell her I've changed my mind?

As I pick up the phone, I see that Mum's followed me inside. Oh God. How am I going to manage this?

"Robyn, hi!" I attempt a natural tone. "How are you?"

OK. I'll just get her off the phone, as quickly as possible.

"Hi! Becky! I'm so glad I got a chance to speak with your mother!" says Robyn. "She seems a lovely lady. I'm so looking forward to meeting her!"

"Me too," I say as heartily as I can. "I can't wait for you to . . . get together."

"Although I was surprised she didn't know about the string orchestra. Tut tut! You really should keep your mom up-to-date, Becky!"

"I know," I say after a pause. "I've just been quite busy . . ."

"I can understand that," says Robyn sympathetically. "Why

don't I send her an information package? It would be so easy to FedEx it over. Then she'll see the whole thing in front of her eyes! If you give me the address—"

"No!" I cry before I can stop myself. "I mean . . . don't worry. I'll pass everything on. Really. Don't . . . send anything. Nothing at all."

"Not even a few menu cards? I'm sure she'd love to see those!"

"No! Nothing!"

My hand is tight around the receiver and my face is sweating. I don't even dare look at Mum.

"Well, OK!" says Robyn at last. "You're the boss! Now, I've spoken to Sheldon Lloyd about the table arrangements . . . ."

As she babbles on, I dart a glance at Mum, who is about three feet away from me. Surely she can hear the phone from there? Surely she just heard the word *Plaza*? Surely she just caught *wedding* and *ballroom*?

"Right," I say, without taking in anything that Robyn's saying, "That all sounds fine." I twist the cord around my fingers. "But . . . but listen, Robyn. The thing is, I've come home to get away from it all. So could you possibly not phone me here anymore?"

"You don't want to be updated?" says Robyn in surprise.

"No. That's fine. You just . . . do your thing, and I'll catch up when I get back next week."

"No problem. I understand. You need time out! Becky, I promise, unless it's an emergency, I'll leave you alone. You have a lovely break now!"

"Thanks. I will. Bye, Robyn."

I put the phone down, shaky with relief. Thank God she's gone.

But I don't feel safe. Robyn's got the number here now. She could phone at any time. I mean, what counts as an emergency in wedding planning? Probably anything. Probably a misplaced rose petal. She only has to say one wrong word to Mum, and both of them will realize what's been going on. Mum will immediately realize why I came back here, what I was trying to say.

She'd be so hurt. I can't allow that to happen.

OK, I have two options. Number one: get Mum and Dad to move house immediately. Number two . . .

"Listen, Mum," I say, turning round. "That woman Robyn. She's . . ."

"Yes?"

"She's . . . deranged."

"Deranged?" Mum stares at me. "What do you mean, love?"

"She . . . she's in love with Luke!"

"Oh my goodness!"

"Yes, and she's got this weird delusion that she's going to marry him."

"*Marry* him?" Mum gapes at me.

"Yes! At the Plaza Hotel! Apparently she even tried to . . . um . . . book it. Under my name!"

My fingers are twisting into complicated knots. I must be crazy. Mum'll never fall for this. Never. Not in a million—

"You know, that doesn't surprise me!" says Mum. "I could tell there was something a bit odd about her straight away. All this nonsense about violins! And she seemed obsessed by what color I was going to wear—"

"Oh, she's completely obsessed. So . . . if she ever rings again, just make an excuse and put the phone down. And whatever she says, even if it sounds quite plausible . . . don't believe a word of it. Promise?"

"All right, love," says Mum, nodding. "Whatever you say."

As she goes into the kitchen, I hear her saying "Poor woman. You have to feel sorry for them, really. Graham, did you hear that? That lady from America who phoned for Becky. She's in love with Luke!"

I can't cope with this anymore.

I need to see Suze.

Thirteen

I'VE AGREED TO meet Suze at Sloane Square for a cup of tea. There's a crowd of tourists milling around when I arrive, and for a moment I can't see her. Then the throng disperses—and there she is, sitting by the fountain, her long blond hair haloed by the sun, and the hugest stomach I've ever seen.

As I see her, I'm all set to rush up to her, exclaim, "Oh God, Suze, it's all a nightmare!" and tell her everything.

But then I stop. She looks like an angel, sitting there. A pregnant angel.

Or the Virgin Mary, perhaps. All serene and lovely and perfect.

And suddenly I feel all messed up in comparison. I'd been planning to unburden the entire situation on Suze, like I always do, and wait for her to think of an answer. But now . . . I just can't. She looks so calm and happy. It would be like dumping toxic waste in some beautiful clear sea.

"Bex! Hi!" As she sees me she stands up, and I feel a fresh shock at how . . . well, how big she looks.

"Suze!" I hurry toward her and give her a huge hug. "You look amazing!"

"I'm feeling great!" says Suze. "How are you? How's the wedding?"

"Oh . . . I'm fine!" I say after a pause. "It's all fine. Come on. Let's go and have some tea."

I'm not going to tell her. This is it. For once in my life, I'm going to sort out my problems on my own.

We go to Oriel and get a table by the window. When the waiter comes, I order hot chocolate, but Suze produces a tea bag and hands it to the waiter.

"Raspberry leaf tea," she explains. "It strengthens the uterus. For labor."

"Right." I nod. "Labor. Of course!"

I feel a little shiver at the base of my spine and smile quickly to cover it.

Secretly, I'm really not at all convinced about this whole giving birth thing. I mean, look at the size of Suze's bump. Look at the size of a full-grown baby. And then tell me *that's* going to fit through . . .

I mean, I know the theory. It's just . . . to be honest, I can't see it working.

"When are you due again?" I say, staring at Suze's stomach.

"Four weeks today!"

"So . . . it's going to grow even bigger?"

"Oh yes!" Suze pats her bump fondly. "Quite a bit, I should think."

"Good," I say weakly, as a waiter puts a cup of hot chocolate in front of me. "Excellent. So . . . how's Tarquin?"

"He's fine!" says Suze. "He's up on Craie at the moment. You know, his Scottish island? They're lambing at the moment, so he thought he'd go and help out. Before the baby comes."

"Oh right. And you didn't go with him?"

"Well, it would have been a bit risky." Suze stirs her raspberry tea thoughtfully. "And the thing is, I'm not *quite* as interested in sheep as he is. I mean, they are really interesting," she adds loyally. "But you know, after you've seen a thousand of them . . ."

"But he'll be back in time, will he?"

"Oh yes. He's really excited! He's been to all the classes and everything!"

God, I can't believe in a few weeks' time Suze will have a baby. I won't even be here.

"Can I touch?" I put my hand gingerly on Suze's stomach. "I can't feel anything."

"That's all right," says Suze. "I expect it's asleep."

"Do you know if it's a boy or a girl?"

"I haven't found out." Suze leans forward earnestly. "But I kind of think it's a girl, because I keep being drawn to all these sweet little dresses in the shops. Like a kind of a craving? And they say in all the books, your body will tell you what it needs. So, you know, maybe that's a sign."

"So, what are you going to call her?"

"We can't decide. It's so hard! You know, you buy these books, and all the names are crap . . ." She takes a sip of tea. "What would you call a baby?"

"Ooh! I don't know! Maybe Lauren, after Ralph Lauren." I think for a few moments. "Or Dolce."

"Dolce Cleath-Stuart," says Suze thoughtfully. "I quite like that! We could call her Dolly for short."

"Or Vera. After Vera Wang."

"*Vera*?" Suze stares at me. "I'm not calling my baby Vera!"

"We're not talking about your baby!" I retort. "We're talking about mine. Vera Lauren Comme des Brandon. I think that's got a really good ring to it."

"Vera Brandon sounds like a character off *Coronation Street*! But I like Dolce. What about if it was a boy?"

"Harvey. Or Barney," I say after a little thought. "Depending on whether it was born in London or New York."

I take another sip of hot chocolate—then look up, to see Suze gazing at me seriously.

"You wouldn't really have a baby in America, would you, Bex?"

"I . . . I don't know. Who can tell? We probably won't have children for years yet!"

"You know, we all really miss you."

"Oh, not you, too, Suze." I give a half-laugh. "I had Mum on at me today to move back to Oxshott."

"Well, it's true! Tarkie was saying the other day, London just isn't the same without you."

"Really?" I gaze at her, feeling ridiculously touched.

"And your mum keeps asking me if I think you'll stay in New York forever . . . you won't, will you?"

"I honestly don't know," I say helplessly. "It all depends on Luke . . . and his business . . ."

"He's not the boss!" says Suze. "You have a say, too. Do you want to stay out there?"

"I don't know." I screw up my face, trying to explain. "Sometimes I think I do. When I'm in New York, it seems like the most important place in the world. My job is fantastic, and the people are fantastic, and it's all wonderful. But when I come home, suddenly I think, Hang on, this is my home. This is where I belong." I pick up a sugar packet and begin to shred it. "I just don't know whether I'm ready to come home yet."

"Oh, come back to England and have a baby!" says Suze wheedlingly. "Then we can be mummies together!"

"Honestly, Suze!" I take a sip of chocolate, rolling my eyes. "Like I'm really ready to have a baby!" I get up to go to the ladies' room before she can say anything else.

On the other hand . . . she has got a point. Why shouldn't I have a baby? Other people do—so why not me? I mean, if I could somehow bypass the actual *having* it bit. Maybe I could have one of those operations where you go to sleep and don't feel anything. And then when I woke up I'd have a baby!

I have a sudden pleasant vision of Suze and me walking up the road together, pushing prams. That might be quite fun, actually. I mean, you can buy loads of gorgeous baby things these days. Like cute little hats, and tiny denim jackets . . . And—yes—doesn't Gucci do a really cool baby sling?

We could have cappuccinos together, and walk round the shops, and . . . I mean, that's basically all mothers do, isn't it? Now that I think about it, I'd be perfect at it!

I must definitely have a chat with Luke.

It's not until we're leaving Oriel that Suze says, "So, Bex, you haven't told me anything about the wedding!"

My stomach gives a little swoop, and I turn my head away, under the pretense of putting on my coat.

I'd kind of managed to forget about the whole wedding issue.

"Yes," I say at last. "Well, it's all . . . um . . . fine!"

I'm not going to bother Suze with my problems. I'm not.

"Was Luke all right about you getting married in England?" She looks anxiously at me. "I mean, it didn't cause a rift between you or anything?"

"No," I say after a pause. "I can honestly say that it didn't."

I hold the door open for her and we walk out into Sloane Square. A column of schoolchildren in corduroy knickerbockers is crowding the pavement, and we stand aside, waiting for them to pass.

"You know, you made the right decision." Suze squeezes my arm. "I was so worried you were going to choose New York. What made you finally decide?"

"Er . . . this and that. You know. So, erm . . . did you read about these new proposals to privatize the water system?"

But Suze ignores me. Honestly, isn't she interested in current affairs?

"So what did Elinor say when you called off the Plaza?"

"She said . . . erm . . . well, she wasn't pleased, of course. She said she was very cross, and . . . er . . ."

"Very cross?" Suze raises her eyebrows. "Is that all? I thought she'd be furious!"

"She *was* furious!" I amend hurriedly. "She was so furious, she . . . burst a blood vessel!"

"She burst a blood vessel?" Suze stares at me. "Where?"

"On her . . . chin."

There's silence. Suze is standing still in the street, her expression slowly changing. "Bex—"

"Let's go and look at baby clothes!" I say hurriedly. "There's that really sweet shop on the King's Road . . ."

"Bex, what's going on?"

"Nothing!"

"There is! I can tell. You're hiding something."

"No, I'm not!"

"You did call the American wedding off, didn't you?"

"I . . ."

"Bex?" Her voice is as stern as I've ever heard it. "Tell me the truth."

Oh God. I can't lie any more.

"I . . . I'm going to," I say weakly.

"You're going to?" Suze's voice rises in dismay. "You're *going to*?"

"Suze—"

"I should have known! I should have guessed! But I just assumed you must have called it off, because your mother kept on organizing her wedding, and no one said anything about New York, and I thought, oh, Bex must have decided to get married at home after all . . ."

"Suze, please. Don't worry about it," I say quickly. "Just stay calm . . . breathe deeply . . ."

"How can I not worry about it!" cries Suze. "How can I not worry? Bex, you promised me you were going to sort this out weeks ago! You promised!"

"I know! And I'm going to. It's just . . . it's been so difficult. Deciding between them. They both seemed so perfect, in completely different ways—"

"Bex, a wedding isn't a handbag!" says Suze incredulously. "You can't decide you'll treat yourself to two!"

"I know! I know! Look, I'm going to sort it out—"

"Why didn't you tell me before?"

"Because you're all lovely and serene and happy!" I wail. "And I didn't want to spoil it with my stupid problems."

"Oh, Bex." Suze gazes at me silently—then puts an arm round me. "So . . . what are you going to do?"

I take a deep breath.

"I'm going to tell Elinor the New York wedding is all off. And I'm going to get married here in England."

"Really? You're completely sure about that?"

"Yes. I'm sure. After seeing Mum and Dad . . . and Mum was so sweet . . . and she has no idea what I've been planning behind her back . . ." I swallow hard. "I mean, this wedding is everything to her. Oh God, Suze, I feel so stupid. I don't know what I was thinking. I don't want to get married at the Plaza. I don't want to get married anywhere else except at home."

"You won't change your mind again?"

"No. Not this time. Honestly, Suze, this is it."

"What about Luke?"

"He doesn't care. He's said all along, it's up to me."

Suze is silent for a moment. Then she reaches in her bag for her mobile phone and thrusts it at me.

"OK. If you're going to do it, do it now. Dial the number."

"I can't. Elinor's in a Swiss clinic. I was planning to write her a letter—"

"No." Suze shakes her head firmly. "Do it now. There must be someone you can call. Call that wedding planner, Robyn, and tell her it's off. Bex, you can't afford to leave it any longer."

"OK," I say, ignoring the leap of apprehension inside me. "OK, I'll do it. I'll . . . I'll call her."

I lift up the phone—then put it down again. Making the decision in my head was one thing. Actually making the call is another. What's Robyn going to say? What's everybody going to say? I wouldn't mind a little time, just to think through exactly what I'm going to tell them . . .

"Go on!" says Suze. "Do it!"

"All right!"

With trembling hands I lift the phone and dial 001 for America—but the display remains blank.

"Oh . . . dear!" I exclaim, trying to sound upset. "I can't get a signal! Oh well, I'll just have to phone later—"

"No you won't! We'll keep walking till you get one. Come on!" Suze starts marching toward the King's Road and I scuttle nervously along behind her.

"Try again," she says as we reach the first pedestrian crossing.

"Nothing," I quaver. God, Suze looks incredible, like the prow of a ship. Her blond hair is streaming out behind her, and her face is flushed with determination. How come she's got so much energy, anyway? I thought pregnant women were supposed to take it easy.

"Try again!" she repeats after every three hundred feet. "Try again! I'm not stopping till you've made that call!"

"There's nothing!"

"Are you sure?"

"Yes!" Frantically I punch at the buttons, trying to trigger a signal. "Look!"

"Well, keep trying! Come on!"

"I am! I am!"

"Oh my God!" Suze gives a sudden shriek and I jump in terror.

"I'm trying! Honestly, Suze, I'm trying as hard as I—"

"No! Look!"

I stop still, and turn round. She's stopped still on the pavement, ten yards behind me, and there's a puddle of water at her feet.

"Suze . . . don't worry," I say awkwardly. "I won't tell anybody."

"No! You don't understand! It's not . . ." She stares at me wildly. "I think my waters have broken!"

"Your what?" I feel a thud of pure fright. "Does that mean . . . Are you going to—"

This can't be happening.

"I don't know." I can see panic rising on Suze's face. "I mean, it's possible . . . But it's four weeks early! It's too soon! Tarkie isn't here, nothing's ready . . . Oh God . . ."

I've never seen Suze look so scared before. A choking dismay creeps over me, and I fight the temptation to burst into tears. What have I done now? As well as everything else, I've sent my best friend into premature labor.

"Suze, I'm so sorry," I gulp.

"It's not your fault! Don't be stupid!"

"It is! You were so happy and serene, and then you saw me. I should just stay away from pregnant people—"

"I'll have to go to the hospital." Suze's face is pale. "They said to come in if this happened."

"Well, let's go! Come on!"

"But I haven't got my bag, or anything. There's loads of stuff I need to take . . ." She bites her lip worriedly. "Shall I go home first?"

"You haven't got time for that!" I say in a panic. "What do you need?"

"Baby clothes . . . nappies . . . stuff like that . . ."

"Well, where do you . . ." I look around helplessly, then, with a sudden surge of relief, spot the sign for Peter Jones.

"OK," I say, and grab her arm. "Come on."

As soon as we get into Peter Jones, I look around for an assistant. And thank goodness, here comes one, a nice middle-aged lady with red lipstick and gold spectacles on a chain.

"My friend needs an ambulance," I gasp.

"A taxi will be fine, honestly," says Suze. "It's just that my waters have broken. So I should probably get to the hospital."

"Goodness!" says the lady. "Come and sit down, dear, and I'll call a taxi for you . . ."

We sit Suze down on a chair by a checkout desk, and a junior assistant brings her a glass of water.

"Right," I say. "Tell me what you need."

"I can't remember exactly." Suze looks anxious. "We were given a list . . . Maybe they'll know in the baby department."

"Will you be OK if I leave you?"

"I'll be fine! Contractions haven't even started."

"You're sure?" I glance nervously at her stomach.

"Bex, just go!"

Honestly. Why on earth do they put baby departments so far away from the main entrances of shops? I mean, what's the point of all these stupid floors of clothes and makeup and bags, which no one's interested in? After sprinting up and down about six escalators, at last I find it, and come to a standstill, panting slightly.

For a moment I look around, dazed by all the names of things I've never heard of.

Reception blanket?

Anticolic teats?

Oh, sod it. I'll just buy everything. I quickly head for the nearest display and start grabbing things indiscriminately. Sleeping suits, tiny socks, a hat . . . a teddy, a cot blanket . . . what else? A Moses basket . . . nappies . . . little glove puppets in case the baby gets bored . . . a really cute little Christian Dior jacket . . . gosh, I wonder if they do that in grown-up sizes too . . .

I shove the lot onto the checkout desk and whip out my Visa card.

"It's for my friend," I explain breathlessly. "She's just gone into labor. Is this everything she needs?"

"I wouldn't know, I'm afraid, dear," says the assistant, scanning a baby bath thermometer.

"I've got a list here," says a nearby woman in maternity dungarees and Birkenstocks. "This is what the National Childbirth Trust recommends you take in."

"Oh, thanks!"

She hands a piece of paper to me and I scan the endless typed list with growing dismay. I thought I'd done so well—but I haven't got half the stuff they say here. And if I miss anything, it'll turn out to be completely vital, and Suze's whole birth experience will be ruined and I'll never forgive myself.

Loose T-shirt . . . Scented candles . . . Plant sprayer . . .

Is this the right list?

"Plant sprayer?" I say bewilderedly.

"To spray the laboring woman's face," explains the woman in dungarees. "Hospital rooms get very hot."

"You'll want the home department for that," puts in the assistant.

"Oh, right. Thanks."

Tape recorder . . . soothing tapes . . . inflatable ball . . .

"Inflatable ball? Won't the baby be a bit young to play with a ball?"

"It's for the mother to lean on," says the woman kindly. "To alleviate the waves of pain. Alternatively she could use a large bean bag."

Waves of pain? Oh God. The thought of Suze in pain makes me feel all wobbly inside.

"I'll get a ball *and* a bean bag," I say hurriedly. "And maybe some aspirin. Extra-strong."

At last I stagger back to the ground floor, red in the face and panting. I just hope I've got all this right. I couldn't find an inflatable ball in the whole of the stupid shop—so in the end I grabbed an inflatable canoe instead, and made the man pump it up for me. I've got it wedged under one arm now, with a Teletubbies bean bag and a Moses basket stuffed under the other, and about six full carrier bags dangling from my wrists.

I glance at my watch—and to my utter horror I see that I've already been twenty-five minutes. I'm half expecting to see Suze sitting on the chair holding a baby in her arms.

But there she is, still on the chair, wincing slightly.

"Bex. There you are! I think my contractions have started."

"Sorry I took so long," I gasp. "I just wanted to get everything you might need." A box of Scrabble falls out of one of the bags onto the ground, and I bend to pick it up. "That's for when you have an epidural," I explain.

"The taxi's here," interrupts the lady with gold spectacles. "Do you need some help with all that?"

As we make our way out to the chugging taxi, Suze is staring at my load in utter bewilderment.

"Bex . . . why did you buy an inflatable canoe?"

"It's for you to lie on. Or something."

"And a watering can?"

"I couldn't find a plant sprayer." Breathlessly I start shoving bags into the taxi.

"But why do I need a plant sprayer?"

"Look, it wasn't my idea, OK?" I say defensively. "Come on, let's go!"

Somehow we cram everything into the taxi. A canoe paddle falls out as we close the door, but I don't bother trying to get it. I mean, it's not like Suze is having a water birth.

"Tarkie's business manager is trying to reach him," says Suze as we zoom along the King's Road. "But even if he gets on a plane straight away, he's going to miss it."

"He might not!" I say encouragingly. "You never know!"

"He will." To my dismay I can hear her voice starting to wobble. "He'll miss the birth of his first child. After waiting all this time. And doing the classes, and everything. He was really good at panting. The teacher made him do it in front of everyone else, he was so good."

"Oh, Suze." I feel like crying. "Maybe you'll take hours and hours, and he'll still make it."

"You'll stay with me, won't you?" She suddenly turns in her seat. "You won't leave me there?"

"Of course not!" I say, appalled. "I'll stay with you all the time, Suze." I hold both her hands tight. "We'll do it together."

"Do you know anything at all about giving birth?"

"Erm . . . yes," I lie. "Loads!"

"Like what?"

"Like . . . um . . . you need hot towels . . . and . . ." Suddenly I spot a baby milk carton poking out of one of the bags. ". . . and many babies require a vitamin K injection after the birth."

Suze stares at me, impressed. "Wow. How did you know that?"

"I just know stuff," I say, pushing the carton out of sight with my foot. "You see? It'll be fine!"

OK, I can do this. I can help Suze. I just have to stay cool and calm and not panic.

I mean, millions of people give birth every day, don't they? It's probably one of those things that *sounds* really scary but is quite easy when it comes to it. Like a driving test.

"Oh God." Suze's face suddenly contorts. "Here it comes again."

"OK! Hang on!" In a flurry of alarm I scrabble inside one of the plastic bags. "Here you are!"

Suze opens her eyes dazedly as I produce a smart cellophaned box. "Bex—why are you giving me perfume?"

"They said get jasmine oil to help ease the pain," I say breathlessly. "But I couldn't find any, so I got Romance by Ralph Lauren instead. It's got jasmine overtones." I rip off the packaging and squirt it at her hopefully. "Does that help?"

"Not really," says Suze. "But it's a nice smell."

"It is, isn't it?" I say, pleased. "And because I spent over thirty quid, I got a free beauty bag with exfoliating body mitt and—"

"St. Christopher's Hospital," says the driver suddenly, drawing up in front of a large redbrick building. We both stiffen in alarm and look at each other.

"OK," I say. "Keep calm, Suze. Don't panic. Just . . . wait there."

I open the taxi door, sprint through an entrance marked "Maternity," and find myself in a reception area with blue upholstered chairs. A couple of women in dressing gowns look up from the magazines they're reading, but other than that, there are no signs of life.

For God's sake. Where is everybody?

"My friend's having a baby!" I yell. "Quick, everyone! Get a stretcher! Get a midwife!"

"Are you all right?" says a woman in white uniform, appearing out of nowhere. "I'm a midwife. What's the problem?"

"My friend's in labor! She needs help immediately!"

"Where is she?"

"I'm here," says Suze, struggling in through the door with three bags under one arm.

"Suze!" I say in horror. "Don't move. You should be lying down! She needs drugs," I say to the nurse. "She needs an epidural and general anesthetic and some laughing gas stuff, and . . . basically, whatever you've got . . ."

"I'm fine," says Suze. "Really."

"OK," says the midwife. "Let's just get you settled into a room. Then we can examine you and take a few details . . ."

"I'll get the rest of the stuff," I say, and start heading back toward the doors. "Suze, don't worry, I'll be back. Go with the midwife and I'll come and find you . . ."

"Wait," says Suze urgently, suddenly turning round. "Wait, Bex!"

"What?"

"You never made that call. You never canceled the New York wedding."

"I'll make it later," I say. "Go on. Go with the midwife."

"Make it now."

"*Now?*" I stare at her.

"If you don't make it now, you'll never make it! I know you, Bex."

"Suze, don't be stupid! You're about to have a baby! Let's get our priorities right, shall we?"

"I'll have the baby when you've made the call!" says Suze obstinately. "Oh!" Her face suddenly twists. "It's starting again."

"OK," says the midwife calmly. "Now, breathe . . . try to relax . . ."

"I can't relax! Not until she cancels the wedding! Otherwise she'll just put it off again! I know her!"

"I won't!"

"You will, Bex! You've already dithered for months!"

"Is he a bad sort, then?" says the midwife. "You should listen to your friend," she adds to me. "She sounds like she knows what she's talking about."

"Friends can always tell the wrong 'uns," agrees the woman in the pink dressing gown.

"He's not a wrong 'un!" I retort indignantly. "Suze, please! Calm down! Go with the nurse! Get some drugs!"

"Make the call," she replies, her face contorted. "Then I'll go." She looks up. "Go on! Make the call!"

"If you want this baby born safely," says the midwife to me, "I'd make the call."

"Make the call, love!" chimes in the woman in the pink dressing gown.

"OK! OK!" I scrabble for the mobile phone and punch in the number. "I'm calling. Now go, Suze!"

"Not until I've heard you say the words!"

"Breathe *through* the pain . . ."

"Hello!" chirps Robyn in my ear. "Is that wedding bells I hear?"

"There's no one there," I say, looking up.

"Then leave a message," says Suze through gritted teeth.

"Another deep breath now . . ."

"Your call is *so* important to me . . ."

"Go on, Bex!"

"All right! Here goes." I take a deep breath as the bleep sounds. "Robyn, this is Becky Bloomwood here . . . and I'm canceling the wedding. Repeat, I'm canceling the wedding. I'm very sorry for all the inconvenience this is going to cause. I know what a lot you've put into it and I can only guess at how angry Elinor will be . . ." I swallow. "But I've made my final decision—and it's that I want to get married at home in England. If you want to talk to me about this, leave a message at my home and I'll call you back. Otherwise, I guess this is good-bye. And . . . thanks. It was fun while it lasted."

I click off the phone and stare at it, silent in my hand.

I've done it.

"Well done," says the midwife to Suze. "That was a tough one!"

"Well done, Bex," says Suze, pink in the face. She squeezes my hand and gives me a tiny smile. "You've done the right thing." She looks at the midwife. "OK. Let's go."

"I'll just go and . . . get the rest of the stuff," I say, and walk slowly toward the double doors leading out of the hospital.

As I step out into the fresh air I can't help giving a little shiver. So that's it. No more Plaza wedding. No more enchanted forest. No more magical cake. No more fantasy.

I can't quite believe it's all gone.

But then . . . if I'm really honest, it only ever was a fantasy, wasn't it? It never quite felt like real life.

This is real life, right here.

For a few moments I'm silent, letting my thoughts drift, until the sound of an ambulance siren brings me back to the present. Hastily I unload the taxi, pay the driver, then stare at the mound of stuff, wondering how on earth I'm going to get it all inside. And whether I really did need to buy a collapsible playpen.

"Are you Becky Bloomwood?" A voice interrupts my thoughts and I look up, to see a young midwife standing at the door.

"Yes!" I feel a tremor of alarm. "Is Suze all right?"

"She's fine, but her contractions are intensifying now, and we're still waiting for the anesthetist to arrive . . . and she's saying she'd like to try using"—she looks at me puzzledly—"is it . . . a canoe?"

Oh my God.

Oh my God.

I can't even begin to . . . to . . .

It's seven o'clock in the evening, and I'm completely shattered. I have never seen anything like that in my life. I had no idea it would be so—

That Suze would be so—

It took six hours altogether, which is apparently really quick. Well, all I can say is, I wouldn't like to be one of the slow ones.

I can't believe it. Suze has got a baby boy. A tiny, pink, snuffly baby boy. One hour old.

He's been weighed and measured, and apparently he's a really healthy size, considering he came early. A nurse has dressed him in the most gorgeous white and blue baby suit and a little white blanket, and now he's lying in Suze's arms, all curled up and scrumpled, with tufts of dark hair sticking out over his ears. The baby that Suze and Tarquin made. I almost want to cry . . . except I'm so elated. It's the weirdest feeling.

I meet Suze's eyes, and she beams euphorically. She's been beaming ever since he was born, and I'm secretly wondering if they gave her a bit too much laughing gas.

"Isn't he just perfect?"

"He's perfect." I touch his tiny fingernail. To think that's been growing inside Suze, all this time.

"Would you like a cup of tea?" says a nurse, coming into the warm, bright room. "You must be exhausted."

"Thanks very much," I say gratefully, stretching out a hand.

"I meant Mum," says the nurse, giving me an odd look.

"Oh," I say flusteredly. "Yes, of course. Sorry."

"It's all right," says Suze. "Give it to Bex. She deserves it." She gives me an abashed smile. "Sorry I got angry with you."

"That's all right." I bite my lip. "Sorry I kept saying, 'Does it really hurt?'"

"No, you were great. Seriously, Bex. I couldn't have done it without you."

"Some flowers have arrived," says a midwife, coming in. "And we've had a message from your husband. He's stuck on the island for the moment because of bad weather, but he'll be here as soon as he can."

"Thanks," says Suze, managing a smile. "That's great."

But when the midwife goes out again, her lips begin to tremble. "Bex, what am I going to do if Tarkie can't get back? Mummy's in Ulan Bator, and Daddy doesn't know one end of a baby from the other . . . I'm going to be all on my own . . ."

"No, you aren't!" I quickly put an arm round her. "I'll look after you!"

"But don't you have to go back to America?"

"I don't have to go anywhere. I'll change my flight and take more vacation days." I give her a tight hug. "I'm staying here with you for as long as you need me, Suze, and that's the end of it."

"What about the wedding?"

"I don't need to worry about the wedding any more. Suze, I'm staying with you, and that's that."

"Really?" Suze's chin quivers. "Thanks, Bex." She shifts the baby cautiously in her arms, and he gives a little snuffle. "Do you . . . know anything about babies?"

"You don't have to know anything!" I say confidently. "You just have to feed them and dress them up in nice clothes and wheel them around the shops."

"I'm not sure—"

"And anyway, just look at little Armani." I reach into the white bundle of blanket and touch the baby's cheek fondly.

"We're *not* naming him Armani!"

"Well, whatever. He's an angel! He must be what they call an 'easy' baby."

"He is good, isn't he?" says Suze, pleased. "He hasn't even cried once!"

"Honestly, Suze, don't worry." I take a sip of tea and smile at her. "It'll be a blast!"

Finerman Wallstein
Attorneys at Law
Finerman House
1398 Avenue of the Americas
New York, NY 10105

Miss Rebecca Bloomwood
251 W. 11th Street, Apt. B
New York, NY 10014

May 6, 2002

Dear Miss Bloomwood:

Thank you for your message of April 30, and I confirm that under the fourth clause I have added the section "(f) I give and bequeath to my gorgeous godson Ernest, the sum of $1,000."

May I draw your attention to the fact that this is the seventh amendment you have made to your will since drawing it up a month ago?

With kind regards,

Jane Cardozo

Fourteen

I STUMBLE UP THE steps of our building. Swaying slightly, I reach for my key—and, after three goes, manage to get it in the lock.

Home again.

Quiet again.

"Becky? Is that you?" I hear Danny's voice from above and the sound of his footsteps on the stairs.

I stare dazedly up, unable to focus. I feel like I've run a marathon. No, make that six marathons. The last two weeks has been a blurry jumble of nights and days all run into one. Just me and Suze, and baby Ernest. And the crying.

Don't get me wrong, I adore little Ernie. I mean, I'm going to be his godmother, and everything.

But . . . God. That *scream* of his . . .

I just had no idea having a baby was like that. I thought it would be *fun*.

I didn't realize Suze would have to feed him every single hour. I didn't realize he would refuse to go to sleep. Or that he would hate his crib. I mean, it came from the Conran Shop! All lovely beech, with gorgeous white blankets. You'd think he would have loved it! But when we put him in it, all he did was thrash about, going "Waaah!"

Then I tried to take him shopping—and when we started out, it was fine. People were smiling at the pram, and smiling at me, and I was starting to feel quite proud of myself. But then we went into Karen Millen, and I was halfway into a pair of leather trousers when he started to yell. Not a cute little whimper. Not a plaintive little wail. A full-throated, piercing "This Woman Has Kidnapped Me, Call the Cops" scream.

I didn't have any bottles or nappies or anything, and I had to run down the Fulham Road, and by the time I got home, I was red in the face and panting and Suze was crying and Ernest was looking at me like I was a mass murderer or something.

And then, even after he'd been fed, he screamed and screamed all evening . . .

"Jesus!" says Danny, arriving downstairs in the hall. "What happened to you?"

I glance in the mirror and feel a dart of shock. I look pale with exhaustion, my hair is lank and my eyes are drained. Tarquin got home three days ago, and he did do his fair share—but that didn't mean I got any sleep. And it didn't help that when I finally got on the plane to fly home, I was seated next to a woman with six-month-old twins.

"My friend Suze had a baby," I say blearily. "And her husband was stuck on an island, so I helped out for a bit . . ."

"Luke said you were on vacation," says Danny, staring at me in horror. "He said you were taking a rest!"

"Luke . . . has no idea."

Every time Luke phoned, I was either changing a nappy, comforting a wailing Ernie, comforting an exhausted Suze—or flat-out asleep. We did have one brief, disjointed conversation, but in the end Luke suggested I go and lie down, as I wasn't making much sense.

Other than that, I haven't spoken to anyone. Mum called to let me know that Robyn had left a message at the house that I should call her urgently. And I did mean to call back. But every time I had a spare five minutes to myself . . . somehow I just couldn't face it. I've no idea what's been going on; what kind of arguments and fall-out there's been. I know Elinor must be furious. I know there's probably the mother of all rows waiting for me.

But . . . I just don't care. All I care about right now is getting into bed.

"Hey, a bunch of boxes arrived from QVC." Danny looks at me curiously. "Did you order a set of Marie Osmond dolls?"

"I don't know," I say blankly. "I expect so. I ordered pretty much everything they had."

I have a dim memory of myself at three in the morning, rocking Ernest on my lap so Suze could have a sleep, staring groggily at the screen.

"Do you know how terrible the telly is in Britain at three in the morning?" I rub my dry cheeks. "And there's no point watching a film, because the minute it gets to a good bit, the baby cries and you have to leap up and start joggling him around, singing 'Old Macdonald Had a Farm, Ee-I Ee-I Oh . . .' and he still doesn't stop crying. So you have to go into 'Oh what a beautiful mooorr-rn-ing . . .' but that doesn't work either . . ."

"Right," says Danny, backing away. "I'll . . . take your word for it. Becky, I think you need a nap."

"Yes. So do I. See you later."

I stumble into the apartment, shove all the post on the sofa, and head for the bedroom, as single-minded as a junkie craving a hit.

Sleep. I need sleep . . .

A light is blinking on our message machine and as I lie down, I automatically reach out and press the button.

"Hi, Becky! Robyn here. Just to say the meeting with Sheldon Lloyd to discuss table centerpieces has been changed to next Tuesday the twenty-first, at two-thirty. Byee!"

I have just enough time to think "That's odd," before my head hits the pillow and I pass out into a deep, dreamless sleep.

Eight hours later I wake up and sit bolt upright.

What was that?

I reach out to the machine and press the "Repeat" button. Robyn's voice chirps exactly the same message again, and the computer display informs me it was left yesterday.

But . . . that doesn't make any sense. The New York wedding's off.

I look disorientedly around the dim apartment. My body clock's so screwed up, it could be any time at all. I pad into the kitchen for a glass of water and look blearily out of the window at the mural of dancers on the building opposite.

I canceled the wedding. There were witnesses. Why is Robyn still organizing table centerpieces? I mean, it wasn't as though I was vague about it.

What's happened?

I drink my water, pour another glass, and go into the living room. It's 4 P.M. according to the VCR clock, so there's still time to call her. Find out what's going on.

"Hello! Wedding Events Ltd.!" says a girl I don't recognize. "How may I help you?"

"Hi! Excuse me, this is Becky Bloomwood. You're . . . you were organizing a wedding for me?"

"Oh, hi, Becky! I'm Kirsten, Robyn's assistant. Can I just say that I thought your *Sleeping Beauty* concept was totally inspired? I told all my friends about it, and they were all, like, 'I love *Sleeping Beauty*! That's what I'm going to do when *I* get married.' "

"Oh. Er . . . thanks. Listen, Kirsten, this might seem like a strange question . . ."

How am I going to put this? I can't say, Is my wedding still on?

"Is my . . . wedding still on?"

"I certainly hope so!" says Kirsten with a laugh. "Unless you've had a row with Luke!" Her tone suddenly changes. "*Have* you had a row with Luke? Because we have a procedure if that happens . . ."

"No! I haven't! It's just . . . didn't you get my message?"

"Which message was that?" says Kirsten brightly.

"The message I left about two weeks ago!"

"Oh, I'm sorry. What with the flood . . ."

"Flood?" I stare at the phone in dismay. "You had a *flood*?"

"I was sure Robyn had called you in England to let you know! It's OK, nobody was drowned. We just had to evacuate the office for a few days, and some of the telecoms were affected . . . plus unfortunately an antique ring cushion belonging to one of our clients was ruined . . ."

"So you *didn't* get the message?"

"Was it the one about the hors d'oeuvres?" says Kirsten thoughtfully.

I swallow several times, feeling almost light-headed.

"Becky, Robyn's just stepped in," Kirsten's saying, "if you'd like to speak to her . . ."

No way. I'm not trusting the phone anymore.

"Can you tell her," I say, trying to keep calm, "that I'm coming into the office. Tell her to wait. I'll be there as soon as I can."

"Is it urgent?"

"Yes. It's pretty urgent."

Robyn's offices are in a plushy building, right up on Ninety-sixth Street. As I knock on the door, I can hear her gurgling laugh, and as I cautiously open the door, I see her sitting at her desk, champagne glass in one hand, telephone in the other, and an open box of chocolates on the desk.

"Becky!" she says. "Come in! I won't be a second! Jennifer, I think we should go with the devore satin. Yes? OK. See you soon." She puts down the phone and beams at me. "Becky, sweetheart. How are you? How was England?"

"Fine, thanks. Robyn—"

"I have just been to a delightful thank-you lunch given to me by Mrs. Herman Winkler at the Carlton. Now, that was a fabulous wedding. The groom gave the bride a schnauzer puppy at the altar! So adorable . . ." Her brow wrinkles. "Where was I going with this? Oh yes! You know what? Her daughter and new son-in-law just left for England on their honeymoon! I said to her, perhaps they'll bump into Becky Bloomwood!"

"Robyn, I need to talk to you."

"Absolutely. If it's about the dessert flatware, I've spoken to the Plaza—"

"It's not about the flatware!" I cry. "Robyn, listen! While I was England, I canceled the wedding. I left a message! But you didn't get it."

There's silence in the plushy room. Then Robyn's face creases up into laughter.

"Ha-ha-ha! Becky, you're priceless! Isn't she priceless, Kirsten?"

"Robyn, I'm serious. I want to call the whole thing off. I want to get married in England. My mum's organizing a wedding, it's all arranged—"

"Can you imagine if you did that?" says Robyn with a gurgle. "Well, of course you couldn't, because of the prenup. If you canceled now, you'd be in for a lot of money!" She laughs gaily. "Would you like some champagne?"

I stare at her, momentarily halted. "What do you mean, the prenup?"

"The contract you signed, sweetheart." She hands me a glass of champagne, and my fingers automatically close round it.

"But . . . but Luke didn't sign it. He said it wasn't valid if he didn't sign—"

"Not between you and Luke! Between you and me! Or, rather, Wedding Events Ltd."

"What?" I swallow. "Robyn, what are you talking about? I never signed anything."

"Of course you did! All my brides do! I gave it to Elinor to pass along to you, and she returned it to me . . . I have a copy of it somewhere!" She takes a sip of champagne, swivels on her chair, and reaches into an elegant wooden filing cabinet.

"Here we are!" She hands me a photocopy of a document. "Of course, the original is with my lawyer . . ."

I stare at the page, my heart pounding. It's a typed sheet, headed "Terms of Agreement." I look straight down to the dotted line at the bottom—and there's my signature.

My mind zooms back to that dark, rainy night. Sitting in Elinor's apartment. Indignantly signing every single sheet in front of me. Not bothering to read the words above.

Oh God. What have I done?

Feverishly I start to scan the contract, only half taking in the legal phrases.

> *"The Organizer shall prepare full plans . . . time frame to be mutually agreed . . . the Client shall be consulted on all matters . . . liaise with service providers . . . budget shall be agreed . . . final decisions shall rest with the Client . . . any breach or cancellation for any reason whatsoever . . . reimbursement . . . 30 days . . . full and final payment . . . Furthermore . . ."*

As I read the next words, slugs are crawling up and down my back.

> *"Furthermore, in the case of cancellation, should the Client marry within one year of the date of cancellation, the Client will be liable to a penalty of $100,000, payable to Wedding Events Ltd."*

A hundred-thousand-dollar penalty.

And I've signed it.

"A hundred thousand dollars?" I say at last. "That . . . that seems a lot."

"That's only for the silly girls who pretend to cancel and then get married anyway," says Robyn cheerily.

"But why—"

"Becky, if I plan a wedding, then I want that wedding to happen. We've had girls pull out before." Her voice suddenly hardens. "Girls who decided to go their own way. Girls who decided to use my ideas, my contacts. Girls who thought they could exploit my expertise and get away with it." She leans forward with glittering eyes, and I shrink back fearfully.

"Becky, you don't want to be those girls."

She's crazy. The wedding planner's crazy.

"G-good idea," I say quickly. "You have to protect yourself!"

"Of course, Elinor could have signed it herself—but we agreed, this way, she's protecting her investment too!" Robyn beams at me. "It's a neat arrangement."

"Very clever!" I give a shrill laugh and take a slug of champagne.

What am I going to do? There must be some way out of this. There *must* be. People can't force other people to get married. It's not ethical.

"Cheer up, Becky!" Robyn snaps back into cheery-chirrupy mood. "Everything's under control. We've been taking care of everything while you were in Britain. The invitations are being written as we speak."

"Invitations?" I feel a fresh shock. "But they can't be. We haven't done a guest list yet."

"Yes you have, silly girl! What's this?"

She presses a couple of buttons on her computer and a list pops up, and I stare at it, my mouth open. Familiar names and addresses are scrolling past on the screen, one after another. Names of my cousins. Names of my old school friends. With a sudden lurch I spot "Janice and Martin Webster, The Oaks, 41 Elton Road, Oxshott."

How does Robyn know about Janice and Martin? I feel as though I've stumbled into some arch-villainess's lair. Any minute a panel will slide back and I'll see Mum and Dad tied to a chair with gags in their mouths.

"Where . . . where did you get those names?" I ask, trying to make it sound like a lighthearted inquiry.

"Luke gave us a list! I was pressuring him about it, so he had a look around your apartment. He said he found it hidden under the bed, or someplace odd. I said, that's probably the safest place to put it!"

She produces a piece of paper, and my eyes focus on it in disbelief.

Mum's handwriting.

The guest list she faxed over to us, weeks ago. The names and addresses of all the family friends and relations who are being invited to the wedding. The wedding at home.

Robyn's inviting all the same people as Mum.

"Have the invitations . . . gone out yet?" I say in a voice I don't quite recognize.

"Well, no." Robyn wags her finger at me. "Elinor's all went out last week. But we got your guest list so late, I'm afraid yours are still with the calligrapher! She's going to mail them off just as soon as she's finished . . ."

"Stop her," I say desperately. "You have to stop her!"

"What?" Robyn looks at me in surprise, and I'm aware of Kirsten lifting her head in interest. "Why, sweetheart?"

"I . . . I have to post the invitations myself," I say. "It's a . . . a family tradition. The bride always, er . . . posts her own invitations."

I rub my hot face, trying to keep cool. Across the room, I can see Kirsten staring curiously at me. They probably think I'm a complete control freak now. But I don't care. I have to stop those invitations from going out.

"How unusual!" says Robyn. "I never heard that custom before!"

"Are you saying I'm making it up?"

"No! Of course not! I'll let Judith know," says Robyn, picking up the phone and flicking her Rolodex, and I subside, breathing hard.

My head is spinning. Too much is happening. While I've been closeted with Suze and Ernie, everything has been steaming ahead without me realizing it, and now I've completely lost control of the situation. It's like this wedding is some big white horse that was trotting along quite nicely but has suddenly reared up and galloped off into the distance without me.

Robyn wouldn't *really* sue me. Would she?

"Hi, Judith? Yes, it's Robyn. Have you . . . you have? Well, that was quick work!" Robyn looks up. "You won't believe this, but she's already finished them!"

"What?" I look up in horror.

"She's at the mailbox already! Isn't that a—"

"Well, stop her!" I shriek. "Stop her!"

"Judith," says Robyn urgently. "Judith, stop. The bride is very particular. She wants to mail the invitations herself. Some family tradition," she says in a lower tone. "British. Yes. No, I don't know either."

She looks up with a careful smile, as though I'm a tricky three-year-old.

"Becky, I'm afraid a few already went into the mailbox. But you'll get to mail all the rest!"

"A few?" I say agitatedly. "How many?"

"How many, Judith?" says Robyn, then turns to me. "She thinks three."

"Three? Well . . . can she reach in and get them back?"

"I don't think so."

"Couldn't she find a . . . a stick or something . . ."

Robyn stares at me silently for a second, then turns to the phone.

"Judith, let me get the location of that mailbox." She scribbles on a piece of paper, then looks up. "You know what, Becky, I think the best thing is if you go down there, and just . . . do whatever you have to do . . ."

"OK. I will. Thanks."

As I put my coat on, I can see Robyn and Kirsten exchanging glances.

"You know, Becky, you might want to chill out a little," says Robyn. "Everything's under control. There's nothing for you to worry about!" She leans forward cozily. "As I often say to my brides, when they get a little agitated . . . it's just a wedding!"

I can't even bring myself to reply.

The mailbox is off the corner of Ninety-third and Lexington. As I turn into the street I can see a woman who must be Judith, dressed in a dark raincoat, leaning against the side of a building. As I hurry toward her, I see her look at her watch, give an impatient shrug, and head toward the mailbox, a stack of envelopes in her hand.

"Stop!" I yell, increasing my pace to a sprint. "Don't post those!" I arrive by her side, panting so hard I can barely speak.

"Give me those invitations," I manage to gasp. "I'm the bride. Becky Bloomwood."

"Here you are!" says Judith. "A few already went in. But you know, no one said anything to me about not mailing them," she adds defensively.

"I know. I'm sorry."

"If Robyn hadn't called when she did . . . they would've been gone. All of them!"

"I . . . I appreciate that."

I flip through the thick taupe envelopes, feeling slightly shaky as I see all the names on Mum's list, beautifully written out in Gothic script.

"So are you going to mail them?"

"Of course I am." Suddenly I realize Judith's waiting for me to do it. "But I don't want to be watched," I add quickly. "It's a very private matter. I have to . . . say a poem and kiss each one . . ."

"Fine," says Judith, rolling her eyes. "Whatever."

She walks off toward the corner, and I stand as still as a rock until she's vanished from sight. Then, clutching the pile of invitations to my chest, I hurry to the corner, raise my hand, and hail a cab to take me home.

Luke is still out when I arrive, and the apartment is as dim and silent as it was when I left it. My suitcase is open on the floor—and as I walk in I can see inside it the pile of invitations to the Oxshott wedding that Mum gave me to pass on to Elinor.

I pick up the second pile of invitations and look from one to the other. One pile of white envelopes. One pile of taupe envelopes. Two weddings. On the same day. In less than six weeks.

If I do one, Mum will never speak to me again.

If I do the other, I get sued for $100,000.

OK, just . . . keep calm. Think logically. There has to be a way out of this. There *has* to be. As long as I keep my head and don't get into a—

Suddenly I hear the sound of the front door opening. "Becky?" comes Luke's voice. "Is that you?"

Fuck.

In a complete panic, I open the cocktail cabinet, shove both lots of invitations inside, slam the door, and whip round breathlessly just as Luke comes in.

"Sweetheart!" His whole face lights up and he throws his briefcase down. "You're back! I missed you." He gives me a huge hug—then draws back and looks anxiously at me. "Becky? Is everything all right?"

"I'm fine!" I say brightly. "Honestly, everything's great! I'm just tired."

"You look wiped out. I'll make some tea, and you can tell me all about Suze."

He goes out of the room and I collapse weakly on the sofa.

What the hell am I going to do now?

THE PINES
43 Elton Road
Oxshott
Surrey

FAX MESSAGE

TO BECKY BLOOMWOOD

FROM MUM

20 May 2002

Becky, love, I don't want to worry you. But it looks like that
deranged woman you were telling us about has gone one step
further and actually printed invitations! Auntie Irene phoned up
today and told us she'd got some peculiar invitation through the
post, for the Plaza Hotel, just like you said. Apparently it was
all bronze and beige, very odd and not like a proper wedding
invitation at all!

The best thing is to ignore these people, so I told her to put it
straight in the bin and not worry about it. And you must do the
same, darling. But I just thought I should let you know.

Much love and talk soon,

Mum xxxxxxxxx

Finerman Wallstein
Attorneys at Law
Finerman House
1398 Avenue of the Americas
New York, NY 10105

Miss Rebecca Bloomwood
251 W. 11th Street, Apt. B
New York, NY 10014

May 21, 2002

INVOICE no. 10956

April 3rd	Receiving instructions to redraft your will	$150
April 6th	Receiving further instructions to redraft your will	$150
April 11th	Receiving instructions for further amendments to your will	$150
April 17th	Receiving further instructions to redraft your will	$150
April 19th	Receiving instructions for further amendments to your will	$150
April 24th	Receiving further instructions to redraft your will	$150
April 30th	Receiving instructions for further amendments to your will	$150

Total: **$1,050**

With thanks

Fifteen

OK. THE REALLY vital thing is to keep a sense of proportion. I mean, let's face it, every wedding has the odd glitch. You can't expect the whole process to go smoothly. I've just bought a new book, called *The Realistic Bride,* which I'm finding very comforting at the moment. It has a huge chapter all about wedding hitches, and it says: "No matter how insurmountable the problem seems, there will always be a solution! So don't worry!"

So the example they give is of a bride who loses her satin shoe on the way to the reception. Not one who has arranged two different weddings on the same day on different continents, is hiding half the invitations in a cocktail cabinet, and has discovered her wedding planner is a litigious nutcase.

But you know, I'm sure the principle's broadly the same.

I've been back in New York for a week now, and during that time I've been to see about seventeen different lawyers about Robyn's contract. All of them have looked at it carefully, told me they're afraid it's watertight, and advised me in the future to read all documentation before signing it.

Actually, that's not quite true. One lawyer just said, "Sorry, miss, there's nothing we can do," as soon as I mentioned that the contract was with Robyn de Bendern. Another said, "Girl, you're in trouble," and put the phone down.

I can't believe there isn't a way out, though. As a last resort, I've sent it off to Garson Low, the most expensive lawyer in Manhattan. I read about him in *People* magazine, and it said he has the sharpest mind in the legal world. It said he can find a loophole in a piece of concrete. So I'm kind of pinning all my hopes on him—and meanwhile, trying very hard to act normally and not crumple into a gibbering wreck.

"I'm having lunch with Michael today," says Luke, coming into the kitchen with a couple of boxes in his arms. "He seems to have settled into his new place well."

Michael's taken the plunge and moved to New York, which is fantastic for us. He's working part time as a consultant at Brandon Communications, and the rest of the time, as he put it, he's "reclaiming his life." He's taken up painting, and has joined a group that power-walks in Central Park, and last time we saw him he was talking about taking a course in Italian cookery.

"That's great!" I say.

"He said we must come over soon . . ." He peers at me. "Becky, are you all right?"

Abruptly I realize I'm drumming a pencil so hard it's making indentations in the kitchen table.

"I'm absolutely fine," I say with an overbright smile. "Why wouldn't I be?"

I haven't said a word about anything to Luke. In *The Realistic Bride* it says the way to stop your fiancé from getting bored with wedding details is to feed them to him on a need-to-know basis.

I don't feel Luke needs to know anything just yet.

"A couple more wedding presents," he says. He dumps the boxes on the counter and grins at me. "It's getting closer, isn't it?"

"Yes! Yes it is!" I attempt a laugh, not very successfully.

"Another toaster . . . this time from Bloomingdale's." He frowns. "Becky, exactly how many wedding lists have we got?"

"I don't know. A few."

"I thought the whole point of a wedding list was that we *didn't* end up with seven toasters."

"We haven't got seven toasters!" I point to the box. "This is a *brioche grill.*"

"And we also have . . . a Gucci handbag." He raises his eyebrows quizzically at me. "A Gucci handbag for a wedding present?"

"It's his-and-hers luggage!" I say defensively. "I put down a briefcase for you . . ."

"Which no one's bought for me."

"That's not my fault! I don't tell them what to buy!"

Luke shakes his head incredulously. "Did you put down his-and-hers Jimmy Choos too?"

"Did someone get the Jimmy Choos?" I say joyfully—then stop as I see his face. "I'm . . . joking." I clear my throat. "Here. Look at Suze's baby."

I've just had three rolls of film developed, mostly of Suze and Ernie.

"That's Ernie in the bath . . ." I point out, handing him photographs. "And that's Ernie asleep . . . and Suze asleep . . . and Suze . . . hang on a minute . . ." Hastily I pass over the ones of Suze breast-feeding with nothing on except a pair of knickers. She had actually bought a special breast-feeding top from a catalogue, which promised "discretion and ease at home and in public." But she got so pissed off with the stupid concealed zip, she threw it away after one day. "And look! That's the first day we brought him home!"

Luke sits down at the table, and as he leafs through the pictures, a strange expression comes over his face.

"She looks . . . blissful," he says.

"She is," I agree. "She adores him. Even when he screams."

"They seem bonded already." He stares at a photo of Suze laughing as Ernie grabs her hair.

"Oh, they are. Even by the time I left, he yelled if I tried to take him away from her."

I look at Luke, feeling touched. He's completely transfixed by these photographs. Which actually quite surprises me. I never thought he'd be particularly into babies. I mean, most men, if you handed them a load of baby pictures—

"I don't have any pictures of myself as a tiny baby," he says, turning to a picture of Ernie peacefully asleep on Suze.

"Don't you? Oh well . . ."

"My mother took them all with her."

His face is unreadable, and tiny alarm bells start to ring inside my head.

"Really?" I say casually. "Well, anyway—"

"Maybe she wanted to keep them nearby."

"Yes," I say doubtfully. "Maybe she did."

Oh God. I should have realized these pictures would set Luke off brooding about his mother again.

I'm not quite sure what happened between them while I was away. All I know is that eventually Luke managed to get through to her at the clinic. And apparently she came up with some lame explanation for why that newspaper article didn't mention Luke. Something about the journalist wasn't interested.

I don't know whether Luke believed her. I don't know whether he's forgiven her or not. To be honest, I don't think *he* knows. Every so often he goes all blank and withdrawn, and I can tell he's thinking about it.

Part of me wants to say, "Look, Luke, just forget it! She's a complete cow and she doesn't love you and you're better off without her."

Then I remember something his stepmother, Annabel, said— when we had that chat, all those months ago. As we were saying good-bye, she said, "As hard as it may be to believe, Luke needs Elinor."

"No, he doesn't!" I replied indignantly. "He's got you, he's got his dad, he's got me . . ."

But Annabel shook her head. "You don't understand. He's had this longing for Elinor ever since he was a child. It's driven him to work so hard; it's sent him to America; it's part of who he is now. Like a vine twisted round an apple tree." And she gave me this rather penetrating look and said, "Be careful, Becky. Don't try to chop her out of his life. Because you'll damage him too."

How did she read my mind? How did she know that I was exactly picturing myself, and Elinor, and an ax . . .

I look at Luke, and he's staring, mesmerized, at a picture of Suze kissing Ernie on the tummy.

"Anyway!" I say brightly, gathering up the photos and shoving them back into the envelopes. "You know, the bond is just as strong between Tarquin and Ernie. You should have seen them together. Tarquin's making a wonderful dad. He changes nappies and everything! In fact, I often think a mother's love is overrated . . ."

Oh, it's no good. Luke isn't even listening.

The phone rings, and he doesn't move, so I go into the sitting room to answer it.

"Hello?"

"Hello. Is that Rebecca Bloomwood?" says a strange man's voice.

"Yes it is," I say, noticing a new catalogue from Pottery Barn on the table. Perhaps I should register there too. "Who's this?"

"This is Garson Low, from Low and Associates."

My whole body freezes. Garson Low himself? Calling me at home?

"I apologize for calling so early," he's saying.

"No! Not at all!" I say, coming to life and quickly kicking the door shut so Luke can't hear. "Thanks for calling!"

Thank God. He must think I have a case. He must want to help me take on Robyn. We'll probably make groundbreaking legal history or something, and stand outside the courtroom while cameras flash and it'll be like *Erin Brockovich*!

"I received your letter yesterday," says Garson Low. "And I was intrigued by your dilemma. That's quite a bind you've got yourself in."

"I know it is," I say. "That's why I came to you."

"Is your fiancé aware of the situation?"

"Not yet." I lower my voice. "I'm hoping I'll be able to find a solution first—and then tell him. You understand, Mr. Low."

"I certainly do."

This is great. We've got rapport and everything.

"In that case," says Garson Low, "let's get down to business."

"Absolutely!" I feel a swell of relief. You see, this is what you get when you consult the most expensive lawyer in Manhattan. You get quick results.

"First of all, the contract has been very cleverly drawn up," says Garson Low.

"Right." I nod.

"There are several extremely ingenious clauses, covering all eventualities."

"I see."

"I've examined it thoroughly. And as far as I can see, there is no way you can get married in Britain without incurring the penalty."

"Right." I nod expectantly.

There's a short silence.

"So . . . what's the loophole?" I ask eventually.

"There is no loophole. Those are the facts."

"What?" I stare confusedly at the phone. "But . . . that's why you rang, isn't it? To tell me you'd found a loophole. To tell me we could win!"

"No, Miss Bloomwood. I called to tell you that if I were you, I would start making arrangements to cancel your British wedding."

I feel a stab of shock. "But . . . but I can't. That's the whole point. My mum's had the house done up, and everything. It would kill her."

"Then I'm afraid you will have to pay Wedding Events Ltd. the full penalty."

"But . . ." My throat is tight. "I can't do that either. I haven't got a hundred thousand dollars! There must be another way!"

"I'm afraid—"

"There must be some brilliant solution!" I push back my hair, trying not to panic. "Come on! You're supposed to be the cleverest person in America or something! You must be able to think of some way out!"

"Miss Bloomwood, let me assure you. I have looked at this from all angles and there is no brilliant solution. There is no way out." Garson Low sighs. "May I give you three small pieces of advice?"

"What are they?" I say with a flicker of hope.

"The first is, never sign any document before reading it first."

"I know that!" I cry before I can stop myself. "What's the good of everyone telling me that now?"

"The second is—and I strongly recommend this—tell your fiancé."

"And what's the third?"

"Hope for the best."

Is that all a million-pound lawyer can come up with? Tell your fiancé and hope for the best? Bloody stupid . . . expensive . . . complete rip-off . . .

OK, keep calm. I'm cleverer than him. I can think of something. I know I can. I just *know* I—

Hang on.

I saunter casually into the kitchen, where Luke has stopped gazing at the pictures of Suze and is staring broodingly into space instead.

"Hi," I say, running a hand along the back of his chair. "Hey, Luke. You've got loads of money, haven't you?"

"No."

"What do you mean, no?" I say, slightly affronted. "Of course you have!"

"I've got assets," says Luke. "I've got a company. That's not necessarily the same as money."

"Whatever." I wave my hand impatiently. "And we're getting married. You know, 'All thy worldly goods' and everything. So in a way . . ." I pause carefully, "it's mine, too."

"Yeee-s. Is this going anywhere?"

"So . . . if I asked you for some money, would you give it to me?"

"I expect so. How much?"

"Er . . . a hundred thousand dollars," I say, trying to sound nonchalant.

Luke raises his head. "A hundred thousand dollars?"

"Yes! I mean, it's not that much really—"

Luke sighs. "OK, Becky. What have you seen? Because if it's another customized leather coat—"

"It's not a coat! It's a . . . a surprise."

"A hundred-thousand-dollar surprise."

"Yes," I say after a pause. But even I don't sound that convinced. Maybe this isn't a brilliant solution after all.

"Becky, a hundred thousand dollars *is* that much. It's a lot of money!"

"I know," I say. "I know. Look . . . OK . . . it doesn't matter." And I hurry out before he can question me further.

OK, forget the lawyers. Forget the money. There has to be another solution to this. I just need to think laterally.

I mean, we could always elope. Get married on a beach and change our names and never see our families again.

No, this is it. I go to the Oxshott wedding. And Luke goes to the New York wedding. And we each say we've been jilted . . . and then we secretly meet up . . .

No! I have it! We hire stand-ins! Genius!

I'm riding up the escalator to work as this idea comes to me—and I'm so gripped, I almost forget to step off. This is it. We hire look-alikes, and they stand in for us at the Plaza wedding, and no one ever realizes. I mean, all the guests there are going to be Elinor's friends. People Luke and I barely know. We could get the bride look-alike to wear a really thick veil . . . and the Luke look-alike could say he'd cut his face shaving, and wear a huge bandage . . . and meanwhile we'd have flown back to England . . .

"Watch out, Becky!" says Christina with a smile, and I look up, startled. I was about to walk right into a mannequin.

"Busy thinking about the wedding?" she adds as I go into the personal shopping department.

"That's right," I say brightly.

"You know, you look so much more relaxed these days," says Christina approvingly. "Your break obviously did you the world of good. Seeing your mom . . . catching up with home . . ."

"Yes, it was . . . great!"

"I think it's admirable the way you're so laid-back." Christina takes a sip of coffee. "You've barely mentioned the wedding to any of us since you've been back! In fact, you've almost seemed to be avoiding the subject!"

"I'm not avoiding it!" I say, my smile fixed. "Why would I do that?"

"Some brides seem to make so *much* of a wedding. Almost let it take over their life. But you seem to have it all under control—"

"Absolutely!" I say, even more brightly. "If you'll excuse me, I'll just get ready for my first client—"

"Oh, I had to switch your appointments around," says Christina as I open the door of my room. "You have a first-timer at ten. Amy Forrester."

"I don't like yellow or orange." Amy Forrester's voice is still droning on. "And when I say dressy, I mean not *too* dressy. Just kind of formal . . . but sexy. You know what I mean?" She snaps her gum and looks at me expectantly.

"Er . . . yes!" I say, not having a clue what she's talking about. I can't even remember what she wants. Come on, Becky. Concentrate.

"So, just to recap, you're after . . . an evening dress?" I risk, scribbling on my notebook.

"Or a pantsuit. Whatever. I can pretty much wear any shape." Amy Forrester gazes complacently at herself in the mirror, and I give her a surreptitious Manhattan Onceover, taking in her tight lilac top and turquoise stirrup leggings. She looks like a model in an ad for some dodgy piece of home exercise equipment. Same tacky blond haircut and everything.

"You have a wonderful figure!" I say, realizing a bit late that she's waiting for a compliment.

"Thank you! I do my best."

With the help of Rollaflab! Just roll away that flab . . .

"I already bought my vacation wardrobe." She snaps her gum again. "But then my boyfriend said, why not buy a few more little things? He loves to treat me. He's a wonderful man. So—do you have any ideas?"

"Yes," I say, finally forcing myself to concentrate. "Yes, I do. I'll just go and fetch some pieces that I think might suit you."

I go out onto the floor and start gathering up dresses. Gradually, as I wander from rail to rail, I begin to relax. It's a relief to focus on something else; to think about something other than weddings . . .

"Hi, Becky!" says Erin, passing by with Mrs. Zaleskie, one of her regular clients. "Hey, I was just saying to Christina, we have to plan your shower!"

Oh God.

"You know, my daughter works at the Plaza," puts in Mrs. Zaleskie. "She says *everyone's* talking about your wedding."

"Are they?" I say after a pause. "Well, it's really no big deal—"

"No big deal? Are you kidding? The staff is fighting over who's going to serve! They all want to see the enchanted woodland!" She peers at me through her spectacles. "Is it true you're having a string orchestra, a DJ, *and* a ten-piece band?"

"Er . . . yes."

"My friends are *so* jealous I'm going," says Erin, her face all lit up. "They're like, you have to show us the pictures afterward! We are allowed to take pictures, right?"

"I . . . don't know. I guess so."

"You must be excited," says Mrs. Zaleskie. "You're a lucky girl."

"I . . . I know."

I can't bear this.

"I have to go," I mutter, and hurry back to the personal shopping department.

I can't win. Whatever I do. Either way, I'm going to let down a whole load of people.

As Amy wriggles into the first dress, I stand, staring blankly at the floor, my heart thumping hard. I've been in trouble before. I've been stupid before. But never on this level. Never so large, so expensive, so important . . .

"I like this," says Amy, staring at herself critically. "But is there enough cleavage?"

"Er . . ." I look at her. It's a black chiffon dress, slashed practically to the navel. "I *think* so. But we could always have it altered . . ."

"Oh, I don't have time for that!" says Amy. "I'm only in New York for one more day. We go on vacation tomorrow and then we're moving to Atlanta. That's why I came out shopping. They're packing up the apartment and it's driving me nuts."

"I see," I say absently.

"My boyfriend adores my body," she says smugly as she clambers out of it. "But then, his wife never bothered with her appearance at all. Ex-wife, I should say. They're getting a divorce."

"Right," I say politely, handing her a white and silver sheath dress.

"I can't believe he put up with her for so long. She's this completely jealous harridan. I'm having to take legal action!" Amy steps into the sheath dress. "You know, she mailed me this really offensive letter. It was like a list of completely insulting stuff about me! Our lawyer says we have an excellent case."

That sounds familiar. I look up, my brain starting to tweak. "You're sure it was her who sent it?"

"Oh yes! I mean, she signed it and everything. Plus it was definitely her writing. William recognized it."

I stare at her, my skin prickling. "What . . . what did you say your boyfriend's name was?"

"William." Her lip curls scornfully. "*She* called him Bill."

Oh my God.

It is. It's the blond intern. Right here in front of me.

OK. Just . . . keep smiling. Don't let her know you suspect anything.

Inside I'm hot with outrage. *This* is the woman Laurel was cast aside for? This stupid, tacky airhead?

"That's why we're moving to Atlanta," Amy says, examining her reflection complacently. "We want to start a new life together, so William asked the firm for a transfer. You know, discreetly. We don't want the old witch following us." She frowns. "Now, I like this one better."

She bends down farther and I freeze. Hang on. She's wearing a pendant. A pendant with a . . . is that green stone an *emerald*?

"Amy, I just have to make a call," I say casually. "Keep trying on the dresses!" And I slide out of the room.

When I eventually get through to Laurel's office, her assistant, Gina, tells me she's in a meeting with American Airlines and can't be disturbed.

"Please," I say. "Get her out. It's important."

"So is American Airlines," says Gina. "You'll have to wait."

"But you don't understand! It really is crucial!"

"Becky, a new skirt length from Prada is not crucial," says Gina a little wearily. "Not in the world of airplane leasing."

"It's not clothes!" I say indignantly—then hesitate for a second, wondering how much Laurel confides in Gina. "It's Amy Forrester," I say at last in a lowered voice. "You know who I mean?"

"Yes, I know," says Gina in a voice that makes me thinks she knows even more than I do. "What about her?"

"I have her."

"You *have* her? What do you—"

"She's in my fitting room right now!" I glance behind me to make sure no one can hear. "Gina, she's wearing this pendant with an emerald in it! I'm sure it's Laurel's grandmother's! The one the police couldn't find."

There's a long pause.

"OK," says Gina at last. "I'll get Laurel out of the meeting. She'll probably come right over. Just don't let . . . *her* leave."

"I won't. Thanks, Gina."

I put down the phone and stand still for a moment, thinking. Then I head back to my fitting room, trying to look as natural as possible.

"So!" I say breezily as I go in. "Let's get back to trying on dresses! And remember, Amy, just take your time over each one. As long as you like. We can take all day, if we need to—"

"I don't need to try on any more," says Amy, turning round in a tight red sequined dress. "I'll take this one."

"What?" I say blankly.

"It's great! Look, it fits me perfectly." She does a little twirl, admiring herself in the mirror.

"But we haven't even started yet!"

"So what? I've made my decision. I want this one." She looks at her watch. "Besides, I'm in a bit of a hurry. Can you unzip me, please?"

"Amy . . ." I force a smile. "I really think you should try on some others before you make a decision."

"I don't need to try any others! You have a very good eye."

"No, I don't! It looks terrible!" I say without thinking, and she gives me a strange look. "I mean . . . there was a wonderful pink dress I wanted to see on you . . ." I grab for the hanger. "Just imagine that on you! Or . . . or this halter neck . . ."

Amy Forrester gives me an impatient look. "I'm taking this one. Please, will you help me out of it?"

What can I do? I can't *force* her to stay.

I glance surreptitiously at my watch. Laurel's office is only a block or two away. She should be here any minute.

"Please, will you help me out of it?" she repeats, her voice hardening.

"Yes!" I say flusteredly. "All right!"

I reach for the zip of the sequined red dress and start to pull it down. Then I have a sudden thought.

"Actually," I say. "Actually, it'll be easier to get it off if I pull it over your head—"

"OK," says Amy Forrester impatiently. "Whatever."

I undo the zip a tiny bit more, then tug the tight-fitting dress up over her hips and right over her head.

Ha! She's trapped! The stiff red fabric covers her face completely, but the rest of her is clad only in underwear and high heels. She looks like a Barbie doll crossed with a Christmas cracker.

"Hey. It's gotten stuck." She waves one of her arms fruitlessly, but it's pinned to her head by the dress.

"Really?" I exclaim innocently. "Oh dear. They do that sometimes."

"Well, get me out!" She takes a couple of steps, and I back away nervously in case she grabs my arm. I feel like I'm six years old and playing blindman's bluff at a birthday party.

"Where are you?" comes a furious muffled voice. "Get me out!"

"I'm just . . . trying to . . ." Gingerly I give a little tug at the dress. "It's really stuck," I say apologetically. "Maybe if you bent over and wriggled . . ."

Come *on*, Laurel. Where are you? I open my fitting room and have a quick glance out, but nothing.

"OK! I'm getting somewhere!"

I look up and feel a plunge of dismay. Amy's hand has appeared out of nowhere and somehow she's managed to grasp the zip with two manicured nails. "Can you help me pull the zipper down?"

"Erm . . . I can try . . ."

I take hold of the zip and start pulling it in the opposite direction from the way she's tugging.

"It's stuck!" she says in frustration.

"I know! I'm trying to get it undone . . ."

"Wait a minute." Her voice is suddenly suspicious. "Which way are you pulling?"

"Er . . . the same way as you . . ."

"Hi, Laurel," I suddenly hear Christina saying in surprise. "Are you all right? Did you have an appointment?"

"No. But I think Becky has something for me—"

"Here!" I say, hurrying to the door and looking out. And there's Laurel, cheeks flushed with animation, wearing her new Michael Kors skirt with a navy blue blazer, which looks completely wrong.

How many times have I told her? Honestly, I should do more

spot-checks on my clients. Who knows what they're all wearing out there?

"Here she is," I say, nodding toward the Barbie-doll-Christmas-cracker hybrid, who is still trying to unzip the dress.

"It's OK," says Laurel, coming into the fitting room. "You can leave her to me."

"What? Who's that?" Amy's head jerks up disorientedly. "Oh Jesus. No. Is that—"

"Yes," says Laurel, closing the door. "It's me."

I stand in front of the door, trying to ignore the raised voices coming from my room. After a few minutes, Christina comes out of her room and looks at me.

"Becky, what's going on?"

"Um . . . Laurel bumped into an acquaintance. I thought I'd give them some privacy." A thumping sound comes from the room and I cough loudly. "I think they're . . . chatting."

"Chatting." Christina gives me a hard look.

"Yes! Chatting!"

The door suddenly opens, and Laurel emerges, a bunch of keys in her hand.

"Becky, I'm going to need to pay a little visit to Amy's apartment, and she'd like to stay here until I come back. Isn't that right, Amy?"

I glance past Laurel into the fitting room. Amy is sitting in the corner in her underwear, minus the emerald pendant, looking completely shell-shocked. She nods silently.

As Laurel strides off, Christina gives me an incredulous look. "Becky—"

"So!" I say quickly to Amy, in my best Barneys employee manner. "While we're waiting, would you care to try some more dresses?"

Forty minutes later, Laurel arrives back, her face alive with animation.

"Did you get the rest of it?" I say eagerly.

"I got it all."

Christina, on the other side of the department, looks up, then looks away again. She's said that the only way she can't fire me for what just happened is not to know about it.

So we're basically agreed, she doesn't know about it.

"Here you are." Laurel tosses the keys to Amy. "You can go now. Give my regards to Bill. He deserves you."

As Amy totters, almost running, toward the escalator, Laurel puts an arm round me.

"Becky, you're an angel," she says warmly. "I can't even begin to repay you. But whatever you want, it's yours."

"Don't be silly!" I say at once. "I just wanted to help."

"I'm serious!"

"Laurel—"

"I insist. Name it, and it'll be there in time for your wedding."

My wedding.

It's as though someone's opened a window and the cold air is rushing in.

In all the excitement and urgency, I'd managed briefly to forget about it. But now it all comes piling back into my head.

My two weddings. My two fiascos.

Like two trains traveling toward me. Quicker and quicker, getting nearer even when I'm not looking at them. Gathering momentum with every minute. If I manage to dodge one, I'll only get hit by the other.

I stare at Laurel's warm, open face, and all I want to do is bury my head in her shoulder and wail, "Sort out my life for me!"

"Whatever you want," says Laurel again, and squeezes my shoulders.

As I walk slowly back to my fitting room, the adrenaline has gone. I can feel a familiar, wearying anxiety creeping over me. Another day has gone by, and I'm no nearer to a brilliant solution. I have no idea what I'm going to do. And I'm running out of time.

Maybe the truth is, I can't solve this on my own, I think, sinking heavily down in my chair. Maybe I need help. Fire rescue trucks and SWAT teams.

Or maybe just Luke.

Sixteen

As I arrive home, I'm surprisingly calm. In fact, I almost feel a sense of relief. I've tried everything—and now I'm at the end of the line. There's nothing else I can do but confess everything to Luke. He'll be shocked. Angry too. But at least he'll know.

I stopped in a café on the way, had a coffee, and thought very carefully about how I was going to tell him. Because everyone knows, it's all in the presentation. When the president's going to raise taxes, he doesn't say, "I'm going to raise taxes." He says, "Every American citizen knows the value of education." So I've written out a speech, a bit like the State of the Union address, and I've memorized it word for word, with gaps for interjections from Luke. (Or applause. Though that's a bit unlikely.) As long as I stick to my text, and no one brings up the question of Ugandan policy, then we should be all right.

My legs are trembling slightly as I climb the stairs to our apartment, even though Luke won't be back yet; I still have time to prepare. But as I open the door, to my shock, there he is, sitting at the table with a pile of papers and his back to me.

OK, Becky, come on. Ladies and gentlemen of Congress. Four score and thingummy. I let the door swing shut behind me, get out my notes, and take a deep breath.

"Luke," I begin in a grave, grown-up voice. "I have something to tell you about the wedding. It's quite a serious problem, with no easy solution. If there is a solution, it will be one that I can only

achieve with your help. Which is why I'm telling you this now—
and asking that you listen with an open mind."

So far so good. I'm quite proud of that bit, actually. The "listen
with an open mind" bit was especially inspired, because it means he
can't shout at me.

"In order to explain my current predicament," I continue, "I must
take you back in time. Back to the beginning. By which I mean not the
creation of Earth. Nor even the big bang. But tea at Claridges."

I pause—but Luke is still silent, listening. Maybe this is going
to be OK.

"It was there, at Claridges, that my problem began. I was presented with an impossible task. I was, if you will, that Greek god
having to choose between the three apples. Except there were only
two—and they weren't apples." I pause significantly. "They were
weddings."

At last, Luke turns round in his chair. His eyes are bloodshot,
and there's a strange expression on his face. As he gazes at me, I feel
a tremor of apprehension.

"Becky," he says, as though with a huge effort.

"Yes?" I gulp.

"Do you think my mother loves me?"

"What?" I say, thrown.

"Tell me honestly. Do you think my mother loves me?"

Hang on. Has he been listening to a single word I've been
saying?

"Er . . . of course I do!" I say. "And speaking of mothers, that is,
in a sense, where my problem originally lay—"

"I've been a fool." Luke picks up his glass and takes a swig of
what looks like whiskey. "She's just been using me, hasn't she?"

I stare at him, discomfited—then notice the half-empty bottle
on the table. How long has he been sitting here? I look at his face
again, taut and vulnerable, and bite back some of the things I could
say about Elinor.

"Of course she loves you!" I put down my speech and go over to
him. "I'm sure she does. I mean, you can see it, in the way she . . .
um . . ." I tail off feebly.

What am I supposed to say? In the way she uses your staff with
no recompense or thanks? In the way she stabs you in the back,
then disappears to Switzerland?

"What . . . why are you . . ." I say hesitantly. "Has something happened?"

"It's so stupid." He shakes his head. "I came across something earlier on." He takes a deep breath. "I was at her apartment to pick up some papers for the foundation. And I don't know why—maybe it was after seeing those photographs of Suze and Ernie this morning." He looks up. "But I found myself searching in her study for old pictures. Of me as a child. Of us. I don't really know what I was looking for. Anything, I guess."

"Did you find anything?"

Luke gestures to the papers littering the table and I squint puzzledly at one. "What are they?"

"They're letters. From my father. Letters he wrote to my mother after they split up, fifteen, twenty years ago. Pleading with her to see me." His voice is deadpan and I look at him warily.

"What do you mean?"

"I mean that he begged her to let me visit," says Luke evenly. "He offered to pay hotel bills. He offered to accompany me. He asked again and again . . . and I never knew." He reaches for a couple of sheets and hands them to me. "Look, read for yourself."

Trying to hide my shock, I start to scan them, taking in phrases here and there.

Luke is so desperate to see his mother . . . cannot understand your attitude . . .

"These letters explain a lot of things. It turns out her new husband wasn't against her taking me with them, after all. In fact, he sounds like a pretty decent guy. He agreed with my dad, I should come and visit. But she wasn't interested." He shrugs. "Why should she be, I suppose?"

. . . an intelligent loving boy . . . missing out on a wonderful opportunity . . .

"Luke, that's . . . terrible," I say inadequately.

"The worst thing is, I used to take it all out on my parents. When I was a teenager. I used to blame them."

I have a sudden vision of Annabel, and her kind, warm face; of Luke's dad, writing these letters in secret—and feel a pang of outrage toward Elinor. She doesn't deserve Luke. She doesn't deserve any family.

There's silence except for the rain drumming outside. I reach out and squeeze Luke's hand, trying to inject as much love and warmth as I can.

"Luke, I'm sure your parents understood. And . . ." I swallow all the things I really want to say about Elinor. "And I'm sure Elinor wanted you to be there really. I mean, maybe it was difficult for her at the time, or . . . or maybe she was away a lot—"

"There's something I've never told you," interrupts Luke. "Or anybody." He raises his head. "I came to see my mother when I was fourteen."

"What?" I stare at him in astonishment. "But I thought you said you never—"

"There was a school trip to New York. I fought tooth and nail to go on it. Mum and Dad were against it, of course, but in the end they gave in. They told me my mother was away, that, of course, otherwise, she would have loved to see me."

Luke reaches for the whiskey bottle and pours himself another drink. "I couldn't help it, I had to try and see her. Just in case they were wrong." He stares ahead, running his finger round the rim of his glass. "So . . . toward the end of the trip, we had a free day. Everyone else went up the Empire State Building. But I sneaked off. I had her address, and I just came and sat outside her building. It wasn't the building she's in now, it was another one, farther up Park Avenue. I sat on a step, and people kept staring at me as they went by, but I didn't care."

He takes a gulp of his drink and I gaze back at him, rigid. I don't dare make a sound. I hardly dare breathe.

"Then, at about twelve o'clock, a woman came out. She had dark hair, and a beautiful coat. I knew her face from the photograph. It was my mother." He's silent for a few seconds. "I . . . I stood up. She looked up and saw me. She stared at me for less than five seconds. Then she turned away. It was as though she hadn't seen me. She got into a taxi and went off, and that was it." He closes his eyes briefly. "I didn't even have a chance to take a step forward."

"What . . . what did you do?" I say tentatively.

"I left. And I walked around the city. I persuaded myself that she hadn't recognized me. That's what I told myself. That she had no idea what I looked like; that she couldn't possibly have known it was me."

"Well, maybe that's true!" I say eagerly. "How on earth would she have—"

I fall silent as he reaches for a faded blue airmail letter with something paper-clipped to it at the top.

"This is the letter my father wrote her to tell her I was coming," he says. He lifts up the paper and I feel a small jolt. "And this is me."

I'm looking into the eyes of a teenaged boy. A fourteen-year-old Luke. He's wearing a school uniform and he has a terrible haircut; in fact he's barely recognizable. But those are his dark eyes, gazing out at the world with a mixture of determination and hope.

There's nothing I can say. As I stare at his gawky, awkward face, I want to cry.

"You were right all along, Becky. I came to New York to impress my mother. I wanted her to stop dead in the street and turn round and . . . and stare . . . and be proud . . ."

"She is proud of you!"

"She isn't." He gives me a tiny half-smile. "I should just give up."

"No!" I say, a little too late. I reach out and take Luke's arm, feeling completely helpless. Completely sheltered and pampered in comparison. I grew up knowing that Mum and Dad thought I was the best thing in the whole wide world; knowing that they loved me, and always would, whatever I did.

"I'm sorry," says Luke at last. "I've gone on too much about this. Let's forget it. What did you want to talk about?"

"Nothing," I say at once. "It . . . doesn't matter. It can wait."

The wedding seems a million miles away, suddenly. I screw up my notes into a tight ball and throw them in the bin. Then I look around the cluttered room. Letters spread out on the table, wedding presents stacked up in the corner, paraphernalia everywhere. It's impossible to escape your own life when you live in a Manhattan apartment.

"Let's go out and eat," I say, standing up abruptly. "And see a movie or something."

"I'm not hungry," says Luke.

"That's not the point. This is place is just too . . . crowded." I take Luke's hand and tug at it. "Come on, let's get out of here. And just forget about everything. All of it."

We go out and walk, arm in arm, down to the cinema and lose ourselves in a movie about the Mafia. Then when it's over we walk a couple of blocks to a small, warm restaurant we know, and order red wine and risotto.

We don't mention Elinor once. Instead, we talk about Luke's childhood in Devon. He tells me about picnics on the beach, and a tree house his father built for him in the garden, and how his little half-sister Zoe always used to tag along with all her friends and drive him mad. Then he tells me about Annabel. About how fantastic she's always been to him, and how kind she is to everyone; and how he never ever felt she loved him any less than Zoe, who was truly hers.

We talk tentatively about things we've never even touched on. Like having children ourselves. Luke wants to have three. I want . . . well after having watched Suze go through labor, I don't think I want any, but I don't tell him that. I nod when he says "or perhaps even four" and wonder whether maybe I could pretend to be pregnant and secretly adopt them.

By the end of the evening, I think Luke is a lot better. We walk home and fall into bed and both go straight to sleep. During the night I half wake, and I think I see Luke standing by the window, staring out into the night. But I'm asleep again before I'm sure.

I wake up the next morning with a dry mouth and an aching head. Luke's already got up and I can hear clattering from the kitchen, so maybe he's making me a nice breakfast. I could do with some coffee, and maybe some toast. And then . . .

My stomach gives a nervous flip. I've got to bite the bullet. I've got to tell him about the weddings.

Last night was last night. Of course I couldn't do anything about it then. But now it's the morning and I can't wait any longer. I know it's terrible timing, I know it's the last thing he'll want to hear right now. But I just have to tell him.

I can hear him coming along the corridor, and I take a deep breath, trying to steady my nerves.

"Luke, listen," I say as the door swings open. "I know this is a bad time. But I really need to talk to you. We've got a problem."

"What's that?" says Robyn, coming into the room. "Nothing to do with the wedding, I hope!" She's wearing a powder-blue suit and patent leather pumps and carrying a tray of breakfast things. "Here you go, sweetheart. Some coffee to wake you up!"

Am I dreaming? What's Robyn doing in my bedroom?

"I'll just get the muffins," she says brightly, and disappears out of the room. I subside weakly onto my pillow, my head pounding, trying to work out what she might be doing here.

Suddenly last night's Mafia film jumps into my mind and I'm struck with terror. Oh my God. It's obvious.

She's found out about the other wedding—and she's come to murder me.

Robyn appears through the door again, with a basket of muffins, and smiles as she puts it down. I stare back, transfixed with fear.

"Robyn!" I say huskily. "I . . . didn't expect to see you. Isn't it a bit . . . early?"

"When it comes to my clients, there is no such thing as too early," says Robyn, with a twinkle. "I am at your service, day and night." She sits down on the armchair next to the bed and pours me out a cup of coffee.

"But how did you get in?"

"I picked the lock. Only kidding! Luke let me in on his way out!"

I'm alone in the apartment with her. She's got me trapped.

"Luke's gone to work already?"

"I'm not sure he was going to work." Robyn pauses thoughtfully. "It looked more like he was going jogging."

"Jogging?"

Luke doesn't jog.

"Now, drink up your coffee—and then I'll show you what you've been waiting for. What we've all been waiting for." She looks at her watch. "I have to be gone in twenty minutes, remember!"

I stare at her dumbly.

"Becky, are you all right? You do *remember* we have an appointment?"

Dimly a memory starts filtering back into my mind, like a shadow through gauze. Robyn. Breakfast meeting. Oh yes.

Why did I agree to a breakfast meeting?

"Of course I remember!" I say at last. "I'm just a bit . . . you know, hung over."

"You don't have to explain!" says Robyn cheerily. "Fresh orange juice is what you need. And a good breakfast. I say the same thing to all my brides: you must take care of yourself! There's no point starving yourself and then fainting at the altar. Have a muffin." She rummages in her bag. "And look! At last we have it!"

I look blankly at the scrap of shimmering silver material she's holding up.

"What is it?"

"It's the fabric for the cushion pads!" says Robyn. "Flown in especially from China. The one we had all the problems with over customs! You can't have forgotten, surely?"

"Oh! No, of course not," I say hastily. "Yes, it looks . . . lovely. Really beautiful."

"Now, Becky, there was something else," says Robyn. She puts the fabric away and looks up with a serious expression. "The truth is . . . I'm getting a little concerned."

I feel a fresh spasm of nerves and take a sip of coffee to hide it. "Really? What . . . what are you concerned about?"

"We haven't had a single reply from your British guests. Isn't that strange?"

For a moment I'm unable to speak.

"Er . . . yes," I manage at last. "Very."

"Except Luke's parents, who accepted a while ago. Of course they were on Elinor's guest list, so they got their invitation a little earlier, but even so . . ." She reaches for my coffee cup and takes a sip. "Mmm. This is good, if I do say so myself! Now, I don't want to accuse anyone of lacking manners. But we need to start getting some numbers in. So is it OK if I make a few tactful calls to England? I have all the phone numbers in my database . . ."

"No!" I say, suddenly waking up. "Don't call anybody! I mean . . . you'll get the replies, I promise."

"It's just so odd!" Robyn muses. "To have heard nothing . . . They did all receive their invitations, didn't they?"

"Of course they did! I'm sure it's just an oversight." I start pleating the sheet between finger and thumb. "You'll have some replies within a week. I can . . . guarantee it."

"Well, I certainly hope so! Because time is ticking on! We've only got four weeks to go!"

"I know!" I say shrilly, and take another gulp of coffee, wishing desperately it were vodka.

Four weeks.

Oh God.

"Shall I refresh your cup, sweetheart?" Robyn stands up—then bends down again. "What's this?" she says with interest, and picks up a piece of paper lying on the floor. "Is this a menu?"

I look up—and my heart stops. She's got one of Mum's faxes. The menu for the other wedding.

Everything's right there, under the bed. If she starts looking . . .

"It's nothing!" I say, grabbing it from her. "Just a . . . um . . . a menu for a . . . a party . . ."

"You're holding a party?"

"We're . . . thinking about it."

"Well, if you want any help planning it, just say the word!" Robyn lowers her voice confidentially. "And a tiny tip?" She gestures to Mum's menu. "I think you'll find filo parcels are a little passé."

"Right. Er . . . thanks."

I have to get this woman out of here. At once. Before she finds anything else.

Abruptly I throw back the sheets and leap out of bed.

"Actually, Robyn, I'm still not feeling quite right. Maybe we could . . . could reschedule the rest of this meeting?"

"I understand." She pats my shoulder. "I'll leave you in peace."

"By the way," I say casually as we reach the front door. "I was just wondering . . . You know that financial penalty clause in your contract?"

"Yes!" Robyn beams at me.

"Out of interest." I give a little laugh. "Have you ever actually collected it?"

"Oh, only a few times!" says Robyn. She pauses reminiscently. "One silly girl tried to run off to Poland . . . but we found her in the end . . . See you, Becky!"

"See you!" I say, matching her bright tone, and close the door, my heart thumping hard.

She'll get me. It's only a matter of time.

As soon as I get to work, I call Luke at work and get his assistant, Julia.

"Hi," I say, "can I speak to Luke?"

"Luke called in sick," says Julia, sounding surprised. "Didn't you know?"

I stare at the phone, taken aback. Luke's taken a sickie? Blimey. Maybe his hangover was even worse than mine.

Shit, and I've nearly given the game away.

"Oh, right!" I say quickly. "Yes! Now you mention it . . . of course I knew! He's dreadfully sick, actually. He's got a terrible fever. And his . . . er . . . stomach. I just forgot for a moment, that's all."

"Well, give him all the best from us."

"I will!"

As I put the phone down, I realize I might have overreacted a teeny bit. I mean, it's not like anyone's going to give Luke the sack, is it? After all, it's his company.

In fact, I'm *pleased* he's having a day off.

But still. Luke getting sick. He never gets sick.

And he never jogs. What's going on?

I'm supposed to be going out for a drink after work with Erin, but I make an excuse and hurry home instead. When I let myself in, the apartment's dim, and for a moment I think Luke isn't back. But then I see him, sitting at the table in the gloom, wearing track pants and an old sweatshirt.

At last. We've got the evening to ourselves. OK, this is it. I'm finally going to tell him everything.

"Hi," I say, sliding into a chair next to him. "Are you feeling better? I called your work and they said you were ill."

There's silence.

"I wasn't in the right frame of mind to go to work," says Luke at last.

"What did you do all day? Did you really go jogging?"

"I went for a long walk," says Luke. "And I thought a great deal."

"About . . . your mother?" I say tentatively.

"Yes. About my mother. About a lot of other things too." He turns for the first time and to my surprise I see he hasn't shaved. Mmm. I quite like him unshaven, actually.

"But you're OK?"

"That's the question," he says after a pause. "Am I?"

"You probably just drank a bit too much last night." I take off my coat, marshaling my words. "Luke, listen. There's something really important I need to tell you. I've been putting it off for weeks now—"

"Becky, have you ever thought about the grid of Manhattan?" says Luke, interrupting me. "Really *thought* about it?"

"Er . . . no," I say, momentarily halted. "I can't say I have."

"It's like . . . a metaphor for life. You think you have the freedom to walk anywhere. But in fact . . ." He draws a line with his finger on the table. "You're strictly controlled. Up or down. Left or right. No other options."

"Right," I say after a pause. "Absolutely. The thing is, Luke—"

"Life should be an open space, Becky. You should be able to walk in whichever direction you choose."

"I suppose—"

"I walked from one end of the island to the other today."

"Really?" I stare at him. "Er . . . why?"

"I looked up at one point, and I was surrounded by office blocks. Sunlight was bouncing off the plate-glass windows. Reflected backward and forward."

"That sounds nice," I say inadequately.

"Do you see what I'm saying?" He fixes me with an intense stare, and I suddenly notice the purple shadows beneath his eyes. God, he looks exhausted. "The light enters Manhattan . . . and becomes trapped. Trapped in its own world, bouncing backward and forward with no escape."

"Well . . . yes, I suppose. Except . . . sometimes it rains, doesn't it?"

"And people are the same."

"Are they?"

"This is the world we're living in now. Self-reflecting. Self-obsessed. Ultimately pointless. Look at that guy in the hospital. Thirty-three years old—and he has a heart attack. What if he'd died? Would he have had a fulfilled life?"

"Er—"

"Have *I* had a fulfilled life? Be honest, Becky. Look at me, and tell me."

"Well . . . um . . . of course you have!"

"Bullshit." He picks up a nearby Brandon Communications press release and gazes at it. "This is what my life has been about. Meaningless pieces of information." To my shock, he starts to rip it up. "Meaningless fucking bits of paper."

Suddenly I notice he's tearing up our joint bank statement too.

"Luke! That's our bank statement!"

"So what? What does it matter? It's only a few pointless numbers. Who cares?"

"But . . . but . . ."

Something is wrong here.

"What does any of it matter?" He scatters the shreds of paper on the floor, and I force myself not to bend down and pick any of them up. "Becky, you're so right."

"*I'm* right?" I say in alarm.

Something is very wrong here.

"We're all too driven by materialism. With success. With money. With trying to impress people who'll never be impressed, whatever you . . ." He breaks off, breathing hard. "It's humanity that matters. We *should* know homeless people. We *should* know Bolivian peasants."

"Well . . . yes," I say after a pause. "But still—"

"Something you said a while back has been going round and round in my head all day. And now I can't forget it."

"What was that?" I say nervously.

"You said . . ." He pauses, as though trying to get the words just right. "You said that we're on this planet for too short a time. And at the end of the day, what's more important? Knowing that a few meaningless figures balanced—or knowing that you were the person you wanted to be?"

I gape at him. "But . . . but that was just stuff I made up! I wasn't being *serious*—"

"I'm not the person I want to be, Becky. I don't think I've ever been the person I wanted to be. I've been blinkered. I've been obsessed by all the wrong things—"

"Come on!" I say, squeezing his hand encouragingly. "You're Luke Brandon! You're successful and handsome and rich . . ."

"I'm not the person I should have become. The trouble is, now I don't know who that person is. I don't know who I want to be . . . what I want to do with my life . . . which path I want to take . . ." He slumps forward and buries his head in his hands. "Becky, I need some answers."

I don't believe it. At age thirty-four Luke is having a midlife crisis.

SECOND UNION BANK
53 WALL STREET
NEW YORK, NY 10005

May 23, 2002

Miss Rebecca Bloomwood
Apt. B
251 W. 11th Street
New York, NY 10014

Dear Miss Bloomwood:

Thank you for your letter of May 21. I am glad you are starting to think of me as a good friend, and in answer to your question, my birthday is October 31.

I also appreciate that weddings are expensive affairs. Unfortunately, however, I am unable to extend your credit limit from $5,000 to $105,000 at the current time.

I can instead offer you an increased limit of $6,000, and hope this goes some way to help.

Yours sincerely,

Walt Pitman
Director of Customer Relations

49 Drakeford Road
Potters Bar
Hertfordshire

27 May 2002

Mr. Malcolm Bloomwood thanks Mrs. Elinor Sherman very much for her kind invitation to Becky and Luke's wedding at the Plaza on 22nd June. Unfortunately he must decline, as he has broken his leg.

The Oaks
43 Elton Road
Oxshott, Surrey

27 May 2002

Mr. and Mrs. Martin Webster thank Mrs. Elinor Sherman very much for her kind invitation to Becky and Luke's wedding at the Plaza on 22nd June. Unfortunately they must decline, as they have both contracted glandular fever.

9 Foxtrot Way
Reigate
Surrey

27 May 2002

Mr. and Mrs. Tom Webster thank Mrs. Elinor Sherman very much for her kind invitation to Becky and Luke's wedding at the Plaza on 22nd June. Unfortunately they must decline, as their dog has just died.

Seventeen

THIS IS GETTING beyond a joke. Luke hasn't been to work for over a week. Nor has he shaved. He keeps going out and wandering around God knows where and not coming home until the early hours of the morning. And yesterday I arrived back from work to find he'd given away half his shoes to people on the street.

I feel so helpless. Nothing I do seems to work. I've tried making him bowls of nourishing, homemade soup. (At least, it says they're nourishing and homemade on the can.) I've tried making warm, tender love to him. Which was great as far as it went. (And that was pretty far, as it happens.) He seemed better for a little while—but in the end it didn't change anything. Afterward, he was just the same, all moody and staring into space.

The thing I've tried the most is just sitting down and talking to him. Sometimes I really think I'm getting somewhere. But then he either just reverts back into depression, or says, "What's the use?" and goes out again. The real trouble is, nothing he says seems to be making any sense. One minute he says he wants to quit his company and go into politics, that's where his heart lies and he should never have sold out. (Politics? He's never mentioned politics before.) The next moment he's saying fatherhood is all he's ever wanted, let's have six children and he'll stay at home and be a house-husband.

Meanwhile his assistant keeps phoning every day to see if

Luke's better, and I'm having to invent more and more lurid details. He's practically got the plague by now.

I'm so desperate, I phoned Michael this morning and he's promised to come over and see if he can do anything. If anyone can help, Michael can.

And as for the wedding . . .

I feel ill every time I think about it. It's three weeks away. I still haven't come up with a solution.

Mum calls me every morning and somehow I speak perfectly normally to her. Robyn calls me every afternoon and somehow I also speak perfectly normally to her. I even made a joke recently about not turning up on the day. We laughed, and Robyn quipped, "I'll sue you!" and I managed not to sob hysterically.

I feel like I'm in free fall. Plummeting toward the ground without a parachute.

I don't know how I'm doing it. I've slipped into a whole new zone, beyond normal panic, beyond normal solutions. It's going to take a miracle to save me.

Which is basically what I'm pinning my hopes on now. I've lit fifty candles at St. Thomas's, and fifty more at St. Patrick's, and I've put up a petition on the prayer board at the synagogue on Sixty-fifth, and given flowers to the Hindu god Ganesh. Plus a group of people in Ohio who I found on the Internet are all praying hard for me.

At least, they're praying that I find happiness following my struggle with alcoholism. I couldn't quite bring myself to explain the full two-weddings story to Father Gilbert, especially after I read his sermon on how deceit is as painful to the Lord as is the Devil gouging out the eyes of the righteous. So I went with alcoholism, because they already had a page on that.

There's no respite. I can't even relax at home. The apartment feels like it's closing in on me. There are wedding presents in huge cardboard boxes lining every room. Mum sends about fifty faxes a day, Robyn's taken to popping in whenever she feels like it, and there's a selection of veils and headdresses in the sitting room that Dream Dress sent to me without even asking.

"Becky?" I look up from my breakfast coffee to see Danny wandering into the kitchen. "The door was open. Not at work?"

"I've taken the day off."

"I see." He reaches for a piece of cinnamon toast and takes a bite. "So, how's the patient?"

"Very funny."

"Seriously." For a moment Danny looks genuinely concerned, and I feel myself unbend a little. "Has Luke snapped out of it yet?"

"Not really," I admit, and his eyes brighten.

"So are there any more items of clothing going?"

"No!" I say indignantly. "There aren't. And don't think you can keep those shoes!"

"Brand-new Pradas? You must be kidding! They're mine. Luke gave them to me. If he doesn't want them anymore—"

"He does. He will. He's just . . . a bit stressed at the moment. Everyone gets stressed! It doesn't mean you can take their shoes!"

"Everybody gets stressed. Everybody doesn't give away hundred-dollar bills to total strangers."

"Really?" I look up anxiously. "He did that?"

"I saw him at the subway. There was a guy there with long hair, carrying a guitar . . . Luke just went up to him and handed him a wad of money. The guy wasn't even begging. In fact, he looked pretty offended."

"Oh God—"

"You know my theory? He needs a nice, long, relaxing honeymoon. Where are you going?"

Oh no. Into free fall again. The honeymoon. I haven't even booked one yet. How can I? I don't know which bloody airport we'll be flying out of.

"We're . . . it's a surprise," I say at last. "We'll announce it on the day."

"So what are you cooking?" Danny looks at the stove, where a pot is bubbling away. "Twigs? Mm, tasty."

"They're Chinese herbs. For stress. You boil them up and then drink the liquid."

"You think you'll get Luke to drink this?" Danny prods the mixture.

"They're not for Luke. They're for me!"

"For you? What have you got to be stressed about?" The buzzer sounds and Danny reaches over and presses the entry button without even asking who it is.

"Danny!"

"Expecting anyone?" he says as he replaces the receiver.

"Oh, just that mass murderer who's been stalking me," I say sarcastically.

"Cool." Danny takes another bite of cinnamon toast. "I always wanted to see someone get murdered."

There's a knock at the door, and I get up to answer.

"I'd change into something snappier," says Danny. "The courtroom will see pictures of you in that outfit. You want to look your best."

I open the door, expecting yet another delivery man. But it's Michael, wearing a yellow cashmere jumper and a big smile. My heart lifts in relief just at the sight of him.

"Michael!" I exclaim, and give him a hug. "Thank you so much for coming."

"I would've been here sooner if I'd realized how bad it was," says Michael. He raises his eyebrows. "I was in at the Brandon Communications offices yesterday, and I heard Luke was sick. But I had no idea . . ."

"Yes. Well, I haven't exactly been spreading the news. I thought it would just blow over in a couple of days."

"So is Luke here?" Michael peers into the apartment.

"No, he went out early this morning. I don't know where." I shrug helplessly.

"Give him my love when he comes back," says Danny, heading out of the door. "And remember, I've got dibs on his Ralph Lauren coat."

I make a fresh pot of coffee (decaffeinated—that's all Michael's allowed these days) and stir the herbs dubiously, then we pick our way through the clutter of the sitting room to the sofa.

"So," he says, removing a stack of magazines and sitting down. "Luke's feeling the strain a little." He watches as I pour the milk with a trembling hand. "By the looks of things, you are too."

"I'm OK," I say quickly. "It's Luke. He's completely changed, overnight. One minute he was fine, the next it was all, 'I need some answers' and, 'What's the point of life?' and, 'Where are we all going?' He's depressed, and he isn't going to work . . . I just don't know what to do."

"You know, I've seen this coming for a while," says Michael, taking his coffee from me. "That man of yours pushes himself too hard. Always has. Anyone who works at that pace for that length of time . . ." He gives a rueful shrug and taps his chest. "I should know. Something has to give."

"It's not just work. It's . . . everything." I bite my lip awkwardly. "I think he was affected more than he realized when you had your . . . heart thing."

"Episode."

"Exactly. The two of you had been fighting . . . it was such a jolt. It made him start thinking about . . . I don't know, life and stuff. And then there's this thing with his mother."

"Ah." Michael nods. "I knew Luke was upset over that piece in the *New York Times*. Understandably."

"That's nothing! It's all got a lot worse since then."

I explain all about Luke finding the letters from his father, and Michael winces.

"OK," he says, stirring his coffee thoughtfully. "Now this all makes sense. His mother has been the driving force behind a lot of what he's achieved. I think we all appreciate that."

"It's like . . . suddenly he doesn't know why he's doing what he's doing. So he's given up doing it. He won't go to work, he won't talk about it, Elinor's still in Switzerland, his colleagues keep ringing up to ask how he is, and I don't want to say, 'Actually, Luke can't come to the phone, he's having a midlife crisis right now . . .' "

"Don't worry, I'm going in to the office today. I could spin some story about a sabbatical. Gary Shepherd can take charge for a bit. He's very able."

"Will he be OK, though?" I look at Michael fearfully. "He won't rip Luke off?"

The last time Luke took his eye off his company for more than three minutes, Alicia Bitchface Billington tried to poach all his clients and sabotage the entire enterprise. It was nearly the end of Brandon Communications.

"Gary will be fine," says Michael reassuringly. "And I'm not doing much at the moment. I can keep tabs on things."

"No!" I say in horror. "You mustn't work too hard! You must take it easy."

"Becky, I'm not an invalid!" says Michael with a tinge of annoyance. "You and my daughter are as bad as each other."

The phone rings, and I leave it to click onto the machine.

"So, how are the wedding preparations going?" says Michael, glancing around the room.

"Oh . . . fine!" I smile brightly at him. "Thanks."

"I had a call from your wedding planner about the rehearsal dinner. She told me your parents won't be able to make it."

"No," I say after a pause. "No, they won't."

"That's too bad. What day are they flying over?"

"Erm . . ." I take a sip of coffee, avoiding his eye. "I'm not sure of the *exact* day . . ."

"Becky?" Mum's voice resounds through the room on the machine, and I jump, spilling some coffee on the sofa. "Becky, love, I need to talk to you about the band. They say they can't do 'Dancing Queen' because their bass player can only play four chords. So they've sent me a list of songs they *can* play—"

Oh fuck. I dive across the room and grab the receiver.

"Mum!" I say breathlessly. "Hi. Listen, I'm in the middle of something, can I call you back?"

"But, love, you need to approve the list of songs! I'll send you a fax, shall I?"

"Yes. OK, do that."

I thrust down the receiver and return to the sofa, trying to look composed.

"Your mom's clearly gotten involved in the wedding preparations," says Michael with a smile.

"Oh, er . . . yes. She has."

The phone starts to ring again and I ignore it.

"You know, I always meant to ask. Didn't she mind about you getting married in the States?"

"No!" I say, twisting my fingers into a knot. "Why should she mind?"

"I know what mothers are like about weddings . . ."

"Sorry, love, just a quickie," comes Mum's voice again. "Janice was asking, how do you want the napkins folded? Like bishops' hats or like swans?"

I grab the phone.

"Mum, listen. I've got company!"

"Please. Don't worry about me," says Michael from the sofa. "If it's important—"

"It's not important! I don't give a shit what shape the napkins are in! I mean, they only look like a swan for about two seconds . . ."

"Becky!" exclaims Mum in shock. "How can you talk like that! Janice went on a napkin-arranging course especially for your wedding! It cost her forty-five pounds, and she had to take her own packed lunch—"

Remorse pours over me.

"Look, Mum, I'm sorry. I'm just a bit preoccupied. Let's go for . . . bishops' hats. And tell Janice I'm really grateful for all her help." I put down the receiver just as the doorbell rings.

"Is Janice the wedding planner?" says Michael interestedly.

"Er . . . no. That's Robyn."

"You have mail!" pipes up the computer in the corner of the room. This is getting to be too much.

"Excuse me, I'll just get the door . . ."

I swing open the front door breathlessly, to see a delivery man holding a huge cardboard box.

"Parcel for Bloomwood," he says. "Very fragile."

"Thanks," I say, awkwardly taking it from him.

"Sign here, please . . ." He hands me a pen, then sniffs. "Is something burning in your kitchen?"

Oh fuck. The Chinese herbs.

I dash into the kitchen and turn off the burner, then return to the man and take the pen. Now I can hear the phone ringing again. Why can't everyone leave me alone?

"And here . . ."

I scribble on the line as best I can, and the delivery man squints suspiciously at it. "What does that say?"

"Bloomwood! It says Bloomwood!"

"Hello," I can hear Michael saying. "No, this is Becky's apartment. I'm Michael Ellis, a friend."

"I need you to sign again, lady. Legibly."

"Yes, I'm Luke's best man. Well, hello! I'm looking forward to meeting you!"

"OK?" I say, after practically stabbing my name into the page. "Satisfied?"

"Lighten up!" says the delivery guy, raising his hands as he saunters away. I close the door with my foot and stagger into the living room just in time to hear Michael saying, "I've heard about the plans for the ceremony. They sound quite spectacular!"

"*Who are you talking to?*" I mouth.

"*Your mom,*" mouths back Michael with a smile.

I nearly drop the box on the floor.

"I'm sure it'll all run smoothly on the day," Michael's saying reassuringly. "I was just saying to Becky, I really admire your involvement with the wedding. It can't have been easy!"

No. Please, no.

"Well," says Michael, looking surprised. "All I meant was, it must be difficult. What with you based in England . . . and Becky and Luke getting married in—"

"Michael!" I say desperately, and he looks up, startled. "Stop!"

He puts his hand over the receiver. "Stop what?"

"My mum. She . . . she doesn't know."

"Doesn't know what?"

I stare at him, agonized. At last he turns to the phone. "Mrs. Bloomwood, I'm going to have to go. There's a lot going on here. But great to talk to you and . . . I'll see you at the wedding, I'm sure . . . Yes, you too."

He puts down the phone and there's a scary silence.

"Becky, what doesn't your mom know?" he says at last.

"It . . . doesn't matter."

"I get the feeling it does." He looks at me shrewdly. "I get the feeling something's not right."

"I . . . It's nothing. Really . . ."

I stop at the sound of the fax machine whirring in the corner. Mum's fax. I quickly dump the box on the sofa and launch myself at the fax machine.

But Michael's too quick for me. He plucks the page from the machine and starts to read it.

"Playlist for Rebecca and Luke's wedding. Date: 22nd June. Venue: The Pines, 43 Elton Road . . . Oxshott . . ." He looks up, a frown on his face. "Becky, what is this? You and Luke are getting married at the Plaza. Right?"

I can't answer. Blood is pumping through my head, almost deafening me.

"Right?" repeats Michael, his voice becoming sterner.

"I don't know," I say at last in a tiny voice.

"How can you not know where you're getting married?"

He surveys the fax again. I can see comprehension slowly dawning.

"Jesus Christ." He looks up. "Your mom's planning a wedding in England, isn't she?"

I stare at him in mute anguish. This is even worse than Suze finding out. I mean, Suze has known me for so long. She knows how stupid I am and she always forgives me. But Michael. I swallow. Michael's always treated me with respect. He once told me I was sharp and intuitive. He even offered me a job with his company. I can't bear for him to find out what a complete mess I've got into.

"Does your mom know *anything* about the Plaza?"

Very slowly, I shake my head.

"Does Luke's mother know about this?" He hits the fax.

I shake my head again.

"Does anyone know? Does *Luke* know?"

"Nobody knows," I say, finally finding a voice. "And you have to promise not to tell anyone."

"Not *tell* anyone? Are you kidding?" He shakes his head in disbelief. "Becky, how could you have let this happen?"

"I don't know. I don't know. I didn't *mean* for it to happen—"

"You didn't mean to deceive two entire families? Not to mention the expense, the effort . . . You realize you're in big trouble here?"

"It'll work itself out!" I say desperately.

"How is it going to work itself out? Becky, this isn't a double-booked dinner date! This is hundreds of people!"

"Ding-dong, ding-dong!" suddenly chimes my wedding countdown alarm clock from the bookshelf. "Ding-dong, ding-dong! Only twenty-two days to go till the Big Day!"

"Shut up!" I say tensely.

"Ding-dong, ding—"

"Shut *up*!" I cry, and hurl it onto the floor, where the clock face shatters.

"Twenty-two days?" says Michael. "Becky, that's only three weeks!"

"I'll think of something! A lot can happen in three weeks!"

"You'll think of something? That's your only answer?"

"Perhaps a miracle will happen!"

I try a little smile, but Michael's face doesn't react. He still looks just as astounded. Just as angry.

I can't stand Michael being angry with me. My head's pounding and I can feel tears pressing hotly at my eyes. With trembling hands I grab my bag and reach for my jacket.

"What are you going to do?" His voice sharpens. "Becky, where are you going?"

I stare back, my mind feverishly racing. I need to escape. From this apartment, from my life, from this whole hideous mess. I need a place of peace, a place of sanctuary. A place where I'll find solace.

"I'm going to Tiffany," I say with a half-sob, and close the door behind me.

Five seconds after I've crossed the threshold of Tiffany, I'm already calmer. My heart rate begins to subside. My mind begins to turn less frantically. I feel soothed, just looking around at the cases full of glittering jewelry. Audrey Hepburn was right: nothing bad could ever happen in Tiffany.

I walk to the back of the ground floor, dodging the tourists and eyeing up diamond necklaces as I go. There's a girl about my age trying on a knuckle-duster of an engagement ring, and as I see her exhilarated face, I feel a painful pang inside.

It seems like a million years ago that Luke and I got engaged. I feel like a different person. If only I could rewind. God, if I could just have the chance. I'd do it all so differently.

There's no point torturing myself with how it might have been. This is what I've done—and this is how it is.

I get into the elevator and travel up to the third floor—and as I step out, I relax even more. This really is another world. It's different even from the crowded, touristy floor below. It's like heaven.

The whole floor is tranquil and spacious, with silver, china, and glassware displayed on mirror-topped cabinets. It's a world of quiet luxury. A world of glossy, cultured people who don't have to worry about anything. I can see an immaculate girl in navy blue examining a glass candlestick. Another girl, heavily pregnant, is looking at a sterling silver baby's rattle. No one's got any problems here. The only major dilemma facing anyone is whether to have gold or platinum edging their dinner service.

As long as I stay here I'll be safe.

"Becky? Is that you?" My heart gives a little flicker and I turn round, to see Eileen Morgan beaming at me. Eileen is the lady who showed me around the floor when I registered my list here. She's an elderly lady with her hair in a bun, and reminds me of the ballet teacher I used to have when I was little.

"Hi, Eileen," I say. "How are you?"

"I'm well. And I have good news for you!"

"Good news?" I say stupidly.

I can't remember the last time I heard a piece of good news.

"Your list has been going very well."

"Really?" In spite of myself I feel the same twinge of pride I used to when Miss Phipps said my pliés were going well.

"Very well, indeed. In fact, I was planning to call you. I think the time has come . . ." Eileen pauses momentously, ". . . to go for some larger items. A silver bowl. A platter. Some antique hollow-ware."

I stare at her in slight disbelief. In wedding list terms, this is as though she's said I should try for the Royal Ballet.

"You honestly think I'm in that . . . league?"

"Becky, the performance of your list has been very impressive. You're right up there with our top brides."

"I . . . I don't know what to say. I never thought . . ."

"Never underestimate yourself!" says Eileen with a warm smile, and gestures around the floor. "Browse for as long as you like and let me know what you'd like to add. If you need any help, you know where I am." She squeezes my arm. "Well done, Becky."

As she walks away, I feel my eyes pricking with grateful tears. *Someone* doesn't think I'm a disaster. *Someone* doesn't think I've ruined everything. In one area, at least, I'm a success.

I head toward the antiques cabinet and gaze up at a silver tray, filled with emotion. I won't let Eileen down. I'll register the best damn antique hollowware I possibly can. I'll put down a teapot, and a sugar bowl . . .

"Rebecca."

"Yes?" I say, turning round. "I haven't quite decided—"

And then I stop, my words shriveling on my lips. It's not Eileen.

It's Alicia Bitch Longlegs.

Out of the blue, like a bad fairy. She's wearing a pink suit and holding a Tiffany carrier bag and hostility is crackling all around her.

Of all the times.

"So," she says. "So, Becky. I suppose you're feeling pretty pleased with yourself, are you?"

"Er . . . no. Not really."

"Miss Bride of the Year. Miss Enchanted Bloody Forest."

I gaze at her puzzledly. I know Alicia and I aren't exactly best buddies—but isn't this a bit extreme?

"Alicia," I say. "What's wrong?"

"What's wrong?" Her voice rises shrilly. "What could be wrong? Maybe the fact that my wedding planner has dumped me with no warning. Maybe that's irking me a little!"

"What?"

"And why has she dumped me? So she can concentrate on her big, important, Plaza-wedding client. Her extra-special, spare-no-expense client Miss Becky Bloomwood."

I stare at her in horror. "Alicia, I had no idea—"

"My whole wedding's in pieces. I couldn't get another wedding planner. She's bad-mouthed me all over town. Apparently the rumor is I'm 'difficult.' Fucking *'difficult'!* The caterers aren't returning my calls, my dress is too short, the florist is an idiot . . ."

"I'm so sorry," I say helplessly. "I honestly didn't know about this—"

"Oh, I'm sure you didn't. I'm sure you weren't sniggering in Robyn's office while she made the call."

"I wasn't! I wouldn't! Look . . . I'm sure it'll all turn out OK." I take a deep breath. "To be honest, my wedding isn't going that smoothly either . . ."

"Give me a break. I've heard all about your wedding. The whole bloody world has." She turns on her heel and stalks away, and I gaze after her, shaken.

I haven't just ruined my own wedding, I've ruined Alicia's too.

I try to turn my attention back to the antiques cabinet but I feel upset and jittery. OK, come on. Let's pick a few things. That might cheer me up. A nineteenth-century tea strainer. And a sugar bowl with inlaid mother-of-pearl. I mean, that'll always come in handy, won't it?

And look at this silver teapot. Only $5,000. I scribble it down on my list and then look up to see if there's a matching cream jug. A young couple in jeans and T-shirts have wandered over to the same cabinet, and suddenly I notice they're staring up at the same teapot.

"Look at that," says the girl. "A five-thousand-dollar teapot. What would anyone want with that?"

"Don't you like tea?" says her boyfriend with a grin.

"Sure! But I mean, if you had five thousand dollars, would you spend it on a *teapot*?"

"When I have five thousand dollars I'll let you know," says the boyfriend. They both laugh and walk off, hand in hand, light and happy with each other.

Suddenly, standing there in front of the cabinet, I feel ridiculous. Like a child playing with grown-up clothes. What do I want a $5,000 teapot for?

I don't know what I'm doing here. I don't know what I'm doing. I want Luke.

It hits me like a tidal wave, overwhelming everything else. Brushing all the clutter and rubbish away.

That's all I want. Luke normal and happy again.

The two of us normal and happy. I have a sudden vision of us on a deserted beach somewhere. Watching the sunset. No baggage, no fuss. Just the two of us, being together.

Somehow I've lost sight of what really matters in all this, haven't I? I've been distracted by all the froth. The dress, and the cake, and the presents. When all that really counts is that Luke wants to be with me, and I want to be with him. Oh, I've been such a stupid fool . . .

My mobile phone suddenly bleeps, and I scrabble in my bag for it, filled with sudden hope.

"Luke?"

"Becky! What the hell's going on?" Suze's voice shrieks in my ear so fiercely, I nearly drop the phone in fright. "I just had a call from Michael Ellis! He says you're still getting married in New York! Bex, I can't believe you!"

"Don't shout at me! I'm in Tiffany!"

"What the hell are you doing in Tiffany? You should be sorting this mess out! Bex, you're not going to get married in America. You just can't! It would kill your mum."

"I know! I'm not going to! At least . . ." I push a hand distractedly through my hair. "Oh God, Suze. You just don't know what's been going on. Luke's having a midlife crisis . . . the wedding planner's threatened to sue me . . . I feel like I'm all on my own . . ."

To my horror I feel my eyes welling up with tears. I creep round the back of the cabinet and sink onto the carpeted floor, where no one can see me.

"I've ended up with two weddings and I can't do either of them! Either way, people are going to be furious with me. Either way it's going to be a disaster. It's supposed to be the best day of my life, Suze, and it's going to be the worst! The very worst!"

"Look, Bex, don't get into a state," she says, relenting slightly. "Have you really gone through all the options?"

"I've thought of everything. I've thought of committing bigamy, I've thought of hiring look-alikes . . ."

"That's not a bad idea," says Suze thoughtfully.

"You know what I really want to do?" My throat tightens with emotion. "Just run away from all of this and do it on a beach. Just the two of us and a minister and the seagulls. I mean, that's what really counts, isn't it? The fact that I love Luke and he loves me and we want to be together forever." As I picture Luke kissing me against a Caribbean sunset, I feel tears welling up again. "Who cares about having a posh dress? Who cares about a grand reception and getting lots of presents? None of it is important! I'd just wear a really simple sarong, and we'd be in bare feet, and we'd walk along the sand, and it would be so romantic—"

"Bex!" I jump in fright at Suze's tone. She sounds as angry as I've ever heard her. "Just stop it! Stop right there! God, you're a selfish cow sometimes."

"What do you mean?" I falter. "I just meant all the trappings weren't important . . ."

"They *are* important! People have made a lot of effort over those trappings! You've got two weddings that most people would die to have. OK, you can't do both. But you can do one. If you don't do either of them, then . . . you don't deserve them. You don't deserve any of it. Bex, these weddings aren't just about you! They're about all the people involved. All the people who have made an effort and put time and love and money into creating something really special. You can't just run away from that! You *have* to face this out, even if it means apologizing to four hundred people individually, on bended knee. If you just run away, then . . . then you're selfish and cowardly."

She stops, breathing hard, and I hear Ernie begin to wail plaintively in the background. I feel completely shocked, as though she's slapped me in the face.

"You're right," I say at last.

"I'm sorry," she says, and she sounds quite upset too. "But I am right."

"I know you are." I rub my face. "Look . . . I will face this out. I don't know how. But I will." Ernie's wailing has increased to lusty screaming, and I can barely hear myself over the noise. "You'd better go," I say. "Give my godson my love. Tell him . . . his godmother's sorry she's such a flake. She's going to try and do better."

"He sends all his love back," says Suze. She hesitates. "And he says remember, even though we might get a bit cross with you, we're still ready to help. If we can."

"Thanks, Suze," I say, my throat thick. "Tell him . . . I'll keep you posted."

I put my phone away and sit still, gathering my thoughts. At last I get to my feet, brush myself down, and walk back out onto the shop floor.

Alicia's standing five yards away.

My stomach gives a little flip. How long has she been there for? What did she hear?

"Hi," I say, my voice crackly with nerves.

"Hi," she says. Very slowly she walks toward me, her eyes running over me appraisingly.

"So," she says pleasantly. "Does Robyn know you're planning to run off to get married on a beach?"

Fuck.

"I'm . . ." I clear my throat. "I'm not planning to run off to a beach!"

"Sounded to me like you were." Alicia examines a nail. "Isn't there a clause about that in her contract?"

"I was joking! It was . . . you know, just being funny . . ."

"I wonder if Robyn would find it funny." Alicia gives me her most ingratiating smile. "To hear that Becky Bloomwood doesn't care about having a grand reception. To hear that her favorite, goody-two-shoes Little Miss Perfect client . . . is going to fly the coop!"

I have to keep calm. "You wouldn't say anything to Robyn."

"Wouldn't I?"

"You can't! You just . . ." I break off, trying to stay composed.

"Alicia, we've known each other a long time. And I know we haven't always . . . seen eye to eye . . . but come on. We're two British girls in New York. Both getting married. In a way, we're . . . we're practically sisters!"

I force myself to place a hand on her pink bouclé sleeve. "Surely we have to show solidarity? Surely we have to . . . support each other?"

There's a pause as Alicia runs contemptuous eyes over me. Then she jerks her arm away from my hand and starts to stride away.

"See you, Becky," she says over her shoulder.

I have to stop her. Quick.

"Becky!" Eileen's voice is behind me and I turn round in a daze. "Here's the pewterware I wanted to show you . . ."

"Thanks," I say dazedly. "I just have to . . ."

I turn back—but Alicia's disappeared.

Where did she go?

I hurry down the stairs to ground level, not bothering to wait for the lift. As I enter the floor I pause and look around desperately, searching for a flash of pink. But the whole place is crowded with an influx of excited, yabbering tourists. There are bright colors everywhere.

I push my way through them, breathing hard, telling myself Alicia wouldn't really say anything to Robyn; she wouldn't really be so vindictive. And at the same time, knowing that she would.

I can't see her anywhere on the whole floor. At last I manage to squeeze past a group of tourists clustered round a case full of watches and reach the revolving doors. I push my way out and stand on the street, looking from left to right. I can barely see anything. It's a blindingly bright day, with low sunlight glinting off plate-glass windows, turning everything into silhouettes and shadows.

"Rebecca." I feel a hand suddenly pulling sharply at my shoulder. In confusion, I turn round, blinking in the brightness and look up.

As my gaze focuses, I'm gripped by pure, cold terror.

It's Elinor.

Eighteen

I SHOULD NEVER HAVE stepped outside Tiffany.

"Rebecca, I need to talk to you," says Elinor coldly. "At once."

She's wearing a long black coat and oversized black sunglasses and looks exactly like a member of the Gestapo. Oh God, she's found out everything, hasn't she? She's spoken to Robyn. She's spoken to Alicia. She's come to haul me in front of the commandant and condemn me to hard labor.

"How did you know where I was?" I falter.

"Michael Ellis told me," she replies crisply.

Michael told her? Doesn't he think I'm suffering enough?

"Well, I'm er . . . busy," I say, trying to duck back inside Tiffany. "I haven't got time to chat."

"This is not chat."

"Whatever."

"This is very important."

"OK, look, it might *seem* important," I say desperately. "But let's get things in perspective. It's only a wedding. Compared to things like, you know, foreign treaties . . ."

"I don't wish to discuss the wedding." Elinor frowns. "I wish to discuss Luke."

"Luke?" I stare at her, taken aback. "How come . . . have you spoken to him?"

"I had several disturbing messages from him in Switzerland. And yesterday a letter. I returned home immediately."

"What did the letter say?"

"I'm on my way to see Luke now," says Elinor, ignoring me. "I would be glad if you accompany me."

"Are you? Where is he?"

"Michael Ellis went to search for Luke this morning and found him at my apartment. I'm on my way there now. Apparently Luke wishes to speak to me." She pauses. "But I wanted to talk to you first, Rebecca."

"Me? Why?"

Before she can answer, a group of tourists comes out of Tiffany and for a moment we're submerged by them. I could make my getaway under their cover. I could escape.

But now I'm curious. Why does Elinor want to talk to me?

The crowd melts away and we stare at each other.

"Please." She nods toward the curb. "My car is waiting."

"OK," I say, and give a tiny shrug. "I'll come."

Once inside Elinor's plushy limousine, my terror recedes. As I gaze at her pale, impenetrable face, I feel a slow hatred growing inside me instead.

This is the woman who screwed up Luke. This is the woman who ignored her own fourteen-year-old son. Sitting calmly in her limousine. Still behaving as though she owns the world; as though she's done nothing wrong.

"So what did Luke write in his letter?" I say.

"It was . . . confused," she says. "Rambling and nonsensical. He seems to be having some sort of . . ." She gestures regally.

"Breakdown? Yes, he is."

"Why?"

"Why do you think?" I retort, unable to keep a sarcastic edge out of my voice.

"He works very hard," says Elinor. "Perhaps too hard sometimes."

"It's not the work!" I say, unable to stop myself. "It's you!"

"Me." She frowns.

"Yes, you! It's the way you've treated him!"

There's a long pause. Then Elinor says, "What do you mean?"

She sounds genuinely taken aback. Is she really that insensitive?

"OK . . . where shall I start? With your charity! The charity that he has spent all his bloody waking hours working for. The charity that you promised him would benefit the profile of his company. But funnily enough didn't . . . because you took all the credit yourself!"

God, that felt good. Why have I never spoken my mind to Elinor before?

Her nostrils flare slightly and I can tell she's angry, but all she says is, "That version of events is skewed."

"It's not skewed! You used Luke!"

"He never complained about the amount of work he was doing."

"He wouldn't complain! But you *must* have seen how much time he was giving you for nothing! You used one of his staff, for God's sake! I mean, that alone was bound to get him into trouble—"

"I agree," says Elinor.

"What?" I'm momentarily halted.

"To use staff from Brandon Communications was not my idea. Indeed, I was against it. It was Luke who insisted. And as I have explained to Luke, the newspaper article was not my fault. I was given the option of a last-minute interview. Luke was unavailable. I told the journalist at great length about Luke's involvement and gave him Brandon Communications promotional literature. The journalist promised to read it but then used none of it. I assure you, Rebecca, it was out of my control."

"Rubbish!" I say at once. "A decent journalist wouldn't completely ignore something like . . ."

Hmm. Actually . . . maybe they would. Now that I think about it, when I was a journalist I always ignored half the stuff the interviewees told me. I certainly never read any of the stupid heavy literature they gave me.

"Well . . . OK," I say after a pause. "Maybe that wasn't entirely your fault. But that's not the main issue. That's not why Luke's so upset. A few days ago, he went looking for family photos in your apartment. But he didn't find any. Instead, he found some letters from his dad. All about how you didn't want him when he was a child. How you weren't interested in meeting him, even for ten minutes."

Elinor's face flinches slightly but she says nothing.

"And that brought back a lot of other really painful stuff. Like when he came to see you in New York and sat outside your building and you refused to acknowledge him? Remember that, Elinor?"

I know I'm being harsh. But I don't care.

"That was him," she says at last.

"Of course it was him! Don't pretend you didn't know it was him. Elinor, why do you think he pushes himself so hard? Why do you think he came to New York in the first place? To impress you, of course! He's been obsessed for years! No wonder he's gone over the edge now. To be honest, given the childhood he had, I'm amazed he's lasted this long without cracking!"

As I break off for breath, it occurs to me that maybe Luke wouldn't want me discussing all his secret neuroses with his mother.

Oh well, too late now. Anyway, someone's got to let Elinor have it.

"He had a happy childhood," she says, staring rigidly out of the window. We've stopped at a crossing and I can see the reflection of people walking past the car in her sunglasses.

"But he loved you. He wanted *you*. His mother. But you just didn't want to see him—"

"He's angry with me."

"Of course he's angry! You leave him behind and go off to America, not even caring about him, as happy as a clam."

"Happy." Elinor turns her head. "Do you think I'm happy, Rebecca?"

I'm halted. With a very slight twinge of shame I realize it's never occurred to me to think about whether Elinor is happy or not. I've only ever thought about what a cow she is.

"I . . . don't know," I say at last.

"I made my decision. I stuck to it. That doesn't mean that I don't regret it."

She takes off her sunglasses and I try not to give away my shock at the way she looks. Her skin is stretched even more tightly than ever and there's slight bruising around her eyes. Although she's just had a face-lift, to my eye she looks older than she did before. And kind of more vulnerable.

"I did recognize Luke that day," she says in a quiet voice.

"So why didn't you go over to him?"

There's silence in the car—and then, her lips barely moving, she says, "I was apprehensive."

"Apprehensive?" I echo disbelievingly.

"Giving up a child is a tremendous step. Taking a child back into one's life is . . . equally momentous. Particularly after such a long time. I wasn't prepared for such a step. I wasn't prepared for seeing him."

"Didn't you want to talk to him, though? Didn't you want to . . . to get to know him?"

"Maybe. Maybe I did."

I can see a slight quivering, just below her left eye. Is that an expression of emotion?

"Some people find it easy to embrace new experiences. Others shrink away. It may be difficult for you to understand that, Rebecca. I know you are an impulsive, warm person. It's one of the things I admire about you."

"Yeah, right," I say sarcastically.

"What do you mean?"

"Come on, Elinor," I say, rolling my eyes. "Let's not play games. You don't like me. You never have."

"What makes you think I don't like you?"

She cannot be serious.

"Your doorpeople don't let me into my own party . . . you try to make me sign a prenup . . . you're never *ever* nice to me . . ."

"I regret the incident at the party. That was an error on the part of the party planners." She frowns slightly. "But I have never understood your objection to a prenuptial contract. No one should get married without one." She looks out of the window. "We're here."

The car stops and the driver comes round to open the passenger door. Elinor looks at me.

"I do like you, Rebecca. Very much." She gets out of the car and her eye rests on my foot. "Your shoe is scuffed. It looks shoddy."

"You see?" I say in exasperation. "You see what I mean?"

"What?" She gives me a blank stare.

Oh, I give up.

Elinor's apartment is bright with shafts of morning sun, and completely silent. At first I think she must be wrong and Luke isn't here—but as we enter the living room, I see him. He's standing at the picture window, staring out with a deep frown.

"Luke, are you OK?" I say cautiously, and he wheels round in shock.

"Becky. What are you doing here?"

"I just . . . ran into your mother at Tiffany. Where have you been all morning?"

"Around and about," says Luke. "Thinking."

I glance at Elinor. She's staring at Luke, her face unreadable.

"Anyway, I'll leave, shall I?" I say awkwardly. "If you two are going to talk . . ."

"No," says Luke. "Stay. This won't take long."

I sit down awkwardly on the arm of a chair, wishing I could shrink into it. I've never liked the atmosphere in this apartment—but right now it's like the temperature's dropped ten degrees.

"I received your messages," says Elinor. "And your letter, which made very little sense." She takes off her gloves with jerky movements and places them on a side table. "I have no idea what you're trying to accuse me of."

"I'm not here to accuse you of anything," says Luke, making a visible attempt to stay calm. "I just wanted to let you know that I've had a few realizations. One of which has been that I've been somewhat . . . deluded over the years. You never really wanted me to live with you, did you? Yet you've allowed me to believe that you did."

"Don't be ridiculous, Luke," says Elinor after a pause. "The situation was far more complicated than you might imagine."

"You've played on my . . . my weakness. You've used me. And my company. You've treated me like a . . ." He breaks off, breathing heavily, and takes a couple of moments to calm himself. "What's a little sad is that one of the reasons I came to New York was to spend time with you. Perhaps get to know you as well as Becky knows her mother."

He gestures toward me and I look up in alarm. Don't bring me into this!

"What a waste of time." His voice harshens. "I'm not sure you're even capable of that kind of relationship."

"That's enough!" says Elinor. "Luke, I can't talk to you when you're in this state."

As he and Elinor face each other, I see that they're more alike than I've ever realized. They both get that blank, scary expression when things are going badly. They both set themselves impossibly high standards. And they're both more vulnerable than they want the outside world to know.

"You don't have to talk to me," says Luke. "I'm leaving now. You won't see me or Becky again."

My head jerks up in shock. Is he serious?

"You're talking nonsense," says Elinor.

"I've sent a letter of resignation to the trustees of the Elinor Sherman Foundation. There should be no other reason for our paths to cross."

"You have forgotten the wedding," says Elinor crisply.

"No, we haven't. I haven't forgotten it at all." Luke takes a deep breath and glances at me. "As of now, Becky and I will be making alternative arrangements for our marriage. Naturally, I'll pay whatever expenses you've incurred."

Wh—

What did he say? I stare at Luke, gobsmacked.

Did he really just say what I—

Did he really just . . .

Am I hallucinating?

"Luke," I say, trying to keep calm, trying to keep steady. "Let me just get this . . . Are you saying you want to pull out of the Plaza wedding?"

"Becky, I know I haven't discussed this with you yet." Luke comes over and takes my hands. "I know you've been planning this wedding for months. It's a lot to ask you to pull out. But under the circumstances, I just don't feel I can go through it."

"You want to pull out of the wedding." I swallow. "You do know there's a financial penalty?"

"I don't care."

"You . . . you don't care?"

He doesn't care.

I don't know whether to laugh or cry.

"That's not what I meant!" says Luke, seeing my expression. "I do care! Of course I care about us. But to stand up in public, and pretend to be a loving son to . . ." He glances at Elinor. "It would be farcical. It would debase the whole thing. Can you understand that?"

"Luke . . . of course I understand," I say, trying to keep the exhilaration out of my voice. "If you want to pull out, then I'm happy to go along."

I can't believe it. I'm saved. I'm saved!

"You're serious, aren't you?" He stares at me incredulously.

"Of course I'm serious! If you want to cancel the wedding, then I'm not going to put up a fight. In fact . . . let's call it off straight away!"

"You are a girl in a million, Becky Bloomwood." Luke's voice is suddenly thick. "To agree without even hesitating . . ."

"It's what you want, Luke," I say simply. "That's all that matters to me."

It's a miracle!

There's no other explanation.

For once in my life, God was actually listening. Either him or Ganesh.

"You cannot do this." For the first time there's a tremor of emotion in Elinor's voice. "You cannot simply abandon the wedding I have organized for you. Funded for you."

"I can."

"It's a highly significant event! We have four hundred people coming! Important people. Friends of mine, of the charity—"

"Well, you'll just have to make my excuses."

Elinor takes a few steps toward him, and I see to my astonishment that she's shaking with rage. "If you do this, Luke, I can promise you. We will never speak again."

"That's fine by me. Come on, Becky." He tugs at my hand and I follow him, stumbling slightly on the rug.

I can see Elinor's face twitching again, and to my extreme astonishment, I feel a bit sorry for her. But then, as we turn and stride together out of the apartment, I squash it. Elinor's been mean enough to me and my parents. She deserves all she gets.

We walk downstairs in silence. I think we're both completely shell-shocked. Luke lifts his hand for a cab, gives our address to the driver, and we both get in.

After about three blocks we look at each other. Luke is pale and shaking slightly.

"I don't know what to say," he says. "I can't believe I just did that."

"You were brilliant," I say firmly. "She had it coming."

He swivels in his seat and looks at me earnestly. "Becky, I'm so sorry about the wedding. I know how much you've been looking forward to it. I'll make it up to you. I promise. Just tell me how."

I stare at him, my mind working fast. OK. I have to play this one very carefully. If I make the wrong move, everything could still fall about my ears.

"So . . . you do still want to get married? You know, in principle."

"Of course I do!" Luke looks shocked. "Becky, I love you. Even more than I did before. In fact, I've never loved you as much as I did in that room. When you made that incredible sacrifice for me, without even a moment's hesitation."

"What? Oh, the wedding! Yes." I compose my features hastily. "Yes, well. It was quite a lot to ask of me. And um . . . speaking of . . . weddings . . ."

I almost can't bring myself to say it. I feel as though I'm trying to balance the last card on top of the pyramid. I have to get it exactly right.

"How would you feel about getting married in . . . Oxshott?"

"Oxshott. Perfect." Luke closes his eyes and leans back on his seat, looking exhausted.

I'm numb with disbelief. It's all fallen into place. The miracle is complete.

As we drive down Fifth Avenue I look out of the window of the cab, suddenly taking in the world outside. Noticing for the first time that it's summer. That it's a beautiful sunshiny day. That Saks has a new window display of swimwear. Little things I haven't been able to see, let alone appreciate, because I've been so preoccupied, so stressed.

I feel as though I've been walking around with a heavy weight on my back for such a long time, I've forgotten what it's like to walk upright. But at last the burden is lifted, and I can cautiously stand up and stretch, and start to enjoy myself. The months of nightmaresville are over. Finally, I can sleep easy.

Nineteen

EXCEPT I DON'T.

In fact, I don't sleep at all.

Long after Luke's crashed out, I'm staring at the ceiling, feeling uncomfortable. There's something wrong here. I'm just not quite sure what.

On the surface, everything's perfect. Elinor is out of Luke's life for good. We can get married at home. I don't have to worry about Robyn. I don't have to worry about anything. It's like a great big bowling ball has arrived in my life and knocked down all the bad ninepins in one fell swoop, leaving only good ones behind.

We had a lovely celebration supper, and cracked open a bottle of champagne, and toasted the rest of Luke's life, and the wedding, and each other. Then we started talking about where we should go on our honeymoon, and I made a strong case for Bali and Luke said Moscow and we had one of those laughing, almost hysterical arguments you have when you're high on exhilaration and relief. It was a wonderful, happy evening. I should be completely content.

But now that I'm in bed and my mind's settled down, things keep niggling at me. The way Luke looked tonight. Almost too exhilarated. Too bright-eyed. The way we both kept laughing, as though we didn't dare stop.

And other things. The way Elinor looked when we left. The conversation I had with Annabel, all those months ago.

I should feel triumphant. I should feel vindicated. But . . . somehow this doesn't feel right.

At last, at about three in the morning, I slide out of bed, go into the living room, and dial Suze's number.

"Hi, Bex!" she says in surprise. "What time is it there?" I can hear the tinny sound of British breakfast television on in the background, and little gurgles from Ernie. "God, I'm sorry I gave you a hard time yesterday. I've been feeling really bad ever since—"

"It's OK. Honestly, I've forgotten all about it." I huddle on the floorboards, pulling my dressing gown tightly around me. "Listen, Suze. Luke had a huge bust-up with his mum today. He's pulled out of the Plaza wedding. We can get married in Oxshott after all."

"*What?*" Suze's voice explodes down the line. "That's incredible! That's fantastic! Bex, I've been so worried! I honestly didn't know what you were going to do. You must be dancing on the ceiling! You must be—"

"I am. Kind of."

Suze comes to a breathless halt. "What do you mean, kind of?"

"I know everything's worked out. I know it's all fantastic." I wind my dressing gown cord tightly round my finger. "But somehow . . . it doesn't feel fantastic."

"What do you mean?" I can hear Suze turning the volume down. "Bex, what's wrong?"

"I feel bad," I say in a rush. "I feel like . . . I've won but I don't want to have won. I mean, OK, I've got everything I wanted. Luke's had it out with Elinor, he's going to pay off the wedding planner, we can have the wedding at home . . . On the one hand it's great. But on the other hand—"

"What other hand?" says Suze. "There isn't another hand!"

"There is. At least . . . I think there is." I start to nibble my thumbnail distractedly. "Suze, I'm worried about Luke. He really attacked his mother. And now he says he's never going to talk to her again . . ."

"So what? Isn't that a good thing?"

"I don't know. Is it?" I stare at the floor for a few moments. "He's all euphoric at the moment. But what if he starts feeling guilty? What if this screws him up just as badly in the future? You know, Annabel, his stepmum, once said if I tried to chop Elinor out of Luke's life it would damage him."

"But you didn't chop her out of his life," points out Suze. "He did."

"Well, maybe he's damaged himself. Maybe it's like . . . he's chopped his own arm off or something."

"Err, gross!"

"And now there's this huge wound, which nobody can see, and it'll fester away, and one day it'll erupt again . . ."

"Bex! Stop it! I'm eating my breakfast."

"OK, sorry. I'm just worried about him. He's not right. And the other thing is . . ." I close my eyes, almost unable to believe I'm about to say this. "I've kind of . . . changed my mind about Elinor."

"You *what*?" screeches Suze. "Bex, please don't say things like that! I nearly dropped Ernie on the floor!"

"I don't *like* her or anything," I say hastily. "But we had this talk. And I do think maybe she loves Luke. In her own weird, icebox Vulcan way."

"But she abandoned him!"

"I know. But she regrets it."

"Well, so what! She bloody well ought to regret it!"

"Suze, I just think . . . maybe she deserves another chance." I gaze at my fingertip, which is slowly turning blue. "I mean . . . look at me. I've done millions of stupid, thoughtless things. I've let people down. But they've always given me another chance."

"Bex, you're nothing like bloody Elinor! You'd never leave your child!"

"I'm not saying I'm *like* her! I'm just saying . . ." I tail away feebly, letting the dressing gown cord unravel.

I don't really know what I'm saying. And I don't think Suze will ever quite understand where I'm coming from. She's never made any mistakes in her life. She's always cruised through easily, never upsetting anyone, never getting herself in trouble. But I haven't. I know what it feels like to do something stupid—or worse than stupid—and then wish, above anything else, that I hadn't.

"So what does all this mean? Why are you—" Suze's voice sharpens in alarm. "Hang on. Bex, this isn't your way of saying you're going to get married in New York after all, is it?"

"It's not as simple as that," I say after a pause.

"Bex . . . I'll kill you. I really will. If you tell me now that you want to get married in New York—"

"Suze, I don't *want* to get married in New York. Of course I don't! But if we abandon the wedding now . . . then that'll be it. Elinor'll never speak to either of us again. Ever."

"I don't believe it. I just don't believe it! You're going to fuck everything up again, aren't you?"

"Suze—"

"Just as everything is all right! Just as for once in your life, you *aren't* in a complete mess and I can start to relax . . ."

"Suze—"

"Becky?"

I look up, startled. Luke is standing there in his boxers and T-shirt, staring in bleary puzzlement at me.

"Are you OK?" he says.

"I'm fine," I say, putting a hand over the receiver. "Just talking to Suze. You go back to bed. I won't be long."

I wait until he's gone and then shuffle closer to the radiator, which is still giving out a feeble heat.

"OK, Suze, listen," I say. "Just . . . just hear me out. I'm not going to fuck anything up. I've been thinking really hard, and I've had this genius idea . . ."

By nine the next morning I'm at Elinor's apartment. I've dressed very carefully and am wearing my smartest linen U.N. diplomatic envoy-style suit, together with a pair of nonconfrontational rounded-toe shoes. Although I'm not sure Elinor quite appreciates the effort I've made. As she answers the door she looks even paler than usual and her eyes are like daggers.

"Rebecca," she says stonily.

"Elinor," I reply, equally stonily. Then I remember I've come here in order to be conciliatory. "Elinor," I repeat, trying to inject the word with some warmth. "I've come to talk."

"To apologize," she says, heading down the corridor.

God, she is a cow. And anyway, what did I do? Nothing! For a moment I consider turning round and leaving. But I've decided to do this, so I will.

"Not really," I say. "Just to talk. About you. And Luke."

"He has regretted his rash actions."

"No."

"He wishes to apologize."

"No! He doesn't! He's hurt and angry and he has no desire to go near you again!"

"So why are you here?"

"Because . . . I think it would be a good thing if the two of you tried to make up. Or at least talk to each other again."

"I have nothing to say to Luke," replies Elinor. "I have nothing to say to you. As Luke indicated yesterday, the relationship is terminated."

God, they are *so* like each other.

"So . . . have you told Robyn yet about the wedding being off?" This is my secret fear, and I hold my breath for an answer.

"No. I thought I would give Luke a chance to reconsider. Clearly this was a mistake."

I take a deep breath. "I'll get Luke to go through with the wedding. If you apologize to him." My voice is a little shaky. I can't quite believe I'm doing this.

"What did you say?" Elinor turns and stares at me.

"You apologize to Luke and tell him . . . well, basically, that you love him. And I'll persuade him to get married at the Plaza. You'll have your big smart wedding for all your friends. That's the deal."

"You're . . . *bargaining* with me?"

"Er . . . yes." I turn to face her square-on and clench my fists tightly by my sides. "Basically, Elinor, I'm here for completely selfish reasons. Luke has been screwed up about you all his life. Now he's decided he never wants to see you again. Which is all fine and good— but I'm worried that's not the end. I'm worried in two years' time he'll suddenly decide he's got to come back to New York and find you and see if you really are as bad as he thinks you are. And it'll all start again."

"This is preposterous. How dare you—"

"Elinor, you want this wedding. I know you do. You just have to be nice to your son and you can have it. I mean, it's not that much to ask!"

There's silence. Gradually Elinor's eyes narrow, as closely as they can since her last bout of plastic surgery.

"You want this wedding too, Rebecca. Please don't pretend this is a purely altruistic offer. You were as dismayed as I was when he pulled out. Admit it. You're here because you want to get married at the Plaza."

"You think that's why I'm here?" I gape at her. "Because I'm upset that the Plaza wedding was canceled?"

I almost feel like laughing hysterically. I almost want to tell her the whole truth, right from the beginning.

"Believe me, Elinor," I say at last. "That's not why I'm here. I can live without the Plaza wedding. Yes, I was looking forward to it and it was exciting. But if Luke doesn't want it . . . that's it. I can drop it just like that. It's not my friends. It's not my home city. I really don't care."

There's another sharp silence. Elinor moves away to a polished side table and, to my utter astonishment, takes out a cigarette and lights it. She's kept that habit very quiet!

"I can persuade Luke," I say, watching her put the box away. "And you can't."

"You are . . . beyond belief," she says. "Using your own wedding as a bargaining tool."

"I know I am. Is that a yes?"

I've won. I can see it in her face. She's already decided.

"Here's what you have to say." I get out a piece of paper from my bag. "It's all the stuff Luke needs to hear. You have to tell him you love him, you have to say how much you missed him when he was a child, how you thought he'd be better off in Britain, how the only reason you didn't want to see him was you were afraid of disappointing him . . ." I hand the paper to Elinor. "I know none of it is going to sound remotely natural. So you'd better start off by saying 'These words don't come naturally to me.' "

Elinor stares blankly at the sheet. She's breathing heavily and for a moment I think she's going to throw it at me. Then, carefully, she folds up the piece of paper and puts it on the side table. Is that another twitch of emotion beneath her eye? Is she upset? Livid? Or just disdainful?

I just can't get my head round Elinor. One minute I think she's carrying round a huge untapped love deep inside her—and the next I think she's a coldhearted cow. One minute I think she completely hates me. Then I think, maybe she just has no idea how she comes across. Maybe, all this time, she's genuinely believed she was being friendly.

I mean, if no one's ever *told* her what an awful manner she has . . . how's she to know?

"What did you mean by saying that Luke might decide to come back to New York?" she says frostily. "Are you planning to leave?"

"We haven't talked about it yet," I say after a pause. "But yes. I think we might. New York's been great, but I don't think it's a good place for us to be anymore. Luke's burned out. He needs a change of scene."

He needs to be away from you, I add silently.

"I see." Elinor draws on her cigarette. "You appreciate I had arranged an interview with the co-op board of this building? At considerable effort."

"I know. Luke told me. But to be honest, Elinor, we would never have lived here."

Her face flickers again, and I can tell she's suppressing some kind of feeling. But what? Is it fury with me for being so ungrateful? Is it distress that Luke's not going to live in her building after all? Part of me is desperately curious, wants to pick away at her facade, nose in, and find out all about her.

And another, more sensible part of me says, just leave it, Becky. Just leave it.

As I reach the door, though, I can't resist turning round. "Elinor, you know how they say inside every fat person there's a thin person struggling to get out? Well . . . the more I think about you, the more I think there might—possibly—be a nice person inside you. But as long as you keep being mean to people and telling them their shoes are shoddy, no one's ever going to know."

There. She'll probably kill me now. I'd better get out. Trying not to look as though I'm running, I head down the corridor and out of the apartment. I close the door behind me and lean against it, my heart thudding.

OK. So far so good. Now for Luke.

"I have absolutely no idea why you want to go to the Rainbow Room." Luke leans back in his taxi seat and scowls out of the window.

"Because I never have, OK? I want to see the view!"

"But why now? Why today?"

"Why not today?" I glance at my watch and then survey Luke anxiously.

He's pretending he's happy. He's pretending he's liberated. But he's not. He's brooding.

Superficially, things have started to get slightly better. At least he hasn't given away any more items of clothing, and this morning he actually shaved. But he's still far from his old self. He didn't go into work today but sat all day watching a triple bill of old black-and-white films starring Bette Davis.

Funnily enough, I'd never seen the resemblance between Bette Davis and Elinor before.

The truth is, Annabel was right, I think as I watch him. Well, of course she was. She knows her stepson as though he were her own child. And she knows that Elinor is right inside Luke, part of his very being. He can't just cut her out and move on. He needs at least the chance of some kind of resolution. Even if it is painful.

I shut my eyes and send a silent plea to all gods. Please let this work. Please. And then maybe we'll be able to draw a line under all of it and get on with our lives.

"Rockefeller Center," says the taxi driver, pulling up, and I smile at Luke, trying to hide my nerves.

I tried to think of the least likely place that Elinor would ever be found—and came up with the Rainbow Room at Rockefeller Center, where tourists go to drink cocktails and gawk at the view over Manhattan. As we head up to the sixty-fifth floor in the lift, we're both silent, and I pray desperately that she'll be there, that it'll all work out, that Luke won't get too pissed off with me—

We walk out of the lift . . . and I can already see her. Sitting at a window table in a dark jacket, her face silhouetted against the view.

As he spots her, Luke gives a start.

"Becky. What the fuck—" He turns on his heel and I grab his arm.

"Luke, please. She wants to talk to you. Just . . . give her a chance."

"You set this up?" His face is white with anger. "You brought me here deliberately?"

"I had to! You wouldn't have come otherwise. Just five minutes. Listen to what she says."

"Why on earth should I—"

"I really think the two of you need to talk. Luke, you can't leave it like you did. It's eating you up inside! And it's not going to get any better unless you talk to her . . . Come on, Luke." I loosen my grip on his arm and look at him pleadingly. "Just five minutes. That's all I'm asking."

He has to agree. If he stalks out now, I'm dead.

A group of German tourists have come up behind us and I watch them milling around at the window, gasping admiringly at the view. "Five minutes," says Luke at last. "That's all." Slowly he walks across the room and sits down opposite Elinor. She glances over at me and nods, and I turn away, my heart beating fast. Please don't let her fuck this one up. Please.

I walk out of the bar and make my way into an empty function room, where I stand at the floor-length window, gazing out over the city. After a while I glance at my watch. It's been five minutes and he hasn't stormed out yet.

She's delivered on her side of the deal. Now I have to deliver on mine.

I get out my mobile phone, feeling sick with dread. This is going to be hard. This is going to be really hard. I don't know how Mum's going to react. I don't know what she's going to say.

But the point is, whatever she says, however furious she gets, I know Mum and I will last. Mum and I are there for the duration.

Whereas this could be Luke's only chance to reconcile with Elinor.

As I listen to the ringing tone, I stare out over the endless silvery blocks and towers of Manhattan. The sun's glinting off one building, only to be reflected off another, just like Luke said. Backward and forward, never leaving. The yellow taxis are so far down they look like Tonka toys and the people scurrying about are like tiny insects. And there in the middle is the green rectangular form of Central Park, like a picnic rug laid down for the children to play on.

I gaze out, mesmerized by the sight. Did I really mean what I said to Elinor yesterday? Do I really want for Luke and me to leave this amazing city?

"Hello?" Mum's voice breaks my thoughts, and my head jolts upward. For a moment I'm paralyzed with nerves. I can't do this.

But I have to.

I have no choice.

"Hi, Mum," I say at last, digging my nails into the palm of my hand. "It's . . . it's Becky. Listen, I've got something to tell you. And I'm afraid you're not going to like it—"

2 June 2002

Dear Becky,

We were a little bewildered by your phone call. Despite your assurances that all will be clear when you have explained it to us, and that we must trust you, we do not really understand what is going on.

However, James and I have talked long and hard and have at last decided to do as you ask. We have canceled our flights to New York and alerted the rest of the family.

Becky dear, I do hope this all works out.

With very best wishes, and with all our love to Luke—

Annabel

June 10, 2002

Miss Rebecca Bloomwood
Apt. B
251 W. 11th Street
New York, NY 10014

Dear Miss Bloomwood:

Thank you very much for your wedding invitation addressed to
Walt Pitman.

After some discussion we have decided to take you into our
confidence. Walt Pitman does not in fact exist. It is a generic
name, used to represent all our customer care operatives.

The name "Walt Pitman" was chosen after extensive focus
group research to suggest an approachable yet competent
figure. Customer feedback has shown that the continual
presence of Walt in our customers' lives has increased
confidence and loyalty by over 50 percent.

We would be grateful if you would keep this fact to yourself. If
you would still like a representative from Second Union Bank at
your wedding, I would be glad to attend. My birthday is March
5th and my favorite color is blue.

Yours sincerely,

Bernard Lieberman
Senior Vice-President

Twenty

OK. DON'T PANIC. This is going to work. If I just keep my head and remain calm, it'll work.

"It'll never work," says Suze's voice in my ear.

"Shut up!" I say crossly.

"It'll never work in a million years. I'm just warning you."

"You're not supposed to be warning me! You're supposed to be encouraging me!" I lower my voice. "And as long as everyone does what they're supposed to, it will work. It has to."

I'm standing at the window of a twelfth-floor suite at the Plaza, staring at Plaza Square below. Outside, it's a hot sunny day. People are milling around in T-shirts and shorts, doing normal things like hiring horse carriages to go round the park and tossing coins into the fountain.

And here am I, dressed in a towel, with my hair teased beyond recognition into a *Sleeping Beauty* style, and makeup an inch thick, walking around in the highest white satin shoes I've ever come across in my life. (Christian Louboutin, from Barneys. I get a discount.)

"What are you doing now?" comes Suze's voice again.

"I'm looking out the window."

"What are you doing that for?"

"I don't know." I watch a woman with denim shorts sit down on a bench and snap open a can of Coke, completely unaware she's being watched. "To try to get a grip on normality, I suppose."

"Normality?" I hear Suze splutter down the phone. "Bex, it's a bit late for normality!"

"That's not fair!"

"If normality is planet earth, do you know where you are right now?"

"Er . . . the moon?" I hazard.

"You're fifty million light-years away. You're . . . in another galaxy. A long long time ago."

"I do feel a bit like I'm in a different world," I admit, and turn to survey the palatial suite behind me.

The atmosphere is hushed and heavy with scent and hairspray and expectation. Everywhere I look there are lavish flower arrangements, baskets of fruit and chocolates, and bottles of champagne on ice. Over by the dressing table the hairdresser and makeup girl are chatting to one another while they work on Erin. Meanwhile the reportage photographer is changing his film, his assistant is watching Madonna on MTV, and a room-service waiter is clearing away yet another round of cups and glasses.

It's all so glamorous, so expensive. But at the same time, what I'm reminded of most of all is getting ready for the summer school play. The windows would be covered in black material, and we'd all crowd round a mirror getting all overexcited, and out the front we'd hear the parents filing in, but we wouldn't be allowed to peek out and see them . . .

"What are you doing now?" comes Suze's voice again.

"Still looking out the window."

"Well, stop looking out the window! You've got less than an hour to go!"

"Suze, relax."

"How can I relax?"

"It's all fine. It's under control."

"And you haven't told anyone," she says for the millionth time. "You haven't told Danny."

"Of course not! I'm not that stupid!" I edge casually into a corner where no one can hear me. "Only Michael knows. And Laurel. That's it."

"And no one suspects anything?"

"Not a thing," I say, just as Robyn comes into the room. "Hi, Robyn! Suze, I'll talk to you later, OK—"

I put the phone down and smile at Robyn, who's wearing a bright pink suit and a headset and carrying a walkie-talkie.

"OK, Becky," she says in a serious, businesslike way. "Stage one is complete. Stage two is under way. But we have a problem."

"Really?" I swallow. "What's that?"

"None of Luke's family have arrived yet. His father, his stepmother, some cousins who are on the list . . . You told me they'd spoken to you?"

"Yes, they did." I clear my throat. "Actually . . . they just called again. I'm afraid there's a problem with their plane. They said to seat other people in their places."

"Really?" Robyn's face falls. "This is too bad! I've never known a wedding to have so many last-minute alterations! A new maid of honor . . . a new best man . . . a new officiant . . . it seems like everything's changed!"

"I know," I say apologetically. "I'm really sorry, and I know it's meant a lot of work." I cross my fingers behind my back. "It just suddenly seemed so obvious that Michael should marry us, rather than some stranger. I mean, since he's such an old friend and he's qualified to do it and everything. So then Luke had to have a new best man . . ."

"But to change your minds three weeks before the wedding! And you know, Father Simon was quite upset to be rejected. He wondered if it was something to do with his hair."

"No! Of course not! It's nothing to do with him, honestly—"

"And then your parents both catching the measles. I mean, what kind of odds is that?"

"I know!" I pull a rueful face. "Sheer bad luck."

There's a crackle from the walkie-talkie and Robyn turns away.

"Yes," she says. "What's that? No! I said radiant *yellow* light! Not blue! OK, I'm coming . . ." As she reaches the door she looks back.

"Becky, I have to go. I just needed to say, it's been so hectic, what with all the changes, there are a couple of tiny additional details we didn't have time to discuss. So I just went ahead with them. OK?"

"Whatever," I say. "I trust your judgment. Thanks, Robyn."

As Robyn leaves, there's a tapping on the door and in comes Christina, looking absolutely amazing in pale gold Issey Miyake and holding a champagne glass.

"How's the bride?" she says with a smile. "Feeling nervous?"

"Not really!" I say.

Which is kind of true.

In fact, it's completely true. I'm beyond nervous. Either everything goes to plan and this all works out. Or it doesn't and it's a complete disaster. There's not much I can do about it.

"I just spoke to Laurel," she says, taking a sip of champagne. "I didn't know she was so involved with the wedding."

"Oh, she's not really," I say. "There's just this tiny little favor she's doing for me—"

"So I understand." Christina eyes me over her glass, and I suddenly wonder how much Laurel has said to her.

"Did she tell you . . . what the favor was?" I say casually.

"She gave me the gist. Becky, if you pull this off . . ." says Christina. She shakes her head. "If you pull this off, you deserve the Nobel Prize for chutzpah." She raises her glass. "Here's to you. And good luck."

"Thanks."

"Hey, Christina!" We both look round to see Erin coming toward us. She's already in her long violet maid-of-honor dress, her hair up in a medieval knot, eyes lit up with excitement. "Isn't this *Sleeping Beauty* theme cool? Have you seen Becky's wedding dress yet? I can't believe I'm the maid of honor! I was never a maid of honor before!"

I think Erin's a tad excited about her promotion. When I told her my best friend, Suze, couldn't make it, and would she like to be maid of honor, she actually burst into tears.

"I haven't seen Becky's wedding dress yet," says Christina. "I hardly dare to."

"It's really nice!" I protest. "Come and look."

I lead her into the sumptuous dressing area, where Danny's dress is hanging up.

"It's all in one piece," observes Christina laconically. "That's a good start."

"Christina," I say. "This isn't like the T-shirts. This is in a different league. Take a look!"

I just can't believe what a fantastic job Danny has done. Although I'd never admit it to Christina, I wasn't exactly counting on wearing his dress. In fact, to be perfectly honest, I was having secret Vera Wang fittings right up until a week ago.

But then one night Danny knocked on the door, his whole face lit up with excitement. He dragged me upstairs to his apartment, pulled me down the corridor, and flung open the door to his room. And I was speechless.

From a distance it looks like a traditional white wedding dress, with a tight bodice, full, romantic skirt, and long train. But the closer you get, you more you start spotting the fantastic customized details everywhere. The white denim ruffles at the back. The trademark Danny little pleats and gatherings at the waistline. The white sequins and diamante and glitter scattered all over the train, like someone's emptied a candy box over it.

I've never seen a wedding dress like it. It's a work of art.

"Well," says Christina. "I'll be honest. When you told me you were wearing a creation by young Mr. Kovitz, I was a little worried. But this . . ." She touches a tiny bead. "I'm impressed. Assuming the train doesn't fall off as you walk down the aisle."

"It won't," I assure her. "I walked around our apartment in it for half an hour. Not even one sequin fell off!"

"You're going to look amazing," says Erin dreamily. "Just like a princess. And in that room . . ."

"The room is spectacular," says Christina. "I think a lot of jaws are going to be dropping."

"I haven't seen it yet," I say. "Robyn didn't want me going in."

"Oh, you should take a look," says Erin. "Just have a peek. Before it gets filled up with people."

"I can't! What if someone sees me?"

"Go on," says Erin. "Put on a scarf. No one'll know it's you."

I creep downstairs in a borrowed hooded jacket, averting my face when I pass anyone, feeling ridiculously naughty. I've seen the designer's plans, and as I push open the double doors to the Terrace Room, I think I know roughly what I'm expecting to see. Something spectacular. Something theatrical.

Nothing could have prepared me for walking into that room.

It's like walking into another land.

A silvery, sparkling, magical forest. Branches are arching high above me as I look up. Flowers seem to be growing out of clumps of earth. There are vines and fruits and an apple tree covered with silver apples, and a spider's web covered with dewdrops . . . and are those *real* birds flying around up there?

Colored lights are dappling the branches and falling on the rows of chairs. A pair of women are methodically brushing lint off every upholstered seat. A man in jeans is taping a cable to the carpet. A man on a lighting rig is adjusting a silvery branch. A violinist is playing little runs and trills, and there's the dull thud of timpani being tuned up.

This is like being backstage at a Broadway show.

I stand at the side, staring around, trying to take in every detail. I have never seen anything like this in my life before, and I don't think I ever will again.

Suddenly I see Robyn entering the room at the far end, talking into her headpiece. Her eyes scan the room, and I shrink into my hooded jacket. Before she can spot me, I back out of the Terrace Room and get into the lift to go up to the Grand Ballroom.

As the doors are about to close, a couple of elderly women in dark skirts and white shirts get in.

"Did you see the cake?" says one of them. "Three thousand dollars minimum."

"Who's the family?"

"Sherman," says the first woman. "Elinor Sherman."

"Oh, *this* is the Elinor Sherman wedding."

The doors open and they walk out.

"Bloomwood," I say, too late. "I think the bride's name is Becky . . ."

They weren't listening, anyway.

I cautiously follow them into the Grand Ballroom. The enormous white and gold room where Luke and I will lead the dancing.

Oh my God. It's even huger than I remember. It's even more gilded and grandiose. Spotlights are circling the room, lighting up the balconies and chandeliers. They suddenly switch to strobe effects, then flashing disco lights, playing on the faces of waiters putting finishing touches to the tables. Every circular table has an ornate centerpiece of cascading white flowers. The ceiling has been tented with muslin, festooned with fairy lights like strings of pearls. The dance floor is vast and polished. Up on the stage, a ten-piece band is doing a sound check. I look round dazedly and see two assistants from Antoine's cake studio balancing on chairs, sticking the last few sugar tulips into the eight-foot cake. Everywhere is the smell of flowers and candle wax and anticipation.

"Excuse me." I jump aside as a waiter wheels a cart past.

"Can I help you?" says a woman with a Plaza badge on her lapel.

"I was just, er . . . looking around . . ." I say.

"Looking around?" Her eyes narrow suspiciously.

"Yes! In case I ever . . . er . . . want to get married." I back away before she can ask any more. I've seen enough, anyway.

I'm not sure how to get back to the suite from here, and this place is so huge I'm bound to get lost, so I head back down to the ground floor and walk as inconspicuously as I can past the Palm Court to the elevators.

As I pass an alcove containing a sofa, I stop. There's a familiar dark head. A familiar hand, holding what looks like a gin and tonic.

"Luke?" He turns round and peers at me blankly—and I suddenly realize my face is half hidden. "It's me!" I hiss.

"Becky?" he says incredulously. "What are you doing here?"

"I wanted to see it all. Isn't it amazing?" I look around to see if I'm being observed, then slide into the chair opposite him. "You look great."

He looks more than great. He's looking completely gorgeous, in an immaculate dinner jacket and crisp white dress shirt. His dark hair is glossy under the lights, and I can just smell the familiar scent of his aftershave. As he meets my eyes, I feel something release inside me, like a coil unwinding. Whatever happens today—whether I pull this off or not—the two of us are together. The two of us will be all right.

"We shouldn't be talking to each other, you know," he says with a little smile. "It's bad luck."

"I know," I say, and take a sip of his gin and tonic. "But to be honest, I think we're beyond superstition by now."

"What do you mean?"

"Oh . . . nothing." I count to five, psyching myself up, then say, "Did you hear about your parents being delayed?"

"Yes, I was told." Luke frowns. "Did you speak to them? Do you know when they'll get here?"

"Oh, soon, I expect," I say vaguely. "Don't worry, they said they would definitely be there to see you walk down the aisle."

Which is true. In its way.

Luke doesn't know anything of my plans. He's had enough to deal with as it is. For once, I'm the one in charge.

I feel like I've seen a completely different Luke over the last few weeks. A younger, more vulnerable Luke, whom the rest of the world doesn't know anything about. After he had that meeting with Elinor, he was very quiet for a while. There was no huge emotional outburst, no dramatic scene. In some ways, he simply went back to normal. But he was still fragile, still exhausted. Still nowhere near being able to go to work. For about two weeks, he just slept and slept, fourteen or fifteen hours a day. It was as though ten years of driving himself too hard were finally catching up with him.

Now he's gradually becoming his usual self. He's getting back that veneer of confidence. That blank expression when he doesn't want people to know what he's feeling. That abrupt, businesslike manner. He's been into the office during the past week, and it's been like old times.

Although not quite. Because although the veneer's back, the point is, I've seen underneath it. I've seen the way Luke works. The way he thinks and what he's scared of and what he really wants out of life. Before all this happened, we'd been together for over two years. We'd lived together, we were a successful couple. But now I feel I know him in a way I never did before.

"I keep thinking back to that conversation I had with my mother," he says, frowning into his drink. "Up in the Rainbow Room."

"Really?" I say warily. "What exactly—"

"I still find it confusing."

"Confusing?" I say after a pause. "Why's that?"

"I've never heard her speak that way before. It didn't seem real." He looks up. "I don't know whether I should believe her."

I lean forward and take his hand. "Luke, just because she's never said those things to you before, it doesn't mean they aren't true."

This is what I've said to him nearly every day since he had the meeting with Elinor. I want to stop him picking away at it. I want him to accept what she said, and be happy. But he's too intelligent for that. He's silent for a few moments, and I know he's replaying the conversation in his mind.

"Some of the things she said seemed so true, and others, so false."

"Which bits sounded false?" I say lightly. "Out of interest?"

"When she told me that she was proud of everything I'd done, from the founding of my company to choosing you as a wife. It just didn't quite . . . I don't know . . ." He shakes his head.

"I thought that was rather good!" I retort before I can stop myself. "I mean . . . you know . . . quite a likely thing for her to say—"

"But then she said something else. She said there wasn't a single day since I was born that she hadn't thought about me." He hesitates. "And the way she said it . . . I really believed her."

"She said that?" I say, taken aback.

There was nothing about that on the piece of paper I gave Elinor. I reach for Luke's gin and tonic and take a sip, thinking hard.

"I really do think she meant what she said," I say at last. "In fact . . . I know it. The point is, she wanted to tell you she loved you. Even if everything she said didn't sound completely natural, that's what she wanted you to know."

"I suppose so." He meets my eyes. "But still. I can't feel the same way about her. I can't go back to where I was."

"No," I say after a short silence. "Well . . . I think that's probably a good thing."

The spell's been lifted. Luke has finally woken up.

I lean over and kiss him, then take another sip of his drink. "I should go and put my frock on."

"You're not wearing that fetching anorak?" says Luke with a grin.

"Well, I was *going* to. But now you've seen it, I'll just have to find something else, I suppose . . ." I get up to go—then hesitate. "Listen, Luke. If things seem a bit strange today, just . . . go with it, OK?"

"OK," says Luke in surprise.

"You promise?"

"I promise." He gives me a sideways look. "Becky, is there anything I should know?"

"Er . . . no," I say innocently. "No, I don't think so. See you in there."

Twenty-one

I CAN'T BELIEVE I'VE made it to this moment. I honestly can't believe it's really happening.

I'm wearing a wedding dress and a sparkly tiara in my hair.

I'm a bride.

As I'm led by Robyn down the empty, silent Plaza corridors, I feel a bit like the president in a Hollywood movie. "The Beauty is on the move," she's muttering into her headset as we walk along the plushy red carpet. "The Beauty is approaching."

We turn a corner and I catch a glimpse of myself in a huge antique mirror, and feel a dart of shock. Of course I know what I look like. I've just spent half an hour staring at myself in the suite upstairs, for goodness' sake. But still, catching myself unawares, I can't quite believe that girl in the veil is me. It's *me*.

I'm about to walk up the aisle at the Plaza. Four hundred people watching every move. Oh God.

Oh God. What am I thinking?

As I see the doors of the Terrace Room, I start to panic, and my fingers tighten around my bouquet. This is never going to work. I must be mad. I can't do it. I want to run away.

But there's nowhere to run. There's nothing else to do but go forward.

Erin and the other bridesmaids are waiting, and as we draw

near, they all begin to coo over my dress. I've no idea what their names are. They're daughters of Elinor's friends. After today I'll probably never see them again.

"String orchestra. Stand by for Beauty," Robyn is saying into her headset.

"Becky!" I look up, and thank God, it's Danny, wearing a brocade frock coat over leather trousers, and carrying a taupe and bronze Ceremony Program. "You look amazing."

"Really? Do I look OK?"

"Spectacular," says Danny firmly. He adjusts the train, stands back for a look, then takes out a pair of scissors and snips at a piece of ribbon.

"Ready?" says Robyn.

"I guess," I say, feeling slightly sick.

The double doors swing open, and I hear the rustle of four hundred people turning in their seats. The string orchestra starts to play the theme from *Sleeping Beauty,* and the bridesmaids begin to walk up the aisle.

And suddenly I'm walking forward. I'm walking into the enchanted forest, carried on the swell of the music. Little lights are twinkling overhead. Pine needles are giving off their scent under my feet. There's the smell of fresh earth and the sound of birds chirruping, and the trickle of a tiny waterfall. Flowers are magically blooming as I take each step, and leaves are unfurling, and people are gasping as they look up. And there's Luke up ahead, my handsome prince, waiting for me.

Finally, I start to relax. To savor it.

As I take each step, I feel as though I'm a prima ballerina doing the perfect arabesque at Covent Garden. Or a movie star arriving at the Oscars. Music playing, everyone looking at me, jewels in my hair and the most beautiful dress I've ever worn. I know I will never experience anything like this again in my life. Never. As I reach the top of the aisle, I slow my pace right down, breathing in the atmosphere, taking in the trees and the flowers and the wonderful scent. Trying to impress every detail on my mind. Relishing every magical second.

I reach Luke's side and hand my bouquet to Erin. I smile warmly at Gary, Luke's new best man—then take Luke's hand. He gives a little squeeze, and I squeeze it back.

And here's Michael stepping forward, wearing a dark, vaguely clerical-looking suit.

He gives me a tiny, conspiratorial smile, then takes a deep breath and addresses the congregation.

"Dearly beloved. We are gathered here together to witness the love between two people. We are here to watch them pledging their love for each other. And to join with them in celebrating the joy of their sharing of that love. God blesses all who love, and God will certainly bless Luke and Becky today as they exchange their vows."

He turns to me, and I can hear the rustling behind me as people try to get a good view.

"Do you, Rebecca, love Luke?" he says. "Do you pledge yourself to him for better for worse, for richer for poorer, in sickness and in health? Do you put your trust in him now and forever?"

"I do," I say, unable to stop a tiny tremor in my voice.

"Do you, Luke, love Rebecca? Do you pledge yourself to her for better for worse, for richer for poorer, in sickness and in health? Do you put your trust in her now and forever?"

"Yes," says Luke firmly. "I do."

"May God bless Luke and Becky and may they have happiness always." Michael pauses and looks around the room, as though daring anyone to argue with him, and my fingers tighten around Luke's. "May they know the joy of a shared understanding, the delight of a growing love, and the warmth of an everlasting friendship. Now let us applaud the happy couple." He smiles at Luke. "You may kiss the bride."

As Luke bends to kiss me, Michael determinedly begins to clap. There's a slightly uncertain pause . . . then a smattering of people join in, and soon the whole room is applauding.

Gary is murmuring something in Luke's ear, and he turns to me, looking puzzled.

"What about the ring?"

"Don't mention the ring," I say through a fixed smile.

My heart is beating so hard, I can barely breathe. I keep waiting for someone to stand up. For someone to say, "Hang on a minute . . ."

But no one does. No one says anything.

It's worked.

I meet Michael's eye for an instant—then look away before anyone notices. I can't relax yet. Not quite yet.

The photographer comes forward and I take Luke's arm firmly in mine, and Erin gives me my bouquet, wiping away her tears as she does so.

"That was such a beautiful ceremony!" she says. "The bit about the warmth of an everlasting friendship really got to me. You know, because that's all I want." She clasps my bouquet to her chest. "That's all I've ever wanted."

"Well, you know, I'm sure you'll find it," I say, and give her a hug. "I know you will."

"Excuse me, miss?" says the photographer. "If I could just get the bride and groom . . ."

Erin gives me my flowers and ducks out of the way, and I adopt my most radiant, newlywed expression.

"But, Becky," Luke says. "Gary says—"

"Take the ring from Gary," I say without moving my head. "Say you're really embarrassed that it got left out, and we'll do it later."

Some guests have come forward to take photographs, and I rest my head on Luke's shoulder and smile happily at them.

"Something else is wrong," Luke is saying. "Michael didn't proclaim us husband and wife. And don't we have to sign something?"

"Sssshh!" There's a bright flash, and we both blink.

"Becky, what's going on?" He pulls me round to face him. "Are we married?"

"That's a good shot!" says the photographer. "Stay like that."

"Are we married?" Luke's eyes scan my face intently.

"Well . . . OK," I say reluctantly. "As it happens, we're not."

There's another blinding flash. When my eyes focus again, Luke's gazing at me incredulously. "We're not married?"

"Look, just trust me, OK?"

"*Trust* you?"

"Yes! Like you just promised to do five seconds ago! Remember?"

"I promised to do that when I thought we were getting married!"

Suddenly the string orchestra launches into the "Bridal March," and a team of minders usher away the guests with their cameras.

"Go," says a crackling, disembodied voice. "Start walking."

Where on earth is it coming from? Are my flowers talking to me? Suddenly my eyes zoom in on a tiny speaker, attached to a rosebud. Robyn's planted a speaker in my bouquet?

"Bride and groom! Walk!"

"OK!" I say to the flowers. "We're going!"

I grab Luke's arm tight and begin to walk down the aisle, back through the enchanted forest.

"We're not married," Luke is saying disbelievingly. "A whole bloody forest, four hundred people, a big white dress, and we're not married."

"Sssh!" I say crossly. "Don't tell everybody! Look, you promised if things were a bit strange you'd go with it. Well, go with it!"

As we walk along arm in arm, rays of sunlight are piercing the branches of the forest, dappling the floor. Suddenly there's a whirring noise, and to my astonishment the branches creakily begin to retreat, to reveal rainbows playing on the ceiling. A heavenly chorus breaks into song, and a fluffy cloud descends from the sky, on which a pair of fat pink doves are reposing.

Oh God. I've got the giggles. This is too much. Are these the tiny additional details Robyn was talking about?

I look up at Luke, and his mouth is twitching suspiciously too.

"What do you think of the forest?" I say brightly. "It's cool, isn't it? They flew the birch trees over from Switzerland especially."

"Really?" says Luke. "Where did they fly the doves over from?" He peers up at them. "Those are too big to be doves. They must be turkeys."

"They're not turkeys!"

"Love turkeys."

"Luke, shut up," I mutter, trying desperately not to giggle. "They're doves."

We're passing row after row of smartly dressed guests, all smiling warmly at us except the girls, who are giving me the Manhattan Onceover.

"Who the hell are all these people?" says Luke, surveying the rows of smiling strangers.

"I have no idea." I shrug. "I thought you might know some of them."

We reach the back of the room for a final session of photographs, and Luke looks at me quizzically. "Becky, my parents aren't here. And neither are yours."

"Er . . . no. They're not."

"No family. No ring. And we're not married." He pauses. "Call me crazy—but this isn't quite how I expected our wedding to be."

"This isn't our wedding," I say, and kiss him for the cameras.

I can't quite believe we're getting away with it. No one's said anything. No one's questioned a thing. A couple of people have asked to see the ring, and I've just flashed them the band of my engagement ring, turned round.

We've eaten sushi and caviar. We've had an amazing four-course dinner. We've drunk toasts. It's all gone according to plan. We cut the cake with a huge silver sword and everybody cheered, and then the band started to play "The Way You Look Tonight" and Luke led me onto the dance floor and we started dancing. That was one of those moments I'll keep in my scrapbook forever. A whirl of white and gold and glitter and music, and Luke's arms around me, and my head giddy from champagne, and the knowledge that this was it, this was the high, and soon it would be over.

And now the party's in full swing. The band's playing a jazzy number I don't recognize, and the dance floor's full. Amid the throng of well-dressed strangers, I can pick out a few familiar faces. Christina's dancing with her date, and Erin is chatting to one of the groomsmen. And there's Laurel, dancing very energetically with . . . Michael!

Well now. That's a thought.

"So. Guess how many people have asked for my card?" says a voice in my ear. I turn round, to see Danny looking triumphant, a glass of champagne in each hand and a cigarette in his mouth. "Twenty! At least! One wanted me to take her measurements, right then and there. They all think the dress is to die for. And when I told them I'd worked with John Galliano . . ."

"Danny, you've never worked with John Galliano!"

"I passed him a cup of coffee once," he says defensively. "And he thanked me. That was, in its way, an artistic communication . . ."

"If you say so." I grin at him happily. "I'm so pleased for you."

"So are you enjoying yourself?"

"Of course!"

"Your mother-in-law is in her element."

We both turn to survey Elinor, who is sitting at a nearby table, surrounded by smart ladies. There's a slight glow to her cheek and she looks about as animated as I've ever seen her. She's wearing a long sweeping pale green dress and huge quantities of diamonds, and looks like the belle of the ball. Which, in a way, she is. These are her friends. This is really her party, not Luke's or mine. It's a wonderful spectacle. It's a wonderful occasion to be a guest at.

And that's kind of what I feel I am.

A group of women go by, chattering loudly, and I hear snatches of conversation.

"Spectacular . . ."

"So imaginative . . ."

They smile at me and Danny, and I smile back. But my mouth is feeling a bit stiff. I'm tired of smiling at people I don't know.

"It's a great wedding," says Danny, looking around the glittering room. "Really spectacular. Although it's less *you* than I would have thought."

"Really? What makes you say that?"

"I'm not saying it's not fantastic. It's very slick, very lavish. It's just . . . not like I imagined you'd have your wedding. But I was wrong," he adds hastily as he sees my expression. "Obviously."

I look at his wiry, comical, unsuspecting face. Oh God. I have to tell him. I *can't* not tell Danny.

"Danny, there's something you should know," I say in an undertone.

"What?"

"About this wedding—"

"Hi, kids!"

I break off guiltily and turn around—but it's only Laurel, all flushed and happy from dancing.

"Great party, Becky," she says. "Great band. Christ, I'd forgotten how much I love to dance."

I survey her appearance in slight dismay.

"Laurel," I say. "You don't roll up the sleeves of a thousand-dollar Yves St. Laurent dress."

"I was hot," she says with a cheerful shrug. "Now, Becky, I hate to tell you." She lowers her voice. "But you're going to have to get going pretty soon."

"Already?" I look instinctively at my wrist, but I'm not wearing a watch.

"The car's waiting outside," says Laurel. "The driver has all the details. He'll take you to Teterboro Airport and show you where to go. It's a different procedure for private planes, but it should be straightforward. Any problems, you call me." She lowers her voice to a whisper, and I glance at Danny, who's pretending not to be listening. "You should be in England in plenty of time. I really hope it all works out."

I reach out and hug her tightly. "Laurel . . . you're a star," I mutter. "I don't know what to say."

"Becky, believe me. This is nothing. After what you did for me, you could have had ten planes." She hugs me back, then looks at her watch. "You'd better find Luke. I'll see you in a bit."

After she's gone there's a short, interested silence.

"Becky, did I just catch the words *private plane*?" says Danny.

"Er . . . yes. Yes, you did."

"You're flying on a private plane?"

"Yes." I try to sound nonchalant. "We are. It's Laurel's wedding present to us."

"She snapped up the private jet?" Danny shakes his head. "Damn. You know, I was planning to get you that myself. It was between that and the eggbeater . . ."

"Idiot! She's president of a plane company."

"Jesus. A private plane. So . . . where are you heading? Or is it still a big secret?" I watch as he takes a drag from his cigarette, and feel a sudden huge wave of affection for him.

I don't just want to tell Danny what's going on.

I want him to be part of this.

"Danny," I say. "How do you feel about going on a little trip?"

It takes me a while to find Luke. He's been trapped in a corner by two corporate financiers, and leaps up gratefully as soon as I appear. We go around the huge crowded room, saying good-bye and thank you for coming to all the guests we know. To be honest, it doesn't take that long.

Last of all, we approach the top table and interrupt Elinor as discreetly as we can.

"Mother, we're going now," says Luke.

"Now?" Elinor frowns. "It's too early."

"Well . . . we're going."

"Thank you for a wonderful wedding," I say sincerely. "It was really amazing. Everyone's been saying how wonderful it is." I bend to kiss her. "Good-bye."

"Good-bye, Becky," she says in that formal way of hers. "Good-bye, Luke."

"Good-bye, Mother."

They gaze at each other—and for a moment I think Elinor's going to say something else. But instead she leans forward rather stiffly and kisses Luke on the cheek.

"Becky!" I feel someone poking me on the shoulder. "Becky, you're not going yet!" I turn round to see Robyn looking perturbed.

"Er . . . yes. We're off. Thank you so much for everything you've—"

"You can't go yet!"

"No one'll notice," I say, glancing around the party.

"They have to notice! We have an exit planned, remember? The rose petals? The music?"

"Well . . . maybe we could forget the exit—"

"Forget the exit?" Robyn stares at me. "Are you joking? Orchestra!" she says urgently into her headpiece. "Segue to 'Some Day.' Do you copy? Segue to 'Some Day.' " She lifts the walkie-talkie. "Lighting crew, stand by with rose petals."

"Robyn," I say helplessly. "Honestly, we just wanted to slip away quietly . . ."

"My brides do not slip away quietly! Cue fanfare," she mutters into her headpiece. "Lighting crew, prepare exit spotlight."

There's a sudden loud fanfare of trumpets, and the guests on the dance floor all jump. The lighting changes from disco beat to a radiant pink glow, and the band starts to play "Some Day My Prince Will Come."

"Go, Beauty and Prince," says Robyn, giving me a little shove. "Go! *One* two three, *one* two three . . ."

Exchanging looks, Luke and I make it onto the dance floor, where the guests part to let us through. The music is all around us, a spotlight is following our path, and all of a sudden, rose petals start falling gently from the ceiling.

This is rather lovely, actually. Everyone's beaming benevolently, and I can hear some "Aahs" as we go by. The glow of pink light is like being inside a rainbow, and the rose petals smell wonderful as they land on our heads and arms and drift to the floor. Luke and I are smiling at each other, and there's a petal in his hair—

"Stop!"

As I hear the voice, I feel a sudden chill, right to the marrow of my bones.

The double doors have opened, and there she is, standing in the doorway. Wearing a black suit and the highest, pointiest black boots I've ever seen.

Everyone turns to look, and the orchestra peters out uncertainly.

"Oh, look!" I hear someone saying in delight. "That's so cute, they even thought of a witch!"

"Alicia?" says Luke in astonishment. "What are you doing here?"

"Having a good wedding, Luke?" she says sweetly, and takes a few steps into the room.

"Come in," I say quickly. "Come on in and join the party. We would have invited you . . ."

"I know what you're doing, Becky."

"We're getting married!" I say, trying to sound lighthearted. "No prizes for guessing that!"

"I know exactly what you're doing." She meets my eye. "I've got friends in Surrey, and they've been checking things out."

No.

Please, no.

"I think you have a teeny little secret you're not sharing with the rest of your guests." Alicia pulls a mock-concerned face. "That's not very polite, is it?"

I need my fairy godmothers, quick. I need someone to zap her with twinkle dust.

Laurel shoots me a horrified look.

Christina puts down her champagne glass.

"Code red, Code red," I hear Robyn's voice crackling from the bouquet. "Urgent. Code red."

Now Alicia's walking around the dance floor, taking her time, relishing the attention.

"The truth is," she says pleasantly, "this is all a bit of a sham. Isn't it, Becky?"

My eye flickers behind her. Two burly minders in tuxedos are approaching the dance floor. But they're not going to get there in time. It's all going to be ruined.

"It all looks so lovely. It all looks so romantic." Her voice suddenly hardens. "But what people might like to know is that this so-called perfect Plaza wedding is actually a complete and utter . . . *arrrgh!*" Her voice rises to a scream. "Put me down!"

I don't believe it. It's Luke.

He's calmly walked up to her and hoisted her up onto his shoulder. And now he's carrying her out, like a naughty toddler.

"Put me down!" she cries. "Someone bloody well help me!"

But the guests are starting to laugh. She starts kicking Luke with her pointy boots, and he raises his eyebrows but doesn't stop striding.

"It's a fake!" she shrieks as they reach the door. "It's a fake! They're not really—"

The door slams, cutting her off, and there's a silent, shocked moment. No one moves, not even Robyn. Then, slowly, the door opens again, and Luke reappears, brushing his hands.

"I don't like gate-crashers," he says dryly.

"Bravo!" shouts a woman I don't recognize. Luke gives a little bow, and there's a huge, relieved laugh, and soon the whole room is applauding.

My heart is thumping so hard I'm not sure I can keep standing. As Luke rejoins me, I reach for his hand and he squeezes mine hard. I just want to go now. I want to get away.

Now there's an interested babble around the room, and I can hear people murmuring things like "deranged" and "must be jealous." A woman in head-to-toe Prada is even saying brightly, "You know, exactly the same thing happened at *our* wedding—"

Oh God, and now here come Elinor and Robyn, side by side like the two queens in *Alice in Wonderland*.

"I'm so sorry!" says Robyn as soon as she gets near. "Don't let it upset you, sweetheart. She's just a sad girl with a grudge."

"Who *was* that?" says Elinor with a frown. "Did you know her?"

"A disgruntled ex-client," says Robyn. "Some of these girls become very bitter. I've no idea what happens to them! One minute they're sweet young things, the next minute they're throwing lawsuits around! Don't worry, Becky. We'll do the exit again. Attention, orchestra," she says urgently. "Reprise 'Some Day' at the signal. Lighting crew, stand by with emergency rose petals."

"You have emergency rose petals?" I say in disbelief.

"Sweetheart, I have every eventuality covered." She twinkles at me. "This is why you hire a wedding planner!"

"Robyn," I say honestly, "I think you're worth every penny." I put an arm round her and give her a kiss. "Bye. And bye again, Elinor."

The music swells through the air again, we start walking again, and more rose petals start cascading from the ceiling. I really have to hand it to Robyn. People are crowding around and applauding— and is it my imagination, or do they look a bit friendlier, following the Alicia incident? At the end of the line I spot Erin leaning eagerly forward, and I toss my bouquet into her outstretched hands.

And then we're out.

The heavy double doors close behind us and we're in the silent, plushy corridor, empty but for the two bouncers, who stare studiously ahead.

"We did it," I say, half laughing in relief; in exhilaration. "Luke, we did it!"

"So I gather," says Luke, nodding. "Well done, us. Now, do you mind telling me what the fuck is going on?"

Twenty-two

LAUREL ARRANGED IT all perfectly. After a quick detour to the West Village for Danny's passport, we arrived at Teterboro to find the plane all ready for us. We arrived at Gatwick at about eight in the morning, where another car was waiting for us. And now we're speeding through Surrey toward Oxshott. We'll be there soon! I can't quite believe how seamless it's all been.

"Of course, you know your big mistake," says Danny, stretching luxuriously back in the leather Mercedes seat.

"What's that?" I say, looking up from the phone.

"Sticking to two weddings. I mean, as long as you're going to do it more than once, why not three times? Why not six times? Six parties . . ."

"Six dresses . . ." puts in Luke.

"Six cakes . . ."

"Look, shut up!" I say indignantly. "I didn't do all this intentionally, you know! It just . . . happened."

"Just happened," echoes Danny scoffingly. "Becky, you needn't pretend to us. You wanted to wear two dresses. There's no shame in it."

"Danny, I'm on the phone—" I look out of the window. "OK, Suze, I think we're about ten minutes away."

"I just can't believe you've made it," says Suze down the line. "I can't believe it all worked out! I feel like rushing around, telling everyone!"

"Well, don't!"

"But it's so incredible! To think last night you were at the Plaza, and now—" She stops in sudden alarm. "Hey, you're not still wearing your wedding dress, are you?"

"Of course not!" I giggle. "I'm not a complete moron. We changed on the plane."

"And what was that like?"

"It was *so* cool. Honestly, Suze, I'm only ever traveling by Learjet from now on."

It's a bright sunny day, and as I look out of the window at the passing fields, I feel a swell of happiness. I can't quite believe it's all fallen into place. After all these months of worry and trouble. We're here in England. The sun is shining. And we're going to get married.

"You know, I'm a tad concerned," says Danny, peering out of the window. "Where are all the castles?"

"This is Surrey," I explain. "We don't have castles."

"And where are the soldiers with bearskins on their heads?" He narrows his eyes. "Becky, you're sure this is England? You're sure that pilot knew where he was going?"

"Pretty sure," I say, getting out my lipstick.

"I don't know," he says doubtfully. "This looks a lot more like France to me."

We pull up at a traffic light and he winds down the window.

"*Bonjour,*" he says to a startled woman. "*Comment allez-vous?*"

"I . . . I wouldn't know," says the woman, and hurries across the road.

"I knew it," says Danny. "Becky, I hate to break it to you . . . but this is France."

"It's Oxshott, you idiot," I retort. "And . . . here's our road."

I feel a huge spasm of nerves as I see the familiar sign. We're nearly there.

"OK," says the driver. "Elton Road. Which number?"

"Number 43. The house over there," I say. "The one with the balloons and the bunting . . . and the silver streamers in the trees . . ."

Blimey. The whole place looks like a fairground. There's a man up in the horse chestnut tree at the front, threading lightbulbs through the branches, and a white van parked in the drive, and women in green and white stripy uniforms bustling in and out of the house.

"Looks like they're expecting you, anyway," says Danny. "You OK?"

"Fine," I say—and it's ridiculous, but my voice is shaking.

The car comes to a halt, and so does the other car behind, which is carrying all our luggage.

"What I don't understand," says Luke, staring out at all the activity, "is how you managed to shift an entire wedding forward by a day. At three weeks' notice. I mean, you're talking the caterers, you're talking the band, you're talking a million different very busy professionals . . ."

"Luke, this isn't Manhattan," I say, opening the car door. "You'll see."

As we get out, the front door swings open, and there's Mum, wearing tartan trousers and a sweatshirt reading "Mother of the Bride."

"Becky!" she cries, and runs over to give me a hug.

"Mum." I hug her back. "Is everything OK?"

"Everything's under control, I think!" she says a little flusteredly. "We had a problem with the table posies, but fingers crossed, they should be on their way . . . Luke! How are you? How was the financial conference?"

"It went er . . . very well," he says. "Very well indeed, thank you. I'm just sorry it's caused so much trouble with the wedding arrangements—"

"Oh, that's all right!" says Mum. "I'll admit, I was a bit taken aback when Becky phoned. But in the end, it didn't take much doing! Most of the guests were staying over for Sunday brunch, anyway. And Peter at the church was most understanding, and said he didn't usually conduct weddings on a Sunday, but in this case he'd make an exception—"

"But what about . . . the catering, for instance? Wasn't that all booked for yesterday?"

"Oh, Lulu didn't mind! Did you, Lulu?" she says to one of the women in green and white stripes.

"No!" says Lulu brightly. "Of course not. Hello, Becky! How are you?"

Oh my God! It's Lulu who used to take me for Brownies.

"Hi!" I say, "I didn't know you did catering!"

"Oh well." She makes a self-deprecating little gesture. "It's just to keep me busy, really. Now that the children are older . . ."

"You know, Lulu's son Aaron is in the band!" says Mum proudly. "He plays the keyboards! And you know, they're very good! They've been practicing 'Unchained Melody' especially—"

"Now, just taste this!" says Lulu, reaching into a foil-covered tray and producing a canapé. "It's our new Thai filo parcels. We're rather pleased with them. You know, filo pastry is very in now."

"Really?"

"Oh yes." Lulu nods knowledgeably. "*No one* has shortcake tartlets anymore. And as for vol-au-vents . . ." She pulls a little face. "Over."

"You are so right," says Danny, his eyes bright. "The vol-au-vent is dead. The vol-au-vent is toast, if you will. May I ask where you stand on the asparagus roll?"

"Mum, this is Danny," I put in quickly. "My neighbor, remember?"

"Mrs. B., it's an honor to meet you," says Danny, kissing Mum's hand. "You don't mind my tagging along with Becky?"

"Of course not!" says Mum. "The more the merrier! Now, come and see the marquee!"

As we walk round to the garden, my jaw drops. A huge silver and white striped marquee is billowing on the lawn. All the flower beds read "Becky and Luke" in pansies. There are fairy lights strung up in every available bush and shrub. A uniformed gardener is polishing a new granite water feature, someone else is sweeping the patio, and inside the marquee I can see lots of middle-aged women sitting in a semicircle, holding notebooks.

"Janice is just giving the girls the team briefing," says Mum in an undertone. "She's really got into this wedding organizing lark now. She wants to start doing it professionally!"

"Now," I hear Janice saying as we approach. "The emergency rose petals will be in a silver basket by Pillar A. Could you all please mark that on your floorplans—"

"You know, I think she'll be a success," I say thoughtfully.

"Betty and Margot, if you could be in charge of buttonholes. Annabel, if you could please take care of—"

"Mum?" says Luke, peering into the marquee incredulously.

Oh my God. It's Annabel! It's Luke's stepmum, sitting there along with everyone else.

"Luke!" Annabel looks round and her entire face lights up. "Janice, excuse me for a moment—"

She hurries toward us and envelops Luke in a tight hug.

"You're here. I'm so glad to see you." She peers anxiously into his face. "Are you all right, darling?"

"I'm fine," says Luke, "I think. A lot's been going on . . ."

"So I understand," says Annabel, and gives me a sharp look. "Becky." She reaches out with one arm and hugs me, too. "I'm going to have a long chat with you later," she says into my ear.

"So . . . you're helping with the wedding?" says Luke to his stepmother.

"Oh, it's all hands to the deck around here," says Mum gaily. "Annabel's one of us now!"

"And where's Dad?" says Luke, looking around.

"He's gone to get some extra glasses with Graham," says Mum. "Those two have really hit it off. Now, who's for a cup of coffee?"

"You're getting on well with Luke's parents!" I say, following Mum toward the kitchen.

"Oh, they're super!" she says happily. "Really charming. They've already invited us down to stay in Devon. Nice, normal, down-to-earth people. Not like . . . that woman."

"No. They're quite different from Elinor."

"She didn't seem at all interested in the wedding," says Mum, her voice prickling slightly. "You know, she never even replied to her invitation!"

"Didn't she?"

Damn. I thought I'd done a reply from Elinor.

"Have you seen much of her recently?" says Mum.

"Er . . . no," I say. "Not much."

We carry a tray of coffee upstairs to Mum's bedroom, and open the door to find Suze and Danny sitting on the bed, with Ernie lying between them, kicking his little pink feet. And hanging on the wardrobe door opposite, Mum's wedding dress, as white and frilly as ever.

"Suze!" I exclaim, giving her a hug. "And gorgeous Ernie! He's got so *big*—" I bend down to kiss his cheek, and he gives me an enormous gummy smile.

"You made it." Suze grins at me. "Well done, Bex."

"Suze has just been showing me your family heirloom wedding dress, Mrs. B.," says Danny, raising his eyebrows at me. "It's . . . quite unique."

"This dress is a real survivor!" says Mum delightedly. "We thought it was ruined, but all the coffee came out!"

"What a miracle!" says Danny.

"And even just this morning, little Ernie tried to throw apple puree over it—"

"Oh, really?" I say, glancing at Suze, who flushes slightly.

"But luckily I'd covered it in protective plastic!" says Mum. She reaches for the dress and shakes out the frills, slightly pink about the eyes. "This is a moment I've been dreaming about for so long. Becky wearing my wedding dress. I am a silly, aren't I?"

"It's not silly," I say, and give her a hug. "It's what weddings are all about."

"Mrs. Bloomwood, Becky described the dress to me," says Danny. "And I can honestly say she didn't do it justice. But you won't mind if I make a couple of teeny tiny alterations?"

"Not at all!" says Mum, and glances at her watch. "Well, I must get on. I've still got to chase these posies!"

As the door closes behind her, Danny and Suze exchange glances.

"OK," says Danny. "What are we going to do with this?"

"You could cut the sleeves off, for a start," says Suze. "And all those frills on the bodice."

"I mean, how much of it do we actually need to keep?" Danny looks up. "Becky, what do you think?"

I don't reply. I'm staring out of the window into the garden. I can see Luke and Annabel walking round the garden, their heads close together, talking. And there's Mum talking to Janice, and gesturing to the flowering cherry tree.

"Becky?" says Danny again.

"Don't touch it," I say, turning round.

"What?"

"Don't do anything to it." I smile at Danny's appalled face. "Just leave it as it is."

By ten to three I'm ready. I'm wearing the sausage roll dress. My face has been made up by Janice as Radiant Spring Bride, only slightly toned down with a tissue and water. I've got a garland of bright pink carnations and gypsophila in my hair, which Mum ordered along with my bouquet. The only remotely stylish thing about me is my Christian Louboutin shoes, which you can't even see.

And I don't care. I look exactly how I want to look.

We've had our photos taken by the flowering cherry tree, and Mum has wept all down her "Summer Elegance" makeup and had to be retouched. And now everyone has gone off to the church. It's me and Dad, waiting to go.

"Ready?" he says, as a white Rolls-Royce purrs into the drive.

"I think so," I say, a slight wobble to my voice.

I'm getting married. I'm really getting married.

"Do you think I'm doing the right thing?" I say, only half joking.

"Oh, I think so." Dad looks into the hall stand mirror and adjusts his silk tie. "I remember saying to your mother, the very first day I met Luke, 'This one will keep up with Becky.' " He meets my eye in the mirror. "Was I right, love? Does he keep up with you?"

"Not quite." I grin at him. "But . . . he's getting there."

"Good." Dad smiles back. "That's probably all he can hope for."

The driver is ringing the doorbell, and as I open the door, I peer at the face under the peaked cap. I don't believe it. It's my old driving instructor, Clive.

"Clive! Hi! how are you?"

"Becky Bloomwood!" he exclaims. "Well, I never! Becky Bloomwood, getting married! Did you ever pass your test, then?"

"Er . . . yes. Eventually."

"Who would have thought it?" He shakes his head, marvelingly. "I used to go home to the wife and say, 'If that girl passes her test, I'm a fried egg.' And then of course, when it came to it—"

"Yes, well, anyway—"

"That examiner said he'd never known anything like it. Has your husband-to-be seen you drive?"

"Yes."

"And he still wants to marry you?"

"Yes!" I say crossly.

Honestly. This is my wedding day. I shouldn't have to be re-minded about stupid driving tests that happened years ago.

"Shall we get in?" says Dad tactfully. "Hello, Clive. Nice to see you again."

We walk out into the drive, and as we reach the car I look back at the house. When I see it again I'll be a married woman. I take a deep breath and step into the car.

"Stooooop!" comes a voice. "Becky! Stop!"

I freeze in terror, one foot inside the car. What's happened? Who's found out? What do they know?

"I can't let you go through with this!"

What? This doesn't make any sense. Tom Webster from next door is pelting toward us in his morning suit. What does he think he's doing? He's supposed to be ushering at the church.

"Becky, I can't stand by and watch," he says breathlessly, plant-ing a hand on the Rolls-Royce. "This could be the biggest mistake of your life. You haven't thought it through."

Oh, for God's sake.

"Yes, I have," I say, and try to elbow him out of the way.

But he grabs my shoulder. "It hit me last night. We belong to-gether. You and me. Think about it, Becky. We've known each other all our lives. We've grown up together. Maybe it's taken us a while to discover our true feelings for each other . . . but don't we deserve to give them a chance?"

"Tom, I haven't got any feelings for you," I say. "And I'm getting married in two minutes. So can you get out of my way?"

"You don't know what you're letting yourself in for! You have no idea of the reality of marriage! Becky, tell me honestly. Do you really envisage yourself spending the rest of your days with Luke? Day after day, night after night? Hour after endless hour?"

"Yes!" I say, losing my temper. "I do! I love Luke very much and I do want to spend the rest of my days with him! Tom, it has taken a lot of time and effort and trouble for me to get to this moment. More than you can possibly imagine. And if you don't get out of my way right now and let me get to my wedding, I'll . . . I'll . . ."

"Tom," puts in Dad. "I think the answer's no."

"Oh." Tom is silent for a moment. "Well . . . OK." He gives an abashed shrug. "Sorry."

"You never did have any sense of timing, Tom Webster," says Clive scornfully. "I remember the first time you ever pulled out into a roundabout. Nearly killed us both, you did!"

"It's OK. No harm done. Can we go now?" I step into the car, arranging my dress around me, and Dad gets in beside me.

"I'll see you there, then, shall I?" says Tom mournfully, and I raise my eyes heavenward.

"Tom, do you want a lift to the church?"

"Oh, thanks. That'd be great. Hi, Graham," he says awkwardly to my father as he clambers in. "Sorry about that."

"That's quite all right, Tom," says my father, patting him on the back. "We all have our little moments." He pulls a face at me over Tom's head and I quell a giggle.

"So. Are we all set?" says Clive, turning in his seat. "Any sudden changes of heart? Any more last-minute protestations of love? Any three-point turns?"

"No!" I say. "There's nothing else. Let's go already!"

As we arrive at the church, the bells are ringing, the sun is shining, and a couple of last-minute guests are hurrying in. Tom opens the car door and dashes down the path without a backward glance, while I fluff out my train to the admiring glances of passersby.

God, it is fun being a bride. I'm going to miss it.

"All set?" says Dad, handing me my bouquet.

"I think so." I grin at him and take his outstretched arm.

"Good luck," says Clive, then nods ahead. "You've got a couple of late ones here."

A black taxi is pulling up in front of the church, and both passenger doors are flung open. I stare ahead incredulously, wondering if I'm dreaming, as Michael gets out, still in his evening dress from the Plaza. He extends a hand back into the taxi, and the next moment Laurel appears, still in her Yves St. Laurent with the sleeves rolled up.

"Don't let us put you off!" she says. "We'll just sneak in somewhere—"

"But . . . but what the hell are you *doing* here?"

"Language," says Clive reprovingly.

"What's the point of being in control of a hundred private jets if you can't fly wherever you want?" says Laurel as she comes over to hug me. "We decided we wanted to see you get married."

"For real," says Michael into my ear. "Hats off to you, Becky."

Dad and I wait until they've disappeared into the church, then make our way down the path to the porch where Suze is excitedly waiting. She's wearing a silvery blue dress and carrying Ernie, who's wearing a matching romper suit. As I peep inside the church, I can see the gathered faces of all my family, all my old friends, all Luke's friends and relations. Sitting side by side, happy and expectant.

The organ stops playing, and I feel a stab of nerves.

It's finally happening. I'm finally getting married. For real.

Then the "Bridal March" starts and Dad gives my arm a squeeze, and we start to walk up the aisle.

Twenty-three

WE'RE MARRIED.

We're really married.

I look down at the shiny wedding band that Luke slid onto my finger in the church. Then I look around at the scene before me. The marquee is glowing in the summer dusk, and the band is playing a ropy version of "Smoke Gets in Your Eyes," and people are dancing. Maybe the music isn't as smooth as it was at the Plaza. And maybe the guests aren't all as well dressed. But they're ours. They're all ours.

We had a lovely dinner of watercress soup, rack of lamb, and summer pudding, and we drank lots of champagne and the wine that Mum and Dad got in France. And then Dad rattled his fork in a glass and made a speech about me and Luke. He said that he and Mum had often talked about the kind of man I would marry, and they'd always disagreed on everything except one thing—"he'll have to be on his toes." Then he looked at Luke, who obligingly got up and turned a pirouette, and everyone roared with laughter. Dad said he'd become very fond of Luke and his parents and that this was more than just a marriage, it was a joining of families. And then he said he knew I would be a very loyal and supportive wife, and told the story of how when I was eight I wrote to Downing Street and proposed my father as prime minister—and then a week later wrote again to ask why they hadn't replied—and everyone laughed again.

Then Luke made a speech about how we met in London when I was a financial journalist, and how he noticed me at my very first press conference, when I asked the PR director of Barclays Bank why they didn't make fashion checkbook covers like they have for mobile phones. And then he confessed that he'd started sending me invitations to PR events even when they weren't relevant to my magazine, just because I always livened up proceedings.

(He's never told me that before. But now it all makes sense! That's why I kept being invited to all those weird conferences on commodity brokering and the state of the steel industry.)

Last of all, Michael stood up, and introduced himself in his warm, gravelly voice, and spoke about Luke. About how fantastically successful he is but how he needs someone by his side, someone who really loves him for the person he is and will stop him from taking life too seriously. Then he said it was an honor to meet my parents, and they'd been so friendly and welcoming to a pair of complete strangers, he could see where I got what he called the "Bloomwood bloom" of good-hearted happiness. And he said that I'd really grown up recently. That he'd watched me cope with some very tricky situations, and he wouldn't go into details, but I'd had quite a few challenges to deal with and somehow I'd managed to solve them all.

Without using a Visa card, he added, and there was the hugest roar of laughter, all around the marquee.

And then he said he'd attended many weddings in his time, but he'd never felt the contentment he was feeling right now. He knew Luke and I were meant to be with each other, and he was extremely fond of us both, and we didn't know how lucky we were. And if we were blessed with children, they wouldn't know how lucky they were, either.

Michael's speech nearly made me cry, actually.

Now I'm sitting with Luke on the grass. Just the two of us, away from everyone else for a moment. My Christian Louboutins are all smeared with grass stains, and Ernie's strawberry-covered fingers have left their mark on my bodice. I should think I look a complete mess. But I'm happy.

I think I'm the happiest I've ever been in my life.

"So," says Luke. He leans back on his elbows and stares up at the darkening blue sky. "We made it."

"We made it." My garland of flowers is starting to fall down over one eye, so I carefully unpin it and place it on the grass. "And no casualties."

"You know . . . I feel as though the past few weeks have been a weird dream," says Luke. "I've been in my own, preoccupied world, with no idea what was happening in real life." He shakes his head. "I think I nearly went off the rails back then."

"Nearly?"

"OK, then. I did go off the rails." He turns to look at me, his dark eyes glowing in the light from the marquee. "I owe a lot to you, Becky."

"You don't owe me anything," I say in surprise. "We're married now. It's like . . . everything's a joint account."

There's a rumbling sound from the side of the house, and I look up to see Dad loading our suitcases into the car. All ready for us to go.

"So," says Luke, following my gaze. "Our famous honeymoon. Am I allowed to know where we're going yet? Or is it still a secret?"

I feel a spasm of nerves. Here it comes. The last bit of my plan. The very last cherry on top of the cake.

"OK," I say, and take a deep breath. "Here goes. I've been thinking a lot about us recently, Luke. About being married, about where we should live. Whether we should stay in New York or not. What we should do . . ." I pause, carefully marshaling my words. "And what I've realized is . . . I'm not ready to settle down. Tom and Lucy tried to settle down too early, and look what happened to them. And I adore little Ernie, but seeing what it was like for Suze . . . It made me realize I'm not ready for a baby either. Not yet." I look up apprehensively. "Luke, there are so many things I've never done. I've never really traveled. I've never seen the world. Neither have you."

"You've lived in New York," points out Luke.

"New York is a great city and I do love it. But there are other great cities, all over the world. I want to see those too. Sydney. Hong Kong . . . and not just cities!" I spread my arms. "Rivers . . . mountains . . . all the sights of the world . . ."

"Right," says Luke amusedly. "So, narrowing this all down to one honeymoon . . ."

"OK." I swallow hard. "Here's what I've done. I've . . . I've cashed in all the wedding presents we got in New York. Stupid silver candlesticks and teapots and stuff. And I've . . . I've bought us two first-class tickets round the world."

"Round the world?" Luke looks genuinely taken aback. "Are you serious?"

"Yes! Round the world!" I plait my fingers together tightly. "We can take as long as we like. As little as three weeks, or as long as . . ." I look at him, tense with hope. "A year."

"A year?" Luke stares back at me. "You're joking."

"I'm not joking. I've told Christina I may or may not come back to work at Barneys. She's fine about it. Danny will clear out our apartment for us and put it all in storage—"

"Becky!" says Luke, shaking his head. "It's a nice idea. But I can't possibly just up sticks and—"

"You can. You can! It's all set up. Michael will keep an eye on the New York office. The London office is running itself anyway. Luke, you can do it. Everyone thinks you should."

"Everyone?"

I count off on my fingers. "Your parents . . . my parents . . . Michael . . . Laurel . . . Clive, my old driving instructor . . ."

Luke stares at me.

"Clive, your old driving instructor?"

"OK," I say hastily, "don't bother about him. But everyone whose opinion you respect. They all think you need a break. You've been working so hard, for so long . . ." I lean forward earnestly. "Luke, this is the time to do it. While we're still young. Before we have children. Just picture it. The two of us, wandering through the world. Seeing amazing sights. Learning from other cultures."

There's silence. Luke gazes at the ground, frowning.

"You spoke to Michael," he says at last. "And he'd really be willing to—"

"He'd be more than willing. He's bored living in New York with nothing to do except go power walking! Luke, he said even if you don't go away, you need a long breathing space. You need a proper holiday."

"A year," says Luke, rubbing his forehead. "That's more than a holiday."

"It could be shorter. Or longer! The point is, we can decide as we go along. We can be free spirits, for once in our lives. No ties, no commitments, nothing weighing us down—"

"Becky, love," calls Dad from the car. "Are you sure they'll let you take six suitcases?"

"It's OK, we'll just pay the excess baggage—" I turn back to Luke. "Come on. How about it?"

Luke says nothing for a few moments—and my heart sinks. I have a horrible feeling he's going to revert back to old Luke. Old, workaholic, single-minded, corporate Luke.

Then he looks up—and there's a wry little smile on his face. "Do I have a choice?"

"No." I grab his hand in relief. "You don't."

We're going round the world! We're going to be travelers!

"These last two are very light!" shouts Dad, and waves the cases in the air. "Is there anything in them?"

"No, they're empty!" I turn to Luke, glowing with delight. "Oh, Luke, it'll be so great! This is our one chance to have a year of escape. A year of . . . simplicity. Just us. Nothing else!"

There's a pause. Luke looks at me, his mouth twitching.

"And we're taking two great big empty suitcases with us because . . ."

"Well, you never know," I explain. "We might pick a few things up along the way. Travelers should always support the local economies—" I break off as Luke starts to laugh.

"What?" I say indignantly. "It's true!"

"I know." Luke wipes his eyes. "I know it is. Becky Bloomwood, I love you."

"I'm Becky Brandon now, remember!" I retort, glancing down at my lovely new ring. "Mrs. Rebecca Brandon."

But Luke shakes his head. "There's only one Becky Bloomwood. Never stop being her." He takes both hands in mine and gazes at me with a strange intensity. "Whatever you do, never stop being Becky Bloomwood."

"Well . . . OK," I say, taken aback. "I won't."

"Becky! Luke!" Mum's voice comes across the lawn. "It's time to cut the cake! Graham, put on the fairy lights!"

"Right-o!" calls Dad.

"Coming!" I shout back. "Just let me put my garland back on!"

"Let me." Luke reaches for the garland of pink flowers and puts it on my head with a little smile.

"Do I look stupid?" I say, pulling a face.

"Yes. Very." He gives me a kiss, then stands up and helps me to my feet. "Come on, Becky B. Your audience is waiting."

As fairy lights begin to twinkle all around us, we walk back over the dusky grass to the wedding, Luke's hand clasped firmly around mine.

PRENUPTIAL AGREEMENT
Between Rebecca Bloomwood
and Luke Brandon

22 June 2002

5. JOINT BANK ACCOUNT

5.1 The joint account shall be used for necessary expenditure on household expenses.

"Household expenses" shall be defined to include Miù Miù skirts, pairs of shoes, and other items of apparel deemed essential by the Bride.

5.2 The Bride's decision regarding such expenses shall be final in all cases.

5.3 Questions regarding the joint account shall not be sprung on the Bride by the Groom with no warning, but submitted in writing, with a 24-hour period for reply.

6. SIGNIFICANT DATES

6.1 The Groom shall remember all birthdays and anniversaries, and shall mark said dates with surprise gifts.*

6.2 The Bride shall demonstrate surprise and delight at the Groom's choices.

7. MARITAL HOME

The Bride shall make the best attempt within her powers to maintain order and tidiness in the marital home. HOWEVER, failure to abide by this clause shall not be regarded as a breaking of the contract.

8. TRANSPORT

The Groom shall not comment on the Bride's driving ability.

9. SOCIAL LIFE

9.1 The Bride shall not require the Groom to remember the names and past romantic history of all her friends including those he has never met.

9.2 The Groom shall make every effort to set aside a significant portion of each week for leisure and relaxing activities.

9.3 Shopping shall be defined as a relaxing activity.

*The surprise gifts shall comprise those items marked discreetly by the Bride in catalogues and magazines, to be left around the marital home in the weeks leading up to said dates.

Acknowledgments

Writing this book was tremendous fun; researching it even more so. I am exceedingly grateful to all, both in Britain and in the States, who gave me so much inspiration, and allowed me to come and ask them lots of stupid questions.

My thanks to Lawrence Harvey at the Plaza, who could not have been more helpful, and to the ever wonderful Sharyn Soleimani at Barneys. Also to Ron Ben-Israel, Elizabeth and Susan Allen, Fran Bernard, Preston Bailey, Clare Mosley, Joe Dance at Crate and Barrel, Julia Kleyner and Lillian Sabatelli at Tiffany, Charlotte Curry at *Brides,* Robin Michaelson, Theresa Ward, Guy Lancaster and Kate Mailer, David Stefanou and Jason Antony, and lovely Lola Bubbosh.

A million thanks, as always, to my wonderful agent Araminta Whitley and to Celia Hayley, Kim Witherspoon, and David Forrer. And of course deep gratitude to the endlessly fantastic team at The Dial Press, with particular thanks to Susan Kamil, Zoë Rice, and Nita Taublib.

And lastly to the people who've been there all the way through: Henry, Freddy, and Hugo, and the purple posse. You know who you are.

Coming in 2004

an all-new

Sophie Kinsella
adventure

introducing her latest hilarious heroine
EMMA CORRIGAN

who has a few secrets . . .

Of course I have secrets.

Everyone has a few secrets. I'm not talking about big, earth-shattering secrets. Not the-president-is-planning-to-bomb-Japan-and-only-Will-Smith-can-save-the-world type secrets.

Just normal, everyday little ones. Like, for example, here are a few random secrets of mine, off the top of my head:

1. My Kate Spade bag is a fake.

2. I love sweet sherry, the least cool drink in the universe.

3. I have no idea what NATO stands for. Or even what it is.

EMMA CORRIGAN HAS SECRETS FROM HER BOYFRIEND . . .

4. I weigh one hundred and twenty-eight pounds. Not one eighteen, like Connor thinks.

5. I've always thought Connor looks a bit like Ken. As in Barbie and Ken.

6. Sometimes, when we're right in the middle of passionate sex, I suddenly want to laugh.

EMMA CORRIGAN HAS SECRETS FROM HER COLLEAGUES . . .

7. When Artemis really annoys me, I feed her plant orange juice. (Which is pretty much every day.)

8. It was me who jammed the copier that time. In fact, all the times.

9. Just sometimes, when I'm reading *Marketing Week* at my desk, I really have *Entertainment Weekly* inside.

EMMA CORRIGAN HAS SECRETS FROM HER PARENTS . . .

10. I lost my virginity in the spare bedroom with Danny Nussbaum, while Mum and Dad were downstairs watching *Ben-Hur*.

11. I've already drunk the wine that Dad told me to lay down for twenty years.

12. The goldfish in the kitchen isn't the same one Mum and Dad gave me to look after when they went to Egypt.

EMMA CORRIGAN HAS SECRETS SHE WOULD NEVER SHARE WITH ANYBODY . . .

13. My G-string is hurting me.

14. I've always had this deep-down conviction that I'm not like everybody else, and there's an amazingly exciting new life waiting for me just around the corner.

15. I often have no idea what people are talking about. None whatsoever . . .

UNTIL SHE SPILLS THEM ALL TO A STRANGER ON A PLANE . . .

The plane suddenly drops down again, and I give an involuntary shriek. "We're going to die!" I stare into his face. This could be the last person I ever see alive. I take in the lines etched around his dark eyes, his strong jaw, shaded with stubble.

"I don't think we're going to die," he says. But he's gripping hard onto his seat arms, too. "They said it was just turbulence—"

"Of course they did!" I can hear the hysteria in my voice. "They wouldn't exactly say, 'OK, folks, that's it, you're all goners!'" The plane gives another terrifying swoop and I find myself clutching the man's hand in panic. "We're not going to make it. I know we're not. This is it. I'm twenty-five years old, for God's sake, I'm not ready to die. I haven't achieved anything. I've never had children, I've never saved a life . . ." My eyes fall randomly on the "30 Things to Do Before You're 30" magazine article in front of me. "I haven't ever climbed a mountain; I haven't got a tattoo; I don't even *know* if I've got a G spot . . ."

"I'm sorry?" says the man, sounding taken aback, but I barely hear him.

"I'm not a top businesswoman!" I gesture half tearfully to my suit. "I'm just a crappy assistant and I just had my first-ever big meeting and it was a total disaster. I don't know what *logistical* means, and I've never read a Dickens novel, and my underwear's too small, and I owe my dad four thousand quid, and I've never really been in love . . ."

AT LEAST, SHE THOUGHT HE WAS A STRANGER . . .

So this is the new big boss. The guy in the baseball cap turns, and as I see his face I feel an almighty thud, as though a bowling ball's landed hard in my chest. Oh my God. It's him. The same dark eyes. The same lines etched around them. The stubble's gone, but it's definitely him. It's the man from the plane—the man I told all my secrets to. What's he doing here at the office? And . . . and why has he got everyone's attention? He's speaking now, and everyone is lapping up every word he says. He turns again, and I instinctively duck back out of sight, trying to keep calm. What's he doing here? He can't— That can't be— That can't possibly be. If this is the new mega-boss, I'm in big, big trouble . . .

CAN YOU KEEP A SECRET?

THE NEW NOVEL COMING FROM
Sophie Kinsella

*The trouble with telling
secrets is . . . you can't get
them back*

And don't miss the novel that introduced
the fabulous Becky Bloomwood!

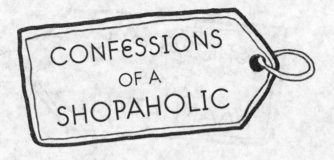

CONFESSIONS
OF A
SHOPAHOLIC

Becky Bloomwood has everything: a fabulous flat in London's trendiest neighborhood, a troupe of glamorous socialite friends, and a closet brimming with the season's must-haves. The only problem is that she can't actually afford it—not any of it. Her job as a financial journalist not only bores her to tears, it doesn't pay much at all. And lately, Becky's been chased by dismal letters from Visa and the Endwich Bank—letters with large red sums she can't bear to read—and they're getting ever harder to ignore. She tries cutting back; she even tries making more money. But none of her efforts succeeds. Becky's only consolation is to buy herself something . . . just a little something . . .

Finally a story arises that Becky actually *cares* about, and her front-page article catalyzes a chain of events that will transform her life—and the lives of those around her—forever.

Sophie Kinsella brilliantly taps into our collective consumer conscience to deliver a novel of our times—and a heroine who grows stronger every time she weakens. Becky Bloomwood's hysterical schemes to pay back her debts are as endearing as they are desperate. Her "confessions" are the perfect pick-me-up when life is hanging in the (bank) balance.

"Packing Light" takes on a whole new meaning

SHOPAHOLIC
TAKES
MANHATTAN

"This expensive, glossy world is where I've been headed all along. Limos and flowers; waxed eyebrows and designer clothes from Barneys. These are my people; this is where I'm meant to be."

—Becky Bloomwood.

With her shopping excesses (somewhat) in check and her career as a TV financial guru thriving, Becky's biggest problem seems to be tearing her entrepreneur boyfriend, Luke, away from work for a romantic country weekend. And worse, figuring out how to "pack light." But packing takes on a whole new meaning when Luke announces he's moving to New York for business—and asks Becky to go with him! Before you can say "Prada sample sale," Becky has landed in the Big Apple, home of Park Avenue penthouses and luxury department stores. Surely it's only a matter of time until she becomes an American TV celebrity, and she and Luke are the toast of Gotham society. Nothing can stand in their way, especially with Becky's bills miles away in London. But then an unexpected disaster threatens her career prospects, her relationship with Luke, and her available credit line! *Shopaholic Takes Manhattan*—but will she have to return it?